DRAGON TOUCHED

THE AWAKENING

DRAGON TOUCHED

THE AWAKENING

C.B. HAIGHT

TO ALL THE TEENAGERS THAT LET ME BE THEIR DUNGEON
MASTER, THANKS FOR THE INSPIRATION. EVEN BETTER,
THANKS FOR THE GRAND ADVENTURES.

"THE WORLD IS FULL OF MAGIC THINGS, PATIENTLY WAITING
FOR OUR SENSES TO GROW SHARPER."
-W.B. YEATS

NE

"Good. That's right, now exhale, and—" The bowstring hummed, and the swift breeze tickled her cheek as she let go. The arrow sped across the field, and the sharp tip struck the target without a sound.

Micah looked down with a raised brow to meet her bright green eyes. Her long, blonde hair cascaded over her shoulder as she stared back at him. A hopeful grin dominated the young woman's face, and those captivating eyes sparkled with confidence.

"Your shot was too quick, Princess," Micah admonished.

"Not so. The shot was true. You saw for yourself," Ahanna protested.

"Was it, then? Let's go see," Micah taunted as he rose from the tall grass to go and investigate.

Confident she felled the rabbit, Ahanna followed her tutor into the field. Her surety shifted into horror when she saw the poor, frightened creature twitching on the ground with blood soaking its hindquarters. The arrow had struck the animal's back but missed killing the rabbit.

"Oh! What have I done?" Ahanna exclaimed as she fell to her knee. Her hand hovered nervously over the protruding arrow as she mentally berated herself for the rushed shot. "Can you help it?"

Micah knelt next to her and gently lifted the suffering animal into his strong hands. He whispered to the rabbit, and the small creature calmed as he gently handled it. "It is not enough to hit your target, Princess. You must do so with mercy," Micah explained.

"I didn't want to put him in agony," Ahanna insisted. "I thought the shot was true. I believed—"

"I know, but your eagerness caused you both pain. Remember this lesson. It is a cruel thing to make any animal or person suffer. If you must kill to eat or protect, do it quickly and with compassion." He placed a large leaf against the wound and chanted as he pulled the arrow free and drew from divine healing powers few could manifest.

Ahanna could only watch in awe. He brought the helpless rabbit close to his chest, petting it gently, as he whispered reassurance and healing prayers. He prayed to the natural forces and his deity, The Creator of Life, Ealoram, to close the wound. Micah's prayers were always different and individual. Yet, they always started the same. With every prayer for healing he offered, Micah always thanked their god for the life in his care first and the gift he was blessed with second.

Listening to the timbre of his voice, Ahanna was carried away by the cadence in his words. Somehow, even when his prayer differed each time, Micah still found a way to add rhythmic balance in the order he used them. She often wondered if that rhythm was born from the magic or found life because of his practiced cadence.

Sweat beaded on his brow as Micah offered a part of himself to the suffering creature. *He's given that to me before*, Ahanna remembered. Still watching him, she noticed that his dark-blonde hair, previously tied back with a strap of leather, had come loose around his face during their hike here. The strands hung over his perfectly rounded ears, framing his shadowed features. Dark lashes shaded his intelligent, blue eyes as he focused his will on the animal in his arms.

Having reached her nineteenth summer, Ahanna was unsure of what to do about the new feelings manifesting in her. Three years her senior, Micah was once like an older brother to her. Since Tisus took him as a ward of the castle when he was still a baby, he grew up with her and her sisters. But when he was barely thirteen, he had surprised King Tisus, and her guilty mind drifted back to that moment.

Young as she was, Ahanna knew Micah didn't want to miss his chance to have a first look at the new stallion that came to Ranoak all the way from Brithel today. He told her that all the best war horses were trained in Brithel. His excitement for the new stallion drove the young boy to double his pace.

"Come on, Ahanna! If you don't hurry, you will miss it," Micah called over his shoulder as he sped down the path. His feet splashed in a small puddle left by the morning rain.

Out of breath, Ahanna blurted, "I'm trying, Micah. You're too fast!"

Micah ignored her complaint and kept running. "Hurry!" he called again.

Ten-year-old Ahanna willed herself to catch up, but her feet didn't carry her far. She tripped hard and tumbled to the ground, scraping her knee and rolling until she smacked her head on a

3

jagged rock stuck in the mud. Embarrassed and hurt, Ahanna cried out, "Micah!"

Micah rolled his eyes, but he stopped. "What now, Princess?" They were only a few feet from the stone building. "You're such a bab—" the derisive comment died when he turned and saw the gash on her head and the blood and mud on her dress. "Ahanna!"

With fear clouding his gentle eyes, Micah rushed back to help her. "Don't move!" he ordered when she tried to get up.

Ahanna's head spun. Micah wanted to see that new horse so badly, and he would be mad if he missed seeing it first. Warm tears mixed with blood and mud left dirty streaks on her face. "I'm coming," she whimpered.

"No, Ahanna, stay there." Micah was at her side before she could rise. There was so much blood coming from the wound that he worried she would pass out. He pressed his hand to her head in an attempt to stem the flow. "It's going to be okay."

"Ow!"

"Don't worry. A healer can fix it."

"My head hurts," Ahanna complained.

"I know. Don't cry, okay?"

"I can't help it," she replied.

"Okay, I know." He pressed harder. "I should go get help."

It hurt when he pressed his hand against the wound, and her head began to burn. With tear-filled eyes, Ahanna looked up at him and pleaded, "Micah, you can't leave me here alone."

"Ahanna, you need a healer."

"Please, Micah. I'll be alright in a minute."

His face pinched with indecision, but he relented. "I'll stay here," he assured her. "Don't worry. Someone's bound to come this way."

Ahanna started to sob again.

"Don't cry, Ahanna," Micah pleaded. "I won't leave you, I

promise."

He did leave her, though. Ahanna's fingers brushed against the scar at the edge of her hairline. By the time her father stumbled across them on his way to see the new horse, Micah had somehow partially closed the wound and stopped the blood flow by praying to Ealoram. When Tisus realized what happened, he made arrangements for Micah to be sent away to expand his newly found abilities.

Two days later, Ahanna's best friend left Castle Ranoak with no fanfare. He hadn't written once during those six long years. Her father insisted he was safe, but she hated that he'd practically ceased to exist.

A year after that, Ahanna's mother disappeared. Tisus hadn't tried to reassure her then because he'd been more worried than anyone else in the months that followed. During those difficult days, Ahanna had wanted her friend back more than ever. She'd needed the boy she looked up to like a brother to help her muddle through the heartache, but he hadn't been there as he'd promised. In time she pushed the resentment away. After all, to her mind, it had been her fault that he was sent away in the first place.

With his training complete, Micah had signed on as a king's ranger and returned home. A year later, King Tisus assigned Micah to teach Ahanna and her sisters basic survival skills and the use of a bow. With his return, Ahanna was so happy to have him back that she refused to mention the lack of contact or the pain it caused her.

With only memories in her mind and the history between them, receiving lessons from Micah and spending hours daily with him sounded exciting and fun. Ahanna foolishly believed she could pick up where they left off, but too much changed for them during those missing years.

The playful boy who'd climbed trees and instigated games of chase was gone. A proud, woodland warrior returned in his stead. He no longer teased her and was consistent in using formality when he addressed her. Worse than his formality was the strange new feelings she had around him.

Ahanna forgot how intelligent and intuitive Micah was. *Or perhaps*, she mused, *the child I was hadn't recognized it.* Now, having to spend time with him for regular lessons, she noticed all of his talents. As a trained ranger, he could hit any target nearly one hundred meters out. His quiet disposition and patience during a hunt was unfathomable, and his knowledge of plants and animals was, in her opinion, unrivaled. All of it made her heart skip beats and her tummy jump.

Little girls barely bothered to notice wild unruly hair, tanned skin from hours in the sun, and bright blue eyes. But, as a young woman entering adulthood, those same traits were at the center of her thoughts all too often, and they fueled her budding crush. Even now, Ahanna was grateful that his deep concentration on the rabbit kept him from noticing her study of him because she couldn't resist looking.

The complexity of these escalating emotions was messing with Ahanna's ability to retain her focus on everything these days. Half the reason that she had rushed her last shot was his proximity and the effect it had on her nerves. The more she was around him, the more she craved their time together.

Of course, she believed Micah was oblivious to her unwelcome feelings. Ahanna did her very best to keep it that way. Micah was her long-time friend, after all. Probably her best friend if she didn't count her sisters. He was dependable and never thought less of her because of her bloodline. Nor did he put her upon a princess pedestal by treating her with ridiculous fragility as most of the castle staff did. When they were together, she was simply

Ahanna. She couldn't stand the idea of losing that friendship and understood the best way to keep it was never to take a risk in the first place.

She kept pretending he was her brother, but nothing she did would erase the butterflies in her belly when Micah smiled at her. No matter how hard she tried, she couldn't stay away or ignore his attention.

Even if he reciprocates my feelings, it will make things worse, she reminded herself. Ignoring the fact that she was the Crowned Princess and destined to be Queen of Ranoak one day, to her mind, her bloodline presented far more complicated conflicts. Ahanna was a half-elf. A racial anomaly most in the realm of Ishreedin were unwilling to associate with, let alone love.

Her heritage was a hidden secret few in Ranoak knew and one that shamed her deeply. Her father went to great lengths to protect Ahanna and her sisters. She rarely ventured outside of the castle grounds. When she did, heavy cloaks were used to cover her slender body, and her attendants always fashioned her hair to hide the tips of her ears.

Even as a 'human' princess, nineteen-year-old Ahanna had never met another elf up close, besides her mother. Her father feared they would recognize the signs of her bloodline and refused to even entertain the idea. If she were to marry, any child from that kind of mixed bloodline would face the same challenges she did, and it would be equally complicated. She often wondered if there was a single man in the entire realm that would accept her.

No, she mused. *Love will not be an option for me. Any man who marries me would likely be bribed with lands and titles in an arranged marriage to make it worth his time and aggravation.* It was another reason she hated the idea of being Queen.

Berating herself for indulging in self-pity, Ahanna forced the depressive thoughts aside as Micah finished tending the wounded rabbit. *I should be paying attention to learn, not gawking at him.*

Still, she stole one more wistful glance at his handsome face, but as if he sensed her staring, Micah looked up. Their eyes locked, and without looking away, he uttered the last few syllables of the healing magic.

TW

S he blushed, and Ahanna's gaze darted away to the newly healed rabbit in his arms. She nervously cleared her throat, "Is he alright now?"

Micah nodded as he set the rabbit down in the tall grass. "Our friend has earned the right to freedom, and we can have supper at the castle instead. We'll try to hunt again another day."

The little animal sprinted away through the brush, and Ahanna's lips tilted in a relieved smile as she watched it disappear.

In truth, Ahanna was never eager to kill it anyway, but King Tisus insisted she learn whatever she could for survival skills, and that included hunting, dressing, and cooking her own meals. She enjoyed using her bow, but today would've been only her second time skinning and preparing her dinner in the wilderness—a skill she had botched the first time as well.

When she finally lost sight of the rabbit, Ahanna looked back to Micah. His eyes were intent upon her as if he was studying her. She ducked her head as those ever-persistent nerves raced through her again, and the heat rose in her cheeks. Her smile faltered. "Um, well, I suppose we should be heading back since we are without a meal and all."

Micah stood and offered her a hand. "Yes, you're right," he said. "The sun wanes, and you must be eager for supper."

Taking his hand, Ahanna rose to her feet. Secretly she wished he would hold on to her for another minute, but he didn't. Instead, he let go of her as if she had a contagious plague and even wiped it on his trousers. Then, turning his back to her, Micah began making his way through the long grass to the tethered horses. "Come along, Princess. You wouldn't want to keep your sisters waiting."

Ahanna gritted her teeth. She hated when he called her Princess. When he said it, for some reason, the words sounded like an insult. "Quit being such a child," she mumbled to herself.

"Did you say something?" Micah asked over his shoulder.

"No, nothing." She shook away her disappointment and the little stab to her pride as she hurried after him.

Before mounting Freesia, she reached up to check her hair again to make sure the swooping braids still covered her ears. Out of the corner of her eye, Ahanna saw Micah frowning at her. Bothered by his reaction, she mounted her horse without another word.

Silence passed between them during the ride back to the stables, and she worried that her growing feelings were becoming transparent. Their trips together were usually filled with conversation.

Her mind replayed that moment when Micah caught her staring at him. *That's why he let me go so quickly*, she reasoned. *He must know.* A thousand scenarios flitted about in her head, and every one of them left her feeling foolish. After circling this new train of thought for several minutes, Ahanna finally settled on the possibility that he would pity her. Or worse, he might joke about it with his friends at the guardhouse.

Poor Ahanna, a silly elf with a childish crush. She almost groaned out loud. *Sweet tender lilies! What if he is laughing at me?* She glanced his way and noticed the tight jaw and his straight back. *That's the posture of an annoyed man,* she thought.

The turmoil within would not abate, and the longer no words passed between them, the more the fear took hold. The more those fears turned Ahanna's thoughts into miserable possibilities, the angrier she became. She tried to will him to look in her direction, but he stubbornly kept his eyes straight ahead.

Why won't he talk to me? she thought, conveniently ignoring the fact that she hadn't said a word to him either.

By the time they reached the stone outbuilding to house the horses, she was fuming, hurt, and frustrated. Dismounting with jerky movements, Ahanna began caring for Freesia as expected, but her actions were rough, and the horse shied away from her temper.

"Princess, you need to be gentle," Micah scolded. "You're frightening Freesia."

"I was gentle!" she insisted, but she wasn't. Feeling guilty on top of everything else, Ahanna sighed and laid her head against Freesia's. *"Goheno nin,"* she said, whispering an Elvish apology to her long-time friend.

Freesia blew hot breath into her hand as if to tell her, *don't worry, I understand.* The mare dipped her head in Micah's direction, and the slightest smile formed on Ahanna's lips, but when she looked back at him with his horse, her smile fell. With raw emotion still clawing at the back of her throat, she picked up a fist full of straw and ran it over her mare's back and sides.

"What's gotten into you?" Micah questioned. "You're acting

strange."

"It's nothing."

Micah came around and gently took her wrist to stay her brushing. "What troubles you?"

"It's nothing," she insisted while trying to pull away, but the sting of tears had embarrassment creeping in. Worse, Micah didn't let go.

Sympathy and possibly understanding entered his eyes. Reaching down, he took her other hand with surprising tenderness.

"What are you doing?"

"Ahanna, I am truly sorry. I could not convince him otherwise, and he is only trying to do what is best for you and the kingdom."

"I'm sorry?" she said with stunned confusion. Staring at his strong hands, Ahanna couldn't process what he was saying.

"I was not informed that he had told you yet. Had I known," he continued, "I would have postponed our trip today."

"What are you talking about?" she asked. "You're not making any sense."

Micah stopped, his brows furrowed with equal confusion. "Leaving has upset you?"

"Leaving?" She finally looked away from his hands and met his eyes.

"In anticipation for your inheritance of the throne, The Enclave will better school you in the ways of the court." Seeing her confusion and the anger building, Micah hesitated before saying, "Surely, this is what upsets you?"

Her eyes widened. "Leaving!"

Micah frowned and let go of her, his own hands falling to his sides. "He has not told you yet."

Ahanna pulled away. Her breathing turned shallow, and it took her a full minute to respond. "He's sending me away?" she asked indignantly.

Micah pulled a hand through his hair, and turning away from her, muttered, "In all the realm, there is no greater fool than I."

"Micah!"

He faced her again. "You didn't know. It wasn't the pending trip to The Enclave that upset you?"

"No." She frantically shook her head. "No. I didn't know."

Micah bowed, "I apologize, Princess. It was not my intent to dishonor the King's trust in me. I'll care for Freesia. You can meet with him right away. Please, extend my apology to your father."

"What do you know, Micah?"

"It is not my place. Your tears…" He sighed, "I made an assumption and misspoke."

"Micah!"

He wouldn't look at her. "Go now, Ahanna."

"Micah! I have a right to know."

He nodded. "Speak with your father."

Micah's loyalty knew no bounds. His steadfast dedication was another thing she admired about him, but Ahanna couldn't keep herself from snapping anyway. "He cannot send me away! Least of all, to The Enclave! What do you know?"

"I will not purposefully betray my King a second time," Micah said firmly and reached to take her horse's reins. "Please. Go to your father. He will explain."

Fiery temper sparked in her eyes, and she snatched her horse's reins away from him. Freesia whinnied at him as if to say, *Don't touch me. I'm mad, too!*

Ahanna snapped, "I shall care for my horse, as my teacher demands of me. Then I'll find my father and tell him I will not be going anywhere." Turning, she pulled on Freesia's reins, and the horse snorted at him as the pair marched to the furthest stall to get away from the Ranger.

Micah's mount, Soros, lowered his head and bumped his shoulder. He accepted the comfort and stroked the horse absent-mindedly. "What have I done, Soros?"

Sighing, Micah ran his hands along the destrier's neck. "I am truly a fool." In truth, he knew that he should have canceled their trip today, but selfishly, he wanted that time with her. He patted Soros' neck and confessed softly, "I don't want her to leave either. But if she stays, I may do something far worse than speaking out of turn to betray my King."

THREE

Riding a roaring tide of fury, Ahanna Nacarian, first daughter to King Tisus and Crowned Princess of Ranoak, ignored acceptable protocol and blew past her father's guards like a raging storm before they could even react. Her eyes sparkled with indignation as she stomped across the stone floor into his private chambers.

"You cannot make me go!"

Caught in the middle of reviewing budget reports with Lord Denaris, King Tisus lifted his dry eyes from the parchment atop his mahogany desk and gave Ahanna his full attention. Seeing the temper in his eldest daughter, he almost smiled, but instead, he raised a brow. "Ahanna."

"I will not go!" she declared.

Caldaren, one of the King's most trusted guards, moved forward, but Ahanna glared at him with icy eyes, and he stepped back again. "Sire?"

"It's alright, Caldaren," Tisus assured him and turned to his advisor. "Denaris, it seems my daughter and I have matters to discuss. The budgets will be waiting for us come morning."

"Most certainly, Your Majesty. I'm famished anyway." Denaris gestured for the guards to leave with a wave of his hand and then turned to Ahanna. "Princess," he said with a curt bow before following the guards and pulling the heavy wooden doors closed behind him.

Rising from his chair, King Tisus reprimanded his daughter with his customary father's glare, but she didn't even wilt from the weight of it this time. He wasn't surprised. Tisus wasn't sure his scathing looks ever swayed his hard-headed child. Standing before him this way, in a fit of anger, Tisus experienced a moment of déjà vu as he saw his beloved wife standing there instead.

It was providence, he supposed, that out of his five daughters, his eldest was the most like his Shelanna. Ahanna inherited the same tall, slender build of the elves, with the lithe grace to match. Her long, blonde hair was straight and left mostly down, with bits of hair from the front pulled back into braids to cover her sharp ears. Her eyes were even the same shade of green as Shelanna's. All of his daughters had green eyes of various shades, but Ahanna's were that same bright emerald green that sparked to life when she was excited or angry. When she'd been born, Tisus had sworn she was an exact copy of her mother, and now that she was grown, he saw the truth of the proclamation.

A pang of longing pricked at his heart as it often did when he thought of his missing wife. For that reason alone, Tisus almost wavered again. He sighed, "Do you want to tell me how you found out, or should we skip to the part when you tell me you're not going again?"

"So it's true?" Ahanna questioned.

"It's true. How did you find out?"

16

"That hardly matters! What does matter is why you would do this? Have I done something wrong?"

Tisus came around his desk but did not hug her as he initially wanted to. "Of course, you haven't done anything wrong. Do you think I want to send you away? It is my worst fear to let go of you."

"Then, why?"

"I am aging, Ahanna, and you are my heir. Therefore, you must learn what is necessary to be Queen. Being the ruler of this land is not something you can muddle through."

"Queen?" she said desperately. "You still won't listen to me. I've said it before. I cannot be Queen."

"Ahanna—"

"No, Father. How can I be Queen? You know how our people will react. By your orders, they don't even know the truth about our heritage. You kept it hidden for good reason. Now you expect to thrust it upon them?"

Tisus shook his head. "When you were first born, the skirmishes in the borderlands were still too fresh, and for your safety, your mother and I decided to keep the knowledge limited, but things have changed. Our people are allies now."

Ahanna scoffed, "That's debatable. A more appropriate description is *not enemies*."

"Exactly," Tisus said. "We need to forge new and better bonds between elves and men. The tyrant King Eduar and his father before him destroyed those relationships long ago. My hope is that you can renew them."

"How do you expect me to do that?"

"I believe you can do anything." When she sighed and sat down, Tisus continued, "You are no longer a helpless child. You have grown into a fine young woman, but you are naive in many ways. I should have sent you sooner, but I was selfish. With some help from The Enclave, you will be a fair and respected queen."

"You can't really think that. You don't believe the people would accept the tainted blood of a half-elf as their Queen. Even you say there is still only tolerance for the elves among the people. Worse, when they learn the truth, no elf would accept me as an ally either. If you make me Queen, it's more likely the wars will start anew and destroy the treaty you signed after you destroyed Eduar." She stood again. "You wish me to lead an entire kingdom full of the same people you worried would reject me, reject all of us?"

He placed his hands on her shoulders and squeezed gently to offer some reassurance. "When you are Queen, they will respect you out of duty, and in time they will respect you because of your deeds."

Pulling away, she laughed at his remark. "I am not like you. I have no great deeds of valor to back me up. Likely, I never will. I don't even want to kill rabbits."

"Deeds of valor are rarely a result of killing."

Ahanna's mouth shut, and she pressed her lips tightly together as she eyed him.

"It was not striking down Eduar that people respected, Ahanna. It was my prior decisions and actions that taught the people to trust me."

It was Ahanna's turn to shake her head. "I have no such choice of history behind me. By your reasoning, even Micah would be a better ruler. All I have is a blood tie to you. How can that possibly make me fit to be Queen?"

"What did you think would happen to this kingdom when I died?"

"I don't want to think about that," she said petulantly and turned her back on him.

Tisus smiled. "I will die, Ahanna. I am, after all, human."

She faced him again. "You are far from your final years, and your blood runs through my veins, too. I am as mortal as you. I could die on the road after you send me away."

He gave her a pitying look. "I did not have Micah train you these last months so you could die on the road. What's more, you are far less aged than I. I'm confident you will live long enough to succeed me."

"Why won't you listen? I lack the temperament for this. I've told you time and time again—Please, this is not for me," she pleaded.

"Ahanna, I never asked to be King. It is not a role I relish, but it is a role I take on for the good of all people. It is a necessary occupation I found myself thrust into. It is not just for my own self that I pour over budgets and listen to complaints. Nor is it for myself that I spend hours working to maintain peace accords and meeting with lords of fiefdoms instead of spending my time with you. If I were to have my way, all of us would live out our days on a quiet farm, but we both know our paths rarely take us the direction we wish."

"Please, Father. Please, don't send me to The Enclave."

Tisus would not sway his resolve. "You need to do this. I fear I have coddled you too long. You must face difficult challenges like this, and in so doing, you will grow in strength. Your mother believed that it is the challenges of the impossible in which we find our greatest selves."

Her temper resurfaced at the mention of her mother. Her eyes glinted, and her face flushed. There were some things Ahanna could not yet understand, and as a result, she could not forgive.

Ahanna snapped, "Do not offer me advice from a woman who abandoned her family. It is *her fault* I have to hide who I am."

Tisus sighed. "What would you have me do, Ahanna?"

19

"I don't know. Maybe you should've thought of all this before you married an elf." Even as the words spilled past her lips, she regretted them. His entire demeanor changed as her words cut through him, and for Ahanna, the sharp retort was simply another reminder as to why her role as Queen would never work.

As her words pierced his heart, Tisus' lips thinned, his eyes hardened, and there was an emptiness inside him. Complete emotional defeat showed in the undefeatable King's features. Then, Tisus moved back to his desk. Removing his crown from his head, he carefully sat down. The precise movements, the weariness in his eyes, and the silence between them strained Ahanna's conscience.

She took note of his greying hair, slumped shoulders, and the way he absently reached for the likeness of her mother he kept inside his pocket. As she waited for his response, Ahanna re-lived those moments eight years before when Tisus realized his wife, Shelanna, was nowhere to be found and when the months of endless searching to bring her home turned up nothing.

Being the oldest, Ahanna had heard the whispers in the castle. She knew what the castle staff thought of her mother's disappearance. They thought her mother flighty. Those few that knew the truth of her heritage believed Shelanna tired of the mortal King and went back to the elves. It was the one place he could not follow.

Watching him, Ahanna always found herself confused as to how someone could grieve so long for a woman that left him without so much as a goodbye. *Could sadness age a man so much?* she wondered, and with that grim thought, Ahanna hated her elven mother even more. "Father, I—"

He lifted a hand to silence her explanation. "What's done is done, and I will not regret it." No justification could take the icy dagger back, and for Ahanna, no argument on his part could make her sympathize with her absent mother.

His tone hardened. "I am grateful for the time I had with her and the children given to me as a result. Maybe one day, you will understand the rare blessing you and your sisters are. In the meantime, I will do all I can to prepare you for whatever may come. I promised your mother I would teach you all I could, and I have. It is time for new lessons. It is time to face your future, Ahanna. All I can do for you now is pray that The Creator will bless you with the courage to see it through."

Her hands shook, and she clenched them at her side to keep them still. "Please—"

"My decision is final. You are my eldest child, and Ranoak is your kingdom when I am gone. As such, you and your sisters will need a proper education. Whether you like it or not, you and Feylynn will be leaving for the Paladin's Enclave within a fortnight for royal training and education.

"I trust your instructors implicitly with your secret and more so with my daughter's safety. Then when you are the Queen, if you are a good queen—an honest, just queen—you will earn the people's trust. Your heritage will not sway them long. Of this, I am sure."

Ahanna's heart started beating so fast that she worried it might burst out of her chest. She pleaded with him, "I would not choose this life. Give the throne to Feylynn. She is far better suited for it, and no one would even know she is elven."

Tisus shook his head. "Feylynn has the heart of a protector, to be sure, and she will be an asset to this kingdom. She is, and will be, your greatest advisor, and you must trust her to be your voice of reason when the need calls for such things. All of your sisters will aid and support you in different ways, but I know you, Ahanna Morningsong Nacarion. I know your strengths and your weaknesses. You are too stubborn to let this kingdom fall into ruin. But, more than that, this kingdom is yours by birthright."

"I refuse that birthright! I will abdicate the throne. I'll leave! You cannot force me to live with these *stuffy, unreasonable, unfeeling* knights for the next three years."

He pinned her with his dark eyes, and this time she saw the flash of temper in them. His voice turned hard once more, "I suggest you use this time away to learn a degree of diplomacy and respect for the Paladins that will bend their knee and swear fealty to you one day."

Ahanna shrank away from the scolding and bit her lip to stem the threat of tears.

His demeanor shifted in the blink of an eye, and King Tisus offered his daughter his honest compassion. "I do none of this to hurt you, only to help you."

She didn't respond as she turned to leave. When she reached for the door, her father said, "I loved her, Ahanna." Looking over her shoulder, she found her father staring out the window into the darkened night. "With every fiber of my soul, I love her still, and your mother loved you girls more than her own life. Maybe one day you will accept that."

Losing the battle to hold back her tears, the wet, salty lines ran down her cheeks, but lifting her head with what little dignity remained in her blood, Ahanna refused to invest any effort in wiping them away. "If she loved us so much, why did she leave?"

King Tisus closed his eyes against the accusation and heard the door close, signaling Ahanna's full retreat. Deep in the pit of his soul, he hated himself for being foolish enough to sign away her fate before she was even born.

Standing there, staring at the glistening stars, he lost track of time. Several minutes passed before he found himself interrupted again. By then, his thoughts had taken a strange turn. "Enter."

"Your Majesty."

King Tisus sensed the movement behind him and knew Micah offered him a formal bow, but he didn't turn to face the young Ranger. "You needn't have come."

"But, Sire, I betrayed your confidence. You must know it was me. For few knew of the arrangements."

"More than you would believe, but yes, I know it was you. However, the fault does not rest with you alone. I should have told Ahanna weeks ago. Even better, I should have prepared her years ago. It was selfish of me to keep the promise hidden this long. I suppose, even early on, I knew how she would react, and I fooled myself into thinking she would go along with it if I told her at the last minute."

Still speaking to his King's back, Micah tried to explain further, "She was upset, Your Majesty, and I assumed you had spoken with her."

"I should have." Turning, Tisus met the young man face to face. "She won't go, you know. You were right before."

"Sire?" Micah questioned.

"When you insisted that The Enclave would shrivel her soul."

"Sire, I spoke out of turn. I am young and do not understand the complexities of your position. I was only frustrated with Lord Denaris. It is not my place to question your plans."

"If no one questions the King, how would a king ever know his faults? It is not only your job as the King's Ranger to question my actions, it is also your responsibility as one of the people under my rule. Only a tyrant would wish unquestioned authority."

Respect shone in the young man's eyes.

"I saw it in her eyes. More than that, I see it in her heart. I think I have always known it would never work for Ahanna. The Order of The Golden Dragon is far too rigid for her. Even if she went, Ahanna would find an escape before long, and she would return here to stay hidden if I allowed it."

"Yes, Sire," Micah agreed with understanding.

King Tisus sighed, "Her soul will wither and die at The Enclave."

"She is not so weak as that," Micah protested.

Tisus smiled as he thought of the Ranger's defense of his daughter, and he recognized how quick he offered it. "They are all so different."

"Yes, Sire."

"How goes her training?"

Micah answered, "Good, Your Majesty. She has a good shot but little patience. She is sharp of mind and has little trouble remembering her lessons."

Tisus nodded. "And the sword?"

"She has a lot of skill there, but again lacks patience. She prefers her bow, but I believe her agile enough to wield two with the proper teacher. However, I do not think I am the right person for that."

Tisus nodded once more. "Even I can be a fool. They need different things. Each of my daughters learns in different ways. All have different talents."

Micah took a step forward. "Your Majesty, perhaps the best way to serve the kingdom is not to send her away for lessons in politics but to hone those talents that come naturally to her. It is Ahanna's unique spirit and passion that gives her strength."

Tisus nodded. "Well said. Still, I made a promise. What's more, we signed an accord that the Golden Dragons would educate the future monarch of my line. I have already postponed it for two years."

"Sire, given the right circumstances, a teacher of a different sort could help, but it would have to be Ahanna's idea. There is someone else that knows what she will need. You have considered it once before."

"Considered, but she is my firstborn and will be Queen. The treaty…"

"If The Enclave temporarily thought Feylynn, the future Queen, it would not compromise the contract. The treaty only states your heir," Micah said.

King Tisus lifted a brow. "That sounds like a conspiracy, young Ranger."

Micah smiled, "It is merely the observation of a young man."

King Tisus held his grin in check. "I see."

"Of course," Micah hedged, "That kind of training… It will be difficult." He shrugged. "Possibly too difficult and dangerous."

"Not much is too difficult for a stubborn child like Ahanna," King Tisus said, rubbing his chin as he considered what Micah was proposing. After a few minutes of silent contemplation, he said, "Very well, then."

Moving to his desk, Tisus sought out fresh parchment and his quill. He applied the black ink with solid and confident strokes. After he finished, he dusted the missive with white powder that hid the symbols from view. Finally, he sealed the letter with his royal mark and handed it to Micah. "Send this to Ellomar right away."

"Yes, Sire."

"Tell no one else."

"I swear, Your Majesty. Consider it done."

As Micah turned to leave, Tisus stopped him. "Make sure she's safe, Micah."

The Ranger turned back to King Tisus with sad resignation but firm resolve. "You can trust me, Sire."

"That I have never doubted. You are as good a man as your father was. Now be swift, for time is short."

"Yes, Sire." Warmed by the compliment, Micah bowed and took his leave.

As Micah hurried to comply with his given orders, Tisus reached into his pocket to pull out the small likeness he carried with him. He rubbed his thumb over the image captured there. A young blonde elf stared back at him with love in her eyes. "I pray I am doing the right thing, Shelanna. May Ealoram himself protect our girls, for this world would swallow them whole given the right chance."

FOUR

"Why are we still doing a lesson if I am leaving in a few days?" Ahanna asked as she pulled on Freesia's reins to keep pace with her instructor.

Upon Soros, Micah gave her a sideways glance, "Do you have something better to do today?"

"I do. I need to pack and plan for the trip."

"Princess, this is probably your last chance to go out before you leave. Do you really wish to waste your time inside pouting?"

Ahanna frowned. "I wasn't pouting," she insisted. Unfortunately his observation was accurate, and it bothered her. Since their argument, she avoided her father at all costs, refused to go to regular meals, and stayed in her room as much as possible.

Micah lifted a knowing brow, and she scoffed. It irritated her more that she liked it when he made that gesture most of the time. Her days with him were numbered to single digits, and she found it difficult to turn her mood around even when she was with him.

He turned his horse toward the woods and pointed to the Feldorian Mountains. "Your view won't be the same since that's where The Enclave is," he explained. "You'll be looking down at Ranoak. Though, you won't be able to see it."

"Have you been there?" Ahanna asked.

He nodded, "I have been to the small village below The Enclave three times. Even though I have never crossed the bridge to go inside, I have seen the huge structure, and it is daunting. The Golden Knights guard that place tightly, and I imagine once you arrive, that kind of protection will increase."

At Castle Ranoak, her father was extremely cautious and protective of his daughters. Even without his protective nature, the truth of her heritage must be carefully protected among the Knights as well. She sighed as she thought about it. "You don't need to remind me. I will be a prisoner wrapped in the glory of fine dresses."

Micah cleared his throat and pointed to the river. "If you cross Cassian's Run and follow the edge of the mountain range there, I stayed in that area for most of my time when I left Ranoak."

"Isn't Pran that way?" Ahanna wondered.

"Right. I traveled all over Ishreedin with El—" he coughed. "My mentor took me to several places, even the edge of the Shilesta Woods, but my home was north of Pran."

Curiosity piqued, Ahanna's mood shifted, "What were the Shilesta woods like?"

"We followed the Silent River and crossed the edge of the Uninhabited Lands. That was a vast place, and I didn't like even being on the edge of it. I never went into the woods themselves but on the border to pass a message to someone. From my view, the forest was dense, thicker than the northern regions. I suppose the mountains are a factor. The rocky range breaks the foliage."

As they rode through the woods, Ahanna listened while

Micah told her about the places he visited and the woods where he lived. Her heart longed to see them too.

He spoke about the wildlife and what she could hunt should she need to survive. Micah also spoke of the land surrounding Ranoak, and it sounded far better than The Enclave, where she would spend the next three years. Even her sister's time to train as a paladin was only two years. Her shoulders slumped, and she frowned as her thoughts drifted back to her problems.

To the people of Ranoak, The Enclave was a legendary architectural structure. People spoke of The Enclave with reverence. It was older than the oldest memory on any existing record. Her father's room had a tapestry depicting the structure's beauty at sunset, and if it were even half as glorious as the artist's creation, seeing it would be a pleasure. Still, wanting to see it and living confined behind its walls were two very different things to Ahanna.

During her distraction, Micah switched topics, "When you are there, you will learn of protocol and politics. I am sure it will be fulfilling in its own way. I much prefer the forests and mountains myself."

Ahanna glared at him. "Are you trying to remind me that I will practically be shackled, Micah?"

He shook his head and avoided her eyes. "No, Princess. I'm sorry, I was only talking to pass the time."

"I know a better way to pass the time," she said and urged Freesia ahead. Ahanna leaned forward and let go of every other thought as her horse took off toward the forest at full gallop.

If only I could run from my duties as easily as Freesia can run from Micah, she thought.

Ahanna let Freesia run to the top of the hill before she reined in. Micah pulled up next to her a few seconds later. She closed her eyes and tipped her head back to let the warmth of the sun fill the emptiness of her cold heart. "I know I have lived a privileged life, and that comes with responsibility, but I loathe what is happening."

"I know this is hard," he said.

"Do you?" she accused and looked at him. "How can you?"

"Princess, I wasn't yet thirteen when your father sent me away."

"But he didn't send you to The Enclave. He didn't expect you to take his place and lead Ranoak. My father didn't ask you to be trapped as a ruler over people that will hate you just because of who you are." She turned away from him when she said, "Who your mother is."

"No. He didn't," Micah conceded. "I never even knew my mother."

"I wish I didn't either," Ahanna said, and her hands unconsciously came up to pull her hair over her ears.

"Ahanna…" Micah started to say.

"I know, Micah."

"I wish there was a way I could help you. If I could, I would take you away to the north to see the forest there."

Ahanna sighed, "But you can't. You are the King's Ranger, and you are trapped in those responsibilities as I will be trapped in mine. We are forever bound to the path fate gives us."

"Princess, don't forget you get to decide what to do with that fate. Even if you are meant to be queen, you do not have to conform to anyone's version of that role, but your own."

Ahanna looked skyward again, and for a minute, she said nothing. Eventually, she sighed, "I suppose we should get on with our lessons for today. It is my last one with you, so I hope you planned a good one."

Micah smiled, "We could talk about poisonous plants, you know, in case you ever find yourself alone in the woods and needing food."

Ahanna smiled, "Have you ever heard of a queen who went exploring alone?"

He smiled with her as his gaze looked over to the beauty of the setting sun. "No, I never have."

Micah arrived back at the castle more than an hour after sunset. After caring for the horses, he went to report to the King. He nodded to the guard, Caldaren, who stood at the stairs.

"Nice to see you back, Micah."

"Is King Tisus available?"

Caldaren gestured for him to pass, "He's alone if that's what you mean."

Micah nodded and quickly took the three steps to the main door and entered. Once he was in the foyer to the King's chambers, he knocked on Tisus' office door.

"Enter," Tisus bade from inside.

As Micah pushed the door open, he found his King sitting at the desk reviewing records from various lords.

When Tisus looked up to see Micah, he grinned. "Tell me."

Micah bowed.

Tisus stood and rounded his desk. Then, taking Micah's shoulder, he said, "Nevermind that, Son, how'd it go?"

"I did my best, Sire. I believe she is thinking about it."

Tisus' brow furrowed, and he dropped his hand. "I should have never agreed to these terms in the treaty, then I wouldn't find myself in such a dilemma."

"Cirus took the letter and should have arrived today," Micah said.

Tisus nodded absently and rubbed his bearded chin. "If she

doesn't run, my hands are tied."

Micah had learned that even as a king, one could rarely do as they wished. "It will be years before we—before *you* can see her again."

"I know, Son. It will be hardest on her sisters, though. My girls are very close. Without their mother, they clung to each other, and while they will see Feylynn at the next festival, and they will be able to write her, Ahanna will have no such contact. I fear for the twins. They rely on their older sisters so much."

"I'll be here, and I will do as much as I can to help," Micah offered.

Tisus smiled, "They are as much your sisters as Ahanna's, aren't they?"

"Yes, Sire."

Tisus patted his shoulder, "It's all up to her now."

"Sire, I could go—"

His suggestion was met with Tisus' shaking head. "She has to do this on her own. If you disappear with her, not only will I have to punish you if caught, but running away with a man will spread rumors that would burden her later. If Ahanna wishes to escape her bindings, she must choose to do it on her own."

Micah pressed his lips together to keep himself from objecting.

"Don't worry, Ellomar has never let me down."

Micah nodded. His mentor had never let him down either, so like Tisus, he would have to trust the old Ranger too.

FIVE

A few days later, Ahanna sat in her bed-chamber and stared at an open trunk filled with gowns, creams, uncomfortable corsets, and everything else her ladies-in-waiting deemed necessary for the long trip she would take tomorrow. Eyeing the green dress for tomorrow, Ahanna groaned aloud, knowing none of it was even remotely practical for a three-week journey on the dusty northern roads. *How am I supposed to relieve myself on the road with all this getup on?*

She glanced longingly at her favored hunting outfit, then back to the oversized box with an expression of pure disdain. Here in the comfort of her room, looking at the dress selected for tonight's dinner, Ahanna's chest tightened with anxiety.

It wasn't as if the dress itself was the problem. Honestly, she loved every one of the dresses that her seamstress Liddia made. But as she stared at the gown, she thought about the walls and turrets of The Enclave, and she was already feeling enclosed.

What will it feel like when I am actually trapped behind them?

A soft knocking on her chamber door interrupted her dark thoughts. Ahanna wiped at the tear that had escaped her control and pasted a fake smile on her face. "Enter."

A small, pixie-like face poked her head into the room. Revienah, Ahanna's youngest sister, grinned mischievously. "Ahanna, you've got to come outside!" she exclaimed as she grabbed her hand. "The Knights have arrived, and you won't believe it till you see it. I love it when they come. They're all so pretty and not like the boring guards out here."

The pressing weight in her chest settled fully as her sister pulled her from the bed and chatted about the arriving Knights. As Revienah continued to pull her along the corridor, Ahanna's stomach twisted and burned.

It was clear that Revienah didn't fully understand the implications that her sister's unwanted fate had arrived in shining armor. By this time tomorrow, both Ahanna and Feylynn would find themselves trapped within the ranks of the Paladin's army, and there would be no chance of escape. That thought alone nearly caused Ahanna to tear her hand from her younger sister's and run down the hall, through the front gates, and away from everything.

When the pair reached the balcony, Ahanna took note of her other sisters respectfully watching the procession below. The hooves of heavy warhorses clattered against the cobbled courtyard, and from here, she heard the Captain's call to halt.

Ahanna's hand went to her throat. She couldn't breathe, and her heart picked up speed as the soldiers reined in their mounts. Her sensitive hearing picked up the hints of scraping metal and worn leather when the Knights adjusted their seats to attention.

Running to the wall to join Resora, her identical twin, Revienah, squealed as she gazed out over the edge, "See! Look at them. They're amazing!"

As she reluctantly approached the balcony, Ahanna faked yet another smile for her youngest sister. *It's the end of everything I know.* Their family would never be the same after today.

She glanced at her closest sister Feylynn as she tucked her lengthy, black hair behind her ears. When Feylynn looked over, their eyes met, and she saw it. That same knowledge weighed on her, but Ahanna's first assumption was incorrect. Her sister did understand. Feylynn—strong, dependable Feylynn—she understood the truth, and she accepted it as an inevitable duty, looked forward to it even. She was eighteen months Ahanna's junior but far more mature in her soul. She favored their father not only in appearance but in spirit as well. She would thrive at The Enclave while Ahanna would wither.

As they stared at one another, her eyes must have displayed fear because Feylynn's filled with compassion.

Ahanna offered a tight nod to her sister as she walked to the balcony's edge, and for a second, she forgot to breathe. Thirty knights in shining gold and silver armor waited in the courtyard. They sat regally upon mighty warhorses at rigid attention. King Tisus approached, and the call of a horn rang out. With precise unity, the legendary Knights lifted fists to their hearts and bowed their heads in salute. Even the horses were trained to lift a single hoof and drop their heads.

As reverent silence filled the area, real panic rose within the Crowned Princess, and her eyes darted about the ranking soldiers, taking in the scene below. Sunlight glinted off of the golden dragon's shields and breastplates. Blue cloaks, pinned to the armor with shining claw-like buckles, fluttered with the light wind. For a moment, her eyes transfixed on the flag adorned with a golden dragon as it danced in that same breeze.

Amazing was not how Ahanna would describe the scene below. *Confining and restrictive* was how it looked. It was no wonder the Knights held such an impressive reputation. Thirty knights in proud formation were more intimidating than two hundred of their regular castle guards.

The rider at the front dismounted and offered King Tisus the customary bow until the King said something to make him rise. Then, the Captain approached, and the two men smiled as they clasped arms in strong solidarity.

"I can't hear what they're saying," Resora complained.

Eager to accommodate her twin, Revienah climbed the short wall to stand on the stone ledge.

"What are you doing?" Enreal scolded.

"What does it look like? I'm trying to get closer," Revienah shot back.

Enreal glowered at her youngest sister and grabbed her arm. "One day, you're going to get yourself killed with these silly stunts you pull."

Fiercely protective and cautious, their middle sister hated all the acrobatic games Revienah played. Their father often teased Revienah, saying she would likely find a way to climb into the celestial fields.

"I'm only trying to hear what they're saying," Revienah protested as Enreal pulled her down. "Who is that speaking to Father?"

"That is Captain Vasjoc, and we are not meant to hear. Otherwise, we would have received an invitation," Feylynn reassured her.

Revienah rolled her eyes.

With her panic rising, Ahanna backed away from the wall. Her breath came in quick short gasps, her eyes filled with tears.

Seeing the fear in her eldest sister's features, Resora moved toward her. "Ahanna, are you sick?"

"I can't do this. I have to leave," she whispered.

"Do what?" Revienah questioned innocently.

"Leave where?" Resora added.

"She does not wish to go with them," Feylynn answered with understanding.

"Why not?" Revienah replied with surprise. "I think it is going to be a grand adventure. Imagine all the places you'll see and the people you'll meet. Father said Resora and I would get a turn to go out into the realm soon. I can hardly wait."

"That's because you're too young to understand what's out there," Ahanna chastised.

"I'm not stupid, Ahanna," Revienah insisted.

Enreal brushed her younger sister's brown hair back lovingly. "Ahanna knows that, and she did not call you stupid."

"See! I can't even speak to my sisters without upsetting them!" Ahanna cried. "How could I ever be a good queen? Enreal is only sixteen, and even she would make a better queen."

Enreal's eyes went wide. "I have no desire to be queen," she insisted.

"I don't want this. Just look at them! Do you know what will happen after this? Arranged marriages, probably to one of those very knights!" Ahanna threw out a hand, pointing toward the men below. "Not to mention politics, finances, impossible decisions… I am too clumsy, too stubborn, too—"

"Wild?" Enreal offered.

"Elven!" Ahanna protested as if that was enough. "I know it's selfish, but I can't go with them. This will never work. I'm not like them, and I'm not like our father. I don't want to be trapped like him. Ranoak deserves better than me. You all do."

"Ahanna, I am sure father would listen—" Resora started, but her sister's shaking head cut her off.

"He won't. He believes I should be Queen. It is my birthright, he insisted. Well, I say it's all your birthright as well. Shouldn't we have a choice?"

Tilting her head, Feylynn said calmly, "We all have choices, Sister. Even a knight sworn to protect the people can choose not to act when the time comes, but how many innocents will suffer if he does? Your choices affect more than just you. Father understands that."

"I know that! Don't you think I know that?" Ahanna pleaded.

"You're saying you want to leave and avoid being Queen, not for yourself but for the kingdom?" Enreal asked.

"It is not I who should be Queen. It should be Feylynn!"

"Me?" Feylynn questioned as she staggered back a step.

"You! You are stronger than I am. Braver." Tears filled Ahanna's eyes. "You are loyal and smart. You are everything I am not."

Still reeling, Feylynn shook her head. "I have no desire to be Queen either. I will guard Ranoak as a Golden Dragon Knight one day, but I do not plan to be its ruler."

"I didn't plan on it either!" Ahanna snapped.

"Someone has to," Enreal said.

"I'll do it!" Revienah offered.

Resora rolled her eyes. "Not likely. You can't even sit still for more than a minute. How will you sit through one hour of an audience with anyone?"

"I'd get people to do it for me," she replied.

Ignoring the twins, Ahanna pleaded with Feylynn. "Can't you see? If made Queen, I will lead this land to ruin. Never would you shy away from a battle or back down from a bully. You always know the right things to say and do. If I can't even shoot a helpless rabbit mercifully, how could I ever issue a merciful judgment? Feylynn, I can't be Queen. I simply can't." Ahanna sank to the ground and began to sob.

Enreal rushed to console her. "Your inability to shoot a

helpless animal shows you are merciful. Killing should never be your first goal."

The twins followed, sinking to their knees on either side of Ahanna. Each of them wrapped their oldest sister up in their arms. Revienah looked to Feylynn with deep, sad eyes. "Please, Feylynn. We have to help her."

Still shocked by her sister's breakdown, she could only stare at her in confusion. "What would you have me do? We are leaving tomorrow. It's too late." But Feylynn *was* thinking about it, even though she didn't want to. They all were.

Enreal looked up. Tears shone in her eyes. "The woods, we can help her hide in the woods until the Knights leave. Micah has trained her. Ahanna could stay there safely for a night or two. Then, if they can't find her, they can't take her."

"The woods are perfect!" Resora agreed. "When they're gone, we can bring you back."

Feylynn was shaking her head, but the younger girls didn't notice.

"I know the perfect way to the stables. We can help you leave right after supper," Revienah offered. "Freesia is one of the fastest horses made. She will help you away. No one will even see us. I use that route sometimes to—" she stopped abruptly when she noted all of her sisters' expressions at her revelation.

Sniffling, Ahanna furrowed her brow and tilted her head to Revienah. She opened her mouth, ready to lecture her youngest sister, but Revienah didn't let her. "Before you think to scold me, remember you need my help."

"And then what?" Feylynn questioned. "What happens next?"

They all turned and stared at Feylynn. For a few seconds, none of them spoke.

"I suppose Father will be a little put out, but she wouldn't have to go," Resora said.

"Feylynn is right," Ahanna replied, drying her tears. "It won't work. I will still be next in line to be Queen, and he can summon them back. It won't change anything."

"We have to do something," Enreal insisted with fierce devotion. "If this causes you so much heartache, we cannot stand by and do nothing."

New tears of love came to Ahanna's eyes, and she squeezed her sister's hands. Shrugging, she said, "It's alright. Feylynn speaks the truth. Leaving for the night or even for a fortnight will not waiver Father's resolve."

"I am only half right," Feylynn said, crouching down before her sisters. As the girls turned their full attention to Feylynn, she heaved a heavy sigh, "Nothing changes if you return."

"You mean she would have to leave?" Revienah questioned with wide eyes. "She can't do that."

Ignoring Revienah, Feylynn focused on Ahanna, "You spoke of choices, and you are right. Everyone has the right to choose, but often our options are limited by circumstance. Be sure of your choice this day, Sister. Be sure about how serious your fears are. The choices you desperately desire are these, leave your home and family behind and never return. Or stay, and prepare for indentured service and schooling, as a servant to the people, with the chance to come back three years hence ready to take on the role of Queen."

"Forever?" Ahanna whispered. "But what about all of you? Will I never see you again?"

Feylynn shrugged. "Either way, when the sun rises tomorrow, our lives will change," she replied, mimicking Ahanna's earlier thoughts.

"What about your promised oaths to The Paladin Enclave?" Ahanna asked.

Feylynn grinned, and Revienah smiled with her as her quick, devious mind pieced together the truth. "She hasn't taken them yet. They can't hold her to a vow she hasn't taken yet."

"What will I do without my sisters?" Ahanna asked.

Feylynn came close and put her hand on her knee. "You will live. And you will find a path to happiness of your choosing."

Enreal sniffled. "We will be here for you when the time to return comes. That will never change."

As all five sisters processed what they were about to do, their heads came together. With saddened hearts, they held tight to one another in a huddle, sharing soft tears of goodbye.

"It's decided then," Feylynn proclaimed after several minutes.

"Tonight after supper, we will help you escape," Enreal finished.

SIX

"I pilfered a bit of food for the road," Enreal said as she entered with bread, cheese, dates, and salted meats, all wrapped in cloth. "Micah was in the kitchens."

Abruptly, Ahanna stopped loading her traveling pack and looked over to her sister. "Micah? What did you tell him?" she asked.

"I told him that I wanted to put together a few of your favorite snacks to ease your journey." Enreal shrugged. "It's true enough. He even helped me select the best foods that keep well."

Relieved, Ahanna finished folding her spare tunic and added it to her pack. "Thanks, Enreal."

"You're really going to go through with it, aren't you?" Enreal questioned. When Ahanna met her eyes, she sniffled. "I cannot imagine what it will be like with both of you gone. I will be the oldest for a time."

Ahanna looked away. "Are you angry with me?"

"No. Not angry. Jealous, maybe. I wish I didn't have to remain here stuck behind stuffy castle walls, wearing fancy dresses, and surrounded by attendants."

Her older sister grinned fondly. "You always were the most like me."

"Maybe. I would miss Father, though. Despite my wish to wander, I'm not sure I would ever have the courage to leave Ranoak."

"I will miss all of you. I wish you could come."

Enreal's head dropped. "I wish you could stay."

Ahanna pulled her sister into a tight embrace, and her tears resurfaced. "If only we could be children again, running through the woods, dragging Micah along in our search for magical ponies."

"If we were children again, Mother would be here, and you wouldn't have to go."

Ahanna's mood soured, and she pulled away to grab her pack. "I'm not gone yet anyway," she teased. "I still need to get to the stables unnoticed."

Enreal smirked. "Revienah will get you there, don't worry. She's been sneaking about for some time now. She's quite skilled, I assure you."

"How did you know?" Ahanna asked.

Enreal smiled. "She uses my window. I am not as heavy a sleeper as she thinks."

Ahanna laughed with her sister, but they sobered quickly when the heavy wooden door opened, and their three other sisters entered. Revienah peered out the door one last time, then quietly closed and locked it once they were all inside.

"Are you ready?" Feylynn asked.

"I am," Ahanna replied.

Feylynn nodded. "As planned, Revienah will take you down

to the stables. In the meantime, I will occupy Captain Vasjoc and Father for as long as I can. Then, Resora and Enreal will feign the need for a night stroll and distract the guards at the southside near the stables."

"Why the guards?" Ahanna turned to Revienah. "Don't you avoid them when you wander about?"

"Are you kidding me? They are all over!" Revienah exclaimed. "Considering Father's idea of protection, we are lucky there are not more. Sometimes I bribe them."

"Blackmail is more like," Enreal teased.

Revienah rolled her eyes. "Anyway, Most times, I can sneak past them when I am by myself." She giggled, "This one time—"

"Later." Feylynn scolded. "We do not have time for stories right now."

Revienah pouted. "Well, two of us sneaking around makes it harder, and the Knights mulling about complicate this even more."

Ahanna frowned.

"Don't look at me like that. You'll jinx us." Revienah complained. "We'll be fine. Enreal and Resora are just additional insurance."

Resora patted her twin's shoulder as she approached Ahanna. "Don't worry, look how pretty Enreal looks tonight. There's not a young knight within one hundred miles that wouldn't be distracted by her."

"That's why you're wearing the red dress. You hate the red dress," Ahanna observed.

Enreal shrugged. "Not so. I'm not too fond of the attention the red dress attracts. I honestly like the dress."

Resora smiled. "A hundred miles, I tell you. They will all be looking at Enreal and her little sister." She paused and reached into her pocket. "I made something for you." Resora placed a wooden charm tied to a leather cord in Ahanna's slender hand.

Ahanna marveled at the woodwork, and she ran her fingers over the precisely carved lines of a little fox. "You made this?"

"It's not such a big thing, but once, while I was studying with Micah, he mentioned the fox and how it's smart and cunning like you. So when I tried to think of something for your trip to The Enclave, this came to my mind."

Ahanna fisted it and pulled it close to her chest. The gift touched her deeply, and her long-withheld tears started to spill freely. "Thank you, Resora."

Never seeing Micah again—and worse—never getting the chance to tell him goodbye had been festering inside her all day. Yet, the risk of going to see him was great. He was too smart and would figure her out before she could even say a word. Worse, he was beyond loyal to King Tisus, and Ahanna believed he would never betray her father by allowing her to leave.

"It's time to go, Ahanna," Feylynn urged.

"You're right." Ahanna wiped her tears quickly and sniffed as she donned her heavy travel pack. She slipped the charm around her neck, and her tears kept flowing.

She broke all their emotional barriers. The five of them fell together, with Ahanna in the middle. They embraced each other as tightly as they could manage, as if trying to cement an unbreakable link that would last for the long separation.

"If only we could hold onto you a little longer," Feylynn said, stepping back but squeezing Ahanna's hand. "I have been holding your hand for as long as I can remember. It's hard to believe I am letting go so easily."

Ahanna sighed. "I love you all, and I promise I will send word as soon as I'm settled so that you may find me should the need arise. I will always come if you call, I swear it!"

Amid tears and running noses, they nodded together in

agreement, and they released their eldest sister.

"Come on, Ahanna, we can use your window," Revienah mumbled as she wiped her tears.

"Why not Enreal's?"

Revienah glared at Enreal. "You told!"

She shrugged. "It seems a moot point now."

Revienah sighed, "The truth is, your window is better, but you sleep like a cat. Apparently, so does Enreal."

"Apparently," Ahanna agreed with a soft smile.

Revienah pulled on her hand. "Come on."

With one final glance back, Ahanna followed her youngest sister outside through the window to make her own fate. The other three watched them drop out of sight with grieving hearts.

After a couple of minutes, Enreal turned to Feylynn. "You do know it won't matter, right?"

"I know," she said firmly.

"What won't matter?" Resora asked.

"If The Enclave suspects Feylynn betrayed her upcoming vows before she even takes them, she may never get the chance to utter them," Enreal explained.

"What?" Resora grabbed Feylynn's arm. "What will you do?"

"It's true that the vow speaks of deception against the King, but they also demand I always do the right thing. Our actions were the right choice. I know it in my heart. Faced with the ultimatum between my sisters or Ranoak, I know the right decision. Likely, I did the right thing for both my sister and for Ranoak."

Resora nodded, relieved.

Enreal shifted to leave the room and enact the rest of their plan. "Do you think they will believe your argument?"

"Does it matter?" Feylynn answered as she followed.

"No. I suppose it doesn't. Let's pray the masters never find out." Enreal turned to her younger sister with a cheerful smile, "Come, Resora, let's go for an evening stroll."

As they left Feylynn alone to head in the opposite direction, the truth burned in her heart. The betrayal of the Crown was a betrayal of the Golden Dragon's code. She had known that truth the moment she offered the idea to her eldest sibling. This plan to help Ahanna could destroy her only chance to be part of the Paladin Enclave. That grim reality would not sway her, though, because Feylynn, second daughter of King Tisus and Shelanna the elf, would always choose her sisters over Ranoak. Family was the only treasure one could not replace. This was the lesson her father instilled above any other.

SEVEN

Revienah hurried along the narrow overhang as nimbly as a cat, and Ahanna struggled to keep up. It wasn't as if she was clumsy. Up until now, she had always considered herself to be surefooted, but her youngest sister put that belief to shame. Revienah was small, and her diminutive size helped, but size was not her only advantage. Her agility far surpassed what anyone would ever suspect from a young princess.

Revienah was agile, daring, and had little fear. She had been climbing things before she could walk, yet it was clear to Ahanna that Revienah had been out on this ledge many times. Even so, she couldn't fathom how this child, not yet thirteen, could maneuver herself so easily and fearlessly, fifty feet above the ground, on a slight overhang no wider than the length of her dagger.

"Slow down," Ahanna whispered sharply. "You're going to break your neck."

Revienah stopped, glared back at her, pointed upward, and

brought her hand back to her lips, indicating that her sister should be quiet.

Ahanna looked up to see the two guards standing watch about fifteen feet above them on the other side of the parapet. Focusing their attention further out, the sentries paid no attention to what was directly below them. Their training centered on keeping enemies out, not keeping princesses in, and it was clear that Revienah took full advantage of this weak point in the castle's security.

Ahanna nodded and gestured for Revienah to continue. Her younger sister moved along but slowed her pace. When they reached the corner, Revienah knelt and worked a small brick free from the wall. Watching her, Ahanna was stunned. She gaped at the contents of her sister's secret cubby and bent down to get a better look. Inside, she kept a waterskin, a rope and hook that she had wedged in the wall, and a box of bandages and ointments. Revienah shrugged and smiled sheepishly and once more reminded her sister to hold her tongue with the same gesture of bringing a finger to her lips.

Closing her open mouth and shaking her head, Ahanna watched in amazement as her sister angled the rope to the south side of the wall. She gestured a few times to make sure Ahanna knew how to hold the lifeline correctly, then she stepped off the ledge backward and scared Ahanna half to death. Peering over the ridge, she watched as Revienah made the descent down the stone as if she were walking down the street backward.

When it was Ahanna's turn, the climb down did not look as polished as her younger sister made it seem. She lost her balance twice, scraped her knee, and received a rope burn on her hand for the trouble. Eventually, she made it to the bottom on shaky legs.

After Ahanna regained her bearings, they ran together across the north side of the grounds toward the gardens. Through the darkness, Revienah guided her older sister through a maze of gardens using small paths and openings between bushes and trees.

They had to backtrack around to the stables using an indirect route to avoid detection. When they came to the edge of their cover, Revienah glanced out to verify whether the coast was clear and froze. When she came back, Revienah gestured for Ahanna to have a look. Several Golden Knights milled about the stables. Many of them leaned over the fence of the exercise arena as the stable boy led Ahanna's horse out for them to admire, and her heart sank.

"Freesia," she whispered.

Revienah came up behind her and gripped her hand in support. Ahanna ducked back and moved deeper into the garden, pulling her sister with her. "What are they doing here?" Ahanna whispered frantically.

"I don't know, but maybe we can wait them out in the gardens. Enreal should be along soon."

Ahanna considered the situation for several minutes. She hated to leave without her horse, but there was no alternative way for her to get another. The Knights were everywhere.

"We can't wait that long," Ahanna countered. "There's no way Enreal and Resora can distract that many. Besides, they are likely already distracting others. Father expects me to meet the Captain within the hour. He will come looking when I don't arrive. I need to be on my way before that."

"On foot?" Revienah asked.

Ahanna glanced back toward the stables longingly. "I don't see that I have any other choice," she replied, keeping her voice low.

Revienah considered Ahanna's response for a second and then offered, "I know a more discreet way out if you don't have a horse. Plus, without Freesia, no one will suspect you left for a bit longer."

Ahanna sighed and shifted her attention back to her horse. "It's probably the best idea. On foot, I can stick to hidden paths and keep any possible tracks hidden."

"I'll take care of her for you until you return."

Ahanna smiled wistfully and looked back to her younger sister. "Promise to ride her every day."

"I promise," Revienah replied.

"Alright then. Show me the way out, Little Raven."

Revienah's brows drew together in a puzzled expression. "What did you call me?"

"Little Raven. You are clever and fast, and it has become clear that you take flight regularly. No wall shall keep you in."

Revienah grinned with pride. "I like that."

"Let's go." Ahanna took her sister's hand.

Together they crept to the back wall bordering the garden and stopped near Cassian's Run, an underground water channel that flowed under the castle wall and provided Ranoak with fresh water.

Even though they were some distance from the stables, the fear of discovery had their hearts racing. In a hushed voice, Revienah explained, "During spring, this river runs too fast, but this late in the year, you can swim it. The grate only goes about eight feet down, although the river bottom has changed over time. Magda has told me that rivers change shape all the time. Storms and animals affect how it flows. She called it natural erosion.

"Anyway, I managed to wiggle between two rocks that moved, and I dug some space between them. It almost took forever because I had to keep coming up for air. The river is also cold. Magda says it's fed snow from the Feldorian Mountains."

"Why did you do this?" Ahanna asked.

"Why not?" Revienah replied. "Once you're through, you

can head for the woods. You should be able to fit, but you'll have to hold your breath awhile."

Ahanna looked at the dark water with trepidation. "How in the realm will I see down there?"

"I'll lead the way since it's dark. I use this." Revienah hesitantly pulled a small glass orb connected to a thin gold chain from her pocket. The glass glowed with a faint blue light.

"Where in all the heavens did you acquire such a treasure?"

"I found it."

"Where?"

Revienah's features pinched. "It doesn't matter."

"Alright, fine, keep your secret." Ahanna glanced again at the icy water and furrowed her brows. "What about my gear?"

Revienah smiled and moved to a cropping of stones behind them. "I keep an oiled skin hidden here and wrap my clothes up inside. It helps. With your pack wrapped in the skin, I am sure it will work, but you'll have to push it through ahead of you. It won't fit on your back. You can tie your bow and short sword outside of it. That way, you won't get caught up by them."

"Just how often do you leave?" Ahanna asked.

Revienah shrugged. "Not so often."

Shaking her head and smiling, Ahanna admitted, "You're a wonder, little sister. I'm only sorry I didn't realize it before today."

Revienah spread the skin out with a sly grin, and the girls set about the task of stripping down to their underclothes for the frigid swim.

Revienah stashed her tunic and trousers behind a rock as Ahanna rolled and stuffed her clothes, including her travel cloak, securely in her pack. Unfortunately, her leather boots would not fit. In the end, Ahanna accepted she would be stuck with wet boots. She decided to tie them together and wore them around her neck.

After the sisters secured the skin around her travel pack, they waded into the mountain water. The cold temperature was jarring and sent chills over their skin. After the initial shock, they pushed themselves in the water. Taking a deep breath, Revienah dove below the surface and Ahanna was close behind as they swam down to the river bottom. Silver-scaled fish darted away from the glowing light wrapped around Revienah's wrist.

When they reached the bottom, Ahanna saw the small opening that nature started, and which her sister had helped along. At first glance, she wasn't as confident she would fit as Revienah was, but she swam hard against the current for the opening anyway. As instructed, Ahanna pushed her pack through the hole first and released it so it wouldn't drag her down.

Her lungs were starting to strain for air, and if Ahanna was going to make it through in time, she needed to move faster. Revienah directed the small light toward the hole for her, and she swam for it with steady strokes. The resistance of the current that condensed at the small opening was much more robust, and it forced her to use the leverage of the rocks and the metal grate to hold her place without exhausting herself.

A slight panic set in when she realized how tight the hole would be—getting her shoulders through required some extra work and creativity. Ahanna put one arm through the hole and shifted, then she gripped the gate on the opposite side to wiggle her other arm out at an angle. She thought she was free when her torso followed, but when her hips met resistance, a tickle of fear settled in her chest.

Ahanna pulled, squirmed, kicked, and the tickle of fear turned to full-blown panic that tried to coax her into opening her mouth and letting go of her precious oxygen. The rough stones tore her undergarments and scraped at her soft skin, leaving painful scratches along her hip. Ahanna's heart thudded in her chest as she put every effort into levering herself free.

Seeing the problem, Revienah pulled and pushed against the barrier from her side. She flipped in the water, took hold of the bars, and tried kicking the loose stone several times. On the fourth try, with Ahanna pulling and Revienah kicking, one of the rocks finally broke free, and dirt and algae clouded the water as the loose stone fell to the bottom of the river bed.

Ahanna pushed against the other stones with all the force she could muster. Kicking her feet hard, she swam for life-giving air. With the momentum she created, Ahanna breached the surface as fast as a flying fish. She sucked in a desperate gulp of air but fell back down into the water. She came up again, sputtering. When she finally regained her bearings, Ahanna tipped her head back and took a few seconds to enjoy the precious commodity of the crisp night around her.

She dove into the water one more time to retrieve her belongings. Breaching the water again, Ahanna tossed her pack to the bank. When the bundle landed on the ground safely, Ahanna turned and swam to the gate that separated her from her sister. Revienah was there waiting, kicking her legs to keep warm. Her sister's tiny hands held onto the iron bars, and Ahanna wrapped her own hands around Revienah's.

Excited, Revienah grinned broadly. "I wasn't sure you'd make it through."

Feeling the sting of fresh scrapes along her thighs, Ahanna shook her head, half in amazement and half in disbelief. "I wasn't either. You really are clever, little sister. Clever, and perhaps a little crazy."

"We all have our strengths."

"I'll miss you," Ahanna chuckled.

Revienah's excitement died, and her smile fell. "I hate this.

What will it be like without you here to scold me?"

"I will send word, I promise. And I shall scold you in my letters. For now, I know there will be many things to scold you for," Ahanna replied.

"It will not be the same anymore. After tonight, everything changes."

She tightened her grip on Revienah's hands. "I suppose that as we get older, changes will be more common, yet that knowledge does little to ease the heartache."

With new tears forming, Revienah sniffled her sorrow away. "Be safe, Ahanna."

"You're telling me such a thing when you could drown in this river at any time?" Ahanna scolded in a sarcastic manner.

"I—" Revienah started to explain, then seeing the sparkle in Ahanna's eyes, she dipped her head bashfully. "You're not serious."

"I had to scold my Little Raven one last time," Ahanna admitted and squeezed her sister's hand again. "In truth, I do wish you would exercise more caution. Be careful while I am away. Don't take many foolish risks."

"I'll do my best," Revienah replied with a mischievous smile. "Take this. You'll need it." She handed her oldest sister the orb.

"I can't, Little Raven. This is yours, and it is clearly precious to you," Ahanna protested.

"It's not." Revienah looked away as she confessed the truth. "I stole it from a trunk in Father's room..." she hesitated. "It's Mother's."

"I see." Ahanna took the miraculous item and rolled it in her fingers.

"I just wanted something of hers, something to connect me to her. When it glowed, I half hoped it was calling to her somehow, but she never came. Now you can have it. She can be with you."

"You didn't steal it," Ahanna insisted. She placed the small orb back in Revienah's hand and closed them in hers. "Mother left it behind, as she left us behind, so rightfully it is yours. You are her daughter. Wherever she is, I am sure she would want you to have it."

"It would help you see in the dark and keep you safe," Revienah protested.

Ahanna was already shaking her head. "It is yours. Besides, if they are looking for me, the light would give me away. Keep it safe, Revienah. Take it on all of your grand adventures, for I am certain you will have many before I return."

Revienah clenched the item in her fist tightly. The action showed Ahanna how much the magical stone meant to her, and she found herself touched that her little sister would even offer it at all.

The bars made it impossible to embrace one another as they wished to, and silence fell around them. Ahanna didn't want to let go, but there was nothing more to say. When Revienah's teeth started the chatter, she knew they could not prolong their goodbye anymore. She squeezed her sister's hand one final time and said, "It's cold, and time is short. Hurry back, so they don't notice you've gone."

They came out here to help Ahanna escape. Now that the moment was upon them, both sisters found it difficult to let go. Making a valiant effort to keep the tears from replacing the river water on her cheeks, Revienah choked out, "You won't forget to come back?"

"Never," Ahanna quietly replied.

"Promise?"

"I swear it."

"You will never be alone out there, Ahanna. We are all with you in spirit."

A fraction of her resolve began to crack. Leaving the throne was nothing. Leaving her home was regretful, but leaving her sisters and her father tore at her soul. Her chest was tight, and there was a ball of emotion forming in her throat. "I love you, Little Raven," she said and somehow found the strength to let go of Revienah's hand. She pushed away from the opening in the wall. "Go! You'll catch your death in these frigid waters."

Revienah nodded. Wiping her tears, she pushed away. Mimicking the same resolve, she swam for the shore.

Before she did the same, Ahanna offered her sister the respect of an Elvish farewell that she had learned from her mother. Closing her eyes and kissing her fingers, Ahanna touched her brow.

After several seconds she let her hand drop and watched until her sister's light reached the riverbank. Knowing Revienah was safe now, Ahanna swam to the opposite side and pulled herself from the grip of the biting river. The chill air pricked at her wet skin. With her teeth chattering now, she pulled her clothing from her pack with fumbling fingers and was pleased to discover the oiled covering had kept everything dry as promised.

After dressing and donning her wet boots, Ahanna hid the oiled skin in a nearby bush for Revienah to retrieve later. Then, she hurried up the hill and took a game path into the woods to avoid detection.

King Tisus stood in front of his throne, with ten Golden Dragon Knights watching as he confronted his daughters. "Where is she?"

"Honestly, Father, I do not know where she planned to go," Feylynn said.

Tisus had to be careful here. If he asked a question incorrectly, his Feylynn would not be able to sidestep her answers as she'd done then. He looked to Revienah, "Where were you before dinner?"

"I went out," Revienah admitted.

Captain Vasjoc asked, "To do what?"

She could hold out even if someone punished her, but Tisus still held his breath until she said, "I went to see the horses. Lots of soldiers were there talking about breeding the stallions."

Vasjoc glanced at one of the Knights near him and the man said, "It's true, sir, there were several men at the stables tonight. If the Princess left, she did not do so on horseback."

"I told you I was there," Revienah quipped.

"Revienah," Tisus scolded. "Do not show disrespect to the Knights."

"Yes, Father."

He eyed his daughters carefully. Next to Revienah, Resora poked her toe at the floor and refused to look up. She pressed her lips so tightly together that he thought she would explode if he questioned her, and Tisus pinched the bridge of his nose in exasperation. "Enreal."

"Yes, Father."

"Did you see Ahanna on your walk tonight?"

She shook her head. "No, Father. We did not see anyone other than the soldiers and the castle guard."

"Then take your younger sisters with you and get to bed. It's far too late for them to be here."

"Yes, Father," Enreal replied and curtsied before she took Resora's arm and left them. Revienah followed without a single hint of a guilty conscience.

Tisus wanted to sigh in relief, but he held it in. He turned to Captain Vasjoc. "Have any of the men found a single clue?"

"No, Sire. There is no sign of the Princess left through the gate."

Tisus huffed, "I have sent Micah Finn, my Ranger, to look for her. She cannot have gone far. We will find her."

The Captain said, "And if we do not locate her before morning?"

Tisus thought about it before saying, "You will have to keep your schedule. This is a temper tantrum of a spoiled princess. She cannot stay away long on her own. If we do not find her by morning, you will take Princess Feylynn as planned, and as the treaty demands, I will bring Princess Ahanna to you myself when I find her."

"I trust you will keep your word, Your Majesty," Vasjoc said.

"Of course, I will keep my word, Captain. Are you questioning my integrity?"

He lifted his hands defensively, "No, Sire. I only want to ensure the heir will be properly trained, as is promised. You swore she would train with us for no less than three years and no more than five."

The King narrowed his eyes. "I am well aware of my promise, Captain. I do not need anyone in The Enclave to remind me of what is on that parchment."

Tisus saw the flicker in Feylynn's eyes. She was surprised by what she was hearing. He had never disclosed that to his daughters before, but today it was important that she understood. He took the steps down to stand closer to Feylynn and met her eyes, "I know my daughters, Captain, I know better than you what they are doing and thinking. If Princess Ahanna ran away, we will not find her until she is ready. When she is, we can discuss what is next, but for now, you are expected to leave tomorrow, and so you shall."

"If she does not come back, I expect you will name Princess Feylynn your heir," Vasjoc said.

"I believe it is too early to discuss changing my heir. I cannot even consider such a drastic decision right now when my daughter is missing."

"Of course, Your Majesty," Vasjoc conceded and pressed his lips together.

"Take Feylynn tomorrow. As for Ahanna, she has until her twenty-third birthday to keep the agreement valid. A few days more will not make much difference. Should I see her, I promise I will bring her to you. I will write to Master Carek today and make sure he is aware."

"Yes, Your Majesty," Vasjoc said.

"Go tend to your men. Make sure you have all you need for your journey."

He bowed, saying, "Yes, Sir," and left the main hall.

Feylynn eyed her father, and he could practically hear her thoughts shouting. He didn't answer any of her unspoken questions, though. "You need rest too. I promise you will understand later."

Feylynn nodded and hugged him. "Goodnight, Father."

"Goodnight," he said and watched her go with a heavy heart. It was the last time he would wish her goodnight for a long time to come. Even worse was the reminder that he hadn't been able to bid Ahanna goodnight at all.

EIGHT

Ahanna hiked all night. By the time the first rays of light turned the sky to a dark blue, she had managed to make her way to a wooded area overgrown with greenery and pine trees, and here she settled for a short rest.

As the morning sun crested the mountain range and cleared off the last bits of darkness, her boots were finally drying out. Her feet inevitably suffered a few blisters from the wet footwear, but she was grateful it hadn't been worse.

Watching the rising sun, she hunkered down low in the brush to wait for the grand procession of Golden Knights to pass. When they finally emerged on the path, Ahanna watched in hopes of catching a glimpse of Feylynn as they made their way down the north road leading toward Dergin's Pass. She could not suppress the need to watch as they marched away despite the danger of being discovered.

The Enclave would not wait for Ahanna to be recovered. It

was something she and her sisters had counted on. They kept a strict schedule, and as predicted, the Knights moved along the road with her sister in tow, precisely at the break of dawn.

A torrent of emotion played through her when Ahanna saw Feylynn's golden mare canter along amid the center of shining armor and regal warhorses. Her sister sat proudly upon her horse, looking every bit a queen with her black hair and her royal blue cloak fluttering in the fall breeze. The sight of Feylynn like that reaffirmed Ahanna's choice to abdicate the throne. It was an image she would store in her memory till she took her last breath, even if that was a hundred or more years away. One day, an artist would render this picture in a storybook—she would make sure of it.

As the procession of Knights passed by her position, Ahanna noticed Feylynn's keen eyes scanning the woods for any sign of her eldest sister. Confident that she could not be seen, Ahanna pressed her fist to her heart in a knight's salute of solidarity and respect. She bowed her head to the woman who would one day be the Queen of Ranoak and whispered an Elvish farewell, *"Mara mǎsta, Nǻsa."*

Unbeknownst to Ahanna, Feylynn did catch a glimpse of her sister hidden among the trees on the hilltop. Sitting upon her horse, with sorrow in her heart, Feylynn kissed her fingers and pressed them to her head, whispering the exact words of farewell in the common tongue, "Good journey, Sister."

Three days later, the shivering wracked her body, and no amount of clenching her jaw would keep her teeth from chattering. The drenching rain soaked her cloak, her tunic, and even seeped into her boots. Three nights had passed since her risky flight from the castle. Still fearing the castle guards looking for her, Ahanna trudged along through the dreary weather. She spent the last few days trying to put distance between herself and her home while trying to decide on a solid plan. Of course, their whole idea was to get her away, but after she had accomplished that feat, she hadn't been smart enough to map out a possible destination.

She would have to find a place to settle eventually but had no idea where to go. The port cities were out of the question. It was the first place her father would look. Her rash decision and the lack of planning led to her current predicament. Reality was a harsh teacher, and right then, Ahanna was an inept student indeed.

For the last two days, she had slept little. The first night after Ahanna bid farewell to Feylynn, her constant worry over being caught kept her hyper-vigilant to any sound, and she had spent most of the night traveling. Worse, she couldn't shake the feeling that someone had been following her. Moving kept her warmer, and it distracted Ahanna from the lonely, black night with its multiple sounds. Her hereditary eyesight made it possible to see in the dim light, but her sight was less than reliable because of her sensitive hearing. Every noise set her on edge, and her eyes darted about with untrained focus. The tension in her muscles made her body ache, and she longed to relax, but the shadows deceived her too often, and fear was her traveling companion.

Refusing to give in to the rising panic, Ahanna walked through that night and into the next day. The proud Princess was afraid of admitting her defeat, more than she feared the sounds on that dark moonless night. She worried that indulging in any weakness would have her skittering back home, so the Princess kept repeating the mantra, "You will not be afraid."

The second night was warmer and utterly spent. That warmth lulled her into a false sense of security. She drifted in and out of sleep under a cloudless sky filled with stars. Enchanted, Ahanna spent that night enjoying the soft breeze and the beauty around her as she acclimated to the sounds.

Before she realized what had happened, the red dawn crested the sky. With a couple of hours of sleep and finally in good spirits, Ahanna pressed on, ignoring the warnings of the impending storm, until it was too late. Now, the storm was not something she could fight or avoid.

"I'm such a fool," she muttered as she mulled over her mistakes these last days. The drenching rain challenged her resolve as no man or beast could.

Ahanna mentally berated herself for not seeking shelter until the raindrops pattered on her head in the middle of the night, waking her. By then, it was fully dark, and it was too late to make a shelter. Forced to huddle under the boughs of a massive pine, Ahanna kept thinking she could wait out the mild storm.

She couldn't have been more wrong. By the time she took out her rations for breakfast, the small sprinkling of water had turned into a downpour that the tree boughs did little to shelter her from. With no choice, she took a deep breath and braved the storm, hoping to find proper shelter.

As she walked through the woods shivering, Ahanna's thoughts shifted from her own stupidity and drifted back home. She thought of her sisters, her father, Micah, and Freesia. "Oh, Freesia," she whined. "If only you were here with me. Stupid knights!"

Having a horse would be an enormous blessing. Ahanna's feet ached, her wet pack pulled against her tired shoulders, and she had sores from the chaffing of wet boots, both from today and from that first night when she escaped.

Miserable, Ahanna kept up her search for proper shelter, but the mountain did not give up its secrets to her as of yet. The afternoon was waning, and nighttime in the storm without adequate protection could kill her.

Micah had talked about the cold and how it could sap your strength. He'd told her repeatedly that staying warm was her first priority, and staying hydrated was the second. *At least hydration isn't an issue*, she thought cynically.

Not for the first time, she stopped to survey her surroundings. Standing at the edge of an embankment, Ahanna pulled her soaked hood back and searched the moody, grey sky in hopes that she would see a break in the storm. A large bird flapped its wings vigorously overhead, and it surprised Ahanna that any bird would bother to go anywhere in such a storm. It couldn't be easy fighting against the rain and wind.

With her attention divided between the bird, the storm, and the shivering cold, Ahanna didn't notice the ground slipping beneath her feet until it was too late.

She shrieked as the mud gave way, and she lost her footing. Flailing, she slid down a muddy embankment, reaching frantically for any handhold to slow her fall. Finally, her fingers closed around a small branch jutting out of the slipping ground and stopped her downward momentum. The twiggy branch cut at her skin with its thorns, but she held fast.

Grimacing through the sting of it, she twisted to reorient herself, but the traitorous plant chose that moment to release its grip on the earth as its roots pulled free of the ground.

Ahanna shrieked a second time as her reflexes failed her. She slammed her rump against the edge of a small boulder. Sharp pain radiated up her spine, but the rock did nothing to slow her. The loose stone gave way on impact and rolled over her ankle as they tumbled down together.

Within the span of a few heartbeats, Ahanna found herself face-first at the bottom of a trench, covered in mud, with her back and tailbone protesting her every move. The unforgiving storm and the collecting water continued to bring more mud down on both sides of the trench around her.

She shifted gingerly and felt a twinge in her tailbone as she tried to move. Her left ankle ached, but testing it, she knew it would bear her weight. After rolling her ankle a few more times to loosen it up, Ahanna pushed up from the ground to her knees. A pitiful whimper escaped her mouth when she shifted her legs to stand fully, but Ahanna bit her lip and ignored the injuries as best she could. As she rose from the ground, the swampy muck sucked and pulled at her as if it were alive and unwilling to release her. Eventually, she made it to her feet, but the physical effort strained her will to continue on even more. Her throat tightened, and tears began to form. She made no effort to push them back.

For a minute, Ahanna wallowed in her stupidity. *How could I have ever believed this would work? In the name of all that is holy, how will I ever survive winter in the wilds?*

At that moment, the defeated young woman reflected on the grim truth. She realized for the first time how inexperienced she was. It's not as if her lessons with Micah covered survival in such extreme conditions.

Sure he taught me to hunt and how to use a bow. He taught me fire-building skills. He even gave me travel advice. But how does any of that paltry information help me when I am knee-deep in a river of muck?

She looked skyward. "How was the knowledge of poison going to help me stay alive if I freeze to death before I even eat a single berry, Micah?" Ahanna shook her head and evaluated her predicament. "Ealoram above, what was I even thinking?"

The trench she'd fallen into was at least ten feet down, and the walls were a sloppy mess of mud and jutting roots, and she'd already discovered most of those were from a thorny bramble. Not only would the branches be unpleasant to grab, but they would also likely give way from the softened ground. Either way, that would not be a pleasant option. Rainwater formed crevices, and small streams of murky brown water continued to soften the ground, filling the trench around her. Ahanna was smart enough to know climbing back up, at least in this area, would be extremely difficult and waste her fading energy.

There were only two choices. She could follow the trench northeast and keep heading away from home or turn south. South would eventually take her back to her father. Her brows drew in, and her heart sank deep in her chest. Chewing on the bottom of her lip again, she glanced in both directions.

A strange warmth started under her shirt, and when Ahanna reached up to rub her chest, her fingers brushed the little fox hanging about her neck. She thought of her sisters and thought of the warmth of home. Sighing, she pulled her left foot free of the clinging mud. Her boot protested and nearly slid off of her foot as Ahanna took a single disappointed step toward home. It was at that same moment she saw the giant bear ambling toward her.

NINE

Ahanna gasped. Her heart nearly burst from her chest in fright. Despite her earlier self-admonishment, she was not a fool. The danger this new visitor posed was unfathomable. The enormous beast ambling toward her was at least fifteen hundred pounds of claws and teeth. Yet, despite its immense size, the bear navigated the muddy trench with ease, a feat she couldn't manage even if she could find a way to remind her shaking legs how to move.

The bear offered a breathy grunt as it moved closer to her. There was nowhere to hide, and the bear would find her by scent even if she tried. She'd be lucky if fifty paces separated them, and still, she couldn't make her clenched fists reach back for her bow. The voice in her head screamed, *draw, draw, draw*, thrumming in time with the pounding of her heart, but her fingers would not obey.

Even though her mind said draw, the truth stared straight at her. An arrow would make no difference against a foe that big. Ten arrows couldn't fell a bear that size. "Ealoram, have mercy," she whispered in fervent prayer as it came closer. Her legs twitched as her conscious mind considered running, but that idea was no less foolish than a single arrow.

Twenty-five paces, twenty. Ahanna forgot to breathe. She absorbed every detail hoping for inspiration to strike—*Male, definitely male. Possibly blind in one eye*, she thought, as she noticed the left eye was clouded over, and garish scars ran across the length of the creature's face.

Of all the bears she could have encountered, she had to meet this horrific, oversized brawler. He approached her unafraid, and her knees trembled. Her eyes darted about for a solution, any solution that could save her from being mauled to death. She wondered if his obvious blind spot would give her a chance, but she still couldn't force herself to take action.

Fifteen paces. Ahanna stood there, frozen in place. It was as if the bear was mocking her as it leisurely made its way toward her. It groaned and growled again, and in her mind, Ahanna imagined the translation was something like, *Some adventurer you are.*

When the bear came within ten paces, her fingers gripped the small weapon sheathed at her belt. The familiar press of the leather-wrapped hilt of her shortsword offered little comfort, and she wasn't fully aware her hand decided to reach for it anyway. Nor did she have any idea what she would do with such a meager weapon when facing such a mighty adversary. She was certain her brain hadn't given the command to fight, she was barely even trained to use a sword, but her mind was as murky as the water that pooled around her legs.

When the bear noticed her unconscious movement, he rose to his hind legs and bellowed angrily at her. His lips rippled and bared a maw of sharpened teeth. Towering at over ten feet, he took a few more steps in her direction.

The terrifying display stilled Ahanna's heart for three full beats. The creature's hot breath floated out against the frigid air, creating a misty fog as it bellowed. The vibration of its angry warning rippled through Ahanna's bones. Water droplets splattered over them both when he shook his head back and forth aggressively.

Ahanna released the breath she'd been holding and gasped as her heart restarted. A terrifying chill skated down her spine. Looking at those massive paws, she figured the bear's claws had to be at least nine inches long and were the perfect weapon for shredding skin. Of course, the titanic maw could swallow her head whole, but Ahanna knew he wouldn't need to because those teeth could crush bones into powder with minor effort.

A pathetic whimpering sound made its way to her ears, but Ahanna didn't realize the noise had come from her own mouth. The threat this forest ruler imposed created a gelatinous sensation that weakened her muscles as it spread through her whole body. Ahanna wasn't sure how or why she was still standing.

Hands shaking, she uncoiled her fingers slowly and held them out in front, sword free, in a non-threatening gesture.

"Shhhh...shhh," Ahanna soothed. "I won't hurt you if you don't hurt me," she said with a voice as shaky as her body.

The bear sat back on its haunches. Then batting a paw while twisting his head to an odd angle. The bear chuffed at her and blew a heavy breath through his scarred nose. Bits of moisture blew out of his nostrils, and Ahanna wasn't sure if it was rainwater or bear snot that landed on her face.

He put his giant front paws down again and clapped his teeth together a couple of times. The sound of his dagger-like teeth smacking together was not comforting in the least.

Somehow, Ahanna finally found the courage to try and pull her foot from the muck to take a step back, but the ordinarily graceful woman was nothing but clumsy in that desperate moment. The thick mud trapped her feet, and Ahanna was horrified to learn that her body had been idle in the mud for far too long. Her body weight caused her feet to sink even deeper. "No, no, no. Come on!" she begged. Panicking, she pulled harder. She stumbled when her left foot finally broke free, and her boot did not.

Her arms reeled about for balance, and the sudden spastic gestures provoked her giant visitor. Before Ahanna could blink, the bear pounced, closing the final distance between them. It bellowed and growled over her this time.

Ahanna forgot that she had lost a boot, forgot how to think, forgot how to breathe. She couldn't even work up a scream as terror gripped her.

Dropping to a crouch, she covered her neck with her arms. Cowering there with a quivering body, it was all she could do to keep her nose and mouth clear of the water. Her shoeless foot was muddy and sodden. The squishy muck seeped in between her toes, and the cold water bit at her soft skin, but she couldn't care about any of that right now.

It took her a full minute to realize the mighty creature did not attack her or tear her to pieces. The rain slid underneath the neck of her tunic and down her back. Instead of sharp teeth, she could feel its hot breath on her neck as it sniffed her hair. He blew out two more heavy breaths, and again she was sure a little bear snot landed on her skin.

The bear's front legs were right by her face. His razor-like claws were hidden beneath the thick, soupy water, but she knew how long those claws were. Ahanna whimpered, "Please. Please don't kill me."

The bear groaned softly, almost whining as she had.

Daring to twist her head a little to the side, she met its one good eye, "Please don't kill me," she repeated.

Looking past her fear, Ahanna thought she recognized an unnatural intelligence in those deep brown eyes. The bear nudged her with his nose and backed up a single step as if he sensed her fear of him. The little push forced Ahanna to drop one arm to keep herself from falling backward. He moaned at her and clapped his teeth again as if he wanted to tell her something.

Ahanna let her knees fall to the ground to relieve the strain on her legs. Watery mud swirled around them both and gave way beneath her. She sank a little deeper as she bravely lifted one icy cold hand, offering it palm up for the bear. She couldn't control the shaking in her hand and could only hope he wouldn't take the appendage as a trophy in a single bite.

The bear sniffed at her scratched, bloody hand, promptly licked it with his large, rough tongue, and turned his head to grunt twice at the hilltop.

It was the second time the bear had glanced at the hilltop. Confused, Ahanna dared to look in the same direction, and this time she spotted the hooded figure atop the embankment.

Ahanna found the courage to stand awkwardly and bit back the cry that nearly escaped when her injured tailbone protested. Since he hadn't killed her yet, the Princess refused to upset this titian further by admitting her physical weakness when there were less than two feet of distance between them.

The figure on the hill drew back the dark hood of his traveling cloak to reveal a graying head of hair that might have been black once and a heavily bearded face. His hair was scraggly and wet, and his face was richened from life outside in the sun. "Well, Allaros says you're not a goblin, and he likes you well enough, I suppose. Up you go then," he called.

Her confusion multiplied. "Allaros?"

The stranger tipped his head toward the bear, "Allaros."

Ahanna looked at the massive creature next to her, "Allaros."

Upon hearing his name on her lips, Allaros made a sound that was a cross between a groan and purr. He bumped her with his head, and Ahanna stumbled against it, but the heavy mud limited her ability to react. She fell on her sore rear, and this time she couldn't hold back the cry of pain. The man on the hill chuckled. "Come on then, up you go. Let's get you out of that river of mud. The ravine is sure to fill up at this rate, and you'll be in a sorry state if you're still down there."

Annoyed with the stranger for stating the obvious, she sought her missing boot with her hands. *As if my current state isn't sorry enough,* she thought. Blindly searching the water, Ahanna looked back up the hill. "Do you have a rope then?" she asked.

"Nope."

"Then how—" Her fingers brushed against the leather boot and tugging on it, she grunted, "Do you propose I get up there?" The boot popped out so suddenly, Ahanna was glad she wasn't standing, as the force of it would have made her lose her balance a third time.

"Allaros," the stranger answered with a grin.

"Allaros?" she huffed.

Allaros groaned and rubbed his head against her like a tame house cat. Except he wasn't a house cat, and he clearly had no idea how big he was. His actions went a long way to temper her fear of the bear. Trying to push him back a little, Ahanna lost her grip on the boot, and it splashed back down into the muck. Allaros lifted his head to groan and growl at the stranger several times as if he was lecturing his master.

Ahanna spent the brief reprieve from the bear's attention to relocate and don her travel boot even though her foot wrappings and the boot were both disgusting. Mud squished in between her toes, but there was little to be done about it. Finished with the grim task, she was splashed by more of the murky water when the bear lifted his front legs and dropped them several times as if throwing a fit.

The stranger's smile widened, and he laughed, "I think he likes you more than I anticipated when I sent him down there. You better mount up before he drags you up by his teeth."

Ahanna's eyes widened. "His teeth! What?"

The man shrugged, "He wants to get out of the mud. He wants to get both of you out of the mud. So if you don't get on his back soon, he's going to figure out a way to rescue you."

Allaros took her cloak in his teeth. Ahanna had an image of him dragging her up the embankment, and she nearly panicked again. "No! Allaros!"

The bear dropped her cloak and sat back with a groan.

The man above them laughed. Then, he called down, "You do want to get out of that trench, don't you?"

Realizing the plan and too grateful to complain about poor communication skills, she was already moving, "Oh, yes, very much."

"Alright then, mount up."

At first, Ahanna looked at the mighty bear and feared to grab his fur to pull herself across his back. The last thing she wanted to do was pull hard enough to hurt or upset this natural hunter. While she was trying to figure out how to get atop the large animal without being offensive, Allaros bowed his head and then laid down in the muck to allow her access. She nearly wept with gratitude as she climbed on his back. "Thank you, Allaros."

Allaros huffed in reply.

Despite her tender tailbone and her scored hands, Ahanna was eager to be out of the filling trench, so ignoring her ailments, she settled upon him quickly. Riding a bear was very different from riding a horse. He moved differently. His stride was more agile, and his back was far wider. Leaning forward, she gripped his fur to keep her seat, but she tried to be gentle. That grip tightened in a hurry when Allaros deftly took the vertical climb up the muddy hill to bring her safely up to the stranger's side.

When they reached the top, relief flooded her. Without the bear, she would have found herself trapped there for hours. Ahanna directed her attention to the stranger, "I cannot thank you enough for the assistance."

He nodded with a grunt as he scrutinized her.

Uncomfortable, Ahanna shifted to dismount. She winced, and Allaros bellowed while shaking his massive head and scoring the earth with his left claw.

The stranger shook his head with another chuckle and pulled his hood back up over his head while moving forward. "I think you better stay up there for now."

Ahanna bit her lip, "Um. . ."

"He likes the way you smell."

"The way I smell?" Ahanna was certain she couldn't smell that good right now.

"Let's go."

"I'm not sure I—"

Ignoring the forming protest, her rescuer looked back at her over his shoulder and said, "Come on, I'll get you out of this rain. It's going to rain on and off for at least another day. When the sunlight is gone, it will be even colder than it is now. It's one night. Tomorrow you can decide what to do when the weather clears."

Looking up at the darkening clouds, Ahanna could only nod.

"Besides," he said matter of factly, "if you leave now, Allaros might drag you along by your sodden boots anyway, and that would be an uncomfortable way to travel."

The bear clicked his tongue and rumbled a low growl twice

as if agreeing.

She wanted to lay down and wrap her arms around the gentle giant. But, instead, Ahanna leaned down and whispered, "Alright, Allaros, you win."

The bear's chest vibrated as he rumbled his approval, and Allaros started ambling along behind the stranger.

Feeling safe, Ahanna laid down against the thick furry warmth of the grizzly bear. Despite his wet fur, the bear's body heat helped her shivering subside, and it wasn't long before her lids began to feel heavy. She closed her eyes. *Just a few minutes won't hurt.*

It didn't matter that her cloak was soaked and muddy. She pulled it around herself to trap in as much warmth as possible and allowed herself to relax for the first time in days. Allaros' back was so broad it was easy to loosen her grip and fall into the gentle motion of the bear's gait.

She didn't sleep. Of course, no one could sleep under a pounding rain such as this, but as Allaros carried her along, Ahanna was able to let go of the stress she'd been harboring for three days. She was a little surprised that the man who had come to her rescue hadn't peppered her with questions yet, but she was grateful for the time he allowed her to recenter herself.

A little over an hour later, a strange sensation pricked at her senses. Ahanna opened her eyes to find her rescuer kept pace with Allaros now and looked at her with shrewd eyes—Eyes that were a brown hue with golden flecks. When she caught him staring at her, he made no move to look away. Nor did he act bothered by the fact that she caught him in the act. Instead, he nodded and kept walking. Ahanna sat up and unconsciously patted Allaros. The sudden loss of heat from the bear made her shiver as she rose, but she wanted to watch the stranger with caution and a clear view.

He moved through the wilderness with quiet ease. Not even the tall vegetation or the wet rocky ground of the inclining mountain hindered his stride. He was fit despite his apparent age. He was also fully armed with a longbow in one hand and quiver across his back. A long sword was sheathed at his belted waist, with a dagger strapped to his thigh. Ahanna wouldn't have been surprised if he had a hidden blade in his boot as well.

She noticed something else that gave her pause. The stranger's cloak was not black as she'd initially thought. It was a very dark green that held a slight sheen to it. Subtle black embroidery was weaved throughout the material. Even more fascinating was how the weather reacted to his covering. The water beaded and rolled completely off his cloak. The moisture refused to seep into the strange garment. Looking closer, she saw his boots reacted similarly. Though they had traveled through muddy conditions, his black boots hardly held a spec of dirt.

Before she could comment, Allaros halted abruptly. The stranger stepped in front of his companion and grabbed the bear's face. He said lovingly, "Let her down, my friend. I'll take it from here." The bear made a few more grunts and noises before the man nodded, "I'll see what I can do."

Allaros went down again to allow her a more comfortable dismount. The pain in her backside protested every movement as she awkwardly eased off. When she turned, the stranger was standing right behind her. She hadn't even noticed him move in so close. Ahanna took a nervous step back and winced.

"Broken, I think," he observed. "Hard to tell, though. We'll see soon enough, I suppose."

"I'm sorry?" she said.

He waved it away with his hand, "Can you make the climb?"

"What climb?"

He pointed to the tree behind her, and Ahanna noted the

way the tree branches formed perfect handholds for climbing. Following the line of the natural ladder up, Ahanna could now see a cleverly hidden shelter built within several trees that had grown up clustered together.

"I can make it," she assured him.

"You sure?"

She nodded.

"Follow me then," he said as he moved past her and began his ascent. "Use the same branches I use, understand?"

Ahanna swallowed, "Yes."

Observing, she followed his exact moves while biting her lip to ignore every agonized spasm to reach the top. The climb was further up than it appeared from below but, determined to get warm and dry, Ahanna forced herself to keep moving. She was nearly there when her rescuer crested the top platform and, turning, reached down to offer her a hand up. Grateful, she took the help, and he pulled her up smoothly as if she weighed nothing. An awkward, "Thank you," was all she could manage as she took a minute to rest.

"Come with me," he beckoned and led her through the shelter. The place was surprisingly large and had spaces sectioned off for different purposes. Instead of being built within the tree, the shelter was more a part of the tree's structure. She realized the shelter held surprising amenities on a quick glance, but he didn't allow her much time to look around.

He led her through a covered bridge that connected two sections of the tree shelter. On the other side of the bridge, within tightly woven branches, was a circular bedroom somehow formed within the tree's trunk without harming the growing organism.

"You can stay here for now. I sleep around the other side," the man explained.

Ahanna marveled at the unique design. Where twining

branches didn't meet, pieces of wood, mud, and dead leaves had been packed into the spaces to create natural walls against the elements. How anyone could coax a tree to grow in such a way was beyond her exhausted reasoning. However, someone had accomplished the feat. The effort and elemental design did not escape her tired eyes.

"This is beautiful," she said as she walked around the room. She passed a washbasin with blue flowers painted on the bowl. Shelves nestled within the tree branches on either side held small jars, and a linen towel hung on a branch next to it. Above the delicate basin, a looking glass, a precious item indeed, was locked in place and decorated by more tree branches woven around it. To the left of the room, a small table and a single handmade chair sat waiting to be used. A feather quill sat atop parchment upon the table, and a delicate blue crystal jar with dark liquid she assumed was ink sat next to that. On the other side of the room, in an inviting alcove, there was a bed that looked deceivingly soft. Ahanna nearly groaned out loud at the sight of it.

Her rescuer pointed at the washbasin, "Wash up. You'll have to dump the clothes, I'm afraid. Do you have a spare set in your pack?"

"Um, yes. Except for a cloak, but that won't be a problem once I wash mine anyway."

He looked at her with raised eyebrows, "We'll see." He moved to the center of the room, where a column of stone stood. Kneeling, he pulled open a small door built into the rock and put flint to steel. With a single flick, an ember clung to the material inside. She heard him mumble softly, and the flame sparked to life. Standing, he gestured to the bed, "Once you wash up, take your rest. We'll talk tomorrow."

"Wait. You're leaving?"

"I won't be far, but you need a good night's sleep. Don't

worry. You'll be safe enough here." He moved to leave.

"I don't even know your name."

"We'll get to that tomorrow. But, for now, take your rest."

"Thank you for helping me today," Ahanna said before he made it out the door.

He merely nodded politely and left her alone.

Ahanna sighed and felt remnants of the long day throughout her entire body. Eager to get dry, she dropped her pack on the floor and unfastened her cloak. As she pulled it off, she realized why he had been skeptical. The garment was torn in several places and covered in mud so thick the fabric weighed at least a couple of extra pounds. Still, she was a princess trained up in proper behaviors, so instead of dropping the ruined cloak to the floor, she carefully hung the soiled item on one of the protruding branches of the tree.

She went to the washbasin and was horrified at the image staring back at her. Bloodshot eyes reflected in the mirror. Mud, leaves, and twigs clung to her long hair. There was so much mud you couldn't tell that she was a blonde. Her face was coated and filthy with what seemed to be more dirt than skin and her ears— Ahanna sighed again. Her sharply pointed ears were visible through the mess of hair plastered to her head. She reached up and gently touched the elvish tips and realized that was why the man had been staring at her so intently before.

While peace between elves and humans had been in place since her father was appointed king, the relationships between the two races remained fragile, and she believed few would want to help an elf in such a way. The elves cursed themselves to that fate. She'd heard about how they treated other races. Besides her mother, Ahanna never met any other elf in person. When the Elven Dignitaries came to Ranoak, her father kept all the Princesses away from them. They would be less receptive to her secret than humans.

With a heavy heart, Ahanna pushed that all aside and examined the small basin, wondering how she would possibly get clean with such a meager amount of water. She took one of the bottles from the shelves by the bowl and sniffed at it. It smelled of lavender and mint leaves. Pleased, she hurriedly pulled the twigs and leaves from her hair and prepared herself for the cold water. Taking a deep breath, she dunked her whole head into the bowl and found herself both surprised and pleased when warm water touched her cold skin. She scrubbed at her hair and face for as long as she could hold her breath and then dipped her arm in and shifted it back and forth across the bowl to let the water clean her skin before doing the same for her other arm. Feeling better by the minute, Ahanna used the soapy contents from the bottle to remove more of the mud from her hair while she scrubbed her scalp.

The water was murky and brown by then, but she resigned to do the best she could. Ahanna turned and unlaced her boots. Discarding them off to the side to clean later, she stripped off her tunic and pants and hung them on one of the hooks for a hopeful revival later. She then realized her undergarments were in the worst shape. The once white material was as brown as the muddy trench water she'd been trapped in earlier. She was sure they would never be white again.

Feeling the weight of the day and the heavy soil on her body along with it, Ahanna stripped the ruined garments away. She wanted to feel as clean as possible, even if her water source was mucky. If anything, she couldn't be much worse. Turning back to the basin, she gasped.

The delicate blue flowers painted on the bottom of the ceramic bowl were visible again. The dirty brown water was clear. Not a speck of dirt had settled on the bottom. Ahanna took up the rag from one of the shelves and, after dipping it into the basin, she lifted it back up to squeeze the clear water out over her left hand. Ahanna laughed lightly as the warm water dripped over her fingers and ran down her arm.

Despite being exhausted, the miracle of clean water tickled her, and her tired mind replayed some of her rescuer's earlier actions. His cloak and the way it didn't absorb moisture, and when he lit the fire, it took on the first strike as he murmured to it. The shelter was not a feat of natural growth. She had heard legends of people that could sing to the trees to shape them. Many said that was a myth, a fairytale for children. Whoever this man was, he wielded magic. It was a strange revelation. Magic in Ishreedin was supposed to be gone. Some believed magic once drove the elves to evil, unforgivable acts against humankind. Most assume that's how the wars started. Today, very few even wielded the power of Creator blessed healing.

Rather than making her nervous or afraid, the idea that her rescuer was a tree singer fascinated her. His possible magic made her feel safe. Ahanna filed away the information for tomorrow and gratefully washed her whole body as the basin replenished each time it became soiled. Then, blessedly clean and beyond exhausted, she donned her spare travel clothes. Limping over to the bed, she gingerly settled between the fur coverings. Ahanna fell asleep within minutes, and as she slept, she dreamed that she heard the ancient Elvish songs, drifting across the expanse, carried by the breeze.

TEN

When Ahanna awoke the following day, it took a moment for her to remember where she was. After that first sense of insecurity passed, she rolled carefully, testing out the sore muscles that rebelled against her every movement. Her body ached, and her tailbone stabbed her with sharp daggers of pain every time she shifted her hips.

The level of discomfort surprised her. Considering the immense effort required for her to escape the bed and rise, Ahanna couldn't fathom how she'd slept so deep. For a brief moment, she contemplated staying in that bed and hiding from her worries, but Ahanna sensed dawn had already come and gone. She mentally shoved her childish desires aside and forced herself to throw back the warm coverlet and stand.

She splashed water on her face. Then, Ahanna fixed her long blonde hair in the habitual braids that covered her ears.

Finished and feeling better than yesterday, Ahanna glanced

at the dried mud caked on her travel boots and grimaced at the sight. She opted to venture through the shelter of trees barefoot. Following the same path as the night before, she stepped out onto the covered walkway. As predicted, the weather hadn't changed. The rain still poured down as if the sky wished to join Ahanna's melancholy mood, or rather, add to it. She squared her shoulders against the sourness and reminded herself that she was at least dry.

Following the bridge, Ahanna moved across the walkway and into the connecting main chamber. More alert today and even more curious, she took a good look around. A small round table big enough for three sat to one side of the room. In the center was another stone column to house the burning fire. This stone fireplace was much larger, and it could accommodate pots and kettles for cooking. Even now, a kettle hung above hot coals. To her right, a wood counter that curved with the natural shape of the tree wall covered lower shelves and cabinets. The counter's surface was cluttered with berries, a mortar and pestle, a few small potted plants, a loaf of bread wrapped in cloth, and a black flask. Various herbs, including lavender, rosemary, and sage, hung upside-down above the clutter and scented the room with their aroma.

She brushed her fingers over the herbs and even pulled the lavender close for a sniff as she moved to the entrance. She peeked out of the doorway she used last night. Looking for her rescuer, she realized how high she truly was. *I must have climbed forty feet to get here,* she imagined. Unwilling to climb down in her search, Ahanna turned back to the room and picked up the mortar to sniff at the bowl.

The unmistakable screech from a bird of prey drew her attention back to the doorway. Stepping out to the platform, Ahanna tracked the white and grey falcon as it dove from the sky

84

and pulled back at the last second, landing gracefully in another nearby tree. The falcon puffed its chest feathers and shifted its weight back and forth until it finally tucked its wings and settled comfortably. The falcon called out again with two shorter sounds. That was when she saw her rescuer hidden within the branches.

The older man sat comfortably on a thick branch in the tall tree. One foot hung loosely while the other was propped upon a smaller branch. He looked relaxed and at home. Reaching out, he hand-fed the falcon a bit of meat.

Ahanna could see that he spoke to the bird, but from her position, and because of the distance, she couldn't make out any of the words. However, the longer she watched, the more she realized that the falcon practically begged him for attention. Each time the man's hand dropped, the bird would ruffle the feathers around its neck and shift closer until it was eventually sitting on his arm.

The older man kept talking to the bird for several minutes before he coaxed it into taking a small item within its sharp talons. The speckled falcon turned its head to look directly at Ahanna, and the man followed suit. He smiled. Lifting his arm, he urged the bird to take flight. The falcon flapped its wings and gracefully took to the sky.

"You're up," called the stranger as he rose from his perch. He swung down on one branch with an agility that belied his apparent years and skittered across another tree branch. The movement reminded her of Revienah.

"Who are you?" Ahanna asked.

"I suppose many have wondered that very question about me. Even I, at one time," the old man answered as he went past her into the shelter. "Come in. I've made some tea for you. I suspect that tailbone of yours is giving you a few fits this morning."

Distracted, Ahanna followed. "It's nothing."

The man chuckled. "I bet it's a great deal more than nothing. I broke mine once, and I was useless for several weeks. Couldn't get out of the chair without whimpering like a child."

Ahanna smiled. "I suppose it is a bit more than nothing."

"Luckily for you, I can help." He picked up a black flask and tossed it to her. "Drink up."

She deftly caught the flask. "I don't think… " Her breath caught in her throat when she turned it around, and her father's dragon mark caught her attention. "I'm not sure whiskey will help long-term. So I'll pass. Thanks anyway."

"It's not whiskey. Drink up. You're going to need your strength," he insisted while pouring water from the kettle into the two mugs.

Ahanna unscrewed the lid and sniffed at the content. It smelled faintly of ash. Her brows drew together in distaste, and she set the flask on the table. "Look, sir, I appreciate your help, but I don't know you well enough to drink anything you order me to drink. I don't even know your name. The only reason I came here was my utter desperation to be dry. So while I am grateful for your assistance, I think I will pass on any ashy concoctions from one of the strangest men I have ever met. For now, I will stick with water."

"Good."

"What?"

"That's good," he repeated.

Her frustration was growing. "What in all the realms are you talking about? What's good?"

"That you won't drink anything you're handed, especially from one of the *strangest* men you've ever met," he winked with blatant mockery. "And here's your first lesson, water from the wrong source can be as dangerous as any other concocted drinks. Oh, and I'm Ellomar."

"Lesson? What are you…" Ahanna paused when his last statement sank in. "Did you say you are Ellomar?" The question came out barely above a whisper.

Ellomar folded his arms over his chest and eyed her with humor written all over his features. "Yes."

"You're—" She almost sat in the tableside chair but thought better about it when her tailbone protested. "I always thought you were dead. The way Father spoke of you—"

"Almost died twice, but I'm still here for now. Who do you think trained Micah?" Ellomar moved toward her, and she back-stepped unconsciously. Ahanna was stunned.

The Ranger picked up the flask and gently put it back in her hand. Still reeling, Ahanna made no move to stop him.

"Drink it, Ahanna. Then we'll sit down and talk. Three good swallows should do the trick."

"How did you—"

"Drink first."

She nodded meekly and gripped the container when he let go. She turned the flask in her hand again and rubbed her thumb over her father's famous mark. Ellomar moved back to the counter and cut bread as Ahanna opened the lid and tasted the drink. It tasted like it smelled—of ash and spice. Although it was not wholly awful to drink, it wasn't pleasant either. Ahanna choked down three large swigs from the flask just as he pulled out honey and cheese from another cubby beneath the counter.

Within a couple of seconds of the first sip, warmth crawled through her body. Ahanna could feel a tightening and tingling burn on her scored hand. Looking down, she watched in amazement as the skin healed, leaving only a slight puckered line. Her bruises and bumps from the last few days all followed that same pattern. It was the strangest sensation. First, there was warmth, then the slight burn, followed by the soothing tingle. Unfortunately, her tailbone was not so comfortable. The injury there took more time, and Ahanna winced slightly as the potion worked through the break.

As if sensing the potion's progress, Ellomar said, "Severe injuries will be a little uncomfortable to heal, but in a minute or two, it will ease."

Even as he said the words, the discomfort passed, and the cooling tingle followed the heat that had spread through her body.

"I've seen grown men cry out from the pain of healing when their injuries are bad enough," Ellomar said as he set the food on the table and gestured for her to sit.

"You're a tree singer," Ahanna observed bluntly.

"No," Ellomar chuckled.

"Then how do you wield such magic? The tree wasn't natural, and the water basin—"

"*I* cannot wield such magic. This shelter was a gift from an old friend, and yes, that friend was a tree singer. Few know this place exists, and it's important to keep it that way. Do you understand?"

Disappointed, Ahanna bit her lip and nodded. Staring at the food, she dared to ask, "Are you going to send me back?"

"That depends."

"On what?" she asked.

"You, my dear." Ellomar slathered honey on a piece of bread and handed it to her.

She accepted the bread and picked at its crust. "The falcon, you sent a message through it, didn't you?"

"I did," Ellomar replied.

"How long do you think I have?"

The Ranger smiled. "As long as I allow you to stay, I suppose."

She looked at him with hopeful eyes as he covered another slice of bread with honey for himself.

"Your father's not a tyrant, Ahanna. Nor is he a fool. On the contrary, he knew your intent likely before you did."

"I... I couldn't go," she confessed.

"No, you couldn't," he agreed. "Even I could see that when you were knee-deep in mud."

"I tried, I packed my box, and I told myself that I could do it. That I could become a queen. But when I saw the Knights, my heart collapsed, and I couldn't breathe. That was when I knew."

Ellomar said nothing in response to her confession and simply ate his bread.

"I'm not a queen, or at least I shouldn't be," Ahanna proclaimed.

"No?" he asked through a mouthful of food.

"No! Nor do I wish to be," she insisted. "Feylynn is far better suited for the task."

"So says Ahanna."

"Yes. Isn't that enough?"

Ellomar finished his bread and brushed the crumbs from his lap. "I suppose we should know our limitations."

"Exactly!"

"But we should not impose those limitations on ourselves before we even know our strength."

Ahanna set her uneaten bread back down. Then she sat back in her chair and cast her eyes down to the floor. "What happens now?"

"I'm presented with a rare opportunity," said Ellomar.

"What's that?"

He reached for the plate of cheese. "I get to repay my debt to a king and, more importantly, a friend."

Feeling confused, Ahanna eyed him. "I don't understand."

"You will stay here with me. Here, in my glen, your wish is mine to grant. As of right now, in this place, you are no longer a princess of Ranoak. You are a student. You will be my student for as long as I tolerate you." He finished with a large bite of cheese.

For the first time in a week, the tightness that had gripped her chest loosened. "You're serious?"

"I am," replied the Ranger.

"Does he know? What if he sends the Paladins after me?"

Ellomar laughed. "It was his idea. Well, a belated idea. Truth be told, it was one he should have had much sooner. The timing is of no consequence now. He was wise enough to send me word and wiser in his knowledge that you had to take the first step for multiple reasons. As for the Paladins, they would have a difficult time finding you. None know this place exists. Not even your father knows of my location."

"I don't understand," said Ahanna.

"You don't have to understand right away. For now, all you need to know is that you are my charge. While under my care, you will obey." Ellomar's chair creaked as he leaned forward to draw her attention away from the bread on the table. When she met his eyes, he said, "Obey, but never without question. Always question. Observe, learn, and maybe as time passes, you will understand a great many more things than you thought possible. Can you do that?"

"I think so."

"Good. Now eat, for we have a full day ahead of us."

"Today?" Ahanna said.

He smiled. "There's no better day than the first one on a new adventure."

Unsure, Ahanna pointedly stared at the rain outside.

Ellomar laughed. "Eat your fill, and then clean up. I'll be back soon."

Ahanna turned in her chair when he stood. "Where are you going?"

"To prepare your second lesson," was his only reply as he withdrew and left her alone.

ELEVEN

The first few days in the glen saw Ahanna doing whatever Ellomar asked. She was so happy to be safe and more delighted that she didn't get sent to The Enclave. She wanted to make sure Ellomar understood the level of her gratitude.

On her third day, Ellomar took Ahanna to Pran. There he purchased her some additional clothing and a new cloak.

She noticed that the villagers didn't call him Ellomar. Instead, they referred to him as Ferrin. She was wise enough not to say anything in town. When Ahanna asked him about it later that night, Ellomar would only say, "It's better that way." She didn't press the issue.

After obtaining proper clothes, something changed in her daily requirements. Every day during that first week, Ahanna believed Ellomar was punishing her for running away. He set her on every labor-intensive task available in the glen. Caring for the free-range goats, fishing, gathering wild nuts and berries, cooking, cleaning, cutting wood, he pushed her to do all of it. Over the next two weeks, she fell into bed each night with sore muscles and heavy eyelids.

When she finally started to adjust to the rigorous schedule, the Ranger added archery lessons to her routine. As the autumn days passed, Ahanna spent hours every afternoon practicing with her bow. The practices were intense and often tiresome. She shot arrow after arrow at designated targets. She shot at hidden targets, close targets, and even targets that were in motion using a pulley system of Ellomar's invention. He wanted her to perfect her shot every time. He constantly reminded her that hitting the edges of stationary targets meant little when a single arrow shaft was the only thing standing between her and survival.

During her weeks with Micah, Ahanna believed that she was skilled with a bow. Now she wouldn't even classify herself as decent at this point. Her fingers swelled and cracked from excessive use. There were nights when her arms ached so bad that Ahanna couldn't lift them without wincing.

It wasn't until the end of her fourth week of practice that Ahanna noticed the changes in her development. Her fingers were beginning to callus nicely, and all the shooting, hiking, and labor-intensive chores, like water retrieval, were shaping her body. Her muscles were getting stronger, her back bothered her less and less, and at the end of each day, Ahanna had more energy to spare.

Her aim improved as well. She loved the feeling of satisfaction that accompanied every target she hit. At this point, she was hitting only one of five targets dead in the center, but she earned every one of them and took pleasure in knowing that. Ellomar assured her that the sensation of hitting two in a row would have her jumping for joy.

The Ranger spent an equal amount of time shaping her mind

as well. Her evenings were left open for cooking and study. Her original belief of punishment shifted into an honest desire to learn. A large part of her training was an education of the region, and it was her favorite part of each day.

Ellomar, with Allaros at his heel, took her along the base of the mountain range to teach her tracking and hunting techniques. She learned how to follow game trails, watch for animal signs, and how to stay downwind. They discussed the names of plants and trees, and each day they covered new animals and their habits. Ahanna wondered if Ellomar would ever run out of wildlife to teach her. His knowledge was so vast, and she absorbed all of it.

Today, he taught her about the borderlands to the north of the Feldorian Mountains, where her father's kingdom ended.

Ellomar pointed to the mountain range, "To the northwest, on the other side of here, is the barbarian lands. Your father still wishes to build treaties with them, but even after the war, they refused."

"Were they a part of King Eduar's defeat?"

Ellomar shook his head. "No. In fact, the barbarians were mostly removed from it. So were fiefdoms like Yanosh."

"How did they avoid it? Weren't the effects of the war spread all over Ishreedin?"

"Yes, but the north did not see those effects as much. The whole of the northern region is theirs, and few would bother to take it from them, least of all the elves.

"It is an unforgivable, cold place that can freeze a man to death in minutes, yet they live and survive. That harsh land makes hard warriors. If they are weak or lax in any way, they would surely perish."

"How do they survive?" Ahanna wondered.

Between them, Allaros growled.

Ellomar patted his back as they walked. "I only know part

of their survival tactics. Some of it is the animal furs they wrap themselves in."

"I see why Allaros is upset," Ahanna said, patting the bear too.

"The barbarians live a nomadic life. They travel following the animal herds that feed them—moving From Kildresh, then to the tundra, and back as the seasons change. As a right of passage to manhood, they must kill a bear on their own. I found Allaros after one such hunt. Both Allaros and the barbarian lad were severely hurt from their battle when I came upon them."

"What happened?"

"I saved them and took the boy back to his tribe. Allaros has followed me since."

Allaros moaned.

Ahanna smiled and rubbed his back a little more. "How did you find his people? The young boy's, I mean."

"I followed his tracks," Ellomar explained. "That was when I learned that deep in the forest on the other side of this mountain is a lake the barbarians call Borith Voch.

"There is not another lake like it in all of Ishreedin. Even in the dead of winter, the lake does not freeze. The sky above is filled with color, and during twilight, those lights are reflected back upon the mirror the water creates. For the tundra barbarians, it is the domain of one of their gods. Maybe their most revered god. I was nearly killed just for appearing there. Had I not had the boy on a liter, I probably would have."

"It sounds like a hard way to live. I thought being sent to The Enclave was bad enough. I cannot imagine being sent to kill a bear at my age."

"Sixteen," Ellomar said.

"They send them at sixteen?" Ahanna said with disbelief.

Ellomar nodded. "At sixteen, they are already seasoned

hunters and likely participated in a raid or two."

"That's unbe—"

"Barbaric?"

Ahanna nodded.

"I told you, it is a harsh land that builds hardened warriors."

They walked in silence for a time as Ahanna considered what he told her.

Ellomar pointed to the base of a slope, "Look, wild rosemary. It is a good herb for cooking."

Each night Ahanna was in charge of supper, and her new mentor often stressed the importance of using her new plant knowledge in her regular meal planning.

She bent down and used her hook knife for collecting herbs to take some off the plant but stopped and turned back to her mentor, "Do you think my father can do it? Make peace with them, I mean?"

Ellomar shrugged, "I have learned with time a great many things can change, while others stay constant. Would they still be hard warriors if he made a treaty with them and eased their way of life? Would their culture survive such a drastic change? But, on the other hand, can they survive such harsh conditions as time passes?"

Ahanna's face grew pensive. "I suppose survival at its core can force us to change, right?"

"Sometimes, but sometimes our stubborn will can deny change until the end."

She turned away from him again and began cutting herbs. "Who could be so stupid to pick death over small change?"

Ellomar held his laugh at the irony of her statement. "I'm not entirely sure," he replied.

Ahanna put the plant stems in her waist pack. "Ready to go practice now? I think I have what I need for dinner."

Ellomar nodded, "Be sure to write what you learned down during your study time. Even knowing a little about the barbarians may save your life one day, for you will surely encounter them sooner or later."

After making their way back and eating dinner, Ahanna was excused from cleaning up to record what lessons she could remember from that day. Then each morning before her wide range of chores, she was given an hour of study time to memorize her notes and figure out how best to apply that knowledge.

She kept them all in a leather journal Ellomar gave her. Her studies had widened each week, but whenever she believed she'd made progress, Ellomar threw her another challenge. Today was no different.

After her archery practice, he instructed her to collect her arrows as he always did. When she returned short of two arrows, Ellomar nodded and said, "Lost arrows are common. Inspect the rest for damage and repair them. Make sure to sharpen all the tips. Any arrows that were lost need replacing."

"Repair them?"

"Yes, we do not have an unlimited supply of ammunition," he replied over his shoulder as he walked away.

Standing there with no further instruction, Ahanna was dumbfounded for several minutes until she realized that Ellomar must believe she knew how to craft the arrows. *What would he think of my so-called capable skill when he learns that I don't even know how to repair an arrow, let alone craft one?*

She'd seen Micah fix her arrows a few times and, she'd had access to a bow since she was seventeen. It was no wonder Ellomar easily made that assumption. "What good are your lessons, Micah?" she muttered under her breath.

"What was that?" Ellomar called back. Over his shoulder.

"Nothing," she said and waved him along.

Determined to impress Ellomar, Ahanna set about the task of fixing her arrows after they returned to the glen. She didn't ask for help because she reasoned it couldn't be too hard. Fixing the warped bolts just required a slight bending, and if they were cracked, She figured she could bind them with the string and glue Ellomar made from fats and sinew.

As for the missing arrows, she was at a loss. Ahanna assumed she needed to find the straightest branches to do the job and reuse as many tips as possible. It seemed like a simple, logical, and straightforward plan. She went to bed that night feeling confident in her repairs.

The next day during her practice, the first arrow she repaired broke on impact. The second one couldn't really fly.

"Problem?" Ellomar asked.

"No, I just let it go too early."

He nodded and continued to watch.

When she heard her bowstring *twang* as she let another warped arrow fly, Ahanna mumbled a sailor's curse. The shaft wobbled wildly, and the arrow flew wide off her target. The second arrow nearly struck Ellomar, who stood ten feet away.

By the end of practice, she gathered her arrows with frustration, and later that night, she went out to try again. Her second batch was not much better. By her count, Ahanna realized she would be replacing a lot more arrows because of the inaccuracy of her shots. Yet, she still refused to admit anything to Ellomar or ask for help.

He hadn't said anything to her yet, and he clearly knew whatever she was doing wasn't working. She was embarrassed by all of it. If he wouldn't help her, she needed a better solution and needed it soon. After the second failed attempt to repair them, she said, "I don't see why we cannot retrieve new arrows from a craftsman in Pran. Back home, we replenish our supply from the blacksmith," she complained to the Ranger. "Isn't it better to get them from a skilled craftsman?"

Ellomar eyed her pensively. "Fine, then."

Unsure, Ahanna hedged, "Fine? Fine, I can buy new arrows instead?"

"Certainly. The next time we go to the village, you can get as many as you like."

"Really?"

"Yes," Ellomar replied.

"So, I don't need to fix these five?" she asked as hope welled within her.

"Not if you believe buying them is best."

Ahanna's tight posture relaxed, and she offered him a grin. "Thank you."

With a smile of his own, Ellomar nodded and started on the path back home.

She collected the shafts and followed him. "What should I do next?"

He shrugged. "I suppose this time is yours to do what you like."

TWELVE

Over the next four days, Ahanna spent extra time wandering the woods, taking naps, and visiting Allaros. Having a lot of leisure time was rejuvenating, but worry settled in by the end of that fourth day of freedom. Her quiver only held six of her original thirty shafts. That morning, as the pair ate boiled eggs and thin flatbread, she asked the Ranger, as she did every day, "Can we go to the village for arrows today?"

Ellomar sensed her eagerness and replied, "Not today. The road is muddy from last night's rain. As you learned, thick mud on the road is nothing to trifle with."

Nervously, she bit her lip and glanced at the quiver hanging on the back of her chair.

"Ready?" Ellomar questioned as he stood up and cleared his plate.

She took her plate to the counter for washing, but her stomach was a twisted knot.

Ellomar took the rope down while Ahanna gathered her bow and slung it over her shoulder. She reached for her nearly empty quiver and followed Ellomar down to the open meadow where they practiced. She shot her six arrows and started to retrieve them as he instructed. Ahanna winced when she realized that she had lost one more to a crack in the middle of the shaft.

As the lesson wore on, Ahanna lost three more. She was beginning to hate that moving target, as it caused most of her losses.

Now with only two arrows left, Ellomar's gaze settled upon her.

"Something wrong?" he asked.

"I only have two good arrows left," she admitted.

His expression was sympathetic rather than angry. "Ah, well, that's still two we can practice with then. We might as well use these two and get as much practice as we can today. After all, who knows when we can go back to town?"

Ahanna nodded and positioned herself to shoot again. Then, grim-faced, she shot the two arrows again and again until the final one snapped.

"Come along then," he said. "We need to head back since you're out of arrows."

Ahanna collected her waterskin. "We'll be going to the village tomorrow, won't we?"

"We'll see about that," Ellomar replied.

That night, Ellomar woke Ahanna from sleep in a rush. His eyes were frantic and alert. He covered her mouth as she opened her eyes, indicating that she should remain silent. Half groggy and dazed, Ahanna nodded and rose quietly. Her heart thumped heavily in her chest when he pointed to her bow on the wall, indicating that she needed it. She nodded again, retrieved the bow, and strung it with nervous fingers. Then, out of habit, she took up her quiver as well.

Ahanna struggled to see as she followed him down to the trees. Her nerves prickled. The night sky was lightless, and clouds covered the stars. The moon was a silver streak, but a dense fog had moved in.

Once more, Ellomar signaled for her to be quiet before he carefully maneuvered into the trees. With her nerves spiking, Ahanna followed him into the surrounding forest, searching for the source of his discomfort. There, at that moment, Ahanna lost sight of him. It was as if the fog swallowed him whole and without a trace.

As Ahanna turned this way and that, every beat of her heart picked up speed. She could not call out for him since Ellomar wanted her quiet, and she had no idea what they hunted. Worry gripped her. She didn't know what to do, and the panicked bubble rose in her throat. *What should I do? A horde of goblins, a troll, or both, could be stalking me right now, and Ellomar is missing.*

Leaves rustled to her left. Ahanna whipped around and took a couple of steps in that direction. The soft wind tickled her skin and sent a shiver through her. The feeling of danger pressed in around her. It was as though the darkness would suffocate her. The scraping sound of steel pulled from its sheath echoed in the still night. *Ellomar.* She resisted the urge to call out his name. *Where is he?* Ahanna gripped her bow tighter to keep her hands from shaking.

A shadow shifted in the distance. Ahanna heard a man's shout, a throaty growl, and Ellomar's cry of agony. She couldn't stay silent any longer. "Ellomar!"

"Ahanna!"

More animal growling filled the night, and Ellomar's grunts and struggles followed. Ahanna ran toward the chaotic noise. Her heartbeat became frantic with fear, and blood roared in her ears as she broke through the soupy fog and found her mentor on the ground fighting off a dangerous mountain cat. Ellomar barely kept its powerful jaws away from his neck. He looked at her as teeth gleamed above him and paws raked at his shoulder. "Ahanna, shoot it! The cat is feral!"

Instinctively, Ahanna reached over her back for an arrow and found her quiver empty. Horror filled her mind. Ellomar would die right here because she had no way to help him. She searched the ground for his quiver but remembered a split second later that he'd only brought a sword.

Desperately, Ahanna fell to her knees in search of anything that could help. *A rock, I can throw rocks!* Tears slid down her cheeks. She was frantic, and all she could think about was poor Ellomar being raked with claws and shredded by razor-sharp teeth. *If I had a club, I could beat the thing back.*

"Ahanna! Help me!" Ellomar's plea was growing weaker.

A club! My bow! How could I be so stupid? Ahanna's breaths were frenzied as her fingers finally closed around the polished wood. She whispered a prayer to The Creator, begging for a miracle.

That was when she sensed the sudden change. Ellomar's cries and pleas for her to shoot the lion were eerily silent. Her skin prickled, cold fear seeped in, and her heart pounded so hard she thought it would burst.

The hairs on the back of her neck stood on end. She heard the heavy breathing first and could feel the heat of the animal's presence next to her. Ahanna lifted her head and stared straight into the glowing eyes of a two-hundred-pound mountain lion.

The big cat roared, and Ahanna's fist clenched the bow so

tightly that she feared it would break apart before she used it. Then, lifting the wooden weapon, she raised her bow, prepared to fight for her life.

It wasn't until that last desperate second, amid the despair of her possible demise, that Ellomar took pity on her. "While I appreciate the valiant effort you are about to make on my behalf, or perhaps even your own, don't you think that an arrow would have served better in this situation?" Ellomar stood to his feet, drew close, and laid a hand atop the cat's head, scratching its ears.

Dazed, Ahanna struggled realize what was happening. With her bow still clenched tightly in her hand, she focused on the pair standing before her, and several emotions flooded through her.

A huge exhalation of pent-up breath escaped her lips. "You're alive!" she cried. Ahanna's bow clattered to the ground as she threw her arms around Ellomar. The profound relief at seeing him unharmed overcame her as she sobbed against him. First out of fear, then from guilt, sorrow, and as the adrenaline ebbed, her whole body shook with exhaustion, and her knees buckled.

Ellomar patted her back and urged her to sit down. He then placed himself next to her on the hard ground, offering her no words. This particular lesson required her to process what had happened, and the reality she faced did not let up for several long minutes.

When she finally reigned in her emotions, the mountain lion sauntered over to join them.

"Ahanna, meet Sindara," Ellomar offered.

Ahanna sniffled. Locking eyes with the big cat, she turned to Ellomar. "I'm sorry. I am very sorry."

Ellomar nodded. "I know."

"I never thought—I guess I didn't think at all."

"It is not enough to practice with your bow day in and day out. You must always be prepared to use it. A weapon is a tool that requires care. If you are lazy or negligent with that care, the tools in your box of survival will fail you when you need them most."

Ahanna nodded. "I should have—"

Ellomar dispelled her feeling of regret with a wave of his hand. "There is always regret when we look back at history and see the hard truths it provides, Ahanna, but there can be no *should have*. Once we make a decision, whether good or bad, we are stuck with the consequences. Those consequences are not always predictable. Instead of regretting our choices, it is better to accept the lesson they offer and adapt. We can likewise learn from those around us, from the choices they've made. Why do you avoid touching a hot pot?"

"Because it is hot, and it will burn me," Ahanna replied.

Ellomar smiled and asked, "Who told you that it would burn you? This lesson comes at the sake of my own experience. Take comfort that you will never face the real thing. Well, unless you are a fool, but we both know that you are not."

Ahanna nodded as she gazed down at the patterns of foliage on the ground. She offered him a weak smile.

Ellomar rose and offered her a hand up. As they walked home, Ahanna realized there was no anger in her heart for the cruel trick. Instead, she held nothing but gratitude for her teacher and tonight's valuable lesson.

However, something he had said made her pause, and she stopped walking. "Did you say you had a similar experience? Did someone you know die from your mistake?"

Ellomar stopped walking, and Sindara rubbed against his leg and purred. He absently reached down and scratched the lion's head. "One of my companions refused to allow me the time to repair my bow on one of our missions in enemy territory. As a result, when another in my party needed my deadly aim, I failed him."

He was still angry at himself, and Ahanna sensed it deeply. "Wasn't my father the leader of your company? He told us some related stories."

"He was," Ellomar replied with a saddened tone.

"Was it he who denied you time?"

"No! Tisus would have never denied me that time."

"Wh—"

Ellomar cut her off. "Come along. It is late, and this tale is much too long for retelling right now."

"Who died?" Ahanna asked as they reached the main tree to Ellomar's home.

He hesitated. Then, he met her eyes. "Kirren Finn," was all he offered her as he began his climb.

She stopped dead in her tracks as her mentor ascended into the trees above her. "Micah's father," she said, barely above a whisper.

She thought of her best friend and what she would do if he died because of her. That harsh reality of possibly losing Micah because of her laziness settled inside Ahanna and left her shaken.

She barely touched her food the next morning as she pondered Ellomar's words from the night before. Her mind circled with the fear a poorly crafted arrow would leave her as defenseless as no arrow at all.

"Ellomar?"

"Yes?" he replied.

"Would you help me? I mean, would you teach me how to make a proper arrow?"

"It is about time you asked."

Ahanna bit her lip. "I know nothing about arrow-crafting,"

she admitted.

He laughed softly, "That's obvious."

Heat rose in her cheeks. "Last night, I dreamt I couldn't save my sisters. I can never let that happen. I just can't."

Ellomar emptied his bowl, set down his wooden spoon, and sat back in his chair. "Isn't it fascinating how often we insist we can do everything by ourselves when, in truth, we don't have to? When I first instructed you to repair and replace your arrows, you did not ask a single question, and when I saw that first one fly, I nearly tumbled to the ground in a fit of laughter. It was a feat of substantial will that kept my face serious that day."

Ahanna allowed herself a small laugh. "They were pretty bad."

"You improved on the next few, but at the rate you were going, I would be an old man before you managed to craft an arrow worth shooting. Stubborn as you are, you still did not seek my help. Instead, you gave up."

She bit her lip again and lowered her gaze to the floor.

"Ahanna, look at me."

She obeyed, but the embarrassment was still in her eyes.

"Ahanna, you are not the first being that allowed pride to come before humility. Nor will you be the last. Take this next lesson into your heart as you took your experience last night. Never allow pride to keep you from asking for help. Did I not tell you, on your first day here, to ask questions? Even if we can accomplish a task by ourselves, more often than not, we shouldn't have to. To live alone is a hard way to live, my dear. Never purposely take that road for any reason."

"You live here alone," Ahanna observed.

"Do I?"

"Well, I suppose you have Allaros." Then on remembering Sindara last night, she added, "Plus a few others."

His face softened, but he kept his tone firm. "I am never alone, Ahanna. The Creator is always with me. It is Ealoram who sends me companions like Allaros and Sindara. Besides that, my friends might not be present, but that does not mean I cannot call on them.

"You will never be alone unless you choose to be. Do not ever fear to ask for help. Never fear learning from another's experience, and more importantly, you should never fear to share your burden so that the weight of your troubles does not crush you. If I could teach you only one lesson, it would be this. One person is strong enough to shift a boulder, an army of allies can often move mountains, but a small group of friends with trust and love—why, they can change the entire course of history."

Ahanna looked thoughtfully at the floor again, and her fingers fidgeted in her lap.

"Come, my dear, let me show you how to make some proper ammunition," Ellomar finally offered.

She lifted her head, smiled, and took his hand. He pulled her to her feet and led her out to search the woods for all the proper materials.

Ellomar took his time. He taught her how to pick the best wood for the shafts and recognize wood with knots, holes, or other types of damage. Next, he carefully instructed her on how to shape the wood and make it pliable with oil and heat to make it stronger. Finally, he checked each of the shafts she formed to ensure they were straight and taught her how to make the necessary corrections.

Ahanna finished crafting ten new shafts, and Ellomar took her out again to find the best source for rocks to craft the deadly points. He explained different tip types and their purposes, as well as the various stone types to use. When Ahanna asked about the bolts from the blacksmith near the castle, Ellomar discussed the steel tips but did not want to cover the forging of those yet.

After the lesson, Ellomar sent Ahanna out alone to collect ten rocks. When she returned, he tested each one to verify its usability. She ended up going back two more times to find replacements for the stones he deemed unworthy of her time.

Finally, he helped her pick fletching feathers from his stockpile. He insisted that she should not rush the selection for an archer's fletching because it is vital to a good flight.

Days passed, but Ahanna was not weary or bored. Instead, she devoured each instruction like a starving child. By the time the sun had set atop the peaks of the Feldorian Mountains on the third day, Ahanna settled next to Ellomar to watch him work. Soon she was transfixed by the swift ease he employed at making a single arrow. When he finished, he turned to her and said, "It is your turn now." But he observed the sun as he rose to his feet and saw daylight was nearing its end. "Tomorrow, you will make your arrows."

"It is a process, isn't it?" Ahanna asked.

"It is, and you must not rush it. It is also not easily completed in the dark."

Ahanna turned to face the setting sun and frowned. She was eager to employ his teachings, but the day was waning.

"Can't I try one?"

"Very well," he replied, seeing she was eager.

Ellomar watched as Ahanna repeated the steps to craft the perfect arrow. She had to stop and think through her actions several times and asked several questions when she became confused. Working the fletching in and tying the sinew was tricky, but after a few mistakes, she got the hang of it.

The arrowhead proved to be the most labor-intensive part of the process, and Ellomar gently guided her through the work of chipping and sharpening stone. The sun's last rays of light had now entirely disappeared, but Ahanna stubbornly worked in the torchlight that Ellomar provided.

Ahanna completed the arrow, much to her disbelief, and the shaft was perfectly straight. She stood, passed the weapon to Ellomar for inspection, and stretched her back as he eyed her work.

Ellomar tested its bend, checked the fletching, and inspected the tip's sharpness. "Well done," he congratulated. "We can see how it flies tomorrow."

Ahanna grinned. "Really?"

Once more, to verify it was straight, Ellomar eyed the shaft by laying his cheek against it and closing the opposite eye. "Ahanna, you may have a little more elf in you than I thought. The work shows here."

Her proud smile slipped, but she covered it quickly. "It's late, and I now realize I am faced with another long day of arrow-crafting. I think I'll head to bed. If that's alright?"

"That's fine then. Go and rest up," he said.

When the sun rose the following morning, Ellomar allowed Ahanna to devote the entire day to crafting her new arrows. He checked on her often and offered his advice when he determined it necessary. Without a single complaint, Ahanna spent her hours that day filling her quiver. She took pride in the work this time and carefully labored over the finest detail.

The previous night had reiterated Ellomar's lessons. Each time she let an arrow fly, the constant practice centered on honing her ability to survive. For the first time in her life, Ahanna wasn't a princess of Ranoak. Ellomar was helping her become far more.

Day fell into dusk, but she continued. Even though her muscles ached and her fingers hurt, Ahanna did not stop for sleep until she finished crafting her last arrows. Rest would be impossible if she did not prepare for the worst this night or any other night in the future. By the time she crawled into bed, dawn had almost broken through the night sky. Ahanna's fingers and hands bared minor cuts and slivers, her back protested her every movement, and her neck pinched. But her quiver was full of thirty new arrows that she crafted with her own hands. Ahanna fell into her bed with a satisfied smile as sleep claimed her.

Later that day, Ellomar woke Ahanna with excitement in his brown-gold eyes. As Ahanna sat up, he handed her the full quiver. "Let's go see how they fly."

Ahanna accepted the quiver from him with a gleam of eagerness in her eyes.

Out on the range, nervous excitement ran through Ahanna as she selected the first arrow and knocked it. She steadied her breathing and centered her thoughts on the target. The chill air circled her, lifting her hair, and she corrected her aim again. As she bit her lip, there was a millisecond of doubt before she tossed it aside, exhaled, and released. The bolt streaked through the air with perfect precision. Not even the slightest wobble shook the shaft.

Thwack!

The sound of the arrow striking the target was like sweet music to Ahanna's ears. Her grin was full as she inspected her aim. She hit it dead in the center, and the sharpened arrowhead was embedded deep into the target.

Ellomar grinned as well. "Bull's eye," he said.

Ahanna glanced at him, then back to her target, and nodded. "Now that was satisfying."

THIRTEEN

Time passed in a blur, and the bare trees that were once hosts to the fallen leaves on the frosted ground each morning signified autumn's end. For Ahanna, the full days of duties and training shifted into a comfortable routine. Her favorite part of the day was early dawn. She loved waking before sunrise and having the chance to see the brilliant golden light peak over the mountain ranges as it melted the icy glaze.

Each morning required that they gathered a variety of fruit, nuts, and sometimes honey from the natural resources near Ellomar's shelter.

Usually, they ate berries fresh, but the bushes were stripped of any usable fruit this late in the year. Ahanna was only able to find a handful, but she wanted the walk, so she decided to look anyway. One of the culprits for the lack of fruit was walking the woods with her. Allaros always accompanied her when she foraged for food, and his presence was yet another reason mornings appealed to her.

Ahanna smiled as she glanced toward the mighty bear and watched as Allaros sniffed and probed each bush for any hint of sweet treats. She noticed how little effort the big bear put into sniffing the bushes today as they walked about the forest. He knew what she knew. There wasn't anything left.

Allaros moaned as he pushed branches down to find the center of the thorny plants bare.

Understanding filled Ahanna. She was as disappointed as Allaros was. "I know, my friend. It's simply too late, and it's getting cold."

She looked at the sky and knew the first winter snow was getting closer every day. Frost greeted them often in the last ten days and the air carried with it the crisp scent of winter.

Allaros sniffed again at more branches and growled his annoyance.

"It won't matter, Allaros. There isn't a bush within miles that has fruit left. I suppose we will have to break our fast this morning with smoked fish and bread."

He sat down with a huff and moaned again. It was as pathetic a sound as she ever heard and Ahanna laughed, "I'm sorry." She approached him and scratched his neck.

Allaros lifted his giant maw toward the sky to allow her better access, and the familiar rumble in his chest voiced his contentment while she devoted a fair amount of time to soothe him.

"Oh, you're as needy as father's hounds," she teased.

Allaros grunted and batted her gently with his oversized paw.

"Alright, mister sensitive, I take that back," she said with a small laugh as she righted herself. "Let's go and see if the river has given us some fish."

Buoyed by the mention of fish, Allaros grunted again and headed toward the river ahead of her.

When she reached the riverbank, Ahanna was pleased to find the small net they left last night had gifted her five silverfish. Allaros bounded about in the river while she cleaned them at the water's edge. Ellomar had taught her to leave the remains near the water because other creatures of the river would benefit from fish innards as a food source. However, whenever Allaros was with her, Ahanna left him the scraps in case he didn't get his fill from the river.

She glanced over at Allaros as he splashed. The fish in his mouth flopped about as he bounded proudly around a jutting rock. He often used the stone as a table of sorts to devour the fish without losing his meal to the current.

Ahanna laughed softly as the fish flopped away from him when he set it down. He played with his meal for a bit longer, and watching, a pang in her heart made her frown. Allaros would be leaving them soon for his winter rest. Ellomar had explained the animal cycles to her, and she honestly hated the idea of losing her morning companion. She would miss him terribly.

Sighing and setting aside her lamentation, Ahanna finished her task and stored the fish in the basket that hung at her waist. She washed her knife and hands, then dried them with her tunic as she rose. Noting that Allaros was still busy, she left him behind and started back home.

She had only gone a short distance when she noticed a pair of small, blue-grey eyes staring back at her. Almost sure this little cub could not be alone, Ahanna stopped and looked around to verify her safety.

The little white wolf pup yipped at her, and as she headed toward it, the cub growled threateningly while backing away at the same time. Ahanna grinned as the wolf pup prepared to attack her. She did not doubt that the little creature believed it could even take on mighty Allaros.

She assessed the wolf's size and compared it to her experiences with her father's hounds, and she thought the pup to be about three months old. Fascinated by the little wolf and afraid she would scare it off if she continued forward, Ahanna reached into her basket and took out the smallest of her catch. Then, after sitting on the damp foliage that covered the forest floor, she tried to coax the young wolf toward her.

For a long time, the cub yipped and growled at her. Then it sniffed the air a few times. Ahanna suspected that it smelled the meal in her hands, but it did not trust her. Its fear of her was far greater than its hunger and she bit her lip as she watched the wolf cub.

Finally, after several more minutes, she gently tossed the fish between them, and the cub skittered back from the projectile. After a couple of tentative steps forward and back, the cub yipped at her furiously. It took a few steps forward again, barked, eyed the meal, barked, sniffed, glanced at her, and barked again. The cycle of mistrust went on until the pup came close enough to inspect the raw meat. As it drew closer, Ahanna was able to verify the little cub was male.

Hungry enough to risk an encounter, the poor creature darted the final distance and snatched the fish's tail up in his little mouth. Then, he backed away into the security of the trees as fast as he could, pulling the fish carcass through the dead leaves that blanketed the ground.

Ahanna wanted to follow, but she was not equipped with the proper gear or instruction to approach a wolf den. Rising to her feet again, she resigned to head back to Ellomar with her four remaining fish, hoping that he could help her track down the pup.

When she saw Ellomar sitting outside, she frowned. Not because he was out waiting. He preferred being outdoors and would often wait for her to make sure she arrived back safely.

Instead, she frowned because he worked the blade of a short sword with a sharpening stone, his expression was serious and thoughtful, and something about the scene demanded a somber attitude. A strange feeling crept into her belly.

In all her weeks here with him, Ahanna never saw Ellomar with that particular sword. His preferred weapon was sheathed at his waist. Thinking about it, she couldn't recall him drawing that blade either. In fact, over the last several weeks, his focus for her training had been solely on the bow.

Curious now, Ahanna watched Ellomar for a few more minutes. He sat upon his favorite stump with the beautifully crafted short sword held across his knees, and he ran a wet stone across the blade with practiced ease.

Looking with admiration at the weapon, Ahanna noted the intricate elvish design. Elvish weapons were rare in human lands. They were distinct in their style and markings and highly coveted, as no two blades were quite the same.

As the stone slid over the metal with an audible *snick*, Ellomar shifted it again, and the sunlight glinted off of the shiny surface. Ahanna's eyes widened, and she gasped when she saw the subtle tint of blue steel. The strange feeling in her belly spread to her blood and her heart. Her mother had told her stories about swords made of blue steel.

Legend said, that once, when magic was natural among the elves during the time of dragons, famous sword makers crafted their weapons during the last day of autumn on the night of the full moon. Like the ancient tree singers, the swordsmith sang the magic of *Luestia*, the Mother Moon, into the metal to achieve the miracle of blue steel.

The short sword was a form of art itself, with an intricate pattern embedded in the tinted metal. These patterns occurred when steel was heated and then folded into itself, again and again, before being drawn out to full length. She'd seen only one other weapon with a similar design, and it was her father's old sword. The sword he gifted to Feylynn two years ago was made with similar patterns.

This blade was nothing like that one. The black hilt had silver lines crisscrossing in a pattern above flecks of sapphire gems. The hand indexing was made for a small hand—a hand smaller than Ellomar's. The crossguard arched smoothly like a dancer's body, curling up on one side to catch an opposing sword and back down the other to protect the owner's fingers. Small leaf accents finished each curving line of the guard, and a large sapphire, as big as a walnut, was bound to the pommel. It glittered in the sunlight, catching Ahanna's eye.

The elves of Ilarith were famous for being able to incorporate both beauty and function in all of their weapon makings, and this sword was no exception.

She did not have any skill in appraising weapons, but it was no small trinket that Ellomar held in his hands.

Shink, shink, shink. The rhythm he used to sharpen the blue steel gave off a steady scraping sound. Ahanna's brow furrowed as she watched him work the blade's sharpness to his desired level of perfection. He treated the sword with great care, as if he had an emotional connection to it, but it couldn't be his sword. This sword was made for an elf, more likely a female elf.

"It's beautiful," Ahanna observed when she approached him.

Ellomar looked up and met her eyes. "Why do you insist on covering your ears?"

Taken aback, her hand reflexively shot up to her ears to ensure her hair kept the tips hidden. She cleared her throat and tried to change the subject. "Allaros is still down at the river."

Ellomar lifted a brow and returned his attention to sharpening the steel.

"I hauled five fish," Ahanna continued as she moved toward him, "but I shared one with this impetuous little cub that crossed my path. Still, the other four are a good enough size. I was hoping… " Her request to find the cub died when she noticed he didn't look up again. She fisted her hand and tapped her side awkwardly. "Allaros was not pleased today. There were no berries to be found."

Ellomar stood and tested the sword with two rapid cuts through the air. Ahanna flinched from the fast, angry movement even though it was not directed at her. Then with a final nod to the weapon, he walked away from her.

"Wait! Where are you going?" Ahanna asked.

"I am done training, and the day is yours to do as you wish," he said without turning around.

She stepped forward. "But the day has barely begun."

"I have no interest in further training at this time," he replied, making sure the icy bite in his tone was strong enough for her to notice.

"What?" Her trepidation rose. He had never treated her so callously. Ahanna removed the basket from her waist, dropped it to the ground, and went after him. "I don't understand."

"I will not continue to commit my time and effort in training someone who refuses to be honest."

"But I have been honest," she protested and dared to put a hand on his arm to stop him. "Never once did I lie to you."

Ellomar turned to face her. "You lie to yourself every day. Each time you use that looking glass to fashion your hair, you are trying to deceive anyone who sees you. Worse, you deceive yourself."

The look in his eyes was so fierce that Ahanna took a step back. "It's only a practical habit to do those things. From childhood I have fashioned my hair this way. It keeps the hair away from my face when I practice. It is not meant to offend anybody."

"It is no habit that has you checking those sharp tips on your ears several times a day to ensure nobody sees. For you, it is a conscious choice. By telling me it is merely a habit, you have lied twice now. First, when you committed the act, and again when you refused to face my question. And it does offend me," he said firmly. "It should offend you."

"I don't understand. Why are you angry?"

"I am not angry, Ahanna. I am disappointed. I've allowed you enough time in hopes that you would let go of whatever fear that keeps you from the truth, but no more. I have not the time or energy to invest in someone so persistent to live cocooned in self-deceit." He started away again. "I'll send for an escort tomorrow."

A sudden coldness shocked her core, and her eyes widened. "What?"

"I am sure the Golden Knights will still take you in," Ellomar said.

"I cannot go back. Not now!" Ahanna pleaded.

Ellomar ignored her and continued walking.

"What do you want from me?" she called after him.

"The truth!" he called back over his shoulder.

"I am telling the truth." Ahanna stomped back to the open glen. She nearly kicked the basket on the ground, but she reigned in.

She couldn't fathom what caused him to focus on such a dumb thing as her hair. She paced about the area, desperately trying to figure out what to do. She chewed her lip as she contemplated her options.

Halting abruptly, Ahanna reached up and began to tear out the straps holding the swooping braids in place. If staying required showing her ears at the glen, she would accommodate him. *It's*

119

not a big deal. Ellomar's the only one here, and he already knows I am part elf, she thought, as she pulled roughly at the strands with her fingers. When she finished, Ahanna tucked the glossy blonde hair behind her ears and hurried to climb the tree.

Deciding she could win him over again, Ahanna stoked the fire and found the wood for smoking. Then, she went about the task of making breakfast, all while keeping her ears exposed for when he returned.

Keeping her hair back was difficult. It left her feeling raw and exposed. But Ahanna wanted him to see that she could do it. She wanted—she *needed* him to know that she was not afraid.

She cooked one fish to share with him and set about smoking the rest for another day. The problem was he didn't return and Ahanna ended up giving all his food to Allaros. By midday, when she still had yet to see him in the glen, her nerves were spiking.

To alleviate her growing fear, Ahanna went to the meadow and spent two hours practicing her shots. Unfortunately, she missed the center of her targets more often than she hit, which only worsened her mood. Nevertheless, she diligently followed their routine and spent another hour sharpening her arrow tips and checking her arrows for cracks.

She hoped Ellomar would come across her efforts and see her hair tucked back while she worked hard on the things he taught her, and all would be well. It never happened. Ellomar didn't return for any meals the whole day. Ahanna even tried looking for him at one point, but her only discovery was the tiny wolf cub with soulful blue eyes that watched her from the distant tree line. Discouraged, she didn't bother to approach him this time, and instead, she walked home with heavy footsteps and sagging shoulders.

As the light faded, Ahanna was emotionally exhausted and devastated that she wouldn't have the chance to make this right.

She cleaned up the evening meal she had set out and went to her room.

To distract herself from the worry and fear of going home, Ahanna lit several candles to study her notes. Then, she hurried to her desk to grab her leather journal, but on passing the looking glass, she froze.

Slowly turning back, she stared at the reflection in the mirror. She walked forward carefully and took note of every detail of the familiar face that stared back at her. Ahanna's eyes watered at the image. She lifted her fingers and lightly touched her high cheekbone, and traced the line down to her thin lips, letting them linger for a second as memories flooded in.

Pulling her hand away from her mouth, Ahanna tucked her long, blonde hair behind both ears again. She ran her fingers over the back of those sharp points down to her lobes. Any human-like features she might have had were barely noticeable to the Princess.

Dropping her hands, she looked deep into her own emerald eyes. It was there that she saw the truth. It was a truth she hadn't known until this very moment. She hated looking in the mirror because she hated the reminder.

"Why do you cover your ears, *Onwë iel Málos*?"

Ahanna hadn't heard Ellomar return or even noticed his entry to her room, but she didn't turn from the looking glass to face him. She couldn't pull her eyes from the image in the mirror. He'd called her *daughter of the forest*, and it pained her to see the truth of his words. As she stared at the face she loathed, Ellomar moved into the room behind her.

A tear trailed down Ahanna's cheek as she looked past her own green irises and met his brown eyes in the mirror. "Because... Because I don't like what I see."

"What do you see?" Ellomar asked.

Ahanna gazed into her own eyes again, eyes that were hers and yet not hers. "I see *her*."

Ellomar leaned against the tree wall with one shoulder. "Was she so bad to you, *Onwë iel Málos*?"

Ahanna closed her eyes tight to shut out the anguish in her heart. He was using that title purposefully because it struck a chord deep in her soul. Her mother used that name. "No, she was beautiful and kind." Ahanna allowed the memory of her mother to flood through her, and she gripped the basin tightly to steady herself. "She told amazing stories, and sang Elvish lullabies to me every night that she was there."

"Why do you hate her so?" Ellomar asked.

Ahanna couldn't bear to open her eyes and see that face anymore. She deliberately turned away from the glass, away from herself, and frantically pulled her long hair back over her ears.

"She left, Ellomar! She left us like a thief in the night. She only came to visit for a few months at a time as it was, and when she was there—"

Ahanna forced back the tears that threatened to spill, and she clung to the anger. Her voice turned quiet. "When she was there, she was perfect. But she was never there when I needed her most. She hated what we were, refused to take us to her home even. She feared what people would say and think. Why should I think any more of what I am than she did?"

"The mind of a child often sees things in the simplest of terms," Ellomar offered.

"I was not so ignorant as a child, Ellomar. My father loved her, loved us even more than any father because he loved her, and we were from her. Not Shelanna. She refused to stay. She *refused* to give him the commitment he craved, and it devastated him. He still pines for her like a fool."

"How do you know such things?" Ellomar asked with a

raised brow.

"I heard them the night she left. I heard my father beg her to stay. To quit leaving and stay with us, with him. He promised her safety and promised to make her happy. He said he would do anything to keep her in Ranoak."

Ellomar tilted his head in sympathy. "How old were you, Ahanna?"

"Old enough."

"How old, Ahanna?"

"I was eleven. I understood enough to know my mother didn't want to stay."

Ellomar heaved a sigh and straightened his back. He reached down to his belt and pulled the short sword from its sheath. Laying it in his hands as if it was a lost relic, he held it out before her. "Do you know where I got this sword?"

"How could I know such a thing?"

"Look closely."

Ahanna examined it as instructed. Again, there was something familiar— "I do not know this sword," she insisted.

"You do. You've seen it before."

Ahanna turned away from it as the sob constricted in her throat. She didn't want to do this.

Ellomar gave her no quarter. "This sword once belonged to one of the greatest elven warriors of all time. That warrior's name was spoken with fear among the armies of men and revered among the elves. This elf was, likely still is, a legend to all the sentient races of Ishreedin. Many tried to seek out this legendary fighter during the war and make a name for themselves by winning in single combat, but none could.

"When not engaged in single combat, this sword's bearer led legions against the tyrant King that had taught the human race to hate. And yet, during that dark time, this elf was one of the very few that showed mercy. I stand before you today because of that mercy. Your father himself lives and breathes because she wanted a better path."

Ahanna wanted to cover her ears. The sob surfaced, and she choked it back.

Ellomar kept pressing her. "This elf wanted the war to end and hated to look upon the killing fields strewn with blood and bodies.

"That warrior was Shelanna Morningsong, daughter to the elven King Verren Morningsong and Queen Jalise Morningsong. That warrior was your mother, Ahanna."

Ahanna's eyes widened. Her father never spoke of her mother's family. Not even once did he mention they were royalty.

Ellomar ignored her surprise. "Whatever you think of her, Shelanna was no thief in the night. She was the reason the treaty with men came to be. When she had your father at the tip of this very sword, she went against The Queen and allied with him instead of killing him. She helped concoct the plan to dethrone King Eduar.

"As a paladin knight of the Golden Dragons, and the man who killed Eduar, your father was forced into the role of King. Now, the race of men only remembers Tisus' role in the war when they speak of the treaty, but without your mother, there would be no peace, no agreement. With your father, Carek, and me at her side, Shelanna spent hours and hours writing the original treaty.

Ahanna was crying now. "Why are you telling me this? It doesn't mean she loved us."

"I am telling you because you need to know. Both of your parents suffered as a result of this choice. After the treaty was signed, her father named Shelanna the Ambassador to the new human King. The only problem was that they already loved each other by then. They married in secret because your father would not degrade her honor with a torrid affair. Whenever she visited, both were happy for a time, but they courted destruction from the beginning.

"When she carried each of her daughters, your mother would hide the beginning stages at home and then go to a friend in the Shilesta Wood under the guise of training before returning to Ranoak. Elven pregnancies are not as common as human pregnancies are. They expect maybe two or three in their entire lifetime, so who could have guessed that Shelanna would have so many daughters with a human so quickly? She wasn't around for you because she went to great lengths to protect you and your sisters, as well as the fragile kingdom as a whole. She left you in the care of trusted nursemaids with tears in her eyes just weeks after each of you were born. It nearly killed her."

Ahanna's stomach twisted and turned as she shook her head in denial. "How did you acquire the sword?" she whispered with tears in her eyes.

"Your mother risked everything to give you and your sisters a happy life, even at the expense of another possible war should anyone find out. Shelanna was an elven princess, first daughter to Queen Morningsong, and betrothed to another. News of their marriage after such a horrific war would have destroyed the treaty. Although she sacrificed everything for the sake of peace, the old wounds and prejudice kept coming back. Even though her regular guard was composed of trusted friends who would never betray her on purpose, secrets in Ranoak never stay hidden indefinitely."

"Tell me. How did you get this sword?" Ahanna begged to know.

"Shelanna cut her bond to the sword and placed it in my hands herself. She believed that someone had betrayed her. She came to me one night alone, without her guard, and confided in me. She was sure someone in the elven court had found out about her union with your father. She was afraid they would learn the truth about you and your sisters.

"She feared there was a spy and couldn't trust anyone in Castle Ranoak. The last time I saw your mother was the last time any of us in Ranoak saw her. Shelanna begged me to ensure that one of her daughters took up *The Sword of Rimithreal*. She begged me to tell your father to keep your heritage hidden and never speak her name in association with you or your sisters. When was the last time you heard your father say her name?"

Ahanna went back and sat on the bed. "This cannot be," she muttered. Ellomar was right, though. For as long as she could remember, Tisus never said Shelanna's name. He only said *'your mother'* when talking about her.

Ellomar followed and sat next to her on the bed. He laid the sword between them. Staring at the sapphires this closely, Ahanna noticed a smooth fluid-like swirling movement within the stones, and it captivated her attention for several minutes. It was as if the gem was speaking. But it wasn't. Some part of her imagined it saying, *wield me.*

Her hand reached forward, but she stopped right above it. Her fingers twitched and hovered there a moment before she pulled her hand away without touching the relic. Despite her reluctance, her undivided attention to the sword did not sway.

Ellomar continued, "It is because of Shelanna's plea that your father eventually gave the order to have your ears covered by the nursemaids. It was never because of disgust or fear for what people would say. He did it out of a sincere conviction that someone would harm you."

"Why? Why would anyone care?" Ahanna asked.

"Because too many sentient beings—elves, men, dwarves, and everything in between—often trigger a craving for power, and the wicked ones would have no problem destroying five innocent girls to defeat a king with higher morals than this land has ever seen. Knowledge of your very existence offered anyone who knew Tisus Nacarian a chance to ruin him and hurt you in the process, all while they destroyed a hard-won treaty.

"Who would carry on the legacy of Tisus the Bold after that? Who could ever replace the orphan boy who clawed his way through the politics of greedy, pompous lords, taking on a rag-tag group of soldiers no one cared about and making them a team? Who would stand in place of the lead Commander of the Knights of the Golden Dragon—the leader who slew a tyrant king, enacted a justice system of fairness, and found peace in a two centuries old conflict?

"Ahanna? If anyone destroyed your family, then who would carry on Shelanna's legacy as a warrior of mercy and love? Your mother was a woman who threw out tradition and expectations to forge a better path for the future. Who would finally close the gap between the two races?"

"Are you saying that she loved us?"

"Oh, Ahanna. She loved you more than she loved her own life. Your father should have told you."

She sniffed. "He tried. He tried so hard to make me believe it, but I remembered how often she was absent. I still remember that night when he begged her not to leave. Then she was gone, and I hated seeing her every time I looked at myself."

"I see more of her in your soul than I do in that looking glass, but only you can choose the path you take from here. This sword is meant to be yours." Ellomar looked down at the weapon between them. "It is an elvish sword that can only be wielded by an elf of royal birth. If it accepts you, it will bond to you. Only you can wield it thereafter, and only you can break that connection. If you are not worthy, the sword will reject you. The gems holding the magic within will turn black, and hereafter, the magic in that sword will die."

"Feylynn," Ahanna insisted. "She never gave up on mother. She will be the next Queen of Ranoak. It will accept her. She deserves this weapon."

Ellomar shook his head. "Shelanna gave me precise instructions to choose the bearer of this sword. She told me that I would know when the time came. I have not even told your father I have The Sword of Rimithreal in my possession."

Ellomar reverently picked up the sword. Going down on one knee, he formally presented it to Ahanna, as a subordinate would do for his queen. Her pretty green eyes, eyes so like Shelanna's, widened and came up to stare at him with surprise and uncertainty.

"So, Ahanna Morningsong Nacarian. Since you finally offered me the truth you've hidden from the world all these years, I will provide you with a final truth of my sincerity with a long-kept secret. I may have been able to delay your title as the Crowned Princess of Ranoak, but I refuse to taint your mother's sword or memory with anything other than her most legitimate royal elven blood.

"You are a Princess of *Ithildan Málos*, granddaughter to Verren and Jalise Morningsong, and daughter of Shelanna Morningsong, the greatest warrior ever to grace the Shilesta Woods. I am not only your mentor, but I am also your friend. I will not force you to take up the Rimithreal. Instead, I will ask you here and now, just once. Are you *Onwë ielor Málos*?"

Ahanna reached out her hand again, and her fingers hovered above the sword a second time. Transfixed, she stared upon the swirling sapphire gems and again thought it was calling out to her. Sadness and indecision danced in her eyes.

Ellomar prayed he had trusted his instincts correctly. It was trusting those very instincts that saved him time and again, so he could live to see this day. He held faith that this time would be no different.

After several heartbeats, Ellomar saw the same defiant fire from one of his oldest friends come to life in her green eyes. The sapphires pulsed with light, and that was when he was sure.

FOURTEEN

CASTLE RANOAK

In the last tenday, something had been budding inside Resora Nacarian. At first, it started like little butterflies in her belly. Then it turned into a tingling. Then, a couple of days ago, the sensation shifted into a strange warm feeling that flared up often.

Initially, Resora thought she was sick, and then she wondered if it might be lady problems. It was, after all, the winter after her twelfth year of birth. But neither seemed to be the cause, and the longer time passed, the more the sensation grew.

It wasn't burning in her belly like that time she ate spicy food at the Fealty Festival. It wasn't painful, but it was foreign, and it scared her.

When she complained to her father, King Tisus summoned a healer straight away. Resora was peppered with questions and carefully examined, but the healer could find nothing wrong. She turned to Tisus and shook her head. "Must be a bit of bad food. There's no fever, Your Majesty, and I see no other symptoms to worry about."

Feeling relieved, Tisus nodded and sent the woman on her way. He took time out of his daily routine to read to Resora as he always did whenever his daughters felt ill. Today, he read her a story of a great black dragon and the three brave warriors that would defeat it.

She'd heard the story several times. It was one of her favorites. Well, besides her personal adventures anyway. A sudden thought occurred to Resora. "Father, do you think Ahanna is on an adventure?"

King Tisus closed the book but kept a finger between the pages. "I think she is learning and growing, and sometimes that includes a little adventure, but she is safe."

Resora wasn't satisfied. "How do you know she isn't fighting a black dragon right now?"

King Tisus smiled patiently. He heard the worry in her voice. "I promise that she's safe. Besides, no one has seen a dragon in a very long time."

"Will Feylynn have adventures like you? She'll be a knight. Will she have to fight in wars?"

Tisus leaned forward. "I think— I know why your belly burns."

"Why?" she asked.

"You worry for your sisters. I should have seen it much sooner."

Resora looked down at her hands and confessed, "I miss them so much."

King Tisus took her small, dainty hands into his big, callused ones. "Oh, my daughter, so do I." He lowered his voice and added, "I'll let you in on a little secret."

"What's that?"

"I have people looking out for your sisters." King Tisus

smiled.

Wide-eyed, she smiled back. "You do?"

Tisus winked. "Indeed, I do. Two people I trust more than any other in the whole realm. They would notify me at the first sign of any trouble."

"What if there is trouble?" Resora asked.

King Tisus squeezed his daughter's hands. "Then I would don my armor, saddle my warhorse, and race to them as if the demons of the abyss were at my heels."

Resora squeezed her father's hand in return.

He continued, "I swear to you, I would charge those abyssal gates with a sword and shield, cutting down any monster in my path to keep my children safe."

"Will you send me away, too?" Resora questioned suddenly.

His brow furrowed. "Not for a while yet. My heart couldn't take having three of my daughters away at the same time. I can barely tolerate having two missing now."

"That's good," she said. "I don't think I would ever want to leave Ranoak. Of course, Revienah wants to go on grand adventures, but I like the idea of staying here much better."

He chuckled, "From the minute she took her first breath Revienah did it with a desire for adventure. I fear I will have to chain that one down to keep her home."

Resora laughed softly too as King Tisus stood, and leaning forward, kissed her brow. Then he brushed her dark hair back from her face. "Put your worries aside, my daughter. Do not allow this fire dragon of fear to grow in your belly any longer. Ahanna is safe, Feylynn is safe, and I will chain Revienah up should you think she's planning to run away." He finished the last part with a wink.

Resora giggled. "Thank you, Father."

"Get some rest. I'll check on you a little later," he said.

She nodded and laid on her pillows as he eased away.

King Tisus set the book on the bedside table and pulled the covers up over her shoulders before he snuffed out the candle on and left her alone to rest.

Resora had heard people talk about becoming sick with worry, but she didn't know it was an actual condition until now. After her talk with her father, Resora figured she must be more worried than she realized. Her father had compared her burning belly to a fire dragon, and she supposed it felt similar. Not an ancient red or anything so ferocious, but a small sleeping fire drake that sent steaming air through her as it slept content in her tummy. Relieved to know that her condition wasn't so serious, Resora drifted to sleep with the thought of dragons swirling in her mind.

Resora dreamed of two dragons, an angry red and a majestic gold. They flew in the sky above her. At first, Resora thought they were playing with each other. Metallic scales shimmered in the bright sunlight, reflecting the rays around the young Princess as the pair spun about above her. Enormous wings beat and snapped against the wind.

On the ground, Resora watched, frozen by the spectacle of creatures of fire and sky dancing in the clouds above. *No, not clouds*, she realized a heartbeat later, *but smoke*. And the dragons weren't dancing playfully in the sky, but rather, they fought against one another. The majestic creatures engaged in deadly aerial combat and flew at each other with a singular purpose. Death to their enemy!

The ancient tales of dragons told by her father came to life right over her head. The red dragon swooped low, and Resora somehow knew the sleek animal born from magic was female. She was so beautiful and terrifying at the same time. Resora also recognized that this red was a wyrm. Wyrms were built long, lean, and fast, with one set of legs and a pair of strong wings.

The mighty wings were adorned with three razor-sharp claws attached to a carpel-type wrist for grabbing prey, climbing, and walking. The wyrm's scales glimmered with multi-faceted hues of red. The various colorations shimmered with black, purple, maroon, and even pink. It was almost a lie to call her red. The hues were dependent on how the light in the sky touched her body.

Feeling fascinated, Resora squinted through the smoke to see the other dragon, and she realized that the proud male gold was what many called a great dragon. In contrast to the wyrm, he had both front and back legs as well as mighty wings that folded close to their body. A single hooked claw could be seen in the middle of each wing at the peak of the fold. They were more robust than any other of the dragon race. They could climb, use all four legs, and his powerful wings allowed him agility in the sky.

Not only were they strong, her father told her that the great dragons were the largest of all dragonkind. He was enormous and majestic, and the sight of him in the sky warmed Resora's heart. The gold dragon's scales, bright and inspiring, reflected rainbows of color on the ground below as he spun in the sky to avoid his opponent.

As the gold attacked, the ancient red's lean body corrected course, faster than should be possible considering its bulk, and she shot up underneath the gold like a flying spear. Her chest glowed right before a breath of red-orange fire escaped her deadly jaws.

Resora was blinded momentarily by and forced to turn away from the glowing ball of explosive fire. A beastly roar of pain filtered out of the thermal barrier that blocked her sight. The wretched sound echoed on for miles. When the light dissipated seconds later, Resora blinked and looked about to clear her vision. It was the first time she noticed the horrific sight on the ground around her.

The dead and dying were all about her upon a blood-soaked field of battle. The source of the billowing smoke burned yards away, broken war machines that had been set aflame to prevent repairs. Farther out, men, dwarves, and elves fought together against the wicked wyverns and other demons from the abyss.

Resora lifted her head skyward and screamed in fear when she realized that the red wyrm clamped down on gold scales with her wicked jaws. The red wyrm tore through the golden scales on her enemy's hind leg, and blood welled around the wound.

In retaliation, the gold whipped its tail around and slapped the female red's face with barbed spikes, taking out one of the evil beast's eyes. Then, twisting around, the gold raked at the red's side with the massive claws of its free leg and bit down hard on the her tail as it came up near his maw.

Thoroughly entwined, the two dragons spiraled down, down, and down. Neither could spread their wings quickly enough to slow the fall. Resora screamed, "Stop! Please Stop!"

The fighting was done out of pure hatred. What had caused such a state of raw emotion? She was left to watch, crying, and wondering like a cursed ghost because she could not force herself awake as they came barreling down to the hard earth. Death surrounded Resora, and her young mind could not process it. She didn't want to process it. She squeezed her eyes shut and tried her best to force the images away. *Wake up, wake up, wake up,* she silently ordered herself.

The warring titans crashed to the ground, and the shockwave ripped over the field. Resora was knocked to the ground, and she cried out. She heard the gnashing teeth and claws scraping natural armor that no man-made sword could penetrate. The ground vibrated as the dragons battled for supremacy over each other. Resora started to sob. She curled into a ball and covered her ears. "Stop!" she screamed, "You have to stop!"

They didn't hear her. The battle came dangerously close, but Resora refused to look up even if it meant having her bones crushed beneath the weight of a dragon's foot.

Something pushed her off the ground and out of the way. The sharp sting of golden scales from a dragon's tail cut her skin when he pushed her away from the red's destructive path.

Still feeling terrified, Resora tried harder to shut it all out of her mind, but the cacophony of this epic battle was too much. The heat of flames scorched her skin. Her nose filled with the scent of the blood as it spilled onto the earth, and the sickening sounds of torn flesh and mortal wounds assaulted her ears. Resora sobbed against it all.

Suddenly, everything stopped. Fear compelled her to remain still, but the courage that her father had ingrained from a young age forced her to stand. She clamored to her feet and readied herself to run, but as she turned to face her fear, Resora came face to face with the enormous head of the red. She screamed and stumbled back, tripping over the ruddy earth and falling on her rump. It took Resora several heartbeats to realize that the dragon remained still. Blood poured from a mortal wound at the magical beast's neck and stained the ground at her feet. The halting broken breaths of inevitable death rose and fell in the dragon's mighty chest.

Another movement drew Resora's attention. She saw next to the dying dragon that another soul also struggled to live. The gold tried to lift his wings to tuck them close to his body, but the left wing wouldn't rise fully. It hung weirdly, and it would never be the same again.

Wounded and sullied by blood and dirt, the gold took a single step, wavered on his feet, and crashed to the ground. Earth came up around him as he collapsed, and the massive weight of his body shuddered on the field.

Resora covered her mouth in horror. With shaky legs, she walked toward the massive beast. He opened his gilded eyes and pierced her with his gaze. His breathing was labored, and he was not long for this world. It saddened her to know that.

"*The promise must be kept, Onwë iel Málos.*" The mighty gold wasn't speaking with his mouth. Instead, the strange words came into her thoughts.

Before she could react to what was happening, Resora fell to her knees at the massive, clawed feet of the mighty creature and sobbed. "*Nyä vanda indo kopo sä,*" Resora heard herself reply. *What promise?* she wondered.

The dying dragon panted in pain. The dirt and weeds stirred around him with each intake and exhalation of his hot breath, and although he spoke to her mind, his following words were slow and broken, as if his thoughts were failing him.

"*Idë —boe -nya yulma —ingóle,*" he uttered as he released a final breath of blue fire that fully engulfed her.

Resora shot straight up in her bed, gasping for air. The dream was so real. Too real. Strangely enough, she could still feel the flames licking her skin and could hear the crackling burn. The acrid scent of smoke filled her throat and lungs, and a flicker of light in her peripheral vision had her turning her head.

Resora's eyes widened in pure terror when she realized the bedside table was fully aflame. As if alive, the flames licked at the bed drapes and melted the gossamer fabric as they reached across her linens, snaking toward her. The dream of death and fire was too fresh, and she still felt the burn of flames on her skin. Resora started screaming as she scrambled away from her bed.

FIFTEEN

Walking down the corridor, his hands clasped behind his back, King Tisus listened attentively as Denaris explained the latest casualty reports from a barbarian attack on Yonosh during the recent full moon. These skirmishes on the outskirts of the Borderlands were escalating, and Tisus was growing tired of them. He turned to Denaris and started to outline his new plan. That was when he heard Resora's terrorized scream. An icy chill rushed through him, and his heart skipped a beat. He had never heard such a scream from any of his girls.

"Resora!" he bellowed and tore down the adjacent corridor toward her room. As King Tisus rounded the corner, Resora barreled into him and stumbled backward. He caught her arm before she tumbled to the floor, and without a second thought, he scooped the frightened girl into his arms. He held her shaking body tight against his chest.

Resora was twelve now, but she'd always been a slip of a

thing, and her meager weight was nothing for the broad-shouldered Paladin King. His armor weighed more than his little girl. "You're alright now. I've got you," he reassured. "What is it? A nightmare?"

Amid sobbing tears, Resora muttered a single word, "Fire."

"A fire?" Lord Denaris interrupted with skepticism as he caught up to King Tisus.

Resora lifted her head and pointed. "In my room!"

By then, Tisus smelled the burning wood. Glancing down the hallway, he saw the billowing black smoke as it escaped the open doorway and crawled down the corridor like a monstrous demon seeking to terrorize his sweet Resora. Tisus set his distraught daughter down behind him. "Denaris, take Resora, and call for water."

His advisor nodded and took Resora's arm, pulling her along. "Fire! Get water!" he shouted down the hallway, hoping someone would hear. Then Denaris saw a castle guard turning the corner. The Lord snagged the young soldier's tunic to turn him around. "Water! Get buckets!"

Looking over her shoulder, Resora saw her father shield his face with the crook of his arm as he entered her burning bed-chamber. A new panic rose in her belly. She broke free of the distracted Denaris to run after the brave Tisus. "Father!"

"Princess!" Denaris yelled after her but hesitated to follow. "Fool child," he muttered.

Resora's sensitive ears heard the grumbling complaint, but she didn't care. Right then, she only cared about her father. She called after him again, but he had already disappeared behind the thick wall of acrid smoke. "Father, please!"

"Fire!" Denaris shouted once more and ran after the distraught Princess.

"Father!" Resora called with renewed tears as she gripped

the wooden door frame at the entrance to her room. She held her breath and listened for his reply, but there was no response. Resora could not see him through the eerie black and gray cloud that filled the entire room now. She coughed violently as the smoke assaulted her senses, but she did not want to retreat and leave her father here alone. She started through the door, but suddenly someone yanked her back.

Denaris' steady hand gripped her upper arm as he tugged her roughly back into the hallway. For a small man, he was relatively strong and was able to force her to come along.

Resora strained against his hold. "Father!" she screamed.

"Quit acting like a spoiled child and come along," Lord Denaris scolded her.

Two more men, dressed in blue and gold tunics that identified them as house guards, came running down the hall carrying buckets of sloshing water. Drops splattered on the floor as they passed, and Resora wondered how much water they would have left by the time they reached her father. Every single ounce of water was precious to her.

Revienah shot around the corner with Enreal at her heels. Again Resora strained against Denaris' hold to run to her sisters, but he didn't release her until Revienah slammed into her identical twin and hugged her tightly.

Satisfied she would stay put, Denaris gruffly folded his arms.

Resora returned her twin's embrace and reached out for Enreal. After a minute or so, her sisters stepped back to get a sense of what had happened. "There's a fire in our room!" Resora explained. "Father's in there."

"A fire? What happened?" Enreal prodded and took Resora's hand.

Resora looked down to her bare feet and shook her head. "I—I don't know. I was sleeping, and in my dream— and then— It was so hot. The fire it—it woke me, I think." Her brow furrowed.

"Your nightgown," Revienah said as she tugged at the white shift of fabric. "It's burned."

"What?" Resora craned her neck to see the burned gown on the bottom left side.

Enreal's eyes widened. "Resora, you could have died. Are you burned?"

"I—I don't think so." She twisted her leg and ankle and found no sores or blisters, but Enreal was already lifting the gown to her thigh to check. Resora's cheeks burned with embarrassment as two more men with buckets of water rushed past the girls while her whole legs were exposed.

"Thank The Creator. You are unharmed!" Enreal exclaimed as she dropped the burned gown to wrap her sister in another hug.

Revienah joined in on the embrace and mumbled against her shoulder, "I would be horribly bored if I had no twin to tease. Never scare me in such a way again."

Lord Denaris said, "Since you are unharmed, Princess, I think it best if we do not worry your father until tomorrow about the gown. He still has many issues to deal with tonight, and if he sees this, he will be overly concerned. It will deny him sleep to know you were so close to the flame."

Revienah glared at him. "I think he already knows she was close to the fire."

As if considering Denaris' advice, Enreal's expression grew pensive.

Coughing erupted down the corridor as King Tisus, covered in sweat and soot, finally emerged from the twin's bed-chamber. The other four men followed a second later. The castle guards succumbed to the coughing fits and bent over to try and catch their breath. Tisus, however, straightened up as he walked down the hall to meet his frightened children.

Lord Denaris took a step in front of the girls before they could rush to their father. "Sire?"

The Princesses had known Denaris their whole lives and were not surprised by the maneuver. He disliked how affectionate King Tisus was with his daughters around the staff. Ahanna once said it was because their father's advisor was a stick in the mud. A then five-year-old Resora had replied, "He's not stuck in the mud. I just don't think he's very happy." Either way, Denaris was not their favorite person in the castle, and the girls rolled their eyes at his back and stepped around him.

Tisus was a big man. Just over six feet, he was broadly built and had honed that build into solid and capable muscles over years of use. He was not the type of king who sat idly and gluttonous on his throne. He denied himself indulgences most men of his station would revel in daily. He worked hard, trained hard, and always provided help where it was needed. King or not, he was a man of action.

When Tisus neared his daughters, he went down on a knee and used those giant arms to pull them closer into the security of his embrace. "It is over, girls. The fire is gone." The rich timbre of his voice was another comfort to the three sisters.

He chuckled, "Although, I am surely in trouble since your dresses will be ruined by the smoke. I will have to commission more, and it is a crime that I should have to suffer a day with Liddia in the castle again so soon."

The girls giggled briefly, and some of the tension eased.

Resora pulled back and met her father's eyes. "I'm sorry, Father."

"Whatever for?" he asked, surprised by her apology.

"The fire, it's my fault."

"Resora, that fire was not your fault."

She shook her head. "No, it's true! I had a terrible dream

142

about a dragon and must have thrashed about. I knocked over the candle."

He let go of his other two daughters and took Resora's chin in his big hand. "My sweet daughter, there is no way you started that fire. I snuffed the candle out before I left you."

"But—" she started to protest.

"Do not fret about this any longer. I will see that your room is put to order. In the meantime, you and your sister can take Feylynn and Ahanna's rooms."

"Father?" Enreal interjected. "I have some gowns that may fit her and Revienah until Liddia comes anyway."

Tisus grinned proudly and gripped her shoulder, squeezing her lightly. "That is kind of you, Enreal." He stood and took an inventory of his tunic. "I suppose I need a replacement, too."

Enreal didn't smile as Tisus thought she would. His middle daughter was thoughtful, generous, and gentle, but she was a somber creature. She was observant and patient, except when something was bothering her. During those times, she was nervous and unsure of herself.

Denaris cleared his throat. "Your Majesty, we have many other matters to see to. It would be best if we leave the Princesses with their attendants and see to your duties before the hour grows too late."

King Tisus waved him off. "Enreal?"

She squared her shoulders as if steeling herself against the emotion that crept in. She glanced at Denaris, then tugged at one of her small braids, "Lord Denaris is right. Resora needs a bath and a new nightgown as well because her's is burned. Our ladies—"

"What?" Tisus interrupted. He turned to Resora, seeing the burn marks. "You're not hurt?" he questioned with resurfacing concern.

"No, Father." Her cheeks turned pink again as he bent and tugged the gown.

Enreal took his hand. "I already checked, Father, and there is nothing to be done by you or your *men*," she said pointedly. "Don't fret. I will take her to my room and see that she gets some new clothes and a bath. You can check in on us later."

Tisus was angered, but he hid it quickly and nodded gratefully to Enreal. Then he turned his attention to the soldiers behind him. "Send for hot water, and bring some attendants to help the girls. Then clean yourselves up."

"Yes, Your Majesty." The two men bowed and hurried off to comply.

Lifting his hands, Tisus gripped the other two first responders on the shoulder. "Thank you for coming so fast. I am grateful to you both."

The profusion of gratitude had both men shuffling their feet. Finally, the older man said, "It weren't less than you would have done if it'd been my own daughter."

"It's our sworn duty, sire," said the younger man.

"All the same, I thank you."

"Sire, we still have the border raids to see to. This matter is resolved for now, but a great many people are in danger and await your response," Denaris chimed in with growing impatience.

Tisus wanted to growl at his advisor. The man always knew what to say to drive him to action. Most days, being King was a constant struggle over what he wanted versus what his morals demanded. *My daughter was in danger!* he thought in frustration. *But so are a great many others in Yanosh.*

He leaned down and kissed each one of his daughters' brows. "Take care of each other while I attend to some other matters. I will come back as soon as I can." He tried to wipe the anger from his eyes and smile, but his daughters, who knew him so well, saw through the facade.

Enreal took Resora gently by the arm, and the sisters fell in step together.

Tisus watched as they hesitated by the burned room. It didn't take very long for his brave girls to turn their eyes from the sight and straighten their spines as they continued on toward the two doors further along the corridor, disappearing into Enreal's chamber.

When he was sure they were gone, Tisus turned to Denaris with fire in his eyes. "Post two of your most trustworthy guards with my daughters at all times until further notice."

"Sire? You can't possibly think—"

"Someone lit that fire, Denaris."

"I'm sure it's not as nefarious as that. The candle—"

"There was no burning candle in her room this night, and no treated wood would take to flames so hot without help. Someone lit that fire, and my daughter was asleep inside that room when they did." He gritted his teeth against the reality of it while thinking of her burned gown. "I will not lose a single one of them as I did their mother."

Denaris faltered under his intense gaze, but he stood firm. He was barely fifteen years old when he saw those eyes for the first time, and now nearly a quarter-century later, Denaris was still compelled under the Paladin's stare. "I will see to it, Your Majesty."

Tisus' heavy boots scraped against the stone floor as he started down the hallway once more. Denaris was forced to follow since his King hadn't finished his tirade. "Two guards, Denaris, no less. Rotate them every two hours if necessary. I will not have sleepy watchmen guarding my daughters. And start an investigation right away."

"Yes, Sire. I will see it done first thing tomorrow."

"Tonight," Tisus insisted.

"It is late, Sire, and the raids still need your attention. The land disagreement between Lord Larath and Lord Mycerin also awaits your review."

"The land dispute can wait. It is nothing more than greedy men unsatisfied with what they have. As far as the Tundra tribes, I tire of these constant raids. Action seems the best course."

Denaris nodded his head. "Agreed. I will send a battalion to deal with it."

"No," said King Tisus.

"Sire?"

"Send a small reserve of troops to the border of Kildresh."

"Sire, that is precariously close to the largest tribe. A small contingent would not fare well."

"Have the men wait for Master Carek and whomever he deems worthy to assist. I want one of the Kildreshians captured. Instruct Carek to find me the biggest and most honorable warrior among that tribe. I want him tried."

"Your Majesty? That is suicide," Denaris protested.

"No, it's not." Tisus smiled, "Well, not for Carek. I am confident he will capture one."

"Carek is an asset we cannot afford to lose right now. Even if you capture one of those tribesmen, how will you get him to submit for the long journey here? He will slit their throats while they sleep."

The King smiled again, "You have to know how to speak their language. Besides, they won't be coming here. I will ride out to meet Carek when it is done."

Denaris rolled his eyes and scoffed, "Ride out... as far as I know, Carek does not speak Kildreshian. What insanity is this?"

"I am talking about the language of warriors, Denaris. Kildresh Barbarians refuse to die less than an honorable death in battle. Their gods will reject the man's soul if he does. Likewise, they believe that killing a warrior they deem their equal by less than honorable means is an affront to the gods that gave them life.

"If you take one prisoner in fair combat and take his god-blessed weapon, especially if it is an ancestral weapon, and then threaten to hang them without it, you deny them an honorable death. Going further, if Carek defeats him, the barbarian would not dare slit Carek's throat in his sleep. His honor would demand fair combat."

Tisus stopped at the stairs to his private rooms. "Carek knows what to do. We already discussed it at length when he was last here. Carek will petition for me on the captured man's behalf. Once the debt is sealed, it is unbreakable, or the tribesman risk imprisonment in an afterlife equivalent to the Abyss."

Denaris furrowed his brows. "It all seems an unnecessary risk. To what end? What could you possibly want one of those heathens brought back here for? You can't think the tribes would pay a ransom?"

"They are not heathens, my friend. They are merely culturally limited, and Carek will not keep him here. He will take the barbarian to The Enclave."

"Your daughter is at The Enclave, and what of her safety?"

"Feylynn will fair well with the education. I pray she will eventually command a unit one day, and seeing one of her adversaries up close will teach her a great many lessons."

"Eradicating the brutes seems a simpler task and far more efficient. Why do you suffer them as they continue to threaten Ranoak?"

"Denaris, it is tolerance and mercy. In all these years together, I'm amazed that you still find it hard to see mercy's blessings. Perhaps it's because, in your young life, few have shown you mercy."

Denaris shook his head. "Practicality is a much better way to look at things. Mercy weakens our kingdom."

Tisus lifted his eyebrows. "Was it not an elf maiden's mercy that allowed this kingdom to come to pass?"

Denaris rolled his eyes. "Has this plan of yours ever worked?"

Tisus shrugged. "I will let you know when Carek returns. I don't think anyone has ever done it before."

"Then what— How?"

"Some years back, a monk told me about a barbarian that owed him a life debt and how he learned about their culture when the tribesman insisted on following him for over a year."

"A monk. Sire, you must reconsider. This is insanity."

"I will not reconsider," Tisus said firmly. In frustration, his demeanor changed from friendship to the authoritative King he was forced to be more often than he wished. "This is my order. I want these raiders to see and know the kind of people they hurt."

"Capturing a single barbarian cannot possibly make such a difference."

Tisus grinned. "If a single boulder rolls down a hill and into a river, does it not change the way the river flows indefinitely?"

"Did your mysterious monk say that, too?"

Tisus put a finger to his nose. "You are an observant man, Denaris."

Denaris threw up his hands. "I still believe this is madness, but I am not the King. I will see that it is done despite my objections."

Tisus clasped his shoulder. "That is all I ask, my friend. You will see the blessings in time."

"I doubt it," Denaris muttered as Tisus took the stairs to his rooms. "Mark my words, you court disaster."

"It is a courtship I am familiar with."

SIXTEEN

W rapped in Enreal's robe, Resora sat on the edge of her sister's bed while her older sister sought a nightgown for herself. She was loads better after her bath and even found that the burning in her stomach was gratefully absent tonight. Maybe her father had been right after all, and it was merely a worry for her sisters. Regardless of that, she was happy to be feeling healthy and even more thrilled to be alive and unharmed after her terrifying ordeal.

Revienah sat behind Resora and combed her hair. A warm feeling of comfort spread among the sisters as they shared a room. Their attendants knew the three sisters didn't want anyone extra in the room when Enreal shooed them away.

Enreal brought a nightgown to her sister and set it on the bedside where Revienah combed and braided Resora's long brown hair. The twins were identical and had straight dark-brown hair and hazel-green eyes. They inherited their mother's elvish build and were small for their age, but they both had their father's smile. Due to their size, many thought the twins were younger than their twelve years of age.

Their shared connection was evident not only in appearance. The twins' bond was stronger than any of the sisters. They often sensed each other's pain and turmoil, and they could communicate easily with small gestures. They understood each other as none other could.

Their shared bond was the reason Enreal and Revienah had rushed to their rooms that night. Revienah had been dancing in the courtyard and enjoying the first snowfall of winter while Enreal played with one of the hounds. Suddenly Revienah stumbled and sucked in a strained breath. A second later, she pulled Enreal along by the hand and told her that Resora was in danger. They hurried from the courtyard and then heard the call for water buckets. Revienah had never run so fast in her whole life.

While they shared so much, the twins were also very different. Resora was quiet and timid, and she rarely voiced her opinion. When she did, her four sisters had learned to listen because it was often valuable advice. Resora was meticulous in weighing her options before she would act. She loved her studies and preferred to spend time reading.

Revienah, on the other hand, was bold, daring, and often rash. She feared little. As young children, she led Enreal and Resora into grand summer adventures while Feylynn and Ahanna were forever trying to keep them out of trouble. Although filled with imagination and fun, Revienah was not so fond of books and preferred to learn by doing.

Resora watched her sisters out of the corner of her eye, and she wondered if she should tell them about the dream. "Ouch!" she exclaimed as Revienah tugged a little too hard on a snarl.

"Sorry," her twin said.

Enreal smiled. "I could've done it instead."

Resora glanced back. "Remind me how hard she pulls next time I agree to let her help me."

"Alright, but you won't listen," Enreal said lightheartedly.

She was right. Her twin needed to do this task herself to settle the incident. Unlike Enreal's calm demeanor, Revienah did not cope well with being idle in a difficult circumstance. Resora wondered, as she often did, if Enreal felt left out sometimes. Resora and Revienah had each other, and Ahanna and Feylynn were barely a year apart, leaving Enreal stuck between her four sisters.

Like all the sisters, she had distinct traits that made her unique. Enreal's personality was a good mix of Resora's and Ahanna's. She lacked Ahanna's stubborn streak but was not as timid as Resora. In contrast to most middle children who loved to draw attention, she preferred to keep to the background. She took pleasure from the outdoors rather than from stuffy castle walls and parties.

In contrast, Resora preferred parties and delicate dresses. She was shy, but like her twin Revienah, she liked to observe other people.

Enreal didn't care much for regular classroom studies but loved the study of gardening and wildlife. She was cunning when she thought the circumstance required it, but she hated the leadership role that had settled on her. Despite that or because of it, Resora still looked up to her older sister's leadership skills.

Enreal's physical makeup was the most balanced of their parents' bloodlines out of all her siblings. Tisus' curly black hair and Shelanna's straight blonde hair somehow mixed to create Enreal's beautiful auburn tone with naturally soft waves. Her eyes were an exotic jade-green with golden brown flecks. Her shape was not as human-looking as Feylynn's, but neither did she favor the elven blood like Ahanna and the twins. Enreal's soft curves often attracted the eyes of many men in the castle. It was yet another reason Resora suspected she preferred solitude.

Nearly sixteen, Enreal had grown into a striking woman. Resora and Revienah heard their attendants comment on Enreal's eye-catching appearance, and often the ladies whispered that despite her bloodline, Tisus would have lords lining up to take Enreal as a wife.

"There, all done," Revienah said, pulling Resora from her musings.

Turning to face Enreal, Resora asked, "Have either of you dreamt of dragons?"

Enreal rolled her eyes. "Did Father read about the great black Fythinisdim again?"

"Yes, but I didn't dream of a black."

Revienah pursed her lips. "What color was it?"

"There were two of them," said Resora as she picked at the embroidered bed coverings.

"Two?" Enreal prodded.

"A large red and an ancient gold," said Resora.

Enreal's brows drew in. "A gold dragon?"

"Gold is the good luck sign," Revienah added.

Resora nodded. "It was a beautiful and horrid dream at the same time. I did not feel any blessing of good luck. Instead, I felt trapped as I watched the wyrm and the great dragon fighting right above me. In the end, right before I woke up, the gold dragon cast its breath on me, and it burned me like… " She paused. The dragon fire was beyond any descriptions her young mind could fathom. "The burning hurt, Enreal. It was all real."

"Well, the burning was real. At the same time, our room was on fire," said Revienah, insinuating that the connection should be obvious.

"It wasn't… " Resora paused.

Her sisters waited for her to explain.

"It wasn't what?" Enreal coaxed.

"I'm not sure how to explain it," she said.

"It was only a dream," Revienah insisted. "You don't have to explain. I dream all the time of falling or flying. Sometimes I'm not sure which, but it hardly matters because it's a dream."

"I suppose," Resora replied. She wasn't sure how to express the realism of what she experienced in her dream. She had always been a dreamer. From a very young age, she experienced vivid imaginative dreams in her sleep. She was used to bright colors, tiny pixies, even the odd dragon finding her amid her rest, but this was different. This dream was filled with blood, screeching dragons in pain, burning skies, and death. This dream also held a promise, a promise she'd made. She said the words and meant them. Even without understanding the purpose or the weight of those words, she wanted to keep the promise. Resora even grieved the dragon. In her heart, it was as if the young Princess of Ranoak had lost a friend, and she couldn't find the words to explain how it truly felt.

Being observant as always, Enreal noticed Resora's glances at the bedroom door and the hidden fear in her eyes. Enreal glanced at the door as well. The dream must have been horrible indeed to unsettle Resora in such a way, "You don't have to sleep in Ahanna's room. You can stay here with me. Both of you can."

Revienah grinned. "That's a great idea!" She leapt from the bed and hurried to the door. She giggled as she pulled the knob. "I'll be right back."

Enreal knew by Resora's faint smile that her heart was not with them tonight. Enreal slid over and pulled back the coverlet. "Come on, then, you might as well get comfortable while she's gone, or she'll occupy all the good space."

Resora obeyed and clamored up the bed to tuck her cold feet beneath the warm coverings. "Thanks for keeping me company tonight."

"The fire was as frightening to us as it was for Father. Don't let your twin fool you, either. Revienah jests now, but in the courtyard, her face drained of all color. She yelled your name while dashing up the stairs and darting around servants to reach you."

Resora nodded. "She thinks I'm fragile."

"No, dear sister, she thinks you're irreplaceable. We all do."

Resora's lips thinned into a tight line, and a tear slid down her cheek.

"Come on now, don't cry," Enreal soothed.

"I'll be alright. It's been a long day. I'm not even sure why I'm crying. We are all safe."

"Unless you're counting the loss of the wardrobe," Enreal teased her.

With a sniffling laugh, Resora pulled away and wiped at her cheeks. "I know it will be nice to see Liddia again."

"That's better," Enreal encouraged and smiled.

The door opened, and Resora's eyes brightened at the sight of Revienah's full arms. "What are you doing?" she asked.

"I raided the kitchen," Revienah replied. "It seems that we are having a bit of fun tonight, and we needed a few staples."

"Pie and breakfast rolls are not staples," Enreal chided as she got up to help Revienah carry her haul.

"I say they are, and don't forget the tarts." She untied a linen sack from her waist and set it upon the bed.

"We'd be sick if we ate all of this tonight," Enreal said, setting down the rolls.

Revienah shrugged. "Well, don't eat all of it."

Enreal shook her head and grinned at Resora as she picked up a pastry roll and tossed it to her little sister. "Come on then. You'd best help us get rid of the evidence of Revienah's crime."

Full of giggles, the girls set aside the memory of the fire outbreak and indulged in the sweet treats, chattering at the same time about every subject that they could think of. They speculated about palace guards and their lady attendant relationships, reminisced on old jokes, and laughed about tutors and annoying daily lessons.

Their antics lasted well after midnight. With full bellies and happy hearts, the three sisters tucked into Enreal's bed together. Revienah, who was positioned in the center, succumbed to sleep first. On either side, Enreal and Resora were not far behind their youngest sister, and soon the room fell quiet. Heavy lids closed, and Resora sighed contentedly.

"Rest easy, Resora," Enreal said softly as her own eyes gave in to the slumber.

Resora snuggled deeper into her pillow. "Enreal?"

"Hmmm?" came Enreal's muffled reply.

"I think I know the dragon's name," Resora confessed in a sleepy whisper.

Too exhausted to think, Enreal nodded in the darkness. She couldn't even remember what they were talking about. "Um-hum."

Resora yawned and mumbled, "Feldorathanosh, the King of Fire."

Enreal didn't reply this time. Instead, her body relaxed, and her breathing became slow and even. There was a distinct memory in her foggy mind as she rode the tide between sleep and wakefulness. Her mother tucked her into bed singing songs of great and powerful dragons. They flittered into her thoughts now, and smiling at the vague memory, Enreal allowed herself to drift away with the image of that beautiful, blonde elf in her mind.

SEVENTEEN

The scraping sound of metal trays and the rippling of heavy window fabric hinted that the morning routine had begun. Groaning, the girls stirred as bright sunlight bathed the room. Resora rubbed her eyes and stretched. Enreal shifted to sit up, and she yawned. Revienah, however, tried to snuggle in deeper between her sisters and covered her eyes with the blanket.

Tisus strode into their room and chuckled at the sight before him. "When Edith finds out you snagged those breakfast rolls and tarts, there will be a scolding in store for you three."

Awake now, Enreal watched their lady attendants shifting about her room. Tisus stood by the table and picked up a pastry for himself. He took a bite. "I'll not be able to save you this time. I hope it was worth it." He wiped the crumbs from his strong hands as he finished the roll and then walked to Resora to check for a fever. "How are you feeling?"

Resora thought about it for a second and realized that her

belly no longer burned. "Much better," she replied.

"That is a relief," said Tisus, letting his hand drop. His gaze shifted to the bulge in the middle of the bed. "Come now, Revienah, get moving. You still need breakfast, and Lady Liddia will be here by midday."

"Lady Liddia is already here, and by the look of it, so is their breakfast," said a small, aging woman in the doorway.

A castle guard escorted Liddia into the room. Two men laden with supplies followed right behind her. She offered a modest curtsy and said, "Your Majesty."

Enreal and Resora grinned brightly. "Lady Liddia!"

Revienah finally popped out from the shelter of the duvet, with mussed hair that was sticking up in every direction. Revienah didn't give her appearance a second thought as she smiled sleepily, yawned, and said, "Good morning." Then she plopped back down into the pillows and pulled up the blankets to ward away the morning chill.

"Ladies," Liddia said with a respectful tilt of her head.

Tisus cleared his throat. "You came quickly—sooner than expected."

"And why should I come any later? Honestly, did you expect I would doddle when I heard?"

"Well, no—" he started.

"These girls needed proper attire for the day, and you expected me to come at midday. What in all the realms did you plan to do with them until then? Allow them to eat sweets while they lay in bed all day?"

"Of course not." Tisus shook his head.

"Then I suppose it is better that I came quickly, don't you think?"

He bowed his head in defeat. "Of course, I am grateful as always. It is good to see you."

A hint of a smile showed in her eyes. "The feeling is mutual. Now that I'm here, it seems I have a fair amount of work to do, and you must have important matters as well."

Tisus raised a brow. "That, I do."

"Then leave these ladies to me. My assistants have already set up in our dressing room."

"Very well, ladies," said Tisus as he bowed to his daughters. Then, he turned to Liddia and offered her the same respectful bow. "Madam, I will leave them in your care."

Liddia walked over to her trunk and pulled out her tape. "Go on then," she said to Tisus. "We'll have new dresses sooner if you let me get to work." Pretending as if King Tisus had already left them, she turned to his Princesses. "Resora, come over here, child. Let's see how much you've grown since I last visited."

"Yes, my Lady."

Satisfied that the girls were safe and well, Tisus left his daughters with Lady Liddia. The girls grinned at him as he winked and closed the door.

Few in Ranoak would ever dare to speak to King Tisus in such a manner as Liddia exhibited. He was an intimidating figure for sure. Liddia, however, treated him as if she was his aunt, and likewise, she spoiled his daughters as if they were her grandchildren or nieces. Although she never outright disrespected him, she consistently demanded his respect.

The relationship between Lady Liddia and King Tisus was an odd one. Liddia was fifteen years older, and many speculated that Liddia had played a part in raising Tisus, for she was certainly familiar enough with him. It was a well-known fact that Tisus never knew his mother since she died during his birth. His father, it was said, had been a bitter and cold man as a result. At least, that was the current rumor. Tisus never really spoke of his childhood either, so few knew whether there was any truth in the gossip.

Since neither Tisus nor Liddia elaborated on the matter, whatever remained unsaid left remarkable room for speculation.

It mattered little to the girls how Liddia became such a central part of their lives. All that mattered to them was that she was there when they needed her. The seamstress and her attendants made their clothes for them since birth, and the girls loved how she personalized every article they wore. Despite the multiple offers from Tisus to have her reside on the castle grounds, Liddia refused to move in with the King. Still, Tisus kept rooms ready for her anyway, and she made use of them every time she visited.

As Liddia measured Resora, she said, "Gracious, child. It's just as well that I came. You've grown at least two inches since I last visited you, which is not very long ago. If you could stop growing so fast, that would be better."

Resora giggled at the all too common remark. "I'll work on that," she promised.

"See that you do. At this rate, I'll have to come back every week to keep you modestly clothed," Liddia added with a sly grin that easily broke her stern features.

"Thanks for coming early to make me new clothes."

"Well, I surely couldn't have anyone else do it. Any other seamstress would likely put you in bright purple, and that would be awful. Your skin tone is not conducive for purple."

Resora's expression shifted as she glanced toward the window. "Ahanna always looked so beautiful in purple."

Enreal bit her lip at the mention of her oldest sister, and under the covers on the bed, Revienah's eyes opened, but she said nothing. An awkward silence filled the room for several seconds.

Liddia shifted and penned something in her notepad. "That's very true. Ahanna *is* stunning in purple, but I'll tell you a secret. She looks hideous in pastels. You, on the other hand, can wear any light color you choose."

Resora nodded sadly, but she would not look up to meet the dressmaker's eyes.

"How are you feeling, Resora?" Liddia questioned. "Word came to me that you've been ill."

Resora pulled her attention from the window and looked back at the older woman. "Honestly, it's only a touch of tummy trouble. I am feeling much better now."

"Do not let her fool you," Enreal objected. "She has been sick for days, and few know why."

"You are looking a bit peaked," Liddia observed.

"I feel a million times better today. Father says it's probably my worry for Feylynn and Ahanna that has my belly burning."

Liddia paused. "Your belly burns, child?"

"Not today. Before the fire. I was even able to eat two tarts last night after the fire."

"I'm glad of that. You are skinny enough as it is." The older woman smiled, but observant and quiet, Enreal noticed it was not a happy one.

"Father has been reading to me, too, and that's nice because I like his stories."

"Do you? I find some of his stories a bit boring," Liddia said with a conspiratorial wink.

Going with the easing tension, Enreal walked closer. "Resora likes the stories of dragons the best."

"Dragons, is it?" Liddia asked.

Resora nodded. "I even dreamed of them last night. A great gold and a red. Have you ever seen a dragon, Lady Liddia?"

Liddia's eyes widened, and her quill faltered, but she did not look up, and so the change in her demeanor escaped them. "I haven't, dear. I'm not that old," she teased. "You dreamed of a red and gold? Together?" Liddia tried hard to keep her voice even but failed, and her pitch indeed went up.

Resora nodded. "They were amazing! They flew high above me amid a burning sky, fighting against each other in a great battle."

"Did they now!" Liddia said with a grandmother's enthusiasm. "It must have been frightening."

"Oh, it was. It felt more like a nightmare than a dream. Except... Well, I liked seeing the colors of their scales. I am not sure why, but I never knew how many colors a single dragon could have."

"How would you know, dummy? You've never seen one," Revienah mumbled from under the covers. Annoyed, Resora stuck her tongue out at her sister.

"Revienah, don't mock your sister," Liddia scolded.

"Yes, my Lady," Revienah muttered.

"And you, Resora. Sticking out your tongue is very unladylike."

She shifted and stared down at her bare feet. "Yes, my Lady."

"Never mind. What happened next in your dream?" Liddia prodded.

Resora's eyes glittered as she looked up. "Oh, the gold one spoke to me."

"Oh?"

She leaned forward and whispered, "He called me a daughter of the forest in Elvish."

"Really? That sounds like a fanciful dream," said Liddia.

Resora's smile fell. "It was a bit scary, especially when he blew fire at me. I wish I could see a dragon for real—not a mean one, but a brilliant gold one like Feldorathanosh. Maybe I should make my own story about dragons. Except I would make it much prettier because, in my story, everyone would live."

Liddia's hands shook a bit as she shifted to cup Resora's face in her hands. "Well, we best set dreams of dragons and pretty stories aside for now and take care of getting you clothed. We have quite a bit of work to do."

Resora grinned in agreement.

"And no more talk of gold dragons. I want you to get some good rest tonight so you will get better, alright?"

"Yes, my Lady."

Liddia inched closer and kissed Resora's brow. "Very well, then." She took her hand. "I've brought some pretty fabrics, raw silk with dainty flowers, and dark velvets from far-off places. Why don't you come take a look?"

Enreal was certain that Resora's dream had upset the older woman more than she revealed. She watched as Lady Liddia moved to the trunks and began pulling out bolts of fabrics for Resora.

Revienah finally rolled from the bed and scratched her wild mane of dark hair. Then, ambling over toward her twin, she said, "Lady Liddia, I was hoping... Well, since you're making me some new dresses, I thought that perhaps I could persuade you to make me another one of those special outfits. Mine is a bit snug. Plus, I mistakenly tore the knee out."

Liddia's stern features returned as she turned to Revienah. "Huh. What exactly were you doing, Princess, that would tear out the knee of your Aranath spider silk jumpsuit?"

Revienah couldn't hide the guilt on her face. Instead of replying, she walked past the dressmaker, stopped at the table where the pastries were, and shoved an entire tart into her mouth. "Um, climbing," she said, chewing around the food in her mouth.

"Really? Climbing?" Liddia asked.

"Uh-huh," Revienah agreed and choked down some of her food. Her mouth was dry from the sweets last night. The abrupt need for water had her regretting her decision to swallow the whole tart at once. Struggling to eat, she poured some water into a cup and drank greedily.

"What?" Liddia questioned.

"What?" Revienah repeated. She poured more water and drank again while her sisters nervously bit their lips but said nothing. They, too, could not hide the guilt on their faces.

The truth was that Revienah had torn the knee of the fabric while she was trying to get back into the castle the night she helped Ahanna escape. Her original path was blocked, and the forced change in plans had caused her to use a more precarious route. She snagged the knee of her jumpsuit on a metal sconce and nearly fell from a free climb up the north wall. At the time, she had been more worried about falling out of favor with Lady Liddia than the possibility of dying. Aranath spider silk was not easy to tear. Nor was it easy to obtain.

"What exactly were you climbing, Princess Revienah?" Liddia asked again.

"Oh, you know, trees and stuff." Revienah stuffed another tart in her mouth. "Honestly, it happened so long ago. I can hardly remember exactly what it was that time."

Liddia glared at Revienah for several minutes until Resora could no longer stand the silence. Resora was terrible under that kind of pressure. "She was helping Ahanna! Please, my Lady! Don't tell Father. We had to help her, you see. She was so miserable." The words tumbled out so fast that Resora didn't realize her mistake until too late.

Revienah sneered at her sister, and Resora immediately lowered her gaze to the floor in shame.

Liddia pursed her lips in thought and returned her attention to the fabrics again. "I suppose you're right."

"I am?" Resora looked up with disbelief.

"She is?" Revienah asked in mild shock.

The dressmaker's eyes brightened as the stern look cleared

away, and she sorted fabric for display. She glanced at Enreal and saw the worry on her face, and she winked at her. "Of course, you had to help Ahanna—she's your sister after all. If I had a sister, my loyalty would certainly be with her. Besides, I hated the idea of Ahanna being in that Enclave."

All three girls' mouths dropped open in surprise. Enreal took a step closer to Liddia as she set out the last bolt of material. "You... you hated the idea, too?"

"Of course, I did. That place is not what it used to be. These days there is too much political intrigue and posturing. Should Ahanna have resided there, the headmasters would have been maneuvering her around to their liking. They were likely planning her wedding."

Revienah's eyes widened. "That's what Ahanna said."

"Of course, she did. She's a smart girl and far too stubborn for that place." Liddia picked up her quill and measuring tools again and glanced over at Revienah. "Come here, Revienah. Let's take your measurements for a new jumpsuit."

Still stunned that Liddia would not only keep their secret but agreed with their action, Revienah walked to the older woman obediently. She looked to Enreal for reassurance and understood that her sister was no less surprised.

"But what of Feylynn?" Enreal asked. "We didn't help her."

She smiled. "Don't worry. Feylynn is going to be fine there. The Enclave will help her in more ways than one. She is suited for that life, and some of the lessons on intrigue will do her good. I suppose they will be hard-learned lessons for honorable Feylynn but necessary for her all the same. Besides, Feylynn is no wilting flower, and she will likely surprise you."

EIGHTEEN

A fter Liddia left the girls, Enreal excused herself and left the twins alone. As she headed for the library, a little shaky feeling started in her belly. Enreal didn't think of herself as intelligent as Feylynn or Resora. Instead of studies, she enjoyed outdoor activities such as cultivating the gardens. Neither did she believe herself to be as cunning as Ahanna or Revienah since she preferred her own company in quiet solace with her pets rather than intrigue and gossip. But, today, her preferences could not matter. She was old enough to know that something was not right.

Enreal did not like how Lady Liddia reacted when Resora spoke of her dream, and she wanted to understand why the older woman had been so afraid. The dressmaker had recognized the name of that dragon, and Enreal was sure of it.

The library was a vast room located in the center of the castle. It was purposefully designed to be windowless to prevent the light from withering old parchments and tapestries filled with the history of Ranoak. Heavy wooden tables were kept at the center of the room with bright lanterns to offer light for those working on restoration or study.

Shelves filled with leather-bound works and rolled parchments lined the walls. Ancient tapestries hung near the front, and library attendants worked tirelessly to restore what had been lost to damage caused by time and wars.

Enreal hurried over to the section that held the stories and legends of dragons. She spent over an hour pulling out scrolls and looking for the name *Feldorathanosh* or anything about the King of Fire.

An aged librarian slowly approached Enreal, but she was too distracted to notice him right away. "Princess, is there something I can help you find?" he asked.

Startled, Enreal dropped the scroll and almost screamed in fright. Calming herself, she bent to pick up the aged scroll and then placed it back on the shelf. "Um, I'm not entirely sure."

He smiled kindly, and the gesture revealed the lines of age in his skin from years of experience. "What is it you seek today?"

Instinct kept Enreal from being specific. She wasn't sure why, but she didn't want to share too much information. "I want to know about dragons."

"That is a vast subject, Princess."

Enreal bit her lip and considered how to narrow her search. "Specifically, metallic wyrms and golden dragons."

The librarian nodded kindly. "Very well," he said and shifted to the shelves near Enreal. He pulled out two leather-bound works and extracted three tubes with ancient scrolls. "The books, you are welcome to take to your rooms. The parchments, however, will require assistance. They are extremely old and not written in the common tongue. You will have to read them here to ensure they will not be ruined."

"In what language are they written?"

"Dwarvish, I'm afraid. Few can read them, but the dwarves kept meticulous records. I am sure your father could come to help you with them."

"No!" Enreal objected a little too quickly.

The librarian's eyes glanced at her curiously.

Enreal clasped her hands to keep from fidgeting. She pasted a sweet smile on her face. "He seems so busy lately, and I do not wish to bother him. Can't you help me?"

"I'm afraid not. I cannot speak or read the language either. I can send for someone, but that could take weeks."

Disappointed and resigned, Enreal picked up the two books. "I'll start with these and let you know. It's only out of curiosity anyhow. Nothing important."

"Very well, I'll leave you to your studies then." He turned to leave.

Enreal read the book titles and frowned. "Excuse me."

The librarian turned back to her. "Yes?"

"Are there not any books for gold dragons here?"

"Oh, I'm sorry, Princess, most of those accounts were destroyed by the previous monarchy. What is left is protected at The Paladin Enclave. They take the preservation of those remaining histories very seriously there."

Enreal did her best to act like it was not a big deal, But she was more discouraged than when she entered. "Alright, thanks for your help."

The librarian bowed respectfully and left her alone.

Enreal took the two books on the subject of silver dragons and headed back to her room. As she walked down the hallway, she opened the first book and skimmed the pages. She heard an oncoming movement that drew her attention before she could delve too deep. Looking up, she saw Lady Liddia turn to enter her father's corridor. Unsure of what was happening but curious and worried for her younger sister, Enreal decided that she would ask Lady Liddia directly why she reacted so strangely rather than sneaking about the library looking for clues.

As Enreal neared the adjoining corridor, she heard her father's voice boom, "What do you mean she's been touched?"

Enreal peaked around the corner but tried to stay out of sight.

"No, you fool, not like that. And keep your voice down. Resora is *Dragon Touched*." Liddia spoke in low undertones. She glanced over her shoulder nervously, and Enreal, with her heart racing, quickly hid herself against the wall at the corner. "Gracious, Tisus, how in all creation could you miss it?"

Enreal wasn't sure why Revienah liked sneaking about all the time. The fear of getting caught made her very uncomfortable. With her hand pressed to her thundering heart, Enreal tried to listen further.

"It's impossible," Tisus.

"Not so impossible," Lady Liddia admonished as Tisus opened the door to enter his rooms.

"No one..." Tisus began, but even Enreal's elvish hearing couldn't hear the rest of the sentence as the pair entered Tisus' chambers.

Enreal peered around the corner, hoping to hear more, but the door was shut firmly behind them. Biting her lip, she considered eavesdropping at the door for a second or two.

"Princess Enreal?"

For the second time that day, Enreal jumped and let out a little squeak of fright. She topped it off when she bumped her head upon the stone wall. Denaris placed a hand on her shoulder to steady her.

"Are you alright? You look pale, have you taken ill?"

Enreal nodded and then shook her head in the negative. Realizing that she was flustered, she quickly clarified, "No, I'm not ill. Yes, I am alright. You startled me, that's all."

"I am sorry, Princess. You were an unexpected find for me as well. You shouldn't be here at this time of day. Your father is very busy. Can I help you with something?"

Rubbing her head, Enreal replied, "No, I was only looking for Lady Liddia, but she has gone to meet with my father, and I do not wish to interrupt."

"I see. A wise choice on your part. A king must deal with all sorts of people in his daily activities. Interruptions can make it difficult to complete his tasks. And lurking about in the halls is unseemly and not at all a princess-like behavior."

Even at fifteen, Enreal recognized condescension when she heard it. Feeling embarrassed, she replied meekly, "I think I'll head back to my room now."

"Very well," said Lord Denaris. "Do you wish me to pass a message on to Lady Liddia?"

"No, thank you. I will catch up with her after my time in the gardens. Good day to you, Lord Denaris."

"Good day, Princess," Denaris said, offering a customary bow of his head. He watched her leave and waited until she turned down the opposite hallway before making his way down the King's corridor. Enreal was not the only one who overheard that conversation in the hall, neither was she the only one willing to risk eavesdropping.

Lord Denaris had followed the young woman when he noticed her sneaking down the hallway, but he waited to see what she was up to before acting. As a former thief in his younger years, Denaris could move about quickly without being noticed. Right now, he intended to do precisely that to hear more of the private conversation between the dressmaker and Tisus. Unlike

Enreal, Denaris had a much better understanding regarding the topic of being Dragon Touched.

NINETEEN

"**W**hat do you suppose it means?" Resora questioned, and she gripped her twin's hand tightly as a sense of fear overtook her.

"It can't be so bad, or Father would have come to you," Revienah reasoned.

Enreal shook her head. "If they don't tell us, then we should find out."

"How?" Resora asked. "You said the library had nothing on the subject."

"No, I said nothing that I could find," Enreal pointed out. "That library is enormous, and I wasn't looking for anything about being dragon touched. The biggest problem is how to search that library without alerting anyone to our purpose. I wouldn't even know where to start."

Revienah snorted. "Why should we care if they know since we don't even know what we are looking for, either?"

Enreal shook her head. "I am not sure why, but there's just something inside me that warns me we don't want to tip them off."

"I agree, and what if there is something wrong with me?" Resora inquired with fear in her eyes.

"I do not believe Father would keep something so important from you, Resora," Revienah insisted.

"He would if he is trying to protect her," Enreal claimed. Silence reigned over the three sisters as the truth slowly sank in. It was true that their father would do anything to keep them from harm, including keeping important secrets from them.

"I'm scared," Resora admitted.

Revienah drew closer to her twin and rubbed her back. "We'll figure this out. Whatever this dragon thing is, we will fix it."

"Ahanna would know what to do," Resora reasoned sadly.

Enreal nodded. She wished Ahanna was there, too. The leadership role that suddenly fell on her in the absence of her older sisters left her wishing she was smarter. But as the thought occurred to her, another idea struck. "We have another resource that we have not explored."

"What resource?" Revienah asked.

"Not what, but who."

"Who?" the twins asked simultaneously.

"Feylynn."

The twins stared at her, puzzled.

Enreal sighed. "Feylynn is at The Enclave. She has access or at least better access to those texts on ancient gold dragons. We'll write to her and ask her to look into it."

Resora looked skeptical. "Father said we had to wait until her first year was complete to write her."

"But Father can write her," Enreal added slyly.

"If we do that, we might as well ask him ourselves," Resora

argued.

Always quick to catch on, Revienah smiled. "Wait, I get it. We can write a letter and use his seal to make it look official. Father doesn't need to know."

"Seems risky," Resora insisted.

"Not if Reveniah gets the seal," Enreal assured her. "We just have to make sure we put it back."

"Who would you get to deliver such a letter? It wouldn't be coming from his hand, so who would believe Father is the one sending it?" Resora wanted to know.

Revienah smiled. "Micah."

Enreal nodded. "Micah has that falcon he used to receive the message from Ahanna. Surely if that falcon can deliver a message to him, it could deliver one to Feylynn. I bet he would do it."

"He's frightfully loyal to Father and might tell him," Resora reasoned.

Her twin rolled her eyes. "Oh, stop worrying so much, Resora. If you want to find out the truth, we'll have to take a few risks. Micah is loyal to Father, but he is our friend and just as loyal to us. Didn't he come right to us with news from Ahanna? He didn't tell Father about that now, did he?"

"Well, no."

Revienah lifted her hands in exasperation as if to say that single letter was proof of the Ranger's loyalty. "Besides, I should think you would want to know the most since you're the one who's been touched by a dragon."

Resora's lips thinned into a tight line. She hated being so sneaky, but her sister had spoken the truth of it. She needed answers. "You're right. What do you need from me?"

Smiling, Enreal took her hand and pulled her from the room.

"You want me to do what?" Micah asked with surprise as he saddled Freesia that afternoon. He made it a habit to take the horse out once a day since Ahanna left.

"Come on, Micah, don't act so surprised. You're the closest thing we have to a brother," Revienah insisted.

"That doesn't make it right. Besides, if I were your brother, I would tell you this is a terrible idea. I'm sorry, ladies, but why would you possibly think I would go against the King's order?"

"Just look at Resora," said Enreal. As instructed before they approached him, Resora stood there wrapped in a blanket, trying her best to look sick even though she was feeling far better than yesterday. The genuine shivering from the cold bite in the air only added to the effect.

Following Enreal's gesture, Micah glanced at the young Princess, and his brows drew in with concern. The idea of Resora being so ill bothered him and Revienah covered her satisfied smile.

Micah shook his head and turned away from the sick girl to pat Freesia on the neck. "Resora, I'm sorry, but I don't see how sending Feylynn a letter helps you get better. You will have to be more specific."

"Father says I am sick with worry. If I could have some reassurance that she fairs well, then it would help a great deal." Resora finished weakly with a small, pitiful cough for good measure.

Micah scoffed. Ahanna's horse Freesia was no better. The beast snorted out a hot breath against the cold air, and the Ranger laughed out loud. "This was your idea, wasn't it, Revi? You won't manipulate me. I am not so easy to bend as the palace guards you bribe." He laughed again, "Even Freesia sees through your ruse."

Annoyed that he was no longer concerned, Revienah glared at him and folded her arms. "How do you know I bribe the guards?"

Micah winked at her. "Soldiers talk, Revi. They talk a lot. Remember that."

"Whatever," she scoffed but mentally filed away his warning. "My plan would have worked if Resora could act. You almost wavered, and I saw that worried look in your eyes. You're not so tough, Micah Finn."

He shook his head and chuckled as he mounted the black mare. "I'll give you credit, Revi. You do come up with the most outrageous plans."

Enreal surprised him. She rushed forward and took the horse's reins under her neck before Micah could wheel her around and take off. She pinned him with her eyes and tried her best to look mature as she pleaded for Resora.

"Micah, this is vitally important. Please, you must help us. You are the only one we trust to do so. You know better than anyone that we would no more disobey Father than you, but we are asking you to trust us this time. Resora's illness is real and far more complicated than a simple case of worry, as Father hopes. I honestly believe Feylynn's access to the archives in The Enclave is our only hope to gain the truth. That's all I can tell you, but I beg of you to have compassion because we are desperate, and only you can help."

Micah stared down at Enreal for several heartbeats, and there was an indecision that danced in his eyes.

Resora stepped forward, and he glanced at her. "Please, Micah. I must get a message to Feylynn."

He turned his gaze to the horizon now to avoid eye contact. The desperation in their innocent green gems was killing him.

Enreal was reasonably certain they had him, but to make sure, she threw out one last dig to tip the scale. "Besides, think of how relieved Feylynn will be to know Ahanna is safe. After all, it was Feylynn's sacrifice that saved her from The Enclave and an *arranged marriage."*

Micah adjusted himself in the saddle and tipped his head skyward. He huffed in defeat. "In all the realms above and beyond, for a woman who speaks little, you may be the best manipulator of them all." Adjusting his gloves and making a fist, Micah stretched his fingers open again. He looked at Revienah. "Revi, you should take lessons from this one. Not one of the guards would stop you if you could twist them up in such a way." He leaned forward in his saddle and shook his head with a resigned laugh.

After a few seconds of waiting, he looked back at Enreal and saw the budding hope in her pretty jade green eyes. He winked to let her know she'd won, then he twisted about and searched the castle grounds to verify no one was eavesdropping. Straightening up in his saddle again, he took up the leather reins in his hands.

"Write your letter, Enreal, but take your time. The Enclave will not recognize Cirus, my falcon, and he does not know Feylynn or the route through the Feldorian range. He's still young. Moreover, the height of winter is upon us. So your letter will have to wait till spring when I can make the journey myself."

"Spring?" Resora questioned.

"It is the best I can offer. There is no way to get through the pass this late in the year. At the first hint of spring, I will find a way to take the letter to The Enclave personally. Letters are risky. Take care what you put in them."

"Thank you, Micah," Enreal said with sincerity as hope filled her heart. The idea of hearing from their older sisters again warded away the winter chill.

Micah gave her a quick nod. "Don't mention it. I mean that, Enreal. None of you can mention your communications with your sisters to anyone. It is more complicated than simple worry on my part, too. There are people in the castle that would wish you harm."

"We swear, Micah. We will keep this letter between us," she said.

"Don't even ask me anymore. Have your letter ready and leave it in my quarters. I will deliver it as soon as I can."

All three nodded. Enreal stepped back from Freesia.

"You really are a good brother, Micah," Revienah added before he could take off.

He yanked on the reins to turn the horse about and winced at the idea that they wouldn't put the thought of brotherhood in Ahanna's head. "I'll have no way to tell you when it's done. You'll have to keep trusting me." With that last proclamation, Micah tapped Freesia's sides twice, and the horse took off, kicking up mud and snow in her wake.

As they watched the horse and rider thunder away, the three girls huddled together. "Do you think he'll do it?" Resora asked Enreal.

Enreal nodded. "He'll do it. The bigger problem is what we do between now and then."

"I suppose I need to figure out how to get that seal. It's a good thing that Liddia is making me a new outfit," Revienah said as she took her twin's hand. "Come on, Resora."

"Where are we going?"

Revienah smiled wickedly. "To scout and make a plan."

"What about me?" Enreal asked.

Resora shrugged. "I suppose since you're the oldest now, you get to write the letter."

TWENTY

"What are we doing?" Resora questioned quietly as her sister pulled her along the corridor, and she stumbled slightly.

Revienah smiled slyly as she pulled her back up and whispered, "We are going to look for our own answers."

"We are supposed to be practicing our writing."

"Writing is boring, and this is more important. Who cares about fancy letters and formal wording anyway?" said Revienah.

"I care," Resora protested. "I'm getting quite good at it."

Revienah sighed, "Then you can do them later. We need to know what is happening to you, and today is the perfect day to find out."

"It is?"

"Of course it is," she insisted. "Father is taking an audience with the people of Ranoak today. He won't be around his room for a long time yet. So we are going to find out what he is keeping secret."

Resora sighed, "Enreal has been looking through books for days, and she found nothing."

"Enreal isn't looking in the right places," Revienah whispered.

Confused, Resora asked quietly, "What are you talking about?"

She stopped suddenly and turned back to her twin, "Think about it. Father must know something about this sickness."

Resora shook her head. "What if you're wrong? What if he doesn't know?"

Revienah retook her sister's hand and dropped her voice barely above a whisper now, "Why would Liddia tell him about this dragon thing then?"

"I don't know."

"Maybe Father has something in his study to help us."

"Why are we whispering?" Resora asked as she hurried to keep up with her twin.

"Because this is a secret mission. We don't want to get caught. We'll surely be scolded for skipping our studies."

Resora lifted her brow as if Revienah made her point for her, "Shouldn't we act normal then? Whispering is suspicious."

Revienah's face turned pensive as she considered her logic. "It's more fun if we whisper."

Resora shrugged. "Maybe, but it's still suspicious."

Revienah rolled her eyes, and Resora smiled smugly.

"Fine," Revienah agreed with average volume. "Come on," she said, tugging Resora's hand again. "We have to hurry before father finishes with the grievances and law stuff."

Hurrying through the castle, the pair carefully made their way to their father's private rooms. As they took the stone steps leading to the main door, Revienah glanced around to ensure no one was watching. Resora mimicked the gesture even though she didn't think anyone would care that they were going to their father's room. This was a place they were always welcome. However, today Revienah wanted to dig a little in her father's study, and that action would not be so welcome.

Carefully opening the door, Revienah peered into the room to ensure none of the staff were there cleaning. This section of the castle consisted of three separate rooms, all for the King. His bed-chamber, his study on the left side, and a receiving room to the right. All of it was connected by a foyer. Since she could not see past the closed doors into each room, she stood there for a couple of minutes, listening for any noise that would indicate people milling about.

When she was fairly certain it was clear, Revienah whispered over her shoulder, "Let's go."

Following her twin into the foyer of their father's private rooms, Resora closed the entry door behind them. At the same time, Revienah opened the door to the study as softly as she could, but the old hinges betrayed them and creaked loudly.

Resora winced at the harsh sound. "Shhhh."

"I'm trying. These hinges are awful," her sister replied. She didn't even try to open it more. Revienah turned sideways to ease through the small opening to avoid making more noise, and Resora followed.

When she turned to close the door, Revienah grabbed her hand. "Leave it open, it makes too much noise, and we still have to sneak back out."

Resora nodded and looked around the room nervously while Revienah went straight to their father's desk. "What exactly are we looking for?" Resora asked.

Revienah shrugged, "I have no idea."

She laughed softly, "Then how will we know if we find it?"

Her sister laughed as well. "I have no idea."

"So let me get this straight," said Resora. "We're looking for anything about something that may be nothing but could be something."

"Exactly!" Revienah agreed with a mischievous smile. They both giggled lightly as she absently shuffled some missives that were on her father's desk into a stack. "Hurry! Help me out, and start looking," she instructed.

Resigned to Revienah's plan, Resora bent down and pulled open the bottom left drawer as she wondered about the wisdom of Revienah's idea to search their father's study for answers. Resora was confident that if her father knew something that could help her, he would have told them. Even now, the fever in her body grew, but she had faith her father would do anything to protect her.

She hated being sneaky and doing this without talking to her father, but this plan helped Revienah cope. Her sister was better at attacking problems than taking time to think about them.

That was the number one reason Resora often found herself pulled into Revienah's grand schemes. Usually timid, Resora concluded that she would never be brave enough to make up her own wild plans filled with adventure, and Revienah always seemed to create new ones, so she never needed to. As a result, she and Revienah balanced each other out.

When it came to puzzles or problems, Resora would spend days thinking about them, and Revienah would simply act. So, in essence, Resora kept Revienah from being rash, and Revienah kept Resora from letting problems fester. She often thought, without Revienah as her twin, she would be a boring individual indeed. Of course, Revienah's legendary ideas often got them into trouble, but their life was filled with scintillating adventures that had their hearts pounding and their senses tingling. Ultimately, the pair always had fun together, and that's all that mattered.

There were many times their father nearly went mad with their crazy antics. Tisus teased them about their mischief regularly, and because of this, Resora knew he loved them both for their wild spirit rather than in spite of it.

In many cases, Tisus struggled to punish them because he found their actions amusing or creative. Ultimately, their punishments had to be nearly as clever as their crimes, but most of the time, Resora could still see the smile in his eyes as he sentenced them to chores or study.

Resora smiled as she thought about it and realized, as always, her nerves were standing on end.

"Why are you smiling?" Revienah asked.

"I was thinking about what Father would say if he catches us."

"He'll scold us for sure," said Revienah, "and we'll get stuck helping in the kitchens again. Since you're sick, I'll end up with all the work. So get looking."

Resora couldn't keep her smile from spreading. "Alright, alright. I'm looking," she said as she went back to searching the drawer. Almost instantly, her fingers brushed a leather book. Curious, she pulled it from the drawer.

"What's that?" Revienah questioned.

"I think it's a journal," Resora explained quietly as she set it upon the desk. "Maybe Father wrote something down that could help. Or maybe there is something in there about Mother even. I would love that."

"I doubt there is anything about Mother in there. And even if he did write about your illness, we won't have enough time to read it," Revienah shot back. "Besides, I looked at that one last time I was here. That's where he keeps letters from the other fiefdoms. He likes to write down his thoughts on the letters in that journal. *This lord needs* and *that lord wants*. It's all horribly boring. I didn't get past the first five pages."

Even more amused, Resora laughed, "That doesn't mean there isn't something important in there. It just means you are as impatient as ever."

Revienah returned her smile with one of her own but did not deny the accusation as she went back to looking through the loose parchments.

Resora stood up. "Maybe we should switch places then."

"Why?"

She looked at the stack of parchment pointedly. "Because you hate reading even more than you hate writing. I doubt you've even looked at any of those documents closely."

Revienah scrunched her nose. "I looked at them."

Resora lifted her brows in disbelief. "Really?"

"Alright! So I only glanced at them. You win," she agreed as she shifted to take Resora's spot. "I don't know why I even argued the point. The drawers are always more fun."

Grinning, Resora reset the stack and started over as Revienah bent down to look inside the drawer.

Hoping to find some answers to her sister's plight, Revienah shifted through the contents of the drawer until her fingertips brushed against the wooden bottom. Her fingers tingled suddenly, and an urge to dig deeper made her search more. She'd scoured this drawer at least five times in her life and never felt this strange urging of invisible pinpricks in her hand. A little frightened by the sensation, Revienah pulled her hand back and stared at it as she flexed it. Finally, the pinpricks eased, and confusion set in. She tilted her head and looked at the side of the drawer as she stretched her hand forward again. Her fingers buzzed again as she reached inside, and Revienah's hand stopped about two inches from the bottom.

"Resora!" she exclaimed. "This drawer has a false bottom."

"What?"

"Look! My hand stops before the bottom."

"Maybe it's just built like that," Resora pointed out, but even she didn't believe that was true.

With her fingers still tingling and her excitement growing, Revienah searched around for a way to access the bottom but couldn't find a latch. "I don't see any way to open it."

With her face scrunched in thought, Resora considered the possibilities. "Maybe it's leverage. Maybe you need to push down on one side or the other."

Revienah grinned and tested the front of the drawer. It didn't move. Refusing to be discouraged, she moved her hand to the back, pressed down, and lifted the false bottom. "Resora, you're a genius."

Smiling at the compliment, she tilted her head to look inside, "There's a small box in there."

Revienah used her other hand to reach inside. The tingle in her hand spread up her arm as she touched the box and a strange image of a golden eye flashed into her mind. Confused, Revienah froze in place.

"Well, come on, pull it out," Resora urged.

Shaking away the weird occurrence with a literal shake of her head, Revienah extracted the small box and let the false bottom back down. Standing, she presented the box to Resora, but the tingle shifted to strange warmth, and Revienah set the box down before Resora could take it.

"What is it?" Resora asked.

"It's a jewelry box," Revienah said sarcastically. Her head hurt a little, and she was cranky because of it.

Ignoring the sarcasm, Resora lifted the lid, "Maybe there's something in it to help us."

As she removed the lid, both girls stared down at a beautiful circular brooch made to look like a gold dragon's head with a topaz for an eye.

Staring down at it, Resora sensed Revienah's headache through their connection. Turning, she asked, "Are you alright?"

Revienah realized she was rubbing her head. Dropping her hand, she explained, "Yes, it's just a headache. Besides, I know you have had one for days, and you said nothing. So don't worry about it. It will pass."

Resora did worry but sensed the sudden ache was easing, so she let it go and turned back to the brooch. "It's pretty, but why is it hidden in this drawer?"

Revienah shrugged. "I don't know. It must be important."

"Maybe it was Mother's," Resora offered.

"I know you miss her, I do too, but not everything is about Mother. Besides, that's too big for a girl, and Father keeps Mother's stuff in a trunk in his room. I've seen it."

"Is there a room in this place that you haven't searched?" Resora asked.

"There is always hope," Revienah said with a grin.

Resora half wanted it to be her mother's. She wanted something to keep her mother in her mind.

"What is bothering you?" Revienah asked.

"Do you think if Mother is alive that she thinks of us?"

Revienah hesitated, but not for long, "Of course she does! Why wouldn't she?"

"Maybe she forgot us," Resora admitted as her fears surfaced again.

Revienah scoffed, "How could she forget her daughters?"

"Do you remember her face?"

Revienah stared at Resora for a minute. She didn't understand what she was worried about. "Yes. Don't you?"

"Sometimes, I think I remember her, but then the image fades.

And now, when I close my eyes, I only see dragons and death from my dream. I'm scared," Resora confessed as she stared at the box with the dragon pin that brought back those frightful images.

"I know," Revienah admitted. Flustered and wanting to be away from the brooch, Revienah went around Resora to the mess of parchment and started to re-stack them neatly. She didn't know what to say to help Resora, and that was the hardest part. For as long as they'd been alive, the twins had shared their burdens, but in this, Resora was alone, and Revienah had no answers.

Resora kept staring at the jeweled dragon, and Revienah couldn't stand seeing the sad defeat in her sister. She paused in her cleaning and glanced back to the brooch. The strange allure it created was still there, and that flash of a serpent's eye assaulted her again. Shaking her head defiantly, Revienah insisted, "There has to be an answer, Resora. We just need to find it."

Resora glanced back to her twin. "I feel like I am going crazy. I keep forgetting things, and my memory is fuzzy. Revienah, I think I am forgetting Mother. We were so little when she disappeared it's hard enough to remember, but now it's even harder. I can't see her anymore."

Revienah turned to her twin. "You won't forget. I won't let you because I won't forget, and I will remind you every day until we figure this out. Her hair was shiny. It was almost white. Is it helping?"

Resora smiled softly.

Revienah grinned, "We could always ask Father for the likeness he carries. And you could look at it every day."

"I suppose, but I wouldn't want to take that from him," Resora said and went back to the drawer. "If Ahanna returns, that would help. Father says she looks just like Mother."

"If Ahanna came back, she'd figure this out," said Revienah. "She's the best at solving big problems."

"I wish she were here, and Feylynn too," Resora admitted.

Before Revienah could answer, the main foyer door opened and the sound of voices carried into the study.

The twins looked at each other with wide eyes. *"Father,"* Revienah mouthed.

The twins rushed to set the room back to rights. Revienah ignored the tingling warmth as she put the dragon brooch back and tried her best to put the other items back in his drawer silently.

Still talking, Tisus and Denaris passed by the study door and moved into their father's bed-chamber. Relieved, the girls hurried to the door that was slightly open and proceeded to sneak out. Revienah made it through without a sound, but Resora bumped the creaky door, which betrayed them. Revienah rolled her eyes, and Resora's filled with apology.

His bedroom door still open, Tisus came to the entrance, "Resora, Revienah, what are you doing here?"

Unable to look at him, Resora looked back toward the study and trusted Revienah to come up with something.

Always quick when facing punishment, Revienah said the first thing that came to her mind. "I have a headache, and Resora was worried I caught her illness. She made me come here."

"We thought you would be in your study."

Tisus pinned them with his infamous stare. "You didn't hear me talking in my room?"

"We weren't sure if it was coming from your room or your study. Everything echoes here," said Revienah.

Tisus eyed them for another minute. He was not as foolish as they hoped, and he moved forward to check her head for a fever. Pressing a hand to Revienah's skin, the heat coming from her allowed his concern to take over, and he let her lie slide. "You are a little warm."

"Really?" the twins both said at once.

Tisus lifted a knowing brow.

"I didn't think I was warm, is all. It's only a headache," Revienah hurried to explain.

"Well, you best get to bed," he said. That was the best punishment he could give for whatever they were doing. If she was sick, rest was best, and if she wasn't, Revienah hated being still and would despise staying in bed for the rest of the day.

He moved to Resora to check her as well and found her fever burning again. His heart sank, and he frowned. "Both of you would be better off with some rest," he said solemnly. "Lord Denaris, could you make sure these two make it back to their room? I have a couple of things I must see to."

"Of course, Your Majesty."

"Go with Lord Denaris, and I will have some lunch brought to you. Then, if I find some time, I'll come read to you later."

"Yes, Father," the twins said in unison.

Tisus kissed their brows and waited till they left to enter his study. He knew they had been in here as soon as he looked at the stack of papers on the desk. What's more, Revienah's curiosity knew no bounds. He understood his children better than they often knew themselves, and Tisus began to suspect his daughters knew more than they were letting on. He had heard of Enreal's frequent studies in the library as well.

"If only I could take it back," he muttered to himself. But then he remembered if he could change his actions those years before, he might not have lived long enough to have daughters in the first place.

Concerned, Tisus let his eyes roam around the room to see what the twins had been up to. He didn't see anything on the shelves out of place. Focusing on his desk, Tisus noticed the shifted parchment stack on the surface. Rounding the desk, he saw the bottom drawer sticking out by a fraction of an inch. It wasn't the first time Revienah had made that mistake, and Tisus smiled. His left bottom drawer was forever sticking when he closed it, but he always ensured it was closed. He pulled the tricky drawer open, and as he checked the contents, he thought about the brooch hidden in the bottom. On an impulse, Tisus reached in and removed everything inside and pushed the false bottom up to make sure it was still there.

When he saw the box, he knew right away it had been disturbed. He was surprised by that. Revienah was sneaky, but she had been in here several times and never noticed the false bottom before. He was pretty impressed that she had this time. Tisus pulled out the box, setting it atop the stack of missives he still needed to read. Placing his hands down on either side and leaning forward, the King stared at the closed box for a long time, remembering what it represented. He hadn't touched it since his wedding night, but as he stared at it now, Tisus considered the possibilities.

He had sworn he would never need that brooch. He hadn't even considered using them when Shelanna disappeared, but now… He dropped down into his chair as his mind circled back to his fears for Resora. *What if Liddia is right,* he thought. His hand trembled as he reached forward and opened the box.

When he saw the gold dragon staring back at him, Tisus shut it quickly, *not yet,* he thought. He wouldn't take that journey unless there were no other choices before him. Tisus tucked it back into his drawer and silently prayed for the hundredth time that Liddia was wrong.

TWENTY-ONE

esora's symptoms worsened within two fortnights, and King Tisus watched helplessly as she succumbed to illness. Resora ate less and less until she would barely eat a couple of bites every night. She tried to act like she was fine, but the fever betrayed her assurances. She tried to smile when he visited and stay awake as he read to her the last few days, but by the end of the month, Resora could barely stand. And though he hated to admit it, Tisus knew what Lady Liddia had spoken was true. He had to act, and he had to do it now.

Grabbing his personal guard, Caldaren, and young Micah, King Tisus readied to leave the castle, claiming he needed to attend a required diplomatic meeting.

At the door to Revienah's room Tisus stood before Enreal and gently took her arms, "Enreal, you must care for your sister in my absence."

She stared at him in shock. She still didn't understand why

he was going but said nothing to stop him and instead nodded compliantly.

"I would not go if I had any choice," he assured her.

"Yes, Father."

Despite her calm reassurance and her timid nature, Tisus saw the storm of conflict in her eyes. She wanted to make him stay, but she trusted his judgment too. "Do all you can to keep her fever down. I promise I will not be any longer than I must."

Enreal nodded and glanced back to Resora's bed. Revienah sat next to her and washed her sister's brow with damp linen.

Tisus sighed, "You know that I will come back as swiftly as I can."

"I will pray for Ealoram to give the horses strength and speed then."

"I love you, Enreal."

She looked at him then and saw the truth. He was afraid to go. "She will be fine. I swear I will care for her."

Tisus met her beautiful jade green eyes, and emotion rose in his throat, nearly choking him. There was a tick in his jaw, and his resolve began to slip away.

Enreal said, "Be safe, Father, and be quick."

He nodded once, adjusted his glove, and pulled her in for a tight hug. Then, with a quick kiss to her brow, Tisus left her to care for Resora.

She could barely believe that her father would leave while her little sister was so ill but knew whatever pulled him away must have been dire, and she would not make him feel guilty for it.

Enreal obeyed her father's request to stay and watch over Resora, and as the days passed, she made sure Revienah ate and slept as well.

More than a week later, she sat in a chair ringing out the rag they used to dab Resora's brow. When she'd finished rinsing it, Enreal handed the rag to Revienah, who was in bed with her twin and renewed her efforts to cool the fever with the wet cloth.

The bedroom door clattered open, startling the girls, and Denaris strode across the floor with intensity. A lady attendant followed at his heels. Enreal jumped from her chair and nervously offered the Lord a curtsy on his abrupt entrance to the solemn, candlelit room.

"My Lord."

He waved away her formal greeting. "How does she fare?"

"Not well," Enreal replied, looking back to Resora.

The lady attendant busied herself taking her temperature and questioning Revienah about her twin sister's health. Denaris barely paid attention to the whispered conversation. Instead, his mind centered on the task he needed to complete, and for a brief moment, his eyes focused on Enreal.

Even with the dark circles under her eyes and the pale weary look on her face, Enreal still held a stunning beauty. It always amazed Denaris how much these girls inherited from their mother. The mixed heritage was, to his mind, more of a blessing than a curse.

Shaking away his mental digression, Denaris forced himself to refocus on the urgent reason for his visit. Clearing his throat, he interrupted the healer, "Princess Enreal, you and your sister need to keep up your strength. The King does not need more than one of you ill at a time. Your attendants tell me you have refused your daily supper and your midday meals as well."

"In truth, I am not hungry," she replied as she gently squeezed Resora's weak hand.

"I beg that you go to the kitchen and try to nibble on a little something so that you might stay strong for Princess Resora. I will insist if I must."

Enreal nodded. "I will, Lord Denaris. As soon as her fever breaks."

"Go now and take Princess Revienah along with you. I will stay with Resora until you return. I promise to keep her cool as you have done. Give the ladies time to see to your needs. When you come back, you will be better for it. I would be remiss if I did not do my part to help my King's family at such a critical time. In my care, Princess Resora will be safe without you."

Enreal looked at Revienah. "Lor—"

"Please, Princess Enreal. I am nearly the equivalent of her uncle, and my worry is no less than yours. I know I am not good at showing my affection, but I swear I will take good care of her."

Enreal bit her lip as she met Revienah's sad eyes. She did look worn out, and they couldn't keep skipping meals.

"Come now, do not try and talk me out of this. I ask no less than the King himself would of you," Denaris urged. "You must take proper care of yourselves in this time of crisis."

Lord Denaris was right. If their father were here, he would insist they eat. Plus, a few minutes away would likely refresh them both. Revienah looked more tired as every day passed, and she wasn't sleeping much either. Eating at least would help even if leaving Resora here was heart-wrenching. "Come on, Revienah. A break will do us good."

"Bu—" Reveniah started.

Enreal cut off her protest. "Let's at least freshen up. We won't be away for too long."

Stroking Resora's hair, Revienah sighed and kissed her fevered brow. "I'll be right back," she whispered.

The nursemaid helped Revienah ease from the bed, and Enreal took her younger sister's hand as they walked to the door.

"We won't be more than a few minutes," Enreal warned.

Denaris nodded. "I have no doubt."

With another last glance back at Resora, the sisters reluctantly let the woman escort them from the room, leaving their sister in Lord Denaris' care.

When he was sure they were gone, Denaris took up the chair and brought it to the edge of the bed. He shook the afflicted Princess to awaken her gently. "Resora, can you hear me?"

She opened her groggy eyes, looked at him, and nodded but closed them again.

"I have something for you," he said as he placed a smooth object in her hand. "This will help."

In her feverish hand, the gem felt cool to the touch. Resora gripped it tightly, clinging to the remarkable contrast against her skin.

"That's right. Hold it tight. Focus on the gem. Can you feel it?"

The young Princess relaxed again and began to drift back into sleep.

"Resora?" He gently laid a hand on her head to check her fever. She was paler than usual, and her current condition made her look malnourished. Finally, he lowered his voice to a soothing level. "Come now, Resora, I know your stomach hurts, and your head must be pounding, but this will help. I promise. Don't go to sleep now," he said as her body began to relax.

"I'm so tired."

Denaris smiled softly, but Resora didn't see it. "I know, Princess, but could you try for me? I need you to think about the stone in your hand."

Resora tried hard to focus on the smooth, round gem she held. Her brow pinched, and she licked her dry lips, tasting the blood from the cracks that had formed.

"That's right. Now, can you think of the heat you feel? Can you imagine a fire in the stone? Pretty blue flames, maybe or perhaps bright orange?"

When Denaris mentioned fire, the imaginary flames licked her hand, but they did not burn. The whole encounter was dream-like. "I'm tired. I want to sleep," she muttered incoherently.

Denaris grinned broadly when the stone was enveloped in a small blue flame, but it flickered out. "Don't give up, Resora. Picture the fire in your hand, give the burning heat to the stone."

The stone flared to life again, but this time the red jade in her hand glowed bright and hot for more than a minute. Then it began to fade as Resora drifted back into a peaceful sleep.

Denaris nodded and eased the stone from her limp hand. "That's right, Resora, sleep now. You'll feel better." He checked her fever again and was pleased to find her cooler. He lifted the stone and rubbed his thumb over it, feeling the smooth texture of the still cool jade. He'd kept this stone for twenty years now but was never sure why he'd held onto this one and its green twin. He knew each jade would have fetched a high price. He'd even had offers, but he always suspected it was more than it appeared. Today, Denaris found himself grateful he'd not sold it those years before.

Hearing noise in the hallway, Denaris tucked the stone back into his pocket. He clasped his hands behind his back and offered a genuine smile in greeting as Revienah and Enreal entered. "Good news, Your Highnesses. Resora's fever has broken for now."

"Really?" Revienah said with relief and rushed to the bed. "Enreal, he's right. She is much cooler."

Enreal eyed Denaris but followed her sister to see for herself. "Thank you for sitting with her, Lord Denaris."

"Think nothing of it. I will come back as my duties allow. It will give you and your sister time to compose yourselves as needed." He approached Enreal and placed a hand on her shoulder. "You must take care not to overdo it. As I said, it would be a tragedy if more than one of you fell ill. Your father would be devastated if anything should happen to you."

Enreal smiled uncomfortably. "We shall do our best, My Lord."

"That's all I ask." He dropped his hand and bid farewell to Revienah, who had climbed into the bed to join Resora again. "Princess," he said with a bow.

Without another word, Denaris left the girls to retire for the evening. As he walked down the quiet corridor, he pulled out the stone once more, rubbed at the soft glow in its center, and grinned in amazement.

TWENTY-TWO

SHILESTA WOOD

King Tisus halted his dapple grey warhorse at the edge of the Shilesta Wood. The animal jerked his head, and his nostrils blew out hot breaths and snorts from the arduous journey that had brought them here. Tisus pushed the horses to their limit these last few days. Time was not on their side. He patted his faithful horse's neck as two more riders caught up to the King's mount and halted on either side of him. All three horses pranced about a few steps before their riders stilled them.

This was as far as he dared go without a formal invitation. His purpose for being here was not one of good tidings. The evening shadows of the midwinter sun reached across the edges of the snow-covered meadow, and Tisus, usually so confident and courageous in bard's tales, felt a desperate fool at that moment.

There was no way to predict how Queen Morningsong would react when he told her the truth. She may even order his death, and here where the woodland elves reigned, there was nothing he could do to stop them. Nor would he be able to try. Nevertheless, Tisus straightened his spine and steeled himself for what he must do.

Coming here to the edge of the Shilesta Wood in the middle of winter with no invitation from the elves, was an act born from a determined or possibly irrational father. Few in Ishreedin could help Resora and Tisus meant what he said to her when he promised to storm the gates of the abyss for his children. Today his battle for her life would have to come in the form of a long-overdue confession. A tick in his jaw was the only sign of his distress. Luckily, the beard that had grown during his days by Resora's bedside, coupled with the long journey here, hid that tick from the loyal men at his side.

"Your Majesty?" Micah questioned when King Tisus did not speak or proceed. Micah and Caldaren were oblivious to the danger they faced, but Tisus knew. If the elves were threatened in any way, this visit could cause more harm than good. Micah glanced over to Caldaren, and the King's personal guard shrugged.

Tisus ignored them both and squinted at the tree line. He searched leafless winter trees for any sign of the archers that hid along the forest's edge. He'd faced those archers once before and knew their deadly aim.

"Sire?" Micah questioned once more.

Tisus shook away the memory for a moment and glanced at him. Sitting on the reddish-brown horse, Tisus saw his old friend Kirren. It had been an elven arrow that killed Micah's father. The arrow Kirren suffered hit him on the other side of this very border during an attempt to rescue Tisus from imprisonment.

He closed his eyes against the image. *What am I doing?* Fear settled in his belly. If they killed him, they would execute the two men with him. So many men died for Tisus, so many died right before his eyes during the war, but the guilt for Kirren's death had never ebbed, and Tisus worried he had made a mistake in bringing the man's only child along with him today.

He forced the fear aside. He had no choice. He needed men he could fully trust to make the journey along the dangerous edge of the Uninhabited Lands and the Shilesta Woods. To travel the route alone would be the same as asking a man to skewer you through the gut. Only dead men traveled alone—those lands were cursed with the remnants of two centuries of war. The scarred ground ran fallow long ago.

Nothing but thick straw-like patches of grass grew there now. The only sign of anything that ever grew there was the scattering of scraggly, dead branches that replaced what might have been living trees. Most believed the Uninhabited Lands was a place haunted by multiple lost souls cast down by ancient wars. Ancient tales of bones still scattered about the land, and ghostly figures crying out in the night was enough to frighten anyone. No man skirted those lands alone, let alone dare to cross the vast region, and few men dared even to try. Not even Tisus had taken that dare.

Opening his eyes once more, he saw Micah's deep concern on the young Ranger's features. He'd come at his King's request without complaint and without any explanation. His cheeks and nose were painted red by the bite from the winter wind, and Tisus knew the journey had been hard on the two younger men. Nevertheless, he'd chosen them because of their loyalty and because neither of them had ties, direct nor indirect, to the Golden Dragons, and he needed secrecy.

"We wait here," Tisus finally offered, still incapable of that explanation. While both of these men knew his daughters were half-elven, neither one understood who their mother was to the elves of Ilarith. He adjusted himself in his saddle and turned to scan the tree line again.

"For what?" Caldaren asked as he blew hot air onto his icy hands to warm them.

In that exact second, a shrill whistle sounded in the trees ahead of them, then a second, and a third. Feeling Micah's nerves, his horse, Soros, sidestepped and snorted. The Ranger patted his neck to reassure him.

"For that," Tisus said and gestured to the lone rider emerging from the treeline.

The new rider kept his horse at a leisure pace as if he wanted to make them wait as long as possible. The elf acted as if he had all the time in the world, and King Tisus was not worthy of any of it. Looking to Caldaren again, Micah did not hide his annoyance. The male's behavior only confirmed the many rumors about the elves' superiority complex. Turning his attention to Tisus and seeing his posture, Micah realized the King was not unfamiliar with this sort of methodical behavior. As he straightened his spine, the Ranger decided to follow Tisus' lead while doing his best not to look cold.

When Tisus recognized the rider, he folded his winter cloak over his shoulder to hide the gold dragon brooch he wore as he grumbled under his breath, "It had to be him."

Tisus peered at the edge of the woods, hoping to see a different familiar face among the elves. He knew there were many more hiding out there, but he could not discern any of their positions. With little choice left, he squared his shoulders and sat up tall in his saddle, and stared straight at the approaching elf.

Confused, Micah also focused on the newcomer's slow approach, and he tried to look past that arrogant posture. The elf had long hair as black as pitch. The straight, shiny hair reached the middle of his back, and the top half was pulled back into thin braids woven together. As he neared them, Micah noted the finely made leather jerkin with ornate gold stitching that complemented the whole design. The elf's cloak and boots were grey with fur accents. The color was clearly used to blend with the winter climate.

As he came closer, Micah realized neither his hair—nor his finely made clothes—were the elf's most outstanding features. No, it was his eyes that stunned. The male elf had eyes so blue that they could have been sapphires plucked from the mythical lake Telenor. And for a moment, Micah could not look away from those eyes as the elf rode to them proudly on a white mare without any saddle. When his attention finally broke, Micah realized even the horse wore decorative braids with strings in various green shades interwoven within the primary lock.

Micah had seen Shelanna in his youth, but he'd been young when he was sent to Ellomar, and the regular images of Ahanna clouded old images of her mother those years. After being sent to Ellomar, he hadn't interacted with many people at all, let alone elves. He'd forgotten the stark contrasts of elvish angled facial features compared to humans. Today, maturity and this closer proximity to a male elf offered him a new perspective.

Micah realized for the first time that while the daughters of Tisus held visible elven features, those genetic traits were nothing compared to the regal appearance of this man. Ahanna's attributes were the most apparent in the sister's elven heritage. Still, somehow, something different in his behavior showed the Ranger a clear contrast between Tisus's eldest daughter and the elf before him.

He wondered for years how Tisus was able to keep the secret because it seemed so obvious to him, but even thinking now, it wasn't nearly the same. People saw what they wanted to see when they looked upon the daughters of their King from a distance.

There was no way this elf could ever manage the same feat. He was slight of build, but his body was still trimmed and muscular.

He was about the same height as Micah, and that stray thought had him unconsciously adjusting to sit taller in his saddle.

Staring at the newcomer, Micah also noticed the male elf had smooth, hairless cheekbones that lent a younger lean appearance to his facial features, but somehow that shaping was still masculine. Rather than the sharp feminine ear tips Micah was used to seeing on Ahanna, this male's ear tips slanted up to a point as piercing as the tip of a dagger, nearly reaching the crown of his head.

Micah identified the precise movements and cautious eyes, and there was no doubt in his mind that this man was as comfortable with a blade in his hand as he was handling a horse with no saddle. However, a quick glance at the warrior's belt had Micah amending his first assumption. The elf would be comfortable with a blade in each hand, and Micah was sure he could draw those swords in the blink of an eye.

The warrior elf sat on his mare with an alertness only an experienced fighter could know. It was the same awareness that Ellomar had trained into Micah, and right now, as he sized up this newcomer, he was extremely grateful for that training.

The elf stopped a few feet from them and bowed his head in greeting. "King Tisus."

"Lord Halidril," Tisus greeted with a similar nod.

"Now that the formalities are out of the way, why have you come, Giant Slayer?" Halidril asked, using one of the honorifics that elves often did for the King. Somehow though, coming from Halidril, it sounded disrespectful.

"I must see your King and Queen," Tisus demanded, ignoring the slight.

Halidril's facial features remained unchanged, but he tilted his head slightly at the tone of King Tisus. "For what purpose?" he asked.

"It is a personal matter but urgent nonetheless."

Halidril's brow lifted slightly, and his lip tilted smugly. "Of course, I can relay your request and send a messenger with an appropriate time and place to meet and address our court."

Tisus tightened his fist around the reins in his hand and clenched his jaw. Regardless of that frustration, he kept his tone even and professional. "I cannot wait that long. I seek an emergency audience with your King and Queen alone, not with the whole court."

This time Halidril did nothing to camouflage his disdain. "You said the words. You know that such a meeting will not be permitted."

Desperate, Tisus pleaded with the elf and tried to inflict as much respect as he could. "I am at your mercy, Lord Halidril, because this is an urgent matter of life and death. I believe your Queen is the only one that can help."

"You will have to do far better than that, Giant Slayer, to gain a personal audience with my Queen. She is far more valuable to us than your pithy problems." Annoyed, Halidril turned his horse around. "I will send a messenger within a few days."

"Halidril!" Tisus snarled, but the elf made no move to stop. He wanted to blurt out the truth, but the words could not form. Instead, he shouted, "The Great Gold has come!"

The elf stopped his mare but did not turn.

"Resora, my daughter," Tisus hesitated. "She shows signs... Her skin burns! She's only twelve, Halidril."

The elf whirled about, his eyes wide. "It's not possible!" he said. "No human has ever been touched, and more to the point, no one has shown new signs in over four centuries. Not even among our people."

"All the same, it'd be just as well if the Queen could come and verify."

Halidril pinned him with eerie blue eyes filled with fierce hatred. "It seems to me that one of the last of my people to travel into your kingdom, my betrothed no less, was never seen again. Now you would dare ask me to risk my Queen's safety, all to save your half-breed child?"

Tisus was rarely surprised anymore, but as Halidril spat the accusation, it was no less surprising than a lightning bolt spearing through his heart would be. His hand, so steady a second before, shook now, and he clenched it tight to cover it up. Speechless, Tisus offered no reply or defense.

Offended to his core, and worried for his King, Micah urged his horse forward a step and gripped the handle of his dirk. "Take care how you speak when referring to Princess Resora, elf."

Halidril gave him a scathing look, and his left hand went to the hilt of the curved sword at his waist. "Take care of whom you speak to, human."

"You will not disrespect any of the daughters of King Tisus," Micah insisted.

"Step back, human. I have no problem ending the treaty by spilling your blood."

Micah's blade was in his hand before he realized it. "You pompous waste of Shilesta air."

The word treaty snapped Tisus back to reality. "Enough!" he snarled. "Micah, stay your blade! I am here for Resora, not to bring about new wars."

Halidril scoffed, "Your sins say differently."

Feeling defeated, King Tisus met Halidril's eyes. "If you know she is Shelanna's, then you know it's possible. I am willing to submit to your King and Queen the whole truth that they might know. How you came upon the knowledge matters little right now. I can accept their hatred and rage, but I cannot accept that they would let Resora die. The offense was mine, not hers. She should not suffer as a result."

Halidril lost his pompous composure. "How long did you think you could hide the truth? How long did you think you could keep five daughters from me? Five daughters that should have been mine! Five pitiful mutts that are ruined because of your inferior blood!" He urged his horse closer to Tisus. His voice changed to fierce resolve, "You stole something precious from me, Giant Slayer, and worse, you failed to keep it safe. Our whole kingdom suffers because of your offense."

"I stole nothing, Halidril. She was not a possession, and you drove her away with your refusal to find peace, and her fear of you finding out the truth was why she ran away from me. Your hatred cost us both."

"So says the deceitful human King, who in the guise of peace tainted our Princess and lied about it for decades."

"I am here to confess. She's dying, Halidril. Shelanna's daughter is being consumed from the inside, and only your Queen can save her."

Halidril's white mare scraped the ground with her hoof and whinnied softly. The elf tugged lightly on her mane to still her. "I have known for some time what you did, and for the sake of Shelanna's reputation, I have kept this knowledge to myself. I will not taint my betrothed's memory by allowing you access to my Queen. Not even for a Dragon Touched. I would die to keep you from destroying her parents with such a sordid tale of deceit."

Knowing the truth as his missing wife told it, Tisus leaned forward and pierced the male elf with his angry gaze. "It is your pride that cannot handle the fallout, Halidril. You are the worst of your kind. It is elves and men like you that caused the war to last for generations. You are no better than the human King I dethroned or the King before him. You stand here and lie even to yourself. It's more likely you fear a half-elf could eventually bring our people into a new age, because we both know the truth here. We both know what her condition could mean, and that threatens your sanctimonious self-righteousness.

"I also know the humiliation of my union with Shelanna is far greater for you than her. Worst case, she would have been cast out, in which case, I would have taken her in. For you, the stakes were far greater. A rejection from Shelanna, the greatest warrior there ever was, and champion of the realm, for a pitiful, short-lived human, would have never gone away. If I enter those woods, it will be your reputation that comes back tainted."

Halidril smirked and turned his mare once more. "It hardly matters anyway," he said over his shoulder, "because the only truth that matters today is that without my Queen, your daughter will never survive long enough for us to find out what will happen. Then maybe the bloodline will start over with a pure blood." He urged his horse forward to head into the cover of the woods before them.

Micah took up his reigns to follow, but Tisus stopped him by grabbing his hands before he could urge Soros forward.

"I pity you, Halidril. A hatred that runs as deep as yours is far more consuming than the affliction my daughter suffers. It will surely cause your death one day," King Tisus shouted. The elf hesitated for a split second, his head tilted, but he continued as if he didn't hear.

As Halidril's figure disappeared within the leafless trees and cold winter fog, Micah asked, "What now, My King?"

Caldaren couldn't hide his concern. "What will happen to Princess Resora?"

Tisus clenched his jaw. "I don't know." Feeling helpless, he stared down at his hands, wishing that those hands—the hands that fought in hundreds of battles and staunched the lifeblood of many wounded companions—could somehow have the power to stop what was happening to Resora.

Never once did he or Shelanna consider his children could be Dragon Touched. There were only a few alive today that even had a clue of how to help, and right now, they were unreachable.

Beside him, Micah met Caldaren's eyes and mouthed, *"Dragon Touched?"*

Caldaren shook his head. The single gesture was filled with bewildered concern.

Between them, Tisus discreetly removed the gold dragon brooch that held his heavy blue cloak in place. Then, closing his eyes, he dropped it to the ground, hoping he was doing the right thing. He stared at the tree line for a minute more, then tugged on his horse's reins and turned about. "For now, I will go to be with my daughter."

He prodded his warhorse to a run. His companions hurried to follow, but it wasn't long before his billowing cloak flapped in the wind and slid free. It settled on the ground, and Caldaren's horse stomped on it as they followed their King.

"Sire!" Caldaren exclaimed with distress.

"Leave it!" Tisus ordered over his shoulder while silently praying for a miracle.

TWENTY-THREE

Whn King Tisus returned to Ranoak, he went straight to his daughter's room to be with her. News came to him that her fever was blessedly stable, and relief flooded Micah and the King when those reports indicated there were fewer spikes in her temperature during his absence. Everyone was grateful that her condition had not worsened. Tisus even wondered if his trip had been rash, but that thought died when he saw her. Resora's color had drained away, leaving her ghostly white. Her lips were cracked from dehydration, and she barely smiled with drowsy eyes when he took her small hand in his. She didn't even return his grip before she fell back into slumber.

The nursemaids complained that no healer could figure out why Resora's condition cycled. mid-mornings were the worst for her, while late afternoons and evenings were far better. Tisus didn't hear any of it. His heart was breaking.

"She still burns and has little appetite," one nurse said.

Another added, "Princess Enreal managed to get her to eat some food. She even walked around for short periods in the afternoons. And Lord Denaris visits at midday to allow her sisters short breaks."

"Find Lord Denaris. I wish to thank him," King Tisus ordered.

"I'll fetch him," Micah offered.

"No need, I am already here," Denaris said from the hallway. "I received word of your return."

Tisus stood and hugged him as if they were brothers. "I could not bear this burden without my friends."

The action clearly surprised Lord Denaris, but he eventually reciprocated and clapped Tisus on the back before pulling free. "I am sorry you could not return to better news," he said regretfully.

"Tell me all you can," Tisus said.

Micah stared at Resora from the doorway while King Tisus and Lord Denaris fell into conversation. He barely heard anything they said. Resora's appearance was hard to see. The Ranger's heart tightened at the memory of Halidril's words. Whatever this curse was, it might kill her because the elves refused to help, and her family could only sit and watch her wither away.

The King had sworn Caldaren and Micah to secrecy. Tisus explained he did not want to frighten the people in the castle or have rumors spreading before they had answers. He swore that help would come before it was too late, but Micah now saw the truth in that false promise. King Tisus, the man who treated him like his blood-born nephew since birth, was terribly afraid.

Resolved to find a way to help, Micah turned on his heel and went to the gardens to find Enreal. As he pulled the oversized doors open and strode outside, he spotted her right away.

She sat on the edge of a short stone wall that bordered the

cobblestone path to the gardens as she stared aimlessly at the dormant gardens. Sitting in her dark blue dress, with her grey and blue fur cloak wrapped around her shoulders, Micah could see the longing for freedom in her posture. He could hear it in the melancholic notes of the song she sang. One of her father's hounds sat next to her with its head laid in her lap. She absently stroked its furred head as she stared with longing toward the frost-covered trees.

Micah hated to interrupt her solitude, but he had little choice. As he took his first steps toward her, the hound lifted his head, and the dog's initial growl shifted to a lolling tongue and a thumping tail when he identified the intruder. Enreal's perfectly pitched song ended as she glanced toward him. "Hello, Micah."

"Princess," he greeted.

She offered him a small smile. "I am uncertain as to whether or not I like this new version of you. There was once a time when you would spin me about by my arms to hear me giggle, and you used my first name with a smile or a curse on your lips, and yet, now you address me so formally."

"There was once a time when you and your sisters being princesses never occurred to me. I must offer you respect, else others will think decorum is not important, and you will lose respect in their eyes."

"But it is only you and I out here."

Micah nodded. "It is better to keep the habit consistent, lest I forget at the wrong time."

She contemplated his defense and smiled. "Or is it better that you say it constantly, lest you forget who Ahanna is?"

A little stunned by her observation, Micah cleared his throat awkwardly and asked, "What is the Dragon Touched?"

It was Enreal's turn to be surprised, and he saw the shock in her eyes before she turned them away. He suspected that her knowledge on the subject was far more than King Tisus believed.

Enreal returned her attention to the dog and stroked his ears nervously. "What are you talking about?"

"Before you pretend, you should know two things. First, I see through you. And second…" Micah hesitated when she tilted her head slightly to look at him again. "Second—" he continued, "I betray my King by even asking you. So tell me the truth, Sister."

Enreal's shoulders slumped, and she sighed as moisture filled her eyes. "I don't know the truth."

Micah nodded. "With the letter, you want Feylynn to find out?"

Enreal sighed, "The records on gold dragons are kept in The Enclave archives. I've learned most histories on dragons were burned by the tyrant Eduar and his father during the war. I was told The Enclave secured what they could salvage and protect them religiously."

"Why should you need to know about golden dragons? They have been gone for more than a thousand years—" Micah abruptly stopped as he remembered Tisus saying the great gold had come and Halidril balling at the possible implications.

"Resora dreamt of an ancient gold and knew his name," Enreal explained. "After the fire, when she mentioned it to Liddia, the dressmaker lost her composure so visibly that I went searching for the name and accidentally overheard Liddia speaking to Father. And that's all I know."

"What is the dragon's name?"

Enreal picked at the nails on her fingers. "Feldorthanosh. For some reason, Father does not speak of it, not even to us, so I do not ask the scholars."

"Good enough."

"What does that mean? Do you know of the dragon?" Enreal asked.

"No, but I swear that I will do all I can to find out." He handed her a slip of parchment. "Rewrite your letter and include these instructions in it. Have Revi get it to me before the sun rises. I will find a way to deliver it."

"Micah, the pass! You won't get through."

"I'll get through. We can't wait till spring or summer for Feylynn to start looking. She will need time, and Resora may not have it."

"Wouldn't it be better if you spoke with Father? If he knows you know, then can't you simply ask?" Enreal reasoned.

Micah shook his head. "It won't work."

"Why not?" she asked.

"Because your father knows precious little himself. Otherwise, he would have fixed this weeks ago. He went to the Shilesta Wood for help, and they refused him. I can't explain it, but he won't even say the words. It is as if he fears the truth. Your father tried to help his way. Now I will try to help my way. I have to do something."

"The elves? They know about us?"

Micah did not want to tell her about Halidril. He didn't want to hurt her any more than she was already hurting. "I'm not sure what they know, but your father was willing to tell the Queen everything to help your sister, and they denied him access to her."

Enreal looked out to the winter landscape toward the Feldorian Mountains and pulled her cloak tighter about her shoulders. "Micah, those mountains are frigid and unforgiving. You said there was no way through."

"Then I will forge one for this." He put a hand on her shoulder. "Spring is not far off. With any luck, winter will abate early."

"If it doesn't?"

"I will find a place in Blackbur to keep warm until it does, but at least I will be closer than I was before I left. Resora cannot hold on indefinitely. If I am careful, we could get news back from Feylynn even before the Fealty Festival."

Turning around, she threw herself into his arms. At first, Micah was surprised by the action, but there was a desperation in her hug, and he fully returned the embrace.

She sniffed, and Micah realized she was crying. "I don't want to lose her," Enreal whispered.

"I won't let that happen. We'll figure this out, Enreal."

She pulled away and wiped her tears. "I'll have a letter for you tonight. We don't want to lose you either. You swear to be careful?"

Afraid his own emotion would betray him if he spoke, Micah could only nod.

Enreal left him at once and hurried off to compose her letter. Micah stood there for a long time, petting the hound at his side and praying he could do good on the promises he'd just made.

TWENTY-FOUR

Micah was confident that the abyss was not filled with fire and brimstone as he'd been taught during his youth. No, a hell realm, for him at least, would be a frozen wasteland. It would be a place that could freeze your fingers and toes until they were painful to touch, and you would thirst for water while surrounded by ice. In that place, your skin would turn red and burn while your lips cracked and bled as an effect of the unforgiving northern winds.

The first week of his journey hadn't been so bad. Micah had brought both Soros and Freesia with him. The decision to care for two mounts in this unpredictable landscape added three layers of security. Firstly, he was able to switch horses regularly to allow each one a respite from carrying him. This plan alone could shorten his journey to three weeks. Second, if his horse were injured or killed along the way, he likely would die in the pass. In this unforgiving climate, getting through Dergin's Pass would be a six-week journey without a horse. He couldn't carry enough supplies and manage the mountain for six weeks. Finally, he'd thought of Ahanna. Leaving Freesia behind weighed on her, and having seen their shared connection for years, Micah understood that.

When he made the questionable decision to brave the pass, he also decided he would journey to his mentor's home right after going to The Enclave. He needed to let Ahanna know about Resora too. Telling Feylynn and not telling her felt like a betrayal. Micah hoped if he had her horse when he delivered the tragic information, it could only help to soften the blow.

He also wanted the chance to present Resora's problem to Ellomar. There was no man in the world Micah trusted more. The issue at hand required discretion. He suspected that the older Ranger might have the experience and power to help. Ellomar was an accomplished healer. The Creator had blessed that man with more healing magic than Micah had ever seen.

Now, almost halfway through Dergin's Pass, Micah wondered if he would make it to either destination. Every step was a challenge, and this second leg of his journey tested his resolve. Winter was waning, and the warmer days, alternating with cold nights, created icy patches that were difficult to traverse. He avoided loose areas whenever possible because he also understood that a single avalanche from one of the higher peaks could kill him and the horses.

As if the terrain wasn't bad enough to navigate, a late storm struck earlier and was fast progressing into a miserable blizzard. He'd promised Enreal he would forge a path, and as if The Creator Ealoram wanted to make him eat those arrogant words, Micah was doing precisely that. The problem was that he couldn't force the storm to stop with the sheer strength of will in the same way he could force his way up through the wintry landscape.

Cirus had left his perch on Micah's shoulder long ago to fly off and find shelter. Micah wasn't worried about the bird. The falcon would return to him later, and the bird was right to seek shelter.

Trusting the bird's instinct and knowing he could not hope to navigate the treacherous climb through a blizzard, not even when fully energized, let alone utterly exhausted, he scanned the landscape for a solution. Thirty minutes later, he spotted a small alcove with a low overhang in the canyon wall and carefully marked it as an option. While the location would help shield him from the biting wind, the problem was that the deep snow all about him was an avalanche waiting to happen.

He searched for another half an hour for a cave in the mountain, but no better options revealed themselves. Ultimately, risking possible danger in the shelter of the alcove versus the inevitable risk to his life in the storm gave him little choice. He veered toward the shelter and set about the grim task of digging through the old snow surrounding it.

It was painstaking work, but a short time later, he was pleased to find the natural overhang kept the snow clear beneath it, and over the winter, it had formed a small shelter surrounded by the frozen walls. It was a stable of sorts for the horses. It wouldn't be perfect, but it would be far better than being stuck in the storm fully exposed. If this blizzard lasted more than a day, he didn't want to be caught unprepared in the open.

Micah dug out a small opening on one side of the surrounding snow for himself to sleep in and maximize his body heat. He worked tirelessly to shovel out enough snow so he could at least lie down. As he worked, Micah thought back to the winter when he'd been twelve years old.

That winter so long ago, Micah had dug out a small snow fort for Ahanna and Feylynn. He smiled at the memory as he could

216

practically hear their childish voices in his head as he packed down the snow inside his makeshift shelter.

He missed Ahanna. It had only been six months since she left, but it felt like years had passed. He wondered if she had missed him when he'd gone to Ellomar years before. His time in the glen had been full of adventure and education, and he wouldn't have traded the experience for anything. However, in the back of his mind, Ahanna was always there.

Is it the same for her? he wondered. *Will she be too busy to think of me?*

Finally finished with his temporary shelter, Micah shoved the thoughts about the Princess aside as he led his horses into the makeshift stall. He unburdened them and did all he could to shelter his gear from the wind. Pulling his waterskin out, he stuffed snow into the small opening until it was packed full. Then with his travel pack in one hand and the waterskin in the other, Micah climbed into his meager shelter to keep warm.

The snow hut was so small, Micah could only sit up if he hunched over, but the size would contribute to keeping him warm. Shuffling a bit, he adjusted and placed his cold waterskin under his jerkin and wrapped his cloak tightly around his shoulders to melt the snow enough to drink rather than chew.

Micah fumbled through his pack with frozen fingers and pulled out some dried meat to fill his growling belly. All the digging expended his energy, and he needed to refuel. Then, suddenly, Cirus appeared at the shelter opening. The white and brown speckled falcon blinked at him expectantly.

"I see you know right when to show up. After the work is done and the food is out," Micah teased, and smiling, he tore away a piece of meat for his companion. The bird swallowed the morsel and hopped in closer to settle upon Micah's knee, begging for more. He laughed and obliged. "Too cold for hunting?" Micah stroked Cirus' head while he finished off the hard meat. "You went and got yourself spoiled, Cirus."

As if to prove his point, the bird shuffled closer and worked its way under the winter cloak. Micah accepted his friend's companionship and the added warmth as he laid down to get some rest.

"Cirus," Micah mumbled in a sleepy tone. "We need a miracle. At this rate, it will take months to reach The Enclave." The bird gave no reply, and Micah drifted off.

Perched on Micah's pack, Cirus screeched. Micah woke with a start, and shot upright like an arrow, slamming his head against the ice ceiling of his cramped shelter. Hissing, Micah rubbed his tender forehead and cursed Cirus's next high-pitched shriek as the bird took flight.

Annoyed, Micah squinted against the sunlight to watch Cirus flap his wings and work his way high into the sky. Then it hit him, and he realized why the falcon was so vocal this morning. The sun was shining in a blue, cloud-free sky. Elated, Micah scrambled out of the snow mound and went out to greet the morning.

He looked up to the sky when he stood. "Thank Ealoram. For this one—I promise I will stop cursing." After a brief pause he said, "At least I will try my best."

When he looked around, he had to squint as the bright sunlight reflected off the surface of the white powder. It took several minutes for his eyesight to adjust fully.

He stretched, and his body resisted. The challenging rigors of the mountain two days before, added to the tiny shelter he'd taken refuge in, had caused every muscle to be sore. "It's too bad I can't heal myself," Micah muttered as several muscle spasms spread simultaneously, but the sun was shining. The relief that came from that single miracle momentarily brushed aside any other inconvenience.

He'd lost far too much travel time to the harsh pass and had worried that the snow would lock him down for days. Of course, the blasted storm would have ended sooner or later, but he was beyond grateful that it was not more than a day and a half of bad weather. What's more, he was thrilled to find the air warmer than he would expect after so much snowfall.

Cheerfully, the Ranger greeted Soros by scratching his neck and rubbing his soft nose. "I don't suppose that was so bad then. We can still get there if we try."

Obviously jealous, Freesia bumped him in the back.

Chuckling, Micah indulged her. "Ah, then, where are my manners? How could I neglect such a pretty girl?"

The mare stomped a foot, and her head bobbed up and down.

Micah patted her neck a few times for good measure. "It's a good omen, Freesia. The sunshine bids us a kind journey. We'll see your mistress soon enough."

Micah rubbed the horses down once to check their legs, and then he inspected their hooves for damage. When he was confident that they'd all come out of the storm unscathed, Micah gave the horses some oats to nibble as he packed gear and loaded everything back up. He took a few bites of frozen hardtack and mounted Soros before Cirus landed on his shoulder. "What say you, my friend?" The falcon blinked at him and twisted his head sideways. Seeing the bird was at ease on his usual perch, Micah pulled on the horses' reins. "On we go. Let's hope we can get there unscathed."

He proceeded with extreme caution. It didn't take long to understand the fresh snowfall presented several problems, the least of which was working with a layer of soft powder on top of crunchy hard snow beneath. The horses would sink to their bellies and have to expend far too much energy breaking free. In addition, carrying gear made their navigation worse. It put them off-balance, especially when they faced steeper areas. Often, Micah was forced to walk and test the sites over and again with a makeshift walking stick he procured on the mountain.

He worked most of the day, breaking trails and seeking safer paths. As evening crept closer, Micah found himself exhausted. The horses were as well, but he was willing to push forward for one more hour before giving in for the day. He mounted Soros again and urged him along slowly.

Uncomfortable, but willing to trust their master, Soros and Freesia fought for every step with broken, jumpy strides. They'd place a hoof down, and when their weight shifted, the deeper heavy snow would suddenly give, pulling their hooves down, and they would try to shift with jerky movements to accommodate the unpredictable terrain.

The last thing Micah needed was a lame horse. He allowed them the slow, rough pace they needed, but it was a brutal way to ride. It did him little good when Freesia suddenly whinnied and panicked as she sank too deep for her liking. Rearing back, snow flew up as she fought against the entrapment. Soros nervously sidestepped away from her and let out his own bray of disapproval when her lead pulled him.

Fearing she would pull them both down, Micah unlooped Freesia's lead from his saddle and pulled to straighten her out, but she tried to break free on the left side, away from Soros. The odd angle pulled at Soros, and he neighed, resisting the tension. Finally, Micah was forced to let go of the lead as his horse reared slightly. The male horse was feeding off her panic, and Soros quivered beneath him.

Freesia could not win against the frozen ground, and the next time she tried to jump free, her legs got caught up in the deep snow. Her cry was horrific as she fell on her side and rolled. Some of the supplies came free as she struggled to get up.

Micah lept from Soros and hurried over to Freesia. She was panicking now and snorting in between her whinnies. If she didn't calm down, Micah knew she would hurt herself if she hadn't already. In his rush to reach her, he tripped over his own feet as the icy ground crunched under his weight. Bits of snow and ice flew about when Micah fell and slid toward her. He had to turn his feet sideways, angling them to keep his balance, he slowed his descent.

Freesia's eyes went wide, her ears laid back, and she cried out as he took her reins. Micah tugged with all his strength to help her get back up. She fought to stand, but now that he was closer, Micah saw his worst fear come true. Freesia's front right leg did not look right.

If she stood, she would compound the injury. Micah stopped pulling and instead focused all of his attention on soothing her. She was frantic, and it was essential to calm her so he could try to help. The problem was, while Micah was gifted with healing magic, he'd never used it on an animal this size before, and never for an injury this bad. Doubt flooded him.

Healing was the last magic any race could call on, and most people in Ranoak believed that was because their Creator had gifted the people with that particular ability. Any other form of magic was considered a curse and not welcome.

According to Ellomar, Micah's father Kirren was one of the best healers in Ishreedin. His father had taught Ellomar, and in turn, Ellomar had taught Micah when Tisus learned he had inherited the ability. Yet, compared to Ellomar, Micah found himself severely lacking. His ability was minor at best, and he often wondered what his deceased father would think of his minimal skill.

"How am I supposed to fix this?" he said. "I barely have the talent to fix small cuts and heal a small rabbit."

Freesia neighed again, and it was a cry of pain. Micah looked skyward. "Help me, Father," he begged. Then, a warm, comforting calm washed over him and set aside his doubt, and he edged closer to the large horse despite her frenzied movement.

Taking the bridle in his hands with a firm, confident grip, Micah started praying as Ellomar taught him. After a minute or so, Freesia stopped trying to jerk away, and her frantic behavior settled some. She blew out shaky breaths of air through her flared nostrils and offered a soft neigh. It was a desperate plea for help if Micah ever heard one.

"Shhhh, there now… I hear you. I know it hurts, but relax now, my pretty girl. That's it… Be still, Freesia. I'm here," Micah soothed and began to pray again. Freesia relaxed a little more as she rested her head down in the snow. Micah let go of her bridle and went to her leg as he prayed.

Even though animals could not speak, Micah knew by her actions that the mare was placing her trust in him, and the weight of that responsibility was not one he took lightly. He could taste the fear in his throat, and the hardtack in his belly was like lead now. If he couldn't help her, he would have to put her down, and he couldn't stomach that grim reality.

Kneeling, he tentatively ran his hands along her front leg and knew right away that she had broken it in two places. He wasn't sure he could mend such a severe fracture, but he refused to walk away without doing everything possible to get her on her feet once more.

TWENTY-FIVE

GOLDEN DRAGON ENCLAVE

Despite the brisk air that accompanied the last days of winter in the snow-covered Feldorian Mountains, Feylynn Nacarian, second daughter of the King of Ranoak, felt the sweat drip down her neck. Her arms tired under the weight of the sword and shield. She tightened her grip on the leather straps and pulled it closer to feel its protection. The weight and feel of her father's old sword offered to her soul a strange sense of comfort, but the sentiment would not win this battle for her.

Her thick black hair was braided back to keep it tame, but wavy tendrils escaped and clung to her damp skin. Her olive-green eyes tracked her opponent's every move. A man's eyes could lie. His body led the dance.

Keeping a safe distance from her opponent, Feylynn circled and watched his torso for further clues as her training required. The sound of his foot scraping the ground as he stepped left

warned her to lift her shield, but instinct told her it was a decep-
tive trick, she held. His body did not shift, and he was feinting to
throw her off.

The blonde swordsman facing her was only slightly taller
than her five-foot, seven-inch frame. He was not much broader
either, but with two swords, he was cunning.

His clever tricks kept Feylynn guessing, and she found
instinct served her best when battling Lord Irel. The last several
minutes had drained her, and he was still toying with her. She had
to find a way to finish the fight.

Lord Irel didn't allow her the respite she craved. Before
Feylynn could consider it further, he sprang to action again. A
splinter of light flashed as the morning sunlight touched his steel
blade. The sound of armored boots clicked against cobblestones
as he spun back.

Leaning to the left, a woosh of air brushed her skin, and she
barely dodged the strike. *Too close*, she thought. Her sword arm
vibrated as she brought it up to block the second sword and push
it wide. Then, taking a half turn, Feylynn raised her shield to
block the following sweep and thrust the wooden shield forward
into him. She hoped to knock him off balance.

He staggered back with the impact but kept his feet. Closing
in fast to defeat his ample reach, Feylynn kicked at his right shin
this time. He hopped backward before she made contact, but
she'd expected that, hoped for it even. Feylynn came in with a
fast thrust at his belly.

When Irel threw up his blade to block the sudden advance,
Feylynn caught the hilt of his sword with her weapon, reversed
her grip, and twirled it back. The metal of the entwined blades
scraped together.

As his grip loosened, she realized she had lost sight of his
other sword. Irel didn't fight the disarmament. Instead, he came

down with his second sword as the other clattered to the ground. During the same instant it took Feylynn to disarm him, her attacker swiped down with his second sword right at her neck, halting the deadly weapon a hair's breadth from her skin.

"Match," called Master Carek. It was their signal to pull back, and both fighters obeyed to stand at attention as he came between them. The instructor scrutinized each person for any animosity, as he always did after these sessions. Hostility and rage were not honorable tactics.

Feylynn stared straight ahead and focused her thoughts on her sisters to clear her mind. Master Carek, the senior combat training instructor, watched her for several seconds. When he was satisfied, he moved back. Carek sat on The Enclave Council and oversaw all the battle training for new students. He was one of the last Golden Dragons proficient in all martial weapons, including a few exotic ones. At forty and three, he had served during the war against the elves.

He spent all of his spare time studying combat and the rest of his time teaching. He had studied with the hidden Monks of Kempour and even trained with the elite elves of the Shilesta Woods after the treaty. Feylynn suspected that age was his only real adversary.

Master Carek turned to her opponent. "Irel, tomorrow you will train with Master Dein. We will revisit this pairing in three fortnights."

"Yes, sir," replied Irel

"Feylynn, you will face Rhushawn next."

She nodded and made a conscious effort not to cringe.

"Take your ten-minute rest, both of you."

"Yes, sir," both students replied simultaneously.

"You're excused."

They walked back toward the water well. Their match was

her third one that day, and Feylynn had two more fights before she would study texts and tomes on ancient law. Exhausted, she tried to prepare for her upcoming match with Rhushawn mentally.

Irel bumped her shoulder, breaking her train of thought. "That was great! You took my sword."

"You took my head," Feylynn replied. "Your sword could be recovered, my head…"

"You nearly had me twice."

Feylynn scoffed.

Irel joined The Enclave last autumn with her. He was a lordling of Blackbur, a fiefdom in her father's kingdom just south of The Enclave and north of Ranoak. It was land granted to his family by her father after the war, and as the firstborn son of Lord Danoral, Irel would likely inherit those lands one day.

His title meant little to her. Here the two of them were equal as students of The Enclave. Since coming here, all that mattered to Feylynn was her betterment as a knight. Irel, on the other hand, enjoyed pranks and fun.

In her early days here, Feylynn was steadfast in her focus and paid little attention to Irel or any of the other students. And the other recruits were all too happy to reciprocate. Few at The Enclave approved of her presence. Even some of the instructors avoided her. She was, after all, a princess in a school filled with men. Her first few weeks here had been lonely. She'd eaten her meals alone, studied alone, and dealt with the glaring looks alone.

Until Irel sat next to her for her evening meal one day. Persistent and friendly, Irel had been the only one to try to befriend her, and any efforts to push him away had proven futile. During those days, Lord Irel sat next to Feylynn during evening meal time every night for seven days before she caved to his goofy charm. Irel made her laugh, and after grueling days of training and long hours of study, as time went on, Feylynn realized that a laugh now and then was therapeutic.

He seemed to get along with almost everyone as if it was his mission here. In fact, after he befriended her, many of the students quit glaring and even smiled at her from time to time. For her part, it had taken Feylynn a little longer to get used to a friend outside her circle of sisters. Her sisters, Micah, and her ladies in waiting, were her only friends growing up, and it was strange to confide in someone new, let alone a young man.

On days like today, the friendship between them made her grateful. As always, Irel joked and teased her after their match to keep her from getting discouraged. After several pairings together, she still hadn't beaten the rhythm of his two-weapon fighting style.

"I am certain that your constant effort to make me feel better goes against our code of integrity. Lying will neither make me a better fighter nor will it keep me humble."

Irel fetched a pail of water and dumped it on his head. Feylynn cringed. It was so cold up here in the mountains that she couldn't imagine the cold water snaking down under her armor. He dipped in a second time and took a long drink as water spilled out from the side of his mouth. Passing her the ladle, Irel leaned against the well's edge. Feylynn drank her fill without spilling a drop.

"My compliments may not make you humble, but it helps me stay humble. If I believe you can defeat me, I will try harder."

Feylynn rolled her eyes at his pretense and took another drink.

"If I must be honest in all things, I think that my humility is far more important than your personal growth."

Feylynn choked on the water, and Irel laughed. When she quit coughing, she faced him. "Irel, I am certain that you were birthed from the womb with that swaggering confidence."

"Possibly." Irel smiled as he glanced across the field where the knights worked and prepped for sparring match-ups. His smile fell, as did Feylynn's.

They both watched as a young barbarian warrior practiced swings with his favored blade. After a minute or two, Irel added, "Rhushawn, that one came from the womb with a chip on his shoulder the size of Ranoak and that sword in his hand is cursed to be sure."

Feylynn watched Rhushawn test the weight of his massive sword. "Possibly," she muttered.

"Seriously, he's not natural. It seems he was bred from a giant."

Feylynn rolled her eyes. She feared the barbarian and hated that truth, and she loathed the idea of sparring with him. Everyone did. His whole demeanor said *stay away from me*, and in his matches, Rhushawn was ruthless in every single one, which rammed that sentiment down to your gut. He constantly skirted the line of honorable battle and had yet to be beaten by any student here.

Rhushawn was a member of a barbarian tribe from the frigid tundra north of the Feldorian Mountains. He had been captured during a raid on a small town. Rather than hang him for his crimes, it was decided he should serve his punishment at The Enclave. That was four months ago. Almost two months ago, he arrived at the keep with a dark shadow of stubble and even darker, wild, wind-swept hair which hung around his warm brown skin. All of that made him look dangerous. The small scar near his nose helped that image too. Most importantly, he arrived in shackles of iron.

In the beginning, Rhushawn resisted the training and edicts, but Master Carek somehow worked him into compliance. Carek was the only Master allowed to oversee his education. Last month, Rhushawn suddenly had a shift in his demeanor and started participating in the sparring lessons. When he finally emerged from his room, all cleaned up, Feylynn had realized the barbarian was probably only a few years older than she was.

Rumor was, it was his sword that swayed him to obey Enclave mandates. He was allowed to use his personal weapon during sparring practice, but Rhushawn was required to return it afterward. Carek called it compliance, but Feylynn still wondered whether his demeanor was compliant now and what it looked like before he was allowed around the students.

She didn't trust his presence here and still wondered what had prompted the decision to bring a barbarian here. *What fool thought he could learn anything here?* Rhushawn was a danger to everyone.

Towering above her at six feet and five inches, with every muscle in his body honed for combat, Rhushawn often overcame his opponents using brute force more often than he did with skill. His favored weapon, the only weapon he would use, was a custom-made bastard sword that carried some sort of ancestral meaning.

Actually, his sword bordered a craftsman's line between a bastard sword and a greatsword. It was longer than usual, but not quite long enough or broad enough to be considered a greatsword. With the added length, the weapon likely weighed close to eight pounds, yet somehow Rhushawn managed to wield it single-handedly and still hold a shield. Feylynn supposed wielding a bastard sword that long wasn't so hard if your arms were as thick as tree trunks.

Rhushawn hated traditional armor and opted for leather skins instead but that's not what bothered her. His eyes bothered her most. His dark brown eyes weren't warm like honey or chocolate. Rather, they were cold, calculating, almost cruel, and more often than not, he turned those wicked eyes her direction. He did not like her, and he made no secret about it.

Rhushawn's very essence intimidated her. This was their third match-up, and the previous two times left Feylynn battered and sore.

Irel rested a hand on her shoulder. "He's got nothing on you."

"Except a hundred and twenty pounds of muscle and a sword with a long reach," Feylynn corrected.

"You're faster. You can take him," Irel insisted.

She gave him a sidelong glance. "I thought we already discussed compromising your integrity with lies."

Irel smiled. "Take out his knees, and a man that big will hit the ground like a stone."

Feylynn rolled her eyes and moved back to the sparring ring. "He hates me. I am not sure why, but he hates me."

"I don't think he hates you. I'm sure it's only a firm dislike."

"If he doesn't like me, he must positively hate you. Besides me, you're the only other person he looks at like that."

"And after all this time, I thought he might be warming up to me," Irel laughed.

Feylynn didn't smile at Irel's quip as she continued watching Rhushawn.The barbarian stepped up to Master Carek for their match and spoke to him in his native language.

"I don't think he likes anybody, Feylynn. Not even Carek."

"Master Carek," she corrected, but Feylynn did not disagree with the assessment.

"This is your match, Princess," Irel added, using her title with heavy formality.

Feylynn ignored him and steeled herself for the match. Then, rolling her shoulders, she stepped up to the fight and set aside everything else. Rhushawn gave Feylynn a curt nod at her approach, but they both knew he only did so because it was required.

His eyes spoke the truth. He despised a battle pairing with a woman, and he hated even more that the woman was a princess.

Feylynn set aside her doubt. She could still hear her father's lessons as she stepped into the circle. *Don't ever stoop to their level, my daughter. What makes a knight different, what makes us different is our strength of character. Even under the worst circumstances, always be better, be kinder, be smarter, be honorable, be merciful, and always be more than they expect. If you do this, you will change the world around you.*

Feylynn bowed low and offered Rhushawn all of her respect as her father would have wished.

Master Carek stepped back to monitor the match. "Begin."

Feylynn knew she needed patience with this one. She had learned twice before that rushing in against him was a bad idea.

Despite his size and build, Rhushawn was quick and unpredictable. He banged his sword against his shield twice and said, *"Hafðu það þitt besta, þú veika dúllan þín."*

"Rhushawn!" Master Carek admonished.

Feylynn suspected whatever he said was insulting. The barbarian grimaced at the scolding but said nothing more. He sized her up. They circled each other for a few heartbeats. A chill skittered down Feylynn's spine a second before he pounced. She barely had time to raise her shield before he slammed his massive sword against it. Metal and might clanged together as the combat started. Her arm buckled slightly against his sheer strength, and that violent vibration traveled the whole length of that arm.

Heavy blows like that would wear her down faster than offensive maneuvering. She swiped out with her long sword. Rhushawn blocked the strike, and Feylynn tightened her muscles to keep her arm from swinging wide and leaving her open.

She shuffled back.

He followed before she could lunge back in.

Feylynn tried a three-point flurry, but he parried her every swing. She used her small size and elvish agility to dart about and continued her barrage of strikes, hoping one would catch him off guard. She was more cautious this time. When she attempted this same style in their last match, he had blindsided her with the pommel of his sword, dislocating her jaw. That match had ended with her unconscious on the ground.

The lesson served her well. When she saw her opponent's muscles bunching, Feylynn knew his strike was coming. Ducking, she shifted sideways with beautiful grace. Lifting her shield for protection while simultaneously striking low with her sword, Feylynn's blade met skin. His fist slammed into her shield in that same strike. She grunted as the impact drove her back.

Blood leaked from a small cut on his leg, but Feylynn could not celebrate the success of her strike. The barbarian roared and attacked with a fury she had not yet seen in any match she ever faced.

She dodged as he tried to slam his shield into her face and had to parry his strike with her shield up high. Rhushawn came at her other side with his fist. Sword still in hand, he furiously beat his fist against her only protection. His knuckles cracked open, but he didn't seem to notice as he drew back and did it a third time. Keeping her shield up, Feylynn tried to step away, but his shield was there, bashing her side with such bruising force that she doubled back.

She sensed the arena had gone quiet and knew that everyone present watched the intense match-up. Heat flamed in her cheeks. She hated being a target for spectators.

Feylynn tried to turn again and strike out with her sword, but Rhushawn surprised her. He kicked out his large booted foot, and something tore in her knee when it connected. She couldn't bite back her cry of pain as her knee buckled.

"Match!" Master Carek called, but Rhushawn was beyond hearing.

Limping back from the blow, Feylynn tried to keep upright, but he struck her shield again, and she fell to the ground. Her head slammed into the pavement. Instinctively, she rolled across the rough cobblestones to get out of his way. Rhushawn came at her with that wicked sword and murder in his eyes. His first blow missed killing her, but the strike took off the end of her braid as she barely escaped. The barbarian was beyond any possible reason.

His weapon came down again, and she managed to use her shield for protection. It split in half and slivers of wood fell upon her. Feylynn cried out again as her arm suffered under the blow. Nausea followed the sharp, crippling pain. Her knee was on fire, and the agony in her arm cut through her like a large razor shaving her bone. Weakened, she willed her body to roll away from him a third time, but her reflexes were slowing.

Rhushawn threw his shield aside, and the flying projectile nearly hit two students. Then, gripping his sword in both hands, he lifted the blade high to bring his full strength down on her. Feylynn knew she could not avoid him indefinitely.

Suddenly, there was another sword blocking the mighty barbarian's. "Match!" Master Carek called again as he somehow held his sword against Rhushawn's strength to protect Feylynn. For several seconds, no one moved.

The only sound in the courtyard was Irel's feet rushing to Feylynn, pulling her out of the ring in case Rhushawn lost his mind again. The two swords remained locked together, neither wavering for more than a minute. Master and student stared each other down, neither willing to budge.

Dazed and in agony, Feylynn leaned into Irel as she strained to rise and see who would win this titian battle of wills. However, darkness claimed her sight and mind before she could, and she crumpled in her friend's arms.

TWENTY-SIX

Feylynn inhaled the scent of burning sage when she awoke a few minutes later. Irel and another student she didn't recognize laid her down upon the straw mat, and she moaned as the movement jarred her tender injuries. Looking around, Feylynn realized she laid in the healer's room. Straw bed rolls lined the wall, and light poured in from the windows. Across from her, a small trail of smoke danced from the bowl of incense. The scent of it had her stomach turning again. A slight breeze from the uncovered window floated about the room.

Keeping her eyes closed to force herself to a state of relaxation, Feylynn regulated her breathing for a few more minutes.

In the background of her meditative state, she heard Irel dismiss the other student, and she listened while he explained what happened to a young healer who sounded no older than Resora and Revienah.

After Irel summarized the injuries inflicted by Rhushawn,

with more flair than Feylynn thought she required, the young woman said quietly, "I'll fetch Milt. He's better suited for this. Keep her still for now."

By the time Irel returned to her bedside, Feylynn's attention centered on her cumbersome armor. She'd removed the padded leather gauntlet from her good hand with her teeth and was working off the other glove very slowly while biting her lip.

"Let me help you," Irel said and started to unbuckle the pauldron covering her shoulder. They worked together for a few more minutes taking her armor away a piece at a time. Feylynn didn't consider the impropriety of a man helping her out of her armor. She was too desperate to get the weight off her bruised body. By the time they reached her legs, she was sweating again, but this time from the pain.

She allowed Irel to finish up, and she laid back to concentrate on her breathing again. Her mind went back to those final moments before she blacked out, and she croaked, "What happened?"

He pulled carefully on her greave. "Do you not remember? Did you hit your head that hard?" Irel questioned with genuine concern.

She gritted her teeth as he pulled. "No. I remember." She sighed as the leg piece finally came away. "I mean, what happened to Rhushawn?"

"Oh," Irel stepped back before he could answer so that the healer, Milt, a middle-aged man with early signs of graying hair, could examine Feylynn's injuries.

The Enclave kept an entire core of healers on hand, and she had met a few of them since her arrival months before. Battle trainers here trained with real weapons. The instructors believed it better conditioned the Knights to understand war and battle in real terms. The threat of a wooden practice sword was nothing compared to the danger of real steel. Many came to the healers after matches. For the most part, Master Instructors oversaw every battle to keep things from getting out of hand, as it nearly had today.

The healer clicked his tongue as he took an inventory of the injuries with probing hands that made her grimace. "Definitely swollen here," he squeezed her knee joint, and Feylynn whimpered.

"Bruising and tearing are both problems. And the arm—" Milt lifted and tested it a few times. Feylynn cried out and struggled not to yank her broken arm away.

"Well," the healer said. "I've seen worse from Rhushawn as a result of his fits. You must have put up a good fight."

Irel smirked and proclaimed, "She drew first blood."

"Ah, hence the fit," Milt observed with a knowing smile.

Feylynn closed her eyes. "I didn't do well at all. If I had, I wouldn't be here."

"Are you kidding yourself?" Irel asked with disbelief. "In the whole time since he arrived, no one has ever bested Rhushawn."

"Now then, that is not entirely true," Milt added.

"That is, if you don't include Master Carek," Irel corrected himself.

Feylynn rolled her eyes. "I did not best him, Irel, so his streak remains intact."

"Ah," the healer injected, "I think what Lord Irel is saying is that you are the first to have drawn blood at all."

With a twinkle in his blue-grey eyes, Irel added, "That's exactly what I was trying to say."

"What?" she groaned.

"First blood, Fey. I'm guessing that's why Rhushawn lost it."

Master Carek entered the healing room. "Why he lost control is of little consequence. Temper will not serve anyone in battle. First blood is of even less consequence. Why is that, Feylynn?"

"Because first blood will not decide an outcome. Only the

final strike matters," Feylynn replied.

Master Carek turned to Irel. "For the remainder of this evening, Irel, you will study at least three histories in which first blood did not help the warrior who drew it. You will report the results of your study and also note ways the bested warriors could have prevailed."

"Right away, sir." Irel feigned humility and wiped the smile off his face, but Feylynn knew he still hid it in his soul. She suspected that Master Carek knew the same. To her young, loyal friend Irel, the fact that she drew first blood was a victory in his mind.

"You are excused," said Carek.

Irel bowed to the Master Knight and left them, but not before he covertly winked at Feylynn behind their instructor's back. Fearing to give him away, she did not react or even smile.

The healer stopped Carek before he could speak. "You will have to wait, Master Carek. This trainee has waited in pain long enough."

"Very well," Carek replied and sat in a chair nearby.

Milt tended Feylynn's knee first. He placed oils and grey powder on her knee and rubbed the injury gently while murmuring words of prayer and healing with his eyes closed.

The itchy flow of magic coursed through her. At first, it was uncomfortable. It started from the tendons and muscles inside and back over her skin outside as the torn tissue renewed itself. It was like a million tiny spiders inside her knee were spinning webs of ligament and bone. Then her joint heated to the point of burning before it chilled like icy water. The hot and cold cycle repeated itself three times before the sensation of blessed relief finally allowed her to relax. Without interrupting the quiet prayer, Milt moved along her body to help the rest of her injuries along. The process took nearly thirty minutes to complete, but Milt stood back and evaluated his patient when he finished. "Better?"

"Yes, much better," Feylynn replied honestly. "Thank you."

"I suppose you won't listen to me if I tell you that you're much too small to take on someone his size."

Feylynn shook her head.

"Well then, I expect we'll see you back here again soon," said the healer on a resigned sigh. "Be careful, Princess. Rhushawn is not one to trifle with." He glanced back to Master Carek. "She's all yours. Don't get her killed."

Carek offered a curt nod in reply, and Milt left them alone. Master Carek watched as she sat up and evaluated her movement for any lingering signs of injury. "You truly do favor your father," he observed.

Feylynn met his gaze with puzzlement. "Sir?"

"I can barely see it in you, unlike your sisters. I wonder if that is for the best or not."

He was speaking of her elvish traits. Unlike her sisters, Feylynn favored the human bloodline of their father. Her hair was dark and curled naturally instead of being straight. The most defining features for elves were their ears, cheekbones, and slender builds. All of those were less pronounced in her.

While her ears were sharper than most humans, it wasn't in an obvious way. Her facial features were rounder and lacked the sharp cheekbones of her siblings. Inheriting her father's height, Feylynn was the tallest of her sisters and was slight of build like elves were. She carried a warrior's stature of broad shoulders, strong arms, and thick human legs. Of course, that muscle definition could be attributed to Feylynn's relentless sword practice as much as her family genetics.

Unlike Ahanna, Feylynn didn't mind being different. She found it often offered her an unfair advantage, and she was intelligent enough to use it. Despite her build, she was lucky enough to inherit the agility of an elf, and her hearing and eyesight were far superior to most humans. The best advantage was that people never accounted for those traits when sizing her up. People were too shortsighted to see the elf in her, or maybe if they did, they counted it as a disadvantage, but Feylynn knew her bloodline was full of favorable traits.

Even though Feylynn did not favor her mother in appearance, her father often said that she was born with a warrior's heart and a strong sense of justice like her mother. She knew so little about her mother, but Feylynn wanted that to be true, so she lived by that firm belief of justice.

Unsure of how to respond to her instructor's observations, she opted not to. Master Carek was one of a select few that knew her mother personally. She was the reason he'd been afforded a chance to train among the elves after the war ended.

Master Carek stood and asked, "Are you fit then?"

"I believe so, sir," she replied after testing the bend in her knee.

"You managed well today," said Carek.

"Not well enough. I only won twice and lost twice in fatal ways."

"That's true, but few can keep their wits when dealing with Rhushawn. For that reason, you will be paired with him exclusively for two fortnights."

Feylynn was alarmed. "Sir? Did I do something wrong?"

"No, but the pairing will benefit you both. This is part of Rhushawn's punishment and your training."

"Part of his punishment?" Feylynn asked.

Carek's face turned grim. "Rhushawn broke the Paladin's Code of Honorable Combat when he tried to kill you today. As a result, he will face the standard consequences."

Her heart sank. The standard for reckless or disobedient

behavior was five lashes that could not be healed with magical aid. The standard for taking a match too far and risking your partner's life was ten. "You can't!" Feylynn exclaimed, standing to her full height.

"You defend him?" Master Carek questioned.

"I—"

"It is our way, Feylynn. We have rules. There is a code, and we must follow it." Master Carek shook his head.

"According to the Code, does he not have to be accused by the offended party first?" Feylynn didn't know what she was doing. Her mind was screaming at her to shut up, but for some reason, she couldn't. Here she stood championing for the man who would have killed her less than an hour earlier if not for Master Carek's intervention.

"Princess, there were a hundred other witnesses. You must know that."

Feylynn stood at attention and stared straight ahead. "I will not accuse him. I accept partial blame for the outcome of the match. I allowed my animosity toward the barbarian to affect my behavior. I drew blood, knowing his temper, and I pushed him over the edge. I will not accuse him of trying to kill me. The match was fought fairly."

"Princess, you must reconsider."

Feylynn said nothing more.

"Do you understand the consequences of your actions?"

"I do," she replied.

"Do you understand that if the Council believes you are deliberately lying, you could face five lashings as well?"

Feylynn swallowed hard. "I do."

"Do you understand what your father would say if you received such a punishment?

"My father is a Golden Dragon. He understands the rules. He

understood them when he agreed to send me here."

"Princess, a lot has changed since then. Your father was not yet King. There are various politics at play here."

"Politics have no bearing on honor, Master Carek. I stand by my statement," Feylynn proclaimed with firm resolve.

"Even if that is true, I was there, Feylynn. I know what happened best," Master Carek said grimly. "Would you question the honor of my decision?"

Feylynn refused to cringe, but her stomach tightened. As the Master of the match, only Carek could challenge her statement. She still wasn't sure why she was taking this stand. "No, sir, but I would state my perspective on the matter as I perceive it."

"Feylynn, the lashings will not kill him."

"Yes, sir."

"He must learn control."

"It is why we come here, sir. To learn our weaknesses and overcome them."

Master Carek stared at her for several minutes. "Mercy can be perceived as a weakness, Princess."

"Mercy is a core principle of justice, Master Carek."

He heaved a heavy sigh. "Fine, considering your admission, it will be my recommendation that both face equal punishment."

Feylynn's knees felt weak at the possibility of being whipped.

He continued, "You will both be rationed to a single daily meal for five days. Furthermore, you will be assigned to help with any needs down in the village bordering The Enclave. You will not miss a single lesson to accommodate this schedule. You will also be paired as sparring partners for two fortnights so you both can better temper your thoughts and actions."

"Yes, sir," Feylynn chipped.

"There is no promise that my recommendation will be accepted. I will ask you once more, do you wish to change your statement?"

"No, sir."

"Very well, you are confined to your quarters until your punishment is decided."

"Yes, sir," Feylynn replied grimly.

As she walked back to her quarters, Feylynn wondered what she was thinking the entire way. *I'm an idiot*, she kept repeating to herself. But, considering the next twenty-eight days of sparring with Rhushawn, she couldn't help wondering whether the lashing wouldn't be a less painful punishment.

TWENTY-SEVEN

Behind the blacksmith's barn, Rhushawn rested his axe on his shoulder and stood with his usual stoic pose. As if he'd been charged to protect Feylynn rather than help her, the barbarian vigilantly scanned their surroundings. She knew better, though. He was only alert in case someone happened to walk by and find him doing nothing.

Pushing her anger aside and shaking her head at the lunacy of it, Feylynn swung her axe over her shoulders. *Crack!* The log on the stump split cleanly through the center. She added the two pieces to the growing pile and glanced at the stump next to hers.

Rhushawn's tree stump still held a large log that needed splitting. For the last two hours, the stubborn barbarian split one log for every ten she did. She'd even taken a mental count, and it was almost exactly ten to one.

He was careful enough to keep the stump loaded and his axe ready should one of the Masters come by and see him. His complacency infuriated her. It was his fault they were relegated to this task, among others, and he couldn't be bothered to help her finish it quickly. It wasn't like splitting wood was even difficult for him. His mighty muscles swung the axe one-handed as if he applied a hammer to nail, and each time he struck, Rhushawn's blade sliced the wood with ease like a hot knife cutting through churned butter.

In contrast, every log she attacked was a trial of strength and energy. The axe was heavy and unwieldy compared to her sword. The forward balance was strange to adapt to. Besides, she had never done a task like this before in Ranoak. Feylynn rarely hit the logs with any skill and often had to yank the axe out and strike it a few times more to get the stubborn logs to split.

The late cold front from yesterday made the assignment worse. A storm last night left a new layer of snow that was melting and made for muddy roads and soggy boots. The heavy labor made her sweaty, and Feylynn could swear the chill air turned that sweat to ice. She was cold, tired, and frustrated.

Feylynn never thought of herself as weak, nor did she believe that, but this task tested her strength on every level. Rhushawn tested her patience as well. Her arms ached, yet Rhushawn was determined to let her do all the work. Worse, there was little she could do about it now. If she recanted her story, they would both face lashings. If they didn't finish their chores, the Council would add another day to their punishment. Feylynn was trapped in this torture of her own making.

She looked at the pile of logs and muttered, "I'm an idiot." She glared at the barbarian. "I should have let them lash you."

Rhushawn gave no reply as she bent to heave another log on her stump. She heard a sharp crack and looked up to see Rhushawn adding his newly split wood to the pile on her right. Turning with surprise, Feylynn saw a rotund, bald man coming up the hill toward them.

Realizing his motivation, the Princess rolled her eyes at Rhushawn's false work ethic and straightened her sore back to greet the newcomer. Master Jonas may have been a fit knight once upon a time, but the years did not favor him. He had traded his sword for parchment and quill and loved to indulge in sweet treats. Last week, Melorn, another first-year student, had snatched Master Jonas' hidden pastries to share with a few of his other friends. She hadn't known until later when Irel recounted the event at lunch the next day and boasted about the creamed puff he'd eaten. It was supposedly a great game to relieve the older Knight of his deserts.

Master Jonas was in charge of paperwork and finance for The Enclave. Rumors said the portly man was never really a very good warrior but that his father had forced it upon him. Then, the Council took pity on him and allowed him to keep records. Master Jonas' red face from the long walk and lack of regular exercise, coupled with the sweat dripping down his bald head, made her inclined to believe the story.

"Master Jonas," Feylynn greeted.

Glaring at the Master, Rhushawn split two more logs in rapid succession. For that reason alone, she could hug the chubby Master

"Princess Feylynn," he huffed. "Rhushawn," he said with a tired half-wave.

Crack! Another log split. Rhushawn looked positively irritated. On a whim and pleased with his irritation, Feylynn gestured to her stump and said sweetly, "You look tired, Master Jonas. Would you like to sit down?"

"Yes, thank you."

Rhushawn glared at her with murder in his eyes. His oversized hand picked up another log, and he dropped his axe upon it without releasing her from his gaze.

"Could I get some water?" the Master asked.

Rhushawn's irritation turned to malice-filled glee. "I get water," he said with thick heavy words and left before she could protest. Feylynn knew right away the poor man would have a long wait for his water.

She found herself surprised to hear the barbarian speak. It was the first time she heard Rhushawn use the common tongue. Any other time he spoke, it was his native language, Kildreshian, and she was sure none of those comments were what one would consider polite.

As the winded Master patted his brow, he took a few more breaths and said, "A letter came for you."

"Me?"

"Yes, from the King. A messenger delivered it this morning. Master Carek bid me to deliver it right away." His pudgy fingers pulled the letter from his shirt pocket and handed it over to her.

"Thank you," Feylynn said excitedly. She clutched the scroll in her hand, and a pure, joyful grin dominated her face when she saw the wax dragon seal that was her father's. She looked forward to every letter from home, but they were rare. Since arriving, this was only her third one. The first informed her Ahanna was safe, but no, she was not coming home. He told her to avoid speaking of her older sister at all costs. There were a few other details in the message that he confided to her. One of those details was that he would not name her as heir. He insisted Ahanna would be back in time. Feylynn held those secrets close to heart as requested before disposing of the letter.

The second letter was sent as a check-up to request a monthly update from Feylynn on her progress. That was when he explained he would not write often but would think of her twice as much.

It wasn't as if her father didn't wish to write to her, but as

King, his letters drew attention—the kind of attention that a student at The Enclave would not want to incite.

As the first woman ever to train as a knight, people already treated her differently. They did not need regular reminders that she was King Tisus' daughter. Even now, the personal delivery of her letter was not normal behavior for recruits. Most received their messages at the end of the day once a week. She tucked the scroll away into the back of her trousers.

"You're not going to read it?" Master Jonas questioned curiously.

"I will later."

"Your father rarely writes to you. I would think you'd be eager to see what he has to say."

"Yes, but I would much rather wait until I finish with the day's work, and I can read it carefully."

"Yes, well, I can take it back to The Enclave for you."

"That's alright. I'll keep it. It seems silly for you to come all this way and then have to take it back," she said.

"It's no trouble," he insisted.

She looked at him quizically and furrowed her brows. "Thank you, but keeping it will help motivate me to get my work done."

His lips thinned, but he relented. "Very well." He scanned the area for Rhushawn and stood. "I suppose I can get water down at the bakery."

"I suppose so," she agreed, knowing he would get more than water at the village bakery.

"Good day, Princess." He scanned the pile of logs. "You should let that barbarian do this heavy work—it should be easy for him. It seems a horrid task for a Princess of Ranoak."

There it was, the very reason her father didn't write often. Her father knew the letters reminded people of her title rather than her merits. "I'll keep that in mind," she assured him.

He nodded and started back down the hill.

Feylynn thought of the letter in her pocket and picked up her axe. She brought it down with a mighty swing, and it wedged in deep but it did not split. She picked up both the log and axe and slammed them on the stump. The axe barely budged. She tried twice more before letting go and yelling. Frustrated, she kicked the log and watched it tumble off the pedestal.

Rhushawn chose that moment to return and stalked up to her with determination in his eyes. He thrust something at her so forcefully she stepped away from him. "Drink!" he ordered. His order was laced with that heavy accent that caused him to roll his r's.

Feylynn looked down and saw the filled tankard in his hand.

"Drink," he said again, pushing it closer.

She accepted the cup and asked, "Did you poison it?"

Rhushawn's eyes flickered. He violently ripped the cup from her hand and took a large swallow himself. Then, he threw it at her feet, spilling its contents over her boots. Turning around, he picked up her axe handle and smacked it down against her stump with one smooth motion. The blade tore through the wood smoothly as if he was cutting parchment, and the two halves tumbled to the ground.

Irritated and feeling the slightest hint of guilt for offending him, Feylynn picked up the now empty cup, inspected it for damage, and set it aside when she didn't find any. It was, after all, the blacksmith's possession, and she did not wish for him to ruin it.

Rhushawn stalked back to his stump. He picked up his axe, rested it on his shoulder, spat on the ground, and assumed his useless position. Her minor guilt disappeared instantly.

Exhausted but desperate to be done with this task, Feylynn picked up a new log and set it in the center of her stump. She took her axe in hand and glanced at Rhushawn as she lifted it. He was picking at his teeth now. Her fury spiked when she realized the barbarian had eaten something.

As part of their punishment, the pair were rationed to a single daily meal, but that son of a carrion crawler had somehow managed to snatch something to eat. The heat rose in her face as her temper boiled.

With fire in her eyes, Feylynn approached him with her axe in hand. She stopped right in front of him. Rhushawn dropped his own axe from his shoulder and let it hang at his side. He straightened to his full height in front of her and lifted a single brow as if challenging her.

She stared at him with hard, angry eyes for a full minute. He was so much bigger than she was, and his stern expression did not waver from her irritated glare, but she refused to cower to this wasted use of human flesh.

Enough, she thought. Feylynn was sick of Rhushawn, sick of his shows of superiority, and sick of staring at the smug look on his face every day! Without considering the consequences if she missed, Feylynn swung her chopping axe around. It cut through the air a hair's breadth from his belly and landed with a heavy thud, embedded into the frozen ground less than an inch from his foot.

To his credit, the barbarian didn't even flinch. Turning away, Feylynn missed the smile on Rhushawn's lips as she took up the empty tankard and stalked off to fetch more water.

TWENTY-EIGHT

Near the well, Feylynn took several, greedy gulps of water and then sank to the ground. She wrapped her tired arms around her legs and settled her head upon her knees. Tears threatened to spill, but she willed them away. She stared at nothing for several minutes until two robins caught her attention.

A smile broke free as Feylynn watched the pair hop about on the ground in a dance. The birds' playful antics sparked pleasant memories of her sisters. She remembered as a young child when Enreal found a helpless baby bluejay that fell from the nest. Their mother helped the girls construct a safe haven for the baby bird and taught them to feed the helpless hatchling.

She remembered they had spent the entire spring season nurturing and tending the little bird until they eventually freed it when it matured enough to fly. Once released, the little bluejay visited them all summer long and often played in the courtyard with Enreal.

Feylynn frowned. Shelanna had disappeared that same fall. Though she missed her mother, the ache from that loss had faded in the last few years. Right now, she missed her father and sisters, and that fresh longing for home and family settled upon her. Feylynn's anger subsided in its wake.

With the sharp sting of anger fading, and the homesickness growing, Feylynn thought of the letter. She sat up and grasped the precious connection to home. She freed the parchment from her pocket and rubbed her thumb over the dragon seal reverently.

Feylynn debated reading the letter here. She really should get back to the wood. She had to spar within the next hour, and there were a lot more logs to split. But, shaking the sense of responsibility away, she broke the seal on the letter.

Feylynn's surprise was complete when she found it did not contain her father's penmanship. Rather, the letter was from her sister Enreal.

Dearest Feylynn,

Father does not know we sent this letter as Revienah took his seal so it would appear official. Father said, until your first trial, you cannot write directly to us. This news could not wait. Much has happened, so much that I fear a single letter would not convey it all. I am pressed for time, and Micah awaits, so I must forge ahead without all the pleasantries. We need your help. Resora needs your help.

Resora is ill, horribly ill. We all are afraid. More important than the illness are the revelations surrounding it. Resora dreamed of an ancient gold dragon named Feldorthanosh and his battle against an evil red during one of her feverish nights. She narrated it to Liddia, and Liddia was unable to hide her concern.

I tried to investigate, and I overheard Liddia and Father saying Resora is Dragon Touched, but Father keeps this information to himself and has not spoken to Resora. I do not understand the reason for his secrecy, but Father must have reasons. For now, I feel it is best that we do likewise and keep this between sisters.

I searched in the library but discovered all archives on golden dragons are kept at The Enclave. This is a problem only you can solve now. We need you to research the dragon by name for us and write back with any insight you can offer. I know I ask for a great deal here, a miracle even. I wouldn't wish to trouble this upon you, but we are running out of options, and Resora worsens every day.

You must also know that Micah received word from Ahanna! She is safe and sound in a secret location. Micah is using his falcon to send her letters. I believe he knows of her location, but he told us we could not tell a soul that we have been in contact with her. Not even Father can hear of it, but you would want to know. We suspect Father knows more than he will say. He says he has someone looking out for her. It is confusing that Micah should keep this from him. Micah made us swear an oath to keep it a secret. Micah also promises to send Ahanna news of Resora's condition.

This last part is essential. Micah will send Cirus, his falcon, to The Enclave, and you are to send a return message on anything you find. The falcon will hopefully find his way to the gatehouse five days after this letter is delivered. When you see him, please give him a small bit of raw meat. That is his signal to take your reply.

I know the news is dire, and I am sorry. But I pray you might find something we can use to help Resora.

All our love,
Resora, Revienah, and Enreal

Feylynn's brows drew in as she read the letter a second time. Resora's condition pierced her heart. The news was almost too much, and a sudden urge to mount her horse to head home straight away rose within. Of all her sisters, Resora was the frailest. Ever since she was born, she often fell ill with fever.

Fear for Resora pressed in on Feylynn, and she started to think of ways to leave The Enclave. She started making a list of her belongings for the long trip home when reason set in. Feylynn recalled when her instructors once took them to the pass during the early days of winter. It was an unforgiving pathway home, and they wanted the students to understand the dangers of the pass. Even with winter ebbing, it would be weeks before the path was clear enough to travel, and she was not trained sufficiently in elemental survival to even attempt such a journey alone. She wouldn't be any good to Resora if she froze to death upon the mountain.

That realization brought forth a curious thought. How had Micah survived the cold mountain? Master Jonas said one of the King's messengers delivered it, not a bird or a falcon. By her sister's confession Micah must have delivered the letter himself. Maybe that's why Master Jonas had been so curious about its contents. Not even the greediest merchants would try the pass for at least another three to four weeks.

Resora must be in a sad state indeed for Micah to even try, she thought. *My sisters need me, and I am stuck here hundreds of miles away chopping firewood.* Her brow furrowed. Tucking the letter away, Feylynn walked back toward the barn. She resolved that she had to figure out a way to look into the mentioned dragon histories.

As if that was not enough pressure, she also had mixed feelings about the news of Ahanna's communication with Micah. It would have been better if she was kept in the dark on that matter. Like her father, if she found herself questioned on the issue, Feylynn was honor-bound to reveal the truth. Of course, the knowledge wasn't alone soothed her soul.

Ahanna was smart, resourceful, and brave, but it was still good that Micah was looking out for her.

She never consciously thought anything terrible would happen to her eldest sister, but subconsciously little bits of doubt had nibbled away at her. It was, after all, her idea that Ahanna should run away. If something unfortunate happened to her sister, Feylynn realized she would have blamed herself. So there was immense relief in knowing that Ahanna was alive and well, and even a small pleasure in knowing that her whereabouts remained unknown to The Enclave.

The Golden Dragon Masters still intended to cement their hold in the kingdom by keeping a paladin in the royal family. It was a funny concept for Feylynn. Rumor was, three lords waited in line for her arranged marriage, and she hated that idea as much as Ahanna did. She even wondered if Irel was among them.

She and her sisters had done the right thing in helping Ahanna escape. She would have withered under the weight of their political tutelage and its resulting obligations. Feylynn herself would be no better if they tried her.

Feylynn's respect for her father had grown tenfold as she watched him maneuver the Captain in the main hall that day. He did not lie once, and he held to the Knight's Code, but he put his daughters first.

Her sisters were wrong. Their father had no idea where Ahanna was, and he wanted to keep it that way. It was the reason for the secrecy in the first place. If Tisus discovered Ahanna's location or even saw his eldest daughter, her father would be duty-bound as King to keep his word. Feylynn realized the pain of that promise must be a terrible sacrifice for her father. He was forced to choose between his daughter's happiness and the possibility of never seeing her again.

Feylynn was grateful that her sisters had the good sense, not to mention Ahanna's location in the letter.

Micah must be running this errand without her father's knowledge. She was duty-bound to report to the King or technically the King's commanders as a Paladin knight, but technically she was not yet a sworn Golden Dragon. It was a gray area of honesty, and Feylynn took that very seriously. Without his example, she may not have justified her deceit, but she reasoned that if her father could find that grey area for Ahanna's sake, so could she.

They had been best friends for as long as she could remember. Whenever Feylynn had a problem she had confided in Ahanna. Whenever she was happy, her older sister had shared it with her. Not getting any updates would sting, and not being able to talk to her left a hole in her heart that would never fill. Still, they had risked everything to help Ahanna run away, and Feylynn did not regret that decision. But she did not want to jeopardize both their futures any more than she already had because of sentimental attachments.

Feylynn made a mental note to tell Enreal to leave out any updates on her older sister in her return letter. It was risk she couldn't take. But, first, she had to focus on finding information for Resora. Five days was not much time. *How will I ever find time for research in such a short period?* She wondered. Her regular schedule was hard enough, but now it would be nearly impossible with her current punishment. Feylynn sighed.

Rising to her feet, she brushed off her trousers, and with heavy footsteps and a heavier heart, she made her way back. As Feylynn passed the front of the blacksmith's barn, she saw the bulky man pounding away at his anvil.

On a whim, she entered the barn. The whole area smelled of

coal dust and molten iron. The heat emanating from the fire filled the barn, and beads of sweat formed on her brow.

Holding out the metal tankard she'd used for water, she approached the blacksmith and smiled at him. "Thank you for the tankard."

He grunted his acknowledgment without looking at her and brought his hammer down on the red hot metal once more.

"Where can I return it to?"

He paused. "Just set it down. My wife will get it later."

"Yes, sir." Feylynn moved to the table near the forging fire. With a quick glance, she verified the blacksmith was still occupied and pounding away upon the steel. Feylynn set the cup down as instructed and covertly tossed the rolled parchment onto the hot coals at the same time. The paper burst into flames and disappeared from sight.

Seeing the message transform into hot ash offered little relief, but Feylynn knew she had to set the problem aside in the meantime. As it was, she abandoned her duties long enough. She rounded the corner behind the barn only to find Rhushawn standing in his usual pose of utter uselessness. Gritting her teeth at him, she took up her axe and returned to work.

TWENTY-NINE

T he setting sun lit the sky aflame with bright oranges, reds, and golden highlights, but Feylynn couldn't spare a second to take it in. Her breath came fast. Her hair, damp with sweat, stuck to her skin. Rhushawn was too fierce, and for a big man, his quick moves defied what should be possible for someone of his size. Off-balance, Feylynn ducked and swung her sword hard. Then, something in her back popped. She wasn't sure if she felt the popping sensation or heard it, but she certainly felt the immediate consequence of debilitating pain radiating through her spine.

Her breath caught in her lungs as if someone punched her in the chest. She opened her mouth to pull in the air but could not force her lungs to respond.

Rhushawn came at her again. She couldn't think past the agonizing spike of pain that assaulted her spine. Months of training urged her to lift her weapon to block and step away, but as

Feylynn shifted her sword, her body betrayed her. Her feet were leaden and would not obey her command to move. She stumbled, falling backward. She couldn't even find the breath to cry out as she hit the ground with enough force to jar teeth loose.

The impact drove the last bit of air out of her lungs. Opening her mouth, she struggled to draw oxygen, but her back and lungs rebelled against her efforts for several seconds. Somehow, through it all, Feylynn stubbornly held on to her sword. Losing her blade was an automatic forfeiture, and it was her desperate hold that kept Carek from calling the match.

Pinpricks of light danced at the edges of her vision, but Feylynn would not cry for mercy. Desperation filled her. *Not again*, she thought as Rhushawn prowled around her like the animal that he was

The thought of losing to this man again pushed her to fight on, and she finally managed to get little gasps of air into her lungs. The gasping was mixed with painful grimaces as she tried to cope with the agony in her spine to focus. Her vision blurred, her back spasmed, and Princess Feylynn knew she couldn't hope to roll out of Rhushawn's path. She had to do something.

His sword came down, and instinct had her lifting her sword horizontally to protect her heart. The pitiful act of defiance paid off. The weight of his infamous, heavy blade drove her sword's tip to the ground on her other side. Being too weak to protest, she let gravity do the work. His weapon slid down the length of hers, and before he was able to retract its weight back, he nearly lost his balance. In the last week, Feylynn had discovered that the massive sword was not easy to pull back once it had momentum. A sliver of satisfaction spread through Feylynn like warm honey, and for about half of a heartbeat, the pain receded.

He advanced again, and she yelled in desperate fury. Feylynn kicked at his shins twice in rapid succession. The barbarian hissed when the first blow connected. They were both surprised by the force of her kick, and he jumped back from her before the second could make contact. His chest heaved, and anger festered in his eyes. Watching her, Rhushawn didn't lift his blade back up. He paced instead. To the crowd, it looked like he was trying to check his temper.

Feylynn made another feeble attempt to kick him and cried out again. This time her cry was born of pain as her back protested the idiocy of her maneuvers. She wanted to curl into herself and hide from it all, but even that would hurt.

She couldn't fathom why, but Rhushawn stared down at her for a couple of seconds as he paced. There was something in his eyes, an unidentifiable emotion—one she could not even begin to process while concentrating on her injury and the intense feelings he invoked in her.

When he finally came at her side, Feylynn knew she was done. Sweat dampened her skin, and under her armor, her tunic clung to her body. Even the slightest movement created spasms so fierce she nearly sobbed. Yet, she refused to give in to that weakness. Feylynn bit the inside of her cheek instead and stared daggers of hatred at him.

Rhushawn stepped in, but before he could lift his blade, Feylynn swung wildly, and somehow the metal clanged as she pushed the ancestor blade out wide with a single desperate strike. Rhushawn scowled as Feylynn's back arched, and she whimpered with the move. Then, unable to hold the weight of the longsword aloft, her arm fell across her chest almost immediately.

Once again, she had moved the blade without thinking. Only Ealoram himself knew how long she could keep this up. Adrenaline and her protective instincts kept her in this fight, but she also understood that time was not on her side.

I will not give in to him again! Feylynn reminded herself.

She hated him. She hated looking at his stupid face every day for the last week. She despised that this beast had made no effort to complete his share on every chore they were given. His face, his attitude, and his wretched ancestral sword—she hated all of it. But, most of all, she *hated* losing to him every blasted day while everyone in The Enclave watched how inadequate she was.

Feylynn despised herself for ever standing up for him. Worse, she knew that even with the hindsight of this moment, she would have taken the same action today as she had a week before. Rogue tears escaped her tight hold, and that moisture was one more reason to hate the barbarian towering over her.

Out of the corner of her blurred vision, Feylynn saw his sword hand shift slightly. Gritting her teeth, she lifted her head and angled her body to defend. She had no hope to win, but for some reason, she could not allow herself to yield either.

As always, their match had turned into a spectacle. Looking around at the crowd, Rhushawn flicked his wrist, and the heavy sword flipped in his hand with impressive ease. The crowd waited with bated breath knowing he would strike. Rhushawn moved in with purposeful strides, but he surprised everyone watching when he stopped and did not take the killing blow.

Instead, he stood there quietly, looking down at her prone form. His fingers twitched as his hand tightened around his sword's hilt. Feylynn's eyes darted from his hand to his face and back as she waited for the final blow. Mimicking his gesture, her own fingers tightened around her hilt.

Her sensitive ears picked up the sound of murmurs and bets spreading through the watching crowd. His intense stare nearly undid her. She could bet he intended to stand there and wait her out, essentially forcing her to forfeit in front of everyone. Like her, he had to know her strength would eventually fail. The heat rose in her cheeks. Whether from anger or embarrassment, she couldn't tell.

"What are you waiting for?" she forced the words through gritted teeth. "Come closer so I can gut you and finish this."

Rhushawn spat on the ground and wiped the blood from the corner of his lips with the pad of his thumb—blood she'd drawn with her wooden shield when she smashed it into his face earlier.

Seething, Feylynn reached deep within to grasp any strength hiding in reserve. Watching him for any hint of attack, she wished her determination alone could finally defeat him. The pain in her back spread with every movement. There was a buzzing in her ears, and her body was weakening by the second. By all accounts, she shouldn't even be conscious. Yet her fingers stubbornly held on to the hilt of her father's old sword. All she had to do was let go, and it would be over. She defiantly lifted the sword to point it directly at him.

Feylynn's bicep quivered, and her back protested. Rhushawn tilted his head as he looked down the length of her sword. She dropped the blade a fraction of an inch under his scrutiny.

She fought against her own weaknesses. *Do not let go!* she ordered herself. She brought the sword back up, hoping to prove that she could still beat him. If Rhushawn brought that cursed weapon down one more time, she would have no chance of blocking it. Her stubborn will alone kept her blade aloft. The barbarian stood there staring at her as if she was a puzzle to take apart. Finally, at her wit's end, Feylynn screamed, "Do something, you coward!"

He lifted a brow.

Feylynn couldn't understand why, but Carek still hadn't called the match even though Rhushawn could easily claim victory. The barbarian took a step closer. She pointed the shaking sword directly at him as if she would impale him if he advanced any further.

She was done for and knew it. More importantly, Rhushawn knew it, but she was Tisus Nacarian's daughter, and she would not give in. Meeting his eyes, she forced herself to tell him exactly that.

"I will not yield!" *Not to him,* she thought. Even if he beat her a thousand times, Feylynn would never concede to him by choice.

Instead of taking the killing blow, Rhushawn licked his split lip, stepped around her, and shocked everyone by handing his infamous sword to Master Carek hilt first, thereby forfeiting the match.

"Match," Rhushawn said with his thick accent, "Is good death."

Stunned, Carek accepted the sword and offered the barbarian a slight nod. "Match," he agreed.

Feylynn closed her eyes and finally dropped her guard. Sighing in relief, she allowed her shaking sword arm to fall. The steel rang out as it clattered against the paved ground. She still did not let go of her firm grip. She wasn't sure she could.

Rhushawn turned and went back to her side. Hearing his approach and unsure of his intent, Feylynn opened her eyes with worry. Her sword scraped against the ground as she pulled it close to her side.

Rhushawn looked down at her and his lips tilted ever so slightly. She glared at him when she realized he found her fear of him amusing.

"Next time, kick higher, *Voinz Dotier,*" Rhushawn instructed as he stepped over her and made his way toward the barracks. She watched as the crowd parted to allow him passage, and not one person would look at his face or meet his eyes as he passed.

Irel was on his knees by her side an instant later. "Can you walk?"

Embarrassed, the tears came more freely. Feylynn let her head drop and used her free arm to cover her eyes to block out reality. She winced as the movement caused new spasms.

Irel sighed. "Come on, Fey. Let's get you up."

"I need a minute," Feylynn confessed through her tears and found herself disgusted by the weak tone in her voice.

"I can carry you," Irel offered. "Give me your sword."

"No," said Master Carek as he joined them.

Feylynn did not look up at him or uncover her eyes, but she confessed to the pain as the tears streamed down her cheeks. "My back, I heard it pop. I need a healer. Something is very wrong with my back."

Carek crouched down before her. "Princess, do not tarry here at their feet as if you are giving up."

Irel scoffed, "You must be joking. She cannot possibly—"

Carek cut him off with a stern glare. He drew closer and said to Feylynn in a low tone, "Rise and show the future Knights of Ranoak that defeat will not keep you down for long."

"I can't," Feylynn admitted pathetically.

"You can. And you will." His tone was so sharp and out of character that Feylynn uncovered her eyes and looked to her Master Mnstructor.

Carek offered her a reassuring smile. "You have already proven your might today when you refused to yield. Do not waste that victory. Now, show them your strength and your will to press on. Be more than they expect, Princess."

His words, the same words her father spoke before she left, gave her the strength she needed. The tears stopped welling, and Feylynn licked her dry lips.

Carek stood and gestured with his hand for Lord Irel to do the same. For the first time since Rhushawn left, Feylynn heard the whispers around them. She took Master Carek's words to heart and rolled to her side. Her spine spasmed, and she bit the inside of her cheek hard enough to draw blood to keep herself from moaning. She rose on her hands and knees and took a couple of fortifying breaths before gripping her sword and using it for leverage to stand.

For several heartbeats, silence filled the training ground. Everyone watched with bated breath as Feylynn took her first limping step forward. Then, after her third step, something strange happened.

One of the trainees she passed patted her shoulder. "Great job!"

Feylynn winced inwardly but nodded in acknowledgment. She didn't trust herself to speak.

Someone else patted her opposite shoulder and said, "You're keeping that brute guessing, I'd wager."

One of the senior recruits, a burly man with a deep voice, called out loudly, "Way to show him, Princess!"

"Huzzah!" another swordsman yelled, and many others shouted the victory cry with him.

The tears threatened again, but for very different reasons. Most of the trainees here struggled with having her in residence, let alone sparring with her. Until this very moment, Irel was the only one who showed her any soldier-like respect. They respected her station well enough, but they'd mostly ignored her or glowered and gossiped behind her back.

As she took another step forward, Feylynn turned to seek out Master Carek, but he was no longer there. With her attention split, she nearly stumbled on her next step, but suddenly Irel was there, taking ahold of her upper arm to offer his discreet assistance.

Irel leaned in close and whispered, "I think you better get inside before you wreck Master Carek's plan to put you on a pedestal."

Feylynn whispered back, "Don't let go. Else I might fall on my face."

Irel chuckled. "We can't have that. A broken nose would not suit you."

As they walked toward the healer's building, Feylynn allowed herself to lean into Irel's help. The crowd slowly dispersed, and the men started back to their evening duties and matches. Behind her back, Feylynn could hear talks of her last fight with Rhushawn and was surprised by the way they embellished the tale in her favor. She couldn't stop the weak smile that formed on her lips.

As they entered the building, Feylynn was relieved to be away from the crowd because her legs would not go any further, and she staggered. She whimpered as Irel took her up in his arms and moved her toward the healing room.

"Thank you, Irel," she whispered weakly.

"Any time, Fey."

THIRTY

"**I** know I shouldn't be surprised, but I'm surprised nonetheless," Milt said as he tested the bulge in Feylynn's spine. She winced as he checked the vertebrae. He dulled the spasm with healing magic before placing both hands on her back and leaning down with his body weight as he snapped the vertebrae back into place.

"Surprised?" Feylynn groaned as he repeated the motion higher up.

"I am rarely surprised with you warriors. You're all a stubborn, unreasonable lot." Milt offered her a hand. "You can sit up now."

"Determined, not stubborn," she gritted through her teeth as he helped her sit up. To Feylynn's relief, the worst spasms in her spine ebbed enough to let her breathe, although there was still substantial discomfort.

Milt chuckled, "Fair enough. Regardless, determination often means predictable among your peers." His fingers ran over the length of her back, testing the tender muscles.

Annoyed, Feylynn pressed her lips together to keep from speaking carelessly.

"Mettle."

Confused, Feylynn glanced back at him. "What?"

"I am surprised by the strength of your mettle," Milt explained.

"My mettle?"

"The mettle forged under the wisdom of Master Carek." He met her eyes, "Seven days ago, I would never have predicted this outcome."

"What outcome? The outcome has not changed. I still find myself in this room every day to repair the damage done by my defeats against Rhushawn."

"You and I see defeat very differently. By all rights, you shouldn't have been able to walk in here today. Nor should a novice warrior half his size and a quarter his strength draw blood on someone as experienced as Rhushawn every day. Even the barbarian sees the matches differently than you. Part of him despises you every time you sneak past his guard. The other part of him sees you as a possible threat. But today, he saw your victory. Now don't move," he ordered.

Frustrated, Feylynn obeyed and held her words as he offered healing prayers. The warm tingling of his magic poured into Feylynn as Milt pushed on pressure points to loosen the muscles. As he finished, Feylynn took her first deep breath since she'd twisted her back out of place. "Thank you."

"You are welcome," he said kindly.

She wanted to clear up his misunderstanding. "Your praise is misplaced. I didn't walk here on my own. Lord Irel helped me stay upright and carried me when I couldn't go any further. And I hardly believe Rhushawn feels threatened by me in combat. He has proven himself enough times that I am sure of it," she said.

"Oh, Princess, you do threaten him," Milt insisted. "You threaten his culture and upbringing. You threaten how he views the world. He forfeited today because you won. Your refusal to give in would have defeated him on any battlefield. If it hadn't defeated his moral conscience, any man witnessing such courage in battle would have come to your side. Had you died in a real battle in such an honorable fashion, your men would have rallied. Your people would use your death for momentum for revenge and justice. That kind of defeat creates martyrs, and martyrs are dangerous fuel in war. Defeating an enemy is not always about steel and might."

Milt moved to the shelves along the far wall and took up his mortar and pestle to crush leaves for a tonic. "That sword you carry was created with fire and repeated strikes of the hammer. It was beaten into proper shape over hours, perhaps days, and with immense effort. Now and again, the steel resists the blacksmith's vision, and the metal is reworked again and again."

"Your adversity has the same effect. Every encounter shapes you and has strengthened your resolve. I no longer doubt that you, like your father, will make one of our finest Golden Dragon Knights we have ever seen," Milt added as he poured tonic from the kettle.

Humbled, and a little embarrassed by his proclamation, Feylynn lowered her head and stared at her small hands. She ran her thumb over her scraped knuckles wishing his words were true. She wanted to follow in her father's footsteps, but these last weeks she feared she would never be able to measure up to the Mighty Tisus and his legendary feats. As a child, she wished for little else than to take the sacred oath and swear fealty to Ranoak and the King. But during this last week, Feylynn couldn't fathom her future as a Golden Dragon would be anything like her father's. All she'd managed to do thus far is look foolish.

Milt pushed the hot tonic toward her, "Drink this, and you'll be well again in no time. Live to fight another day and such."

Live——Oh, Resora! Her sister's plight rushed through her mind. Here she sat wallowing in self-pity while Resora was possibly dying. She took the cup from the healer and sipped as an idea struck her. Time was short, and books would take days to sort through. Plus, Feylynn didn't know where to start. Whereas Milt, a renowned healer, stood right before her. She couldn't think of a better source for information. "Milt, can I ask you a question?"

"You can, but I make no promises as to whether or not I can answer," he teased.

"It's a serious question."

"Then I'll do my best to be serious," he said.

Feylynn stared into her cup to avoid letting her eyes give anything away. "Can you tell me about an affliction, a sickness, referred to as Dragon Touched?"

When he said nothing right away, she dared to glance up. Milt's smile had faltered. He glanced back at the entrance, then back to Feylynn with a sharp look in his eyes.

Her heart dropped to her stomach. She feared she made a colossal error in judgment by asking him so bluntly.

"Why do you ask?" he questioned.

She shrugged. "It's merely something I heard about. I was curious. Is it dangerous?"

"It's not a sickness, Princess," he said grimly. "It is a curse. An evil, incurable curse that started the first war between elves and men. Thankfully, that curse and all those afflicted with it died long ago."

Her stomach began to twist in knots. She had to know. "How—How did it... " She swallowed hard. Fear gripped her heart. "They. How did they die?"

"The curse drove elves into frenzied madness. They killed

many innocent people, and in the end, those cursed were annihilated. Of course, this was centuries ago during the first uprising. It hasn't manifested itself in any elf since. You will learn of the first uprising in your second year of studies. Unfortunately, after that, the wars were built on revenge for those slain on both sides. Don't worry. You'll study all of this eventually."

"Oh. So only elves suffer— I mean suffered, this curse?" Feylynn said as casually as she could manage, but her heart was breaking.

Milt nodded, "So history tells us. It was hereditary."

Feylynn had to ask. "This curse, where did it come from?"

"The evil machinations of a red dragon. As it was dying, it used the last of its magic to incite the curse upon the elves a great many centuries ago."

"A red? Are you certain?"

"Princess, you look a bit pale. Are you still in pain?"

"What? Oh, no!" She scrambled for an explanation. "I'm fine. The tonic, it never sits well with me."

"You barely drank any."

"Exactly," she said as if that explained it, and standing, she handed him the nearly full cup. "I think I would like to lie down for a little while. Thanks for your help today."

"Are you sure?"

She hastily headed to the entrance. "I am. I feel much better, thanks again. I am sure I'll be back soon enough, anyway." Before Milt could form a reply, Feylynn was scurrying away.

Her mind was racing, and she bit her nails as she walked down the corridor. She didn't even notice when Irel waved at her as she passed the common room. Instead, she went directly to the Paladin archives praying Milt was wrong. She spent the rest of the night pouring over records hoping that she could find something, anything to help. *Resora cannot be dying! There has to be a cure,* she thought.

She asked every Master in the archives for help to find lore on the great gold dragons they were named after. Feylynn poured over every record they gave her, but all of it was vague. Slapping her hands down on the table, she snarled, "There has to be more!"

One of the historians approached. "Princess? Is something wrong?"

"I am looking for gold dragons by name. There is nothing in these records to that effect. Can you help me?"

"I am sorry, Princess, very few of those records survived the war. Many were burned by King Eduar. Those that remain are not kept here."

"Take me to those records," Feylynn demanded.

"I'm sorry, Princess, but you need permission from the King himself."

Despair clawed at her belly. She couldn't ask her Father for permission, and there wasn't enough time to find them on her own with her current punishment. Milt's words swirled about in her head.

"Princess," the woman said, "why don't you retire since it is nearly dawn?"

Feylynn couldn't even believe the entire night had passed. She nearly conceded, but she needed something to tell her sisters. Swallowing hard, she asked, "What about reds? What do you have on the accursed red dragons?"

"My dear… "

"Please," Feylynn begged. "It's crucial."

The woman nodded and motioned for her to follow. Eager to comply, Feylynn trailed after her to the farthest corner of the archives. "I have two records on the Stealer of Souls," the woman said.

"You speak of a singular red," Feylynn observed. The record

keeper stood on tiptoe to pull out an old scroll of parchment wrapped with red ribbon.

"Yes, it is the only red we have by name. The rest of the records on the mighty red are conceptual. *Thaydarianasha* was different. These scrolls are old and both written by two bards of some renown. Thaydarianasha nearly tore our world apart, or so both records indicate. She was an ancient red, filled with blood lust. All the races upon the continent allied against her. When she was defeated several millennia ago, it is said she cursed the land and all who wielded magic. One bard, a dwarf, speaks of a curse she placed to steal magic from mankind. I suspect you cannot read dwarven."

"You're right. I can't."

"The other record… "

"What?" Feylynn pressed.

"Here," she said, handing Feylynn the scroll. "This one was written in Elvish. Though there is some argument about whether the elven bard Jalathin actually penned the record, its authenticity is questionable. Either way, this also names a curse."

Feylynn moved to the nearest table and pulled the lantern close. As she unrolled the scroll, her eyes darted across the elegant script, and her heart sank.

Shrinking with despair, Feylynn handed the scroll back to the woman with shaky fingers. She left the archives and went to her private chamber without a word. Distracted, she did not see Rhushawn waiting for her in the hallway as she passed him. He frowned at her appearance when he saw her behavior, but said nothing as Feylynn opened the chamber door like a ghostly wraith living in undeath.

The weight of the truth suffocated her. Feylynn had no idea how to send back such horrible news. Shutting the door to her room, she held on to the handle as she thought about it.

How am I supposed to tell my sisters that Resora is either dying or going mad?

She let go of the door and sat down at the small desk in her room. She tucked the hair behind her ear. "Is this why Father hasn't talked to them? Does he know?"

Taking up her quill with shaky fingers, it hovered above the parchment for several minutes. Eventually, she decided she couldn't do it. She couldn't tell her younger sisters the truth, even though her code demanded it. There had to be something more. *Why would the tyrant Eduar burn the records? Why would Father hide the rest?* If it killed her, Feylynn vowed she would keep Resora from this dire fate.

Instead of the whole truth, Feylynn told her sisters about possible insanity and a dragon's curse, but nothing she found offered strong conclusions and that she would keep searching for answers. Fearing they could find the same information, she wouldn't even tell her sisters the name of the ancient red dragon. Instead, she instructed them to find her an interpreter of the dwarven language. Feylynn couldn't bear to tell them the full truth and deny their hope, but she refused to give up.

THIRTY-ONE

C old wind cut through his damp cloak like sharpened steel, and he was acutely aware of the heavy mud caked on his boots. They were all filthy and exhausted. Sitting upon Soros, Micah's head bobbed with fatigue as the loyal horse plodded along at a slow, steady pace as if the destrier understood it was necessary.

Following along with a slight limp in her gait, Freesia trusted Micah and Soros to lead her through the worst of the sludge pulling at them with every step they took. He likely should have rested the night before, but understanding how close he was to his destination, combined with his knowledge of the woods, he chose to press on. Part of his decision rested on the hope that the cold night air would chill the ground enough to reduce the muddy conditions. It helped to be sure, but the long days traveling and the lack of rest that night dragged him down into unconsciousness.

His eyelids drooped as he patted the horse beneath him. He

275

half-heartedly mumbled, "A couple of minutes, my friend. Just a few..." Micah didn't even finish the thought before drifting off. Loyal Soros didn't falter as his master fell asleep and leaned forward in the saddle.

Micah wasn't sure how long he slept or what woke him first. Perhaps it was instinct or the sunlight filtering through the trees. It could have been the sound of movement on his left or the fact that the rhythmic plodding of his horse ceased. Maybe it was a combination of everything. Micah blinked several times and squinted against the bright sunlight assaulting his senses. Taking in his surroundings, the strain of the last month melted away like winter snow. Soros had brought them home.

Elated, the young Ranger dismounted and walked around to face his faithful horse. He tugged the reins down gently and laid his forehead against the horse's to thank him. *"Elin annon,* my friend. Your steadfastness is a debt I will never be able to repay."

"A good friend does not require a payment for his valor," offered a familiar voice.

At the sound of Ellomar's voice, Micah grinned and released the horse to face his old mentor. "Because a good friend acts on behalf of others, so often it is merely a way of life."

"So, it seems you did pay attention during your lessons."

"A good friend is like the old man who stands before me. Humility and kindness are at the core of his soul."

Ellomar shook his head and laughed lightly, "You need not flatter me. I am no longer in charge of you."

Warmth filled him, and Micah approached his mentor with open arms. "Well, if that's the case, I will have to work on some new insults."

They embraced with genuine affection. "It's so good to see you, Micah."

"Aye, it is good to be seen by your old eyes. How did you

know to find me here?"

"I have told you before. The forest speaks," Ellomar pulled back and squeezed Micah's shoulder. "Besides, my eyes are not so old. I can still outmaneuver you."

Micah tilted his head, and his eyes sparkled with challenge. "I think we should test that."

"No need, I followed you for at least a mile before you finally roused. Had I been your enemy, you would be dead." Still feeling light-hearted, Ellomar turned his attention to the mare behind them. "Nor am I so old that I can't see the limp in this beauty."

His light mood turned serious when he glanced back to Freesia, "She broke it, in a panic fighting the deep snow in the pass. The injury is severe."

Ellomar examined the front leg and rubbed his hands down the swollen joint.

"I did all I could for her."

"And then some, I'd wager," Ellomar said to assuage Micah's guilt. Upon examining the wound, he took note of the extensive healing upon the double break. "Your skills have improved since you left the glen."

"As you can see, it isn't completely healed. I could use your help," Micah explained.

Ellomar nodded. It was heartening for the old ranger to see Micah's healing abilities had progressed so far at such a young age. To heal her this much would have taken extreme patience and energy. A level of skill, not even Ellomar had when he was Micah's age. The young Ranger would have needed several long sessions to repair the mare's leg enough to bear weight.

As if reading his thoughts, Micah said, "It took three days using my gifts to get her to walk again. And with all my efforts, it still pains her a fortnight later. Can you help her?"

"There's reforming, but I think I can—" Micah's explanation

for the injury struck Ellomar suddenly. He glanced back at him with surprise in his eyes, "Wait! The pass? Dergin's pass?"

Micah nodded.

"What in all the realm could persuade you to attempt such an insane feat this time of year? You know better, Micah Finn! It's a wonder you came out of that pass alive at all, let alone with horses."

Feeling like a scolded child, Micah could not meet Ellomar's eyes. "It's the only route to The Enclave."

Ellomar scowled but understood Micah was not a fool. "What are you doing here, Lad? Why not send Cirus?"

"Dire news, I'm afraid."

"Could you not have sent—"

Micah cut him off with a shake of his head, "I could not send Cirus. He was not familiar with such a journey until now, and he awaits Princess Feylynn's response at The Enclave." He paused then corrected himself, "Though she should have sent that by now, so Cirus is likely back at Castle Ranoak."

Worried, Ellomar stood up straight. "The King? Has something happened?"

Micah shifted his feet and shook his head again, "No, not the King."

Relief flooded Ellomar until Micah pinned him with raw fear in his eyes. "It's Princess Resora. She's taken ill."

"It must be serious, indeed, for you to make such a dangerous journey."

"As I stand before you now, I have no way of knowing if Resora still lives," Micah admitted.

Untying Freesia's tether, Ellomar paused. "She's dying?"

"I do not know, but it does not look good."

"Tisus sends for his daughters then?" When Micah offered no response, Ellomar glanced over his shoulder and noted the young Ranger's reservations. "King Tisus does not know you have come. He did not send you to The Enclave."

"No. Nor did I go there to retrieve Feylynn. There is a far more complicated explanation for that."

"What more?"

Micah scanned the woods, "Ahanna?"

"She is training, closer to home. You may speak freely," Ellomar said and took hold of Freesia's reigns.

Likewise, Micah took up Soros' reigns once more and could not meet his mentor's eyes as they walked together. "What can you tell me of the Dragon Touched?"

Elomar gripped Micah's arm and forced him to look up. The older man stared at him in shock with his gold-flecked eyes. "What did you say, Lad?"

"Resora, King Tisus believes her Dragon Touched."

"You're sure? He told you this?"

"No. In truth, he barely speaks of it at all. He has not even told his daughters. King Tisus took me and one other across the frozen lands all the way to the edge of the Shilesta Wood to beg for help. We met with one named Halidril. I merely happened to be along for the ride when he did so. Why King Tisus entrusted me with this, I do not know."

Ellomar's jaw clenched as he took in his words.

Micah feared Ellomar would contact King Tisus and tell all, but the importance of the issue outweighed any consequences he may face, so he confessed everything. "Enreal is no fool, though, and she discovered the truth. She and Revi begged me to journey to The Enclave in search of answers. Or rather to implore Feylynn to look for answers in the ancient library."

"When?"

"I left Ranoak three fortnights past."

Ellomar shook his head, "No, when did Tisus journey to the

elven wood?"

Micah sighed, "We returned from the wood three days before I left for the Enclave."

Staring at the ground, Ellomar calculated the time and whispered, "Eight weeks." He glanced back at Micah. "How long has Princess Resora been ill?"

"Too long, I fear, the first signs struck her at the beginning of winter, and to my eyes, she worsens with each passing day."

Ellomar stared straight ahead toward the glen he called home and said nothing for a long time, and Micah did not press him. Finally, the old Ranger sighed, "Take the horses, fetch Ahanna, and brush these two down. I need a minute to think."

"Will you not tell me?"

"I fear I have little to tell, but Ahanna should hear of her sister from you. I need to clear my thoughts before I help Freesia in any case. Take the Princess her horse. The sight of Freesia will help soften the blow. I will tend the wound when I have properly prepared."

"How did you know the mare was Freesia?"

"Ahanna speaks of her often."

Trusting in Ellomar, Micah conceded with a nod and started away, but before he had gone two steps, he stopped. Without turning around, he said, "It's bad, isn't it?"

"Yes."

"Can Resora be cured?"

"Go see Ahanna, Lad."

His heart dropped and his shoulder's slumped.. Ellomar's failure to comment spoke volumes. He offered another nod of assent and left Ellomar alone.

As he followed the game trail with the horses in tow, Micah tried to compose himself to break the news to Ahanna, but all coherent thoughts fled when he entered the glen and saw her.

THIRTY-TWO

His breath caught in his throat, and all words failed him when Micah came upon the Princess during her sword practice. He remembered his days training here in the glen, but he was confident it looked nothing like the vision before him now.

Her long, blonde hair whipped around as Ahanna spun and brought her sword across the straw dummy in a downward block against an invisible strike. Then, turning back with lightning speed, she slashed upward against another straw foe. Stretching out one leg and bending the other knee, Ahanna dropped low and slashed at her opponent's legs. The sword was sharp, and it easily cut through the straw dummy's pole. As one attacker fell, she twisted around, came up fast, and impaled the other by driving her sword behind her.

Every move, every strike led her into the next. Just as Ellomar had taught him that no energy should be wasted, her two short swords were precise compliments of one another. Her slender frame lent her grace, her newly developed muscle offered her strength, and with both married together, Ahanna's fluid motions flowed together to create an exquisite dance of death.

To Micah's travel-weary eyes, she was a vision of absolute beauty. He could have stood there silently watching her sword-play for a long time yet, but upon seeing her mistress, Freesia had other ideas. The black mare let out a loud whinny, and stunned by the sound, Ahanna faltered in her graceful dance.

"Freesia?" she said.

If he lived a thousand years, Micah would never forget the way her eyes lit up when Ahanna realized the horse was indeed her mare.

"Freesia!" she squealed, and sheathing her weapons, she hurried over to them.

The horse whinnied once more as Ahanna came near, and the Princess laughed as she took the horse's head in her small hands and kissed her velvet nose. "Oh, how I have missed you, my sweet girl."

"She missed you," Micah said.

Ahanna turned her head to meet his eyes, "Micah! How did you even get here?"

"Not easily, I assure you. My mud-laden boots are a testament to the rigors of the early spring thaw."

"Mud laden boots aside, it's so good to see you." Ahanna ran her hands over Freesia's neck. "It's so good to see both of you," she said to Freesia as the horse leaned into her. Ahanna stumbled under her weight and laughed at Freesia's insistence for attention. She obliged the jealous mare and crooned accolades to her in Elvish.

As she doted on the mare, Micah realized the horse was not the only one capable of jealousy. He cleared his throat, "I see you've found some skill with the blade."

"Some," she said with a sly smile that weakened his knees.

As the gooey sensation filled his chest and belly, Micah's eyes caught sight of Ahanna's hair tucked behind her sharp ears. He lifted an awkward hand and almost touched it, but at the last second, he gestured to it instead, "You've changed it finally."

"I did," she said, blushing. "It still feels a bit strange."

"I like it."

She tilted her head away from him and rubbed Freesia's chin, "Thank you."

A warm buzzing started in his head, and Micah couldn't make his brain think of anything else. As the awkward moment pressed on, Ahanna turned her attention back to the horse. When she began to whisper promises to Freesia of a long ride together in grassy meadows, the buzzing in his head died, and Micah winced inwardly. Guilt replaced all other thoughts and settled in his chest like the weight of the heavy mud on his boots. "Princess, she cannot bear you. At least, not yet. I am so sorry."

Concern filled Ahanna's eyes. "Why? What's wrong with her?"

Micah pointed to the right front leg. "She broke it in Dergin's Pass. I've healed it as much as I can. Ellomar assures me he can heal her further. Until he does, it's best not to add any additional weight to it."

Ahanna bent low to run her hands along the injured leg. "Ellomar has been teaching me. Maybe I could help her."

"You have the gift?" Micah said with surprise.

"It awakened in me over the winter. I suspect my time with Ellomar opened me up to the possibility. Who knows, it could even be this place. There's something here that makes me feel—"

"Connected," Micah finished.

"Yes, exactly! You understand, then?"

Micah grinned, "I do."

Ahanna glanced back. Their eyes met, and her cheeks reddened. She quickly looked away from him again and focused on her old friend as she probed the injury more carefully. "Should I give it a go?"

Micah gripped Freesia's bridle to hold the mare in case she shied away, but trusting her mistress completely, Freesia lifted the leg as if offering Ahanna access.

"You are welcome to try, Princess, but Ellomar is far more experienced with animals as they are more difficult to heal. Their bodies are far different than ours. I know his gift far surpasses my own."

Ahanna pursed her lips, "You're probably right. I suppose it's best to wait for his guidance. I still have little control of healing magic and have barely used it to heal Ellomar's minor scrathes."

"In the meantime, both horses would appreciate a good brushing and some oats. Is there any left from the winter stores?"

Ahanna stood and brushed her hands together to clear off the dirt. "They're both in luck," she said as she took the mare's bridle and led her away.

Micah turned and rubbed his stallion's neck. "You hear that, Soros? The pretty girl has some oats for you."

Walking through the glen, Micah spotted an oddity in the distant tree line. "You have a spy in your midst."

Ahanna followed gaze, and seeing the young white wolf watching them, she smiled. "He comes about now and again. Won't come any closer than that though. I tried to coax him with a meal or two."

"I'm sure Ellomar's animal friends have a place in that. Their scent has to be all over this area."

"Maybe, but I think he's alone. I hate that."

"You can only do so much, Princess," Micah said as they set

the horses up with some feed. "You'll win him over eventually."

"You think so?"

Micah thought about his own feelings and knew the young wolf had no hope of resisting her. "I'm certain of it."

As they cared for the horses together, they fell into a familiar routine of hoof-checks, brushing, and feeding. Micah knew he should be telling her everything, but her smile was so genuine he couldn't take that from her yet. So, he kept the problems from home to himself a while longer. "Is Allaros awake yet?"

She grinned, "Of course you know about Allaros."

"I did live here for several years. He used to steal the berries I picked."

Ahanna laughed, "He does love his berries."

Grinning, Micah kept working the mud off Soros.

"Allaros hasn't crawled out of his cave yet. I took a hike up there three days ago and left him some fish in case he wanted a snack."

"He'll be grateful for that, no doubt," Micah said playfully as he checked Soros' back hooves.

Brushing the caked mud upon Freesia spiked Ahanna's curiosity, "Micah?"

"Yes, Princess?"

"Why are you here? I'm grateful that you brought Freesia to me, but why would my father send you to Dergin's Pass?"

Micah's hand hesitated, but he quickly corrected himself as he put his focus back into his task. His whole purpose for coming was to tell her what was happening back home. Now was his chance to do just that, but he found that he didn't want to be the one to break her heart.

"Micah?" she questioned with concern.

"Your father didn't send me," he said. "I went to The Enclave."

"The Enclave." Her eyes widened and she took a step closer.

"Feylynn! What's happened?"

Micah lamented the loss of her smile moments before. He loathed the idea of telling her about Resora, but he couldn't stall any longer. Resigned, he walked around Soros to face Ahanna. "Resora is ill. Terribly so."

Ahanna gripped his arm, "Resora?"

Micah nodded. "She has been ill for some time, and no one understands the truth of what plagues her. I traveled to The Enclave to leave word with Feylynn."

"How could this happen? The healers should help her."

Shaking his head, Micah explained, "They have exhausted every effort to help, and nothing is working." He took Ahanna's hand and rubbed his thumb over her cold skin. He poured his attention into the details of her hand because he couldn't face the sadness in her eyes. "There's more."

"What more?"

"Resora has been haunted by vivid dreams. Dreams of fire and dragons."

"Well, Father tells enough stories, I am sure—"

"No, Ahanna. Her dreams are specific and filled with peculiar insights. If what Enreal says is true, these dreams are terrifying and almost prophetic. She speaks of a gold dragon by name. A name no one has ever heard of, or at least no record exists. Nothing about this is recorded at the castle. Any records of gold dragons are kept at The Enclave. We asked Feylynn to seek information in the archives there."

"Micah, I don't understand. None of this makes sense."

"When Resora told Liddia of the dreams, Enreal knew the dressmaker was hiding something by her reactions. Then Enreal overheard your father and Liddia speak of something called Dragon Touched. Though he keeps this information to himself, the King's fear of whatever this sickness is, drove him to seek the elves in the Shilesta Woods."

"The elves, are they coming?"

Micah glowered, "No."

As he hesitated, Ahanna pleaded, "What is it? What do you know?"

"I was there with your father at the edge of the wood. He trusted me to travel with him. He trusted me with Resora's condition," Micah admitted with disbelief and a heavy heart.

"What happened?" Ahanna pressed.

Micah's expression turned dark as he remembered the elf with black hair and cold eyes. "There was an elf, Halidril by name. He refused to grant King Tisus access to the Queen. He spoke of tainting your mother's memory by allowing him to pass. They will not help us." He kept Halidril's caustic words about the Princesses to himself. He had no wish to upset Ahanna any more than he had to.

Ahanna pulled her hand away and turned to Freesia. She absent-mindedly ran her hand over the sleek black coat on the mare's back. In response, Freesia craned her neck and whinnied softly.

"Micah, is she— Is my sister dying?"

His eyes filled with sympathy. "I don't know, Princess."

"I have to go back," she whispered.

Micah's eyes widened. "Ahanna, if they see you—"

"I know."

"I don't think you do. Your father signed a treaty before you were born. He regrets it, of course, but he is no less bound to it than he was before you left. The Enclave will force you to go back with them. They will force you into an arranged marriage. If you refuse, it could create a whole new war. A war your father cannot win. How can he win a war against his own military?"

"Ellomar explained everything to me."

"Oh."

For a time, they said nothing, but when Micah couldn't stand the silence any longer, he said, "You cannot go back. Resora would not want that for you."

Ahanna sighed, "No, she wouldn't, but for my sisters, Micah, I will take any risk. I cannot cower here while Resora dies."

"Ahanna."

She shook her head, "I will accept whatever fate they throw at me."

"You won't have to accept anything," said Ellomar as he came upon them.

"I'm going back, Ellomar. I have to," Ahanna insisted.

He lifted his hands in surrender, "I agree. You should. But if we do this correctly, no one will even know."

"How?" Micah questioned.

"The festival," Ellomar offered. "By my calendar, the Fealty Festival approaches."

Micah calculated the days of his journey in his head. "It's close to be sure."

Ellomar shook his head, "Traveling through the pass has muddled your brain. The Golden Dragons will be making their own way through the pass in a week's time."

"That soon?" Micah questioned. His journey through the pass had nearly killed him. He had a hard time imagining it was clear enough for the gold and blue Knights.

"The journey from The Enclave to the glen must have taken you at least fourteen days. With a lame horse and the heavy mud, likely longer," Ellomar stated.

Micah nodded and thought about it. "I stayed at the inn several days to rest Freesia."

"Think now, that's nearly a month of warm spring days since you took the pass, Lad. Dergin's Pass will be much more hospitable by now."

Ahanna started counting the days herself. "He's right. The Fealty Festival is at the end of this month."

"If we go during the festival as merchants, and if we are careful with your appearance, no one will ever know you were there," Ellomar explained.

Ahanna stared at her mentor with worry in her eyes, "That's a long time to wait, Ellomar. What if she worsens?"

He approached her and placed his patient hands on her shoulders, "Ahanna, can you trust me in this? I promise you we will get there, but there is no reason to be foolish in the way you go about it."

Micah shook his head, "Ellomar, the might of the entire Enclave will be there. That's the worst time for her to be in Ranoak."

"Very few in The Enclave leadership would even bother to seek her out, and only a handful of those could recognize any of The Princesses. The long-kept secret of King Tisus is our biggest advantage. The festival is a celebration, and few can celebrate so hard as rigid soldiers that have been given far too many rules. Plus, traders, bards, and merchants will be coming in from all the regions of Ranoak. The crowds will be big enough to slip in and out without notice."

Micah didn't like it, but he trusted Ellomar. "Princess?"

"Promise we will get there in time," Ahanna begged.

"I cannot make you any such promise. You know that," Ellomar replied.

Ahanna bit her lip nervously.

"I'll leave right away," Micah injected. "If Resora is worse, I'll send word with Cirus."

Ahanna nodded her agreement.

"You will not leave without a proper meal and some rest. You can leave at first light," Ellomar corrected.

"I am—" Micah began.

Ahanna cut him off, "Ellomar's right. You're tired, and so is Soros. Take tonight. Even if I were to go, I would have to wait."

Micah nodded once. "Very well, one night."

THIRTY-THREE

RANOAK

Travel-weary and dirty, Micah rode through the gates of Ranoak. His shoulders sagged, his spine ached, and he wanted nothing more than a night's rest in a warm bed. The scent of spiced meats greeted him as he entered the city, and his belly rumbled, reminding him how meager his meals had been lately. After a while, surviving on trail rations made a man pine for a warm meal, but he didn't dare stop to enjoy one. He'd need to wait until he made it back to the castle.

The Ranger maneuvered Freesia through the streets toward the castle proper. After healing the mare in the glen, Ellomar insisted Micah take her back to Ranoak and leave Soros with them. Freesia was too recognizable to chance Ahanna and the horse ride together. No one loved the arrangement, but both Ahanna and Micah respected the wisdom of it.

Micah noticed the merchants getting ready with decorations for the Fealty Festival. Over the years, the festival had expanded, and the entire city was enveloped in the mood. It was no longer exclusive to the castle attendees as it had been in the beginning. In the coming weeks, the frivolity was extended throughout the entire city. Vendors and performers could be found in every tavern and throughout the market square.

He saw one of his favorite bakeries strung up flags, and seeing the Ranger, the baker waved.

"Will you be stopping in for some sweet rolls, young Ranger?"

Micah grinned. "I see you have new blue and gold banners for this year."

"Nah, not this year. Got them last year, but they held up nice. Seems like everyone's already hung theirs. I'm a bit late this year."

Micah glanced around and noted that the baker was right. Most of the shops have already set up their decorations. Likewise, a few traveling vendors already occupied some of the temporary vendor spaces.

"I suppose the biggest event in Ranoak deserves the best decorations," Micah observed.

"That's the truth," the baker agreed. "Been nigh on twenty-three years now since King Tisus saved us from King Eduar and the elves. We should make sure he knows how grateful we are. Too many sons and daughters were lost in those days. King Tisus deserves all we have."

Micah nodded. He learned the history at Tisus' feet, and he realized King Tisus didn't see it that way.E duar forced people into conscription, and during those years, King Eduar just chose his knights for political reasons.

In contrast, on the day he was crowned, Tisus offered any soldier the opportunity to swear fealty or request retirement from their military. The honorable retirement of any man wishing to vacate his role as a peace-keeping soldier was also included in the festival. Whether it was a single year, or twenty, Tisus recognized the importance of their contribution. He shook each man's hand as an equal, and all of them were given accolades based on their service.

Over the years, King Tisus made it a point to honor any who protected his kingdom. He learned as many names as he could and made every man who attended feel as though they mattered. Tisus offered the men who fought for him the dignity of choice and the respect of an equal.

"How's your leg doing?" Micah asked. This baker was one of those who retired after the war. He'd been injured during the time he served under Eduar's forced military.

"Oh, the winter weather makes it hard, but it's nothing I can't manage."

"Good to hear," Micah said. "Can I help you here and convince you to pack me some sweet rolls for the Princesses? It will be a nice surprise when I return."

"Sure thing," the baker said and stepped off his ladder.

Micah dismounted and tied Freesia to a post. Then, he took the baker's place and finished hanging the flags for the older man. As he did, he thought about what the festival meant for most people the baker's age.

The festival was a reminder of freedom. They were free from war, free from authoritarian rule, and free to choose their own paths. Tisus insisted all who served him should have the choice to enlist. There was not a single man that Tisus judged a coward.

Many lords thought him a fool for his award to past soldiers. But in the end, many of those same lords watched in horror as Tisus called them out for war crimes and mistreatment of those that served them in their own fiefs. Under King Tisus' new edicts, their lands were passed to more worthy men.

According to Ellomar, the process of weeding out the wicked

lords and securing a new military took over a year, but it reshaped the kingdom. A year after that, the entire Enclave, led by Master Carek, marched to Ranoak and swore their fealty to King Tisus a second time as a gesture of respect. Thus, a tradition was born. Now every year, the Paladins travel down from the mountain to swear allegiance to their King.

The baker came back with a small box in hand, "One roll for each princess, and one for yourself as well."

Grinning, Micah took the box. "How do you manage all the work during the five whole days of the festival by yourself?"

"Oh, I'm not really by myself anymore. I hired a lad for deliveries, and two young ladies help me in the kitchen now. I'm too old to do it all."

"It's good to hear you have help."

"In fact, I may even go watch the games during one of the days. It's been a few years since I saw would-be knights compete. The butcher's son is joining in this year. I think he's hoping the Master Knights will offer him a scholarship to The Enclave. He's a big kid. Should do well."

Competitors from the outlying fiefdoms engaged in challenges and matches every day so the Masters from The Enclave could evaluate the candidates for skilled new recruits. Some were offered paid scholarships, and they were announced the final night at the ball. The selected candidates left the festival's last day with the Knights and spent the next two years training at The Enclave before coming back and taking the oath.

"I hope he makes it. He'll train with Princess Feylynn if he does," Micah said.

The baker patted his back, "You best be on your way. You look beat, and I am sure you still need to see the King."

"Yes, I will tell him you are well. He asks about you now and then."

"Best thing I ever did was serve under King Tisus," the baker said.

"Me too," Micah said sincerely and mounted Freesia.

As he left, he thought about the upcoming events. Once the Knights arrived, King Tisus would be busy. The first night he would meet with the fiefdom Lords, and they would have dinner while renewing their oaths. The second night was devoted to the watch. And the third went to the castle guards. On each of their nights, they would get to renew their oaths and spend personal time with the King.

The entirety of the fourth evening was given to any paladin that could attend. A grand ball was held that night, but more so for graduates of The Enclave. Before the first pipe rang in playful melody, budding knights who passed their two-year training were offered the chance to kneel before the King with a fist to their heart. In years past, even the elves sent one or two representatives from Ilarith to attend the final night of the festival. However, Micah heard that practice stopped after their Ambassador Shelanna Morningsong disappeared.

"If the elves still came, what would they think of Ahanna now?" Micah wondered aloud.

Most of the people were relieved when they stopped coming, but Micah wondered if that instilled more fear in Tisus' daughters. Even though many in Ranoak were intrigued by the mysterious elves, the tense relationship between the races still left most people uneasy.

What the elves think doesn't matter, Micah reminded himself. *Ahanna will be a symbol just like her father one day.*

In his single act of mercy, which many thought foolish, Tisus had become a symbol of unity and loyalty. He once told Micah there was more power in one-hundred men who wanted to fight to preserve their way of life than one-thousand men who were forced to fight and were ambivalent to their causes. Seeing the streets every year, Micah knew he was right.

This year would be Micah's first chance to swear fealty to the King formally. He wasn't a Golden Dragon, nor was he a part of the city watch. As a ranger, Micah wasn't expected to take the oath. Rangers weren't really soldiers. Although rangers were still valuable, most were motivated by their own causes and reasons.

Being a ranger was more of a way of life. Micah wasn't a conscripted serviceman that followed orders and had a chain of command. Instead, rangers were hired out as guides or guards on the road. Men like Micah served the King or lords in the outlying lands directly, but they did so at their own desire for a contracted fee.

Still, Micah had asked King Tisus if he could take the oath months ago. Tisus was like a father to him, and Micah wanted the chance to show his gratitude and appreciation. So King Tisus set him up to participate in the oath on the fourth night after the Paladins since it was his first time.

Micah reached the inner gates, and the soldiers flagged him down. "Micah, where have you been?"

"I had an important matter to deal with."

"King Tisus requested an audience with you upon your return."

Micah dismounted and patted Freesia's neck affectionately. "Very well, I'll take care of Freesia and find him."

The guard let Micah pass, and he led Freesia back to the stables. He met up with one of the stable hands and passed the mare's care off to the young boy. "Make sure she gets some carrots. I promised her."

"Yes sir, I will," he replied.

Micah ruffled the boy's hair. "Thank you."

He hadn't made it two strides before the boy questioned,

"Sir? Where is Soros?"

Micah responded, "He was injured. An old friend will bring him along in a few days."

"I do hope he's alright."

"He's fine. Now go on. Freesia's tired. Brush her down and get her those carrots."

"Yes, sir," the boy said, leading the mare away.

Turning on his heel, Micah headed toward the castle. He passed under one of the gangway bridges and was knocked off balance when a crying young lady jumped into his arms.

"Micah! You're back!" Revienah said, muffled against his chest.

It took him a minute to orient himself. Micah was used to Revi jumping out from hidden places. What he didn't expect were her tears and the fierce way she clung to him. "What's this now? Resora is she... " He tried to say the words but couldn't force them out as he hugged her tightly.

Revienah shook her head against him, and he set her down to take her pixie-like face in his hands. She sniffled, "I'm just glad you're back, that's all." She pushed his hands away and struggled for that sassy attitude he was so familiar with.

"Revi?" He was the only one that consistently used the nickname, and it always made her feel special.

"It's true," she insisted. "I saw you, and well, I don't know. I can't explain it. Something just broke."

Micah reached out with one hand and wiped away her tears. "You're exhausted, Revi. The dark circles under your eyes tell me that. Have you been sneaking about at night?"

Ignoring the question, Revienah glared at him, "Are you saying I look like horse dung?"

He smiled, "Not dung, but kind of like an overcooked pie."

She folded her arms indignantly, "A pie?"

"Yeah, a little burnt around the edges, but still good."

"You're an idiot," she said with a smirk.

"You still laughed."

Revienah's smile widened, but she rolled her eyes.

He put an arm around her shoulders and started walking. "Come, I must find your father. He has requested that I report to him upon my return."

"He wants to ask you to stand with him when he receives the Knights."

Surprised, Micah asked, "What are you talking about? The castle commander stands with him."

"I heard things. That's all I know. You probably should bathe first. Father will smell you coming long before he sees you, and he might change his mind."

He raised a brow. "Are you saying I smell like horse dung?"

"That's precisely what I am saying."

Micah chuckled. "Fair enough."

"Get yourself cleaned up. I'll let Father know you're here. He's with Resora now anyway."

Micah's expression turned serious. "How is she?"

Revienah shook her head. "No change."

"At least she hasn't worsened while I was away."

Feeling melancholy again, Revienah stared down at her feet as they walked. "Micah?"

Understanding her concerns even without voicing them, Micah said, "Not here, Revi."

"Just tell me, are they okay?"

He nodded, "They both fair well."

"That's good. I was worried. I thought maybe... You know."

Micah took her arm and stopped her, "Thought what?"

"That maybe they would get sick too."

Stunned, he questioned, "Why in all the realms would you

think that?"

She shrugged, "No reason."

"Revi? What is it?"

"It's nothing."

His stomach dropped, and his eyes widened. He grabbed her again and checked for a fever. "Revi, are you sick? Enreal?"

"No! No, it's nothing like that. I swear," she said, pulling free.

"What is it then? What's bothering you?"

She turned her head away from him.

"Revi, talk to me."

"I'm scared," she admitted.

Micah saw the tears welling in her eyes again. He put a hand on her shoulder. "We're going to figure this out, Revi."

She nodded.

"I mean it. I swear on my father's grave, I will not stop until we have answers. You know none of us will."

"Father has given up," Revienah said. Her tone was laced with unexpected anger.

He hugged her again. "No, Revi, he would never."

"He won't even tell us the truth."

"Maybe he doesn't know any more than you do."

Revienah shook her head and pulled a small piece of paper from her pocket. "See for yourself."

"What's this?" Micah questioned as he unrolled the small paper. Revienah said nothing and let him read Feylynn's letter. "This can't be," he insisted.

"Are you saying Feylynn is lying?"

Micah scowled, "No, of course not, but she does not have any basis of fact. This is all hearsay. We have no way to know his reasoning for hiding the records."

"Does it matter? Resora is dying, and the only way to help

her is locked away at my own father's orders."

"You don't know that. You don't know if those records even contain anything that can help."

"What about the red dragon? What about the curse? That healer seems to know a lot."

"Lower your voice," Micah scolded.

She did and came closer so no one would hear, "All I know is we have no answers and more questions. Father knows something. I can see it in his eyes, but he tells us nothing. Meanwhile, Resora's dreams grow more vivid each day, and we know nothing more about these dragons, Feldorathanosh and Thay... Thaydarish... Oh! Whatever her name is. Without the records, we have no way of knowing how to help Resora."

Her words struck him like a blow to the face as Micah gripped her arms. "What did you say?" he asked, as her mouth closed, and her lips thinned into a tight line when she realized her mistake.

"Revi, what did you say?"

"It's nothing."

"Revienah, you know... Do you know the red's name? Did Resora tell you?" Somehow, he knew the truth before she answered. It was why her eyes were so tired and why the tears came so quickly.

"No."

He knelt before her, "Revi, talk to me."

She shook her head. "I don't want to."

"You've dreamed of it? Like Resora?"

Revienah nodded.

"How many times? How often?"

She refused to look at him. "I'm not sick," she mumbled.

He squeezed her arms, "How many times, Revienah?"

Sighing, she confessed, "She's come to me three times now."

His brows furrowed. "The red, it was female?"

300

Revienah nodded and tried to pull free, but Micah didn't release her as the rest of what she said hit him. "Wait. What do you mean, *come* to you?"

"It's like she talks to me. I don't like her." Revienah shivered at the memory of the terrifying red wyrm that haunted her.

"What does she say?"

Revienah waved it away with her hands, "It doesn't matter. It's only stupid dreams."

"What is her name?"

"I can't say it. It's a big name. Why does it matter?"

"You have to tell your sisters," Micah insisted.

"I can't. Enreal already has so much to worry about. I don't want to scare her, and Ahanna and Feylynn aren't here. There's nothing to be done about it anyway, and the last thing I need is a hoard of people watching my every move. You can't say anything, Micah. You have to promise."

"Revi."

"Micah, Enreal can't handle any more right now. I swear if it gets worse, I will speak up, but you have to promise you won't tell her."

Micah rubbed the back of his neck in frustration, then let his hand drop. "Fine, I won't tell Enreal. For now." He would, however, send word to Ellomar tonight.

Pointing her finger at him, she said, "Or Father."

He glared at her, and she demanded again, "Swear it, Micah."

He shook his head, "I can't promise you that, Revi. But for right now, I won't say anything, at least until after the festival."

"I suppose that's fair."

"You may not think so when I tell you I want a promise in return."

Annoyed, Revienah folded her arms again. "What?"

"You have to come tell me if you dream of her again."

She looked toward the castle, "I told you, I'm fine."

Micah mimicked her indignation and folded his arms as well. "Maybe so," he said, "but either you'll swear it to me, or I'll go right now and tell your father the truth."

"Fine."

He lifted a brow.

"Fine, I promise I will tell you if it happens again."

"Good enough."

THIRTY-FOUR

A t any given time, each fiefdom was assigned a garrison of sixty to two-hundred to five-hundred knights to protect their people and borders. Each Lord of those lands was responsible for feeding, ongoing training, and the general care of these men. Having been knights themselves, many lords were honor-bound to do so and took the responsibility seriously. The others were happy to have the King's might to keep them safe, so they accepted the trade-off required.

The Enclave housed nearly two-thousand hundred knights, and on average, two-hundred of those soldiers were trainees who hadn't earned the right to take the oath yet. A large number of the paladin army assigned to separate fiefdoms, made the long journey to the castle every year. Because they were so spread out and assignments often changed, the evening before the festival's first day, they all came together in a designated meadow as fellow soldiers.

Upon her horse, Feylynn looked at all the men eager for tomorrow's festivities. She looked to Irel, "I have seen the knights enter the city time and time again since I was a child, but it all was so formal. I saw them as proud and strong and nothing more. Looking at them now, you can see they are having the time of their lives seeing each other."

"Of course they are," Irel said. His whole face was smiling as he looked around. "Master Vasjoc told me that tonight is for the knights only. In some ways, it's a private party we look forward to when we are doing drills in the freezing rain. It only happens once a year. In this meadow, everyone gets to see old friends and share older stories around the warm light of the fire."

Feylynn realized here among the large group of men that he was in his element. Irel was a very social person, and this was the perfect place to be.

"Princess," Master Carek said as he approached. He had already dismounted and walked his horse behind.

Feylynn dismounted before she answered, "Yes, Master Carek?"

"Your tent will be near mine. It's already set up. The first group of troops to arrive usually set things up so later groups like us can still enjoy the evening."

"Yes, Sir."

"Fey," Irel said, putting a hand on her arm.

She turned to him, but not before she saw Master Carek's disapproval at Irel's lack of formality.

If Irel saw Carek's look, he didn't let it bother him. "I'm going to see some old friends. I'll catch up with you later."

Feylynn nodded.

After he left, Carek's expression made her want to squirm. "I know I should correct him, but it's nice to have a person that is comfortable around me. Do you always use my father's title when you speak to him?"

"Yes."

Feylynn sighed, "I merely wanted..." she stopped. "I'll talk to him."

Master Carek nodded. "I'll show you to your tent, Princess."

After she settled her horse and put her armor inside her tent, she tried to go out among the men to meet some more people and talk with her fellow trainees. The first problem occurred when Carek insisted on going with her, the second was her gender, and the third was her status. Walking around the camp was awkward at best. Men from the other fiefdoms bowed when she passed, and all eyes were drawn to her. Half gave her strange annoyed glances, and the other half offered lewd ones.

She was, after all, the first woman to join their ranks and the daughter of their King besides. Even though they all offered proper respect, none really wanted to spend the evening joking or competing in games of strength with her. It didn't take long for her to understand she would not easily find a group of men to spend the evening hours talking to. She went back to her tent and built a small fire. At her insistence, Carek left her as well to check on some other small matters.

Feylynn didn't let her lonely evening bother her. Accepting her lot, she found comfort in her father's teachings, *"Remember Feylynn. They will always see you differently. They cannot see past your title. In many ways, it is essential. In other ways, it is inconvenient. Even my oldest friends saw me in a different light when I was made King. I will not lie to you and tell you that's an easy thing, but there will come a day when you will understand the necessity."*

From out of nowhere, Rhushawn had come to her small fire without invitation, interrupting her thoughts.

She glared at him, "Rhushawn?"

He grunted and pushed one of two bowls of stew toward her.

Feylynn almost got up to leave him there and retire to her tent, but she suddenly realized the stubborn fool must feel as alone as she did. It wasn't as if the Knights would welcome a barbarian to compete in games of strength or share some mead with him.

So rather than scorn him, Feylynn did the honorable thing. She reached up and took the bowl he offered. "Thank you."

He nodded once and sat down with his own bowl.

Neither spoke a word, but at the very least, they weren't alone, and Feylynn found small comfort in that. They ate their meal together, and he stayed for a long time after, watching the groups around them. Then suddenly, when he deemed it late enough, Rhushawn stood and walked away without so much as a goodbye.

Feylynn huffed a small laugh and went inside her tent to get some rest. *Tomorrow will be a big day.*

Despite long days of travel and the ache in her shoulders, Princess Feylynn held her back straight. As she sat regal and proud upon her white destrier stallion, her royal blue cloak fluttered in the wind, and her polished armor glinted in the early afternoon sunlight. Excitement danced in her soul when she caught her first sight of home.

A little over four weeks had passed since the Knights of The Golden Dragon Enclave marched toward Ranoak. The journey dragged on too long for the Princess, but seeing Ranoak Castle set upon the hillside, her deep longing for home swelled to a crescendo. The dark grey stone, long ramparts, and the royal blue flag had never looked so beautiful. The flag fluttered with the same spring breeze that had freed tendrils of her dark hair from its braid. For Feylynn, the banner seemed to wave to her, welcoming her home.

It took a great deal of effort to maintain discipline and follow the slow procession of knights when she wanted nothing more than to gallop through the castle gates and find her father and her sisters.

Riding among the first line of soldiers, Feylynn understood the people would be watching. She would not falter in her training. Especially here, in this place that had given her everything, a home she cherished to the depths of her soul.

People from all over the region were traveling to Ranoak for the annual fealty festival. As a sign of respect, horses and wagons moved aside at the sight of the infamous knights as they made their way toward the castle. Tradition dictated that the gates would not open for the day until the procession of Knights came upon it.

Feylynn had never realized how much pomp and ceremony went into being a knight. So much of what they did was for show as much as it was for discipline. At midmorning, everyone mounted their horses with fresh faces, clean armor, and excitement for the holiday ahead. To Feylynn, meeting together a day early in order to march into the city as a mighty contingent rather than marching in as a smaller, weaker garrison in random intervals was far more about pride and showmanship than anything else. The horses were even taught to bow. How all of that could make her a better knight was beyond her.

Now, as Feylynn obediently kept her place in the procession, she watched as people moved to allow them passage. She noted the level of respect a whole contingent commanded as they walked the road to their King with stoic expressions and firm resolve.

Children waved with bright smiles, and men of various stations bowed or saluted with a fist to the heart. The people acted as if the Knights marched to war rather than into a week of frivolity. *And the women!* Feylynn thought with a roll of her eyes. The women blushed and tittered as some of the handsome younger warriors broke rank to sneak a grin or a wink in their direction. Irel, one of the ringleaders, offered silent flirtations from his seat.

The Masters at the head of the procession did not engage in any flirtatious games, and neither would she. Veterans of the old war sat proud and strong upon the largest warhorses available. Feylynn suspected the twenty Masters leading the army would have commanded the same level of respect on their own without the might of the soldiers behind them or the horses that bore them.

Master Carek nodded to the man riding to his left when they approached the massive gates leading to the city. Obeying the senior Knight, Master Raytheon pressed his lips to the legendary horn many said came from an ancient golden dragon, a king of fire. Master Raytheon blew, and the horn sounded off two alternating notes announcing their arrival to the city.

The sound of the horn vibrated in her chest, and being one of the Knights for the first time, the power and comfort the call offered filled her heart. In the distance, a second horn answered the first. It was the King's Call. She'd stood next to her father for years as he blew the returning call, welcoming his knights home. As a child, the emotion of that moment had been lost on her. However, today that sound meant everything to her. For today, she was home.

The groaning of the massive gates opening was as beautiful to her as the music of Enreal's voice. The Paladins didn't have to stop or slow, as the gates were timed perfectly to the marching contingent.

As practiced during their early drills at The Enclave, every row would drop back, allowing room for the two soldiers on the outside of each row to take up positions behind those they rode next to minutes before. This was done to accommodate the narrow streets in the city. Still, like everything else the Knights did, there was a sharp precision to their maneuvering, and a great many onlookers came to the gates that morning to watch the beauty of their formations.

On the other side of the gates, five-hundred knights assigned to Ranoak adorned with ceremonial armor and vivid blue capes lined the streets to welcome their brothers in arms home. Raytheon blew a short burst from the traditional horn at the front of the procession next to Master Carek. The sound of shifting armor clinked together when, as one, the Knights stood at attention with feet together, bowed their heads, and brought their gauntlet-covered fists to their chests.

The experience was a first for Feylynn. She'd never been down in the city when the procession arrived. In years past, she greeted the men at Castle Ranoak with her father. The warriors lining the streets would wait until the last row passed, then they would file in behind them and follow the rest of their brothers up to the castle.

Even though she understood the traditions set many years before, Princess Feylynn had never seen the significance of those traditions until this very moment. For the first time in her life, she was moved by the ceremony.

Then it was her turn to ride through, and Raytheon blew his horn one more time as Feylynn passed through the gates. Then, for the first time in twenty-three years, a second King's call sounded from Castle Ranoak.

The men lining the street took a knee to honor the Princess's return home. The essence of the gesture shook Feylynn to her core. Her eyes darted back and forth as the men held this respectful pose until she passed, and looking back over her shoulder, she realized they rose again and assumed their previous stance. As the shock wore off, she took a steadying breath and nodded to as many of them as she could, offering her own gesture of respect.

And hidden in the shadows behind an apothecary wagon that arrived in Ranoak yesterday afternoon, Ahanna Nacarian allowed the wet tears to slide down her cheeks as Ellomar's comforting hand rested on her shoulder.

THIRTY-FIVE

W hen they reached the castle, the Knights fell into their proper formation to greet their King, who stood upon the steps awaiting their return. Denaris stood on Tisus' left, and Feylynn was surprised to see Micah on her father's right, but she gave it little thought when she spotted her younger sisters. Enreal and Revienah, dressed in ornate gowns, stood near the castle doors according to custom. They both grinned as soon as they spotted their older sister, and despite all her formality earlier, Feylynn could not contain the beaming smile that slipped past her guard. Even the mighty Tisus grinned when he saw his daughter among the multitude.

Carek called the soldiers to attention, and with precise unity, the Knights lifted their fists to their hearts and tipped their heads in salute. This time though, Feylynn Nacarion, and her white stallion, bowed with the rest of them. The Princess looked at Tisus, and their eyes met. Father and daughter silently conveyed their thoughts. Feylynn saw the pride in his eyes, and Tisus saw the wonder of the day in her's.

Master Carek dismounted and approached him. He took three stairs and bowed. "Well met, Your Majesty."

King Tisus came down to stand before Carek, a gesture of great respect. Then he returned the same bow to the only other man who could have or possibly should have filled the role as King all those years before. "It is good to see you, my old friend."

Behind him, Denaris winced at the display of weakness in front of so many.

Grinning at each other like old fools, the two men gripped each other's arms in a boisterous forearm shake. Then, Tisus laughed, "Master Carek, the seasons pass so swiftly, and still, I feel as though it has been an age since you returned."

Carek lifted his free hand and gripped Tisus' shoulder, "It has been an age, maybe two, Your Majesty."

"Dismiss this lot then and let them have a bit of fun today. You and I shall go inside and reminisce about long ago battles as old men do."

Carek eyed him carefully. He knew Tisus better than any other despite the light tone and the laugh, so his obvious scrutiny had Tisus doing his best to appear unburdened. His old friend said nothing, but he could tell the Master Paladin saw something there by his expression.

Carek was no fool, though, and would wait for the opportune time to ask. Instead, he grinned and said, "So we shall." Carek turned to the men, "You are dismissed for the rest of the day. Report to your company commanders at dawn for further instructions and schedules."

There was a collective cheer that sounded as the Knights were given leave. Feylynn dismounted her stallion in a rush and led the horse through the throng of bodies to the people she wanted to see most in all the world.

There he is, she thought when she saw her father waiting on the stone steps. Enreal and Revienah didn't even let her get that far. They rushed to greet her with eager grins.

"Feylynn!" Revienah squealed as she jumped at her. Feylynn dropped the horse's leathers and caught her youngest sister in a tight embrace. Enreal didn't even wait for her turn. She simply wrapped her arms around them, and Feylynn used one arm to pull her in closer.

"Young Micah?" Carek called.

Watching the reunion between the Princesses with a smile on his face, Micah turned his attention to the Paladin. "Yes, Master Carek?"

"I am certain that Princess Feylynn would appreciate it if someone could tend her horse."

"Oh, yes, of course," Micah agreed.

When Tisus had asked Micah to stand with him today, the Ranger could not hide his surprise. He even tried to decline. Tisus could still see that confusion and awkwardness in Micah's actions. The young Ranger was more than ready to escape the formal event for quieter areas.

As if reading his mind, Micah asked, "Sire, do you require me for anything further?"

"No, not right now, Son. Like the others, take the day off, but it's best you're back by dinner tonight. I want you to join me with the Lords. As my Ranger, you should get to know all of them."

"Yes, Your Majesty, of course. I shall take my leave. Master Carek," he said respectfully.

"Micah," Carek returned.

The young Ranger descended the steps and passed the bundle of sisters. Then, taking up the obedient stallion's reins to lead him away, Micah turned and smiled at Feylynn, "Welcome home,

Princess."

Watching the girls huddled together, King Tisus felt a pang in his chest. *They should all be here together*, he thought with regret. The burden in his heart grew heavier every day. He'd known that Micah went to The Enclave. The boy had confessed as much to Tisus upon his return. What Micah hadn't admitted was that he'd seen Ahanna. Ellomar sent a message ahead of him.

For Tisus, the young man's loyalty to both his King and the King's daughters at the same time was impressive. Tisus intended to use that as long as Ahanna was forced to remain in exile. He would not have the future Queen of Ranoak uninformed. It was one of two reasons Tisus kept Micah close.

"Distance is a hard thing, old friend," Carek observed while Enreal wiped her joyful tears, and the girls laughed about something Revienah said that only they could hear.

"That it is," Tisus agreed.

"Where is Princess Resora? I expected she'd be here as well."

From behind them, Denaris cleared his throat, "Princess Resora is ill."

Carek turned to the Lord and offered his hand to acknowledge him formerly, "Denaris, you've hardly aged a day. How do you fair these days?"

Denaris ignored the proffered hand. "Well enough, I suppose. King Tisus keeps me busy." He said it as if being busy was a proclamation of his importance.

Denaris never got on well with Carek. As a former thief and a sworn paladin of truth, the two were ever at odds regarding the gray area of right and wrong during their traveling days. Carek was always careful to respect the man who was ten years his junior, but they never bonded so well as Tisus and Denaris. So Denaris was less than warm toward the Weapons Master for as long as they had known each other.

Next to Tisus now, Carek gripped his friend's shoulder again and smiled at Denaris. "Good enough then. I'm glad you're able to serve this stubborn ox and keep him in check."

Tisus laughed, "I fear that is an impossible task, but Denaris manages to do it better than any other. He has not tried splitting my head with a war hammer in his frustration at least."

"That was an accident," Carek protested.

"Yes, well on that note," Denaris interrupted. "I do have matters to attend to. Your Majesty," he bade while offering a half-bow and scurried off.

"Well, time may move swiftly, but some things never change," Carek said, thinking about Denaris and his cold shoulder.

Watching his daughters, Tisus said absently, "As our old masters used to say, change is inevitable, but while there is always change around us, at the core, few things actually do."

"I always hated that quote," Carek admitted. "But as I have grown in experience, I have learned the wisdom those words offer. Mankind is often doomed to repeat the same cycles. They all too easily set aside the lessons of the past when they feel life has swayed in their favor or disfavor."

Watching the two men tease each other, Feylynn grinned and disengaged from her sisters to approach her father. Stopping two steps below him, the Princess offered her father the respectful salute of fist to heart that had been ingrained in her at The Enclave. Tisus was having none of that formality. The big man grabbed her up with the same enthusiasm Revienah displayed minutes before.

Feylynn's heart sang as his hold nearly crushed her ribs even through her armor. "Hello, Father," she grunted.

"Welcome home, my girl."

When he finally set her down again, her smile was beaming. Revienah took Feylynn's hand, "Hurry. We must go see Resora. She is so eager to see you and pouted for hours that she couldn't be here, but she is far too sick to stand in the sun."

The King's smile wavered, and Enreal's whole demeanor shifted as if the weight of a large stone sat upon her small shoulders. Feylynn could feel Master Carek watching her, and lack of surprise at hearing her sister was ill might have given her away. Feylynn ignored his scrutiny and turned to her sisters, "Take me to her. For I have long hoped to see her too."

"Do you regret it?" Ellomar asked Ahanna as they set out bottles for selling later this afternoon. The pair had entered the city late yesterday and found this open spot to set up shop. Ellomar decided they should stick to their natural skills and suggested a guise as healers to not raise suspicion.

He managed to come up with apothecary elixirs and even made Ahanna concoct more than a few of them to sell. The common practice for healers included wearing traditional grey clothing, a white cap for men, and white head dressings for women. They did this to distinguish them from others and help those in need. It was a believable disguise. Health elixirs were a popular item in the city, especially the draughts used for stomach ailments. According to Ellomar, too many people indulged far too much during the festival.

Ahanna braided her long hair into a crown and pinned it tightly on top of her head. The headdress covered her whole head and neck, hiding her thick braid and even her ears.

"So?" Ellomar prodded.

She set down the last bottle and looked toward her mentor, "Humm?"

"Do you regret leaving?"

"No. Why would I?"

"Today, I thought, maybe..." Ellomar hedged.

Ahanna offered him a warm, wistful smile. "No, today comforted me. It assured me that I had made the right choice. Did you see her, Ellomar? She was brilliant."

"I saw her, but who's to say you would have been any less brilliant."

"I say."

He lifted a brow, "Why do you say? Should a leader not be chosen by those they lead?"

Ahanna shrugged, "It's never worked that way before."

Ellomar smirked, "You'd be very wrong about that. Many great battles in history have been key moments where the people made a choice about who they would follow."

Annoyed, she shook her head. "It doesn't matter anyway. I don't want the job."

Ellomar laughed this time, "You think your father wished for such a curse? The best leaders are the best because they don't covet the title in the first place."

"Were you even looking today? They *have* chosen her. She has their loyalty. Plus, I am nothing like him, and—" She looked around to make sure no one was close enough to hear. Then she lowered her voice. "Feylynn is just like him. She will be a far better queen."

"So *you* say."

Ahanna faced him with her hands on her hips, "I do say. Besides, there's no going back in any case."

Before Ellomar could press her anymore, Ahanna saw Micah jogging down the street, checking each wagon as if searching for them.

"Micah!" Ahanna called and waved her hands so he would see her.

Micah smiled when he saw them and hurried over. "This is a

bit different, then," he said when he finally reached them.

Ahanna pulled at her skirts. "And uncomfortable. I'd forgotten how cumbersome a dress that isn't made by Liddia can be." She chuckled, "Remind me to thank her if I ever see her again."

Micah's smile spread. "It's good to see you, Prin—"

"Anna," she said pointedly.

"Oh, yes, Anna," he said, catching on.

Noting the farmer watching them suspiciously, Ahanna offered a girlish giggle, "Honestly, I should be offended that you can't remember my name." Then, she pouted dramatically to sell it. "I thought I meant far more to you."

With his back to the farmer, Micah was unaware of the play and simply tilted his head quizzically. "You did?" Ahanna pinned him with a glare, and he tripped over his tongue, "I mean, you do! Of course, you do. That is . . ."

Ahanna rolled her eyes, and Ellomar covered his laugh with an awkward cough. Seeing Micah fumble made the farmer chuckle to himself, and he went about checking his produce once more.

"Nevermind," she murmured. Then, taking his hand, she pulled him away from the farmer closer to her own cart of wares.

"Aha... Anna," he caught himself this time. "Anna, if I hurt you, I swear it was not my intent."

Ellomar chortled, and putting his hand on Ahanna's shoulder, he said quietly, "If you want, I can play the role of the angry father and give him a boot to his backside for his stupidity."

She laughed with him, and Micah finally realized he had missed some part of the situation. "I'm not sure what happened here, but I'm going to guess it doesn't matter."

Still smiling, Ahanna agreed, "No, it doesn't matter. Just make sure you call me Anna while I'm in the city."

"I can do that."

Her smile fell, "What news, Micah? How is she?"

Micah furrowed his brow at the sight of her dismay. "She has not worsened, but she has not improved." Ahanna bit her lip as he continued, "She is too weak to walk on her own, and her fever persists."

Ellomar tipped his head. "Yet she has not worsened?"

"No. Gratefully, she has not worsened."

"I need to see her," Ahanna pleaded.

Micah took her by the shoulders, "I know, and I have a plan."

"What plan?" Ellomar questioned.

"I have spoken to Revienah and Enreal. They are expecting you. We have not told Resora. We fear in her condition she may say too much during her fits of delirium. After you have left the city, it won't matter if she mentions you."

"After I leave the city?" Ahanna said, confused. "We won't leave for days."

"I know, but I cannot get you to Resora until the final night."

"What?" Ahanna snapped. "I cannot wait that long."

Micah offered her a look of sympathy and lowered his voice, "You must be reasonable. Reasonable and patient. It is the best night to accomplish our goal."

Ellomar nodded, "He's right."

Ahanna threw her hands up and looked skyward, "Why? Why is he right?"

"Calm yourself, Anna," Ellomar said pointedly as people were looking at them now.

She closed her eyes and searched for some semblance of reason.

"Listen now," Ellomar insisted. Then, he gestured to Micah, "Go ahead, Lad."

"Every night during the festival, The Golden Dragons will be milling about the castle grounds. Many of them will be staying in assigned tents within the keep. The rest will be about the city, but make no mistake, their eyes will be ever watchful. You know this."

"I do," Ahanna agreed.

"Right then, getting past a few men the night you left was hard enough. Try to imagine getting past hundreds when the moon is full and bright."

Her stomach flipped at the thought. "This is stupid. Maybe I should turn myself in. At least then I could see her."

Micah held up his hands to slow her down before she acted rashly. "Think about it, the ball. On the last night, the whole of the Paladins attending will be in the castle to witness the Enclave's new members and their first oath to Tisus. After that, they will be trolling for ladies or enjoying the food at the ball."

"There will be few people about that night," Ellomar explained further. "Even the servants will be attending to the needs of celebration."

"Exactly!" Micah said excitedly. "You could have several hours with Resora rather than minutes."

"It could work," Ahanna said as she thought about it.

"It will work," Micah insisted. "Revienah says you know the way in, and it's a bit wider now. She will get you a stableman's outfit to help you stay inconspicuous when you are on the grounds, and she told me that she would leave it for you by the rock. I pray you understand her because she would not explain any further."

"I do. I know what she's talking about," Ahanna assured him.

"Good. Once you make it to the stables, hide there. I will stall Freesia earlier in the day, and you can stay with her. I will come for you when the coast is clear. Revienah and Enreal will attend the ball as expected, then as the night wanes and after you have seen Resora, they will meet you in the gardens, so they might steal a moment to see you as well."

"What of Feylynn?" she asked.

Micah swallowed hard. He winced as he glanced at Ellomar, then back to her. "You must understand."

Ahanna turned her head away from the pity in his eyes. "She's not coming."

"Feylynn sent a letter, weeks back, requesting they not tell her of your whereabouts, nor is she to even know if you are in the city. For both your sakes, she cannot risk knowing."

Ahanna nodded, but tears formed in her eyes.

Ellomar's heart filled with sympathy. "She cannot lie, and she would never wish to betray you. It is a double-edged sword."

"I know," Ahanna said quietly, and she wiped the tears with her sleeve. "It is a sword of my own making." She took a steadying breath before she met Micah's eyes once more. "I know, she's right," she said louder this time to assure him. "Can you tell her..." Ahanna squeezed her eyes shut again to keep the emotion back. "Will you tell her I love her?"

Micah shook his head, "No."

Ellomar folded his hands over his chest, and Ahanna's nose scrunched up with new irritation. "And why not?"

"Because you will tell her yourself."

"How do you propose I do that?" she asked.

Micah picked up the quill from a record book resting next to him and handed it to her. "With this."

Catching on, Ahanna rolled the stem of the quill between her fingers. "Oh."

"Have a letter ready for me for both Feylynn and your father by tomorrow, and I will deliver them when the time is right."

"You must be very cautious of what you say in those letters," Ellomar warned. "Not even your father knows of your where-abouts. He only knows that you are in my care."

"I understand," Ahanna said and chewed her bottom lip

nervously.

"Good enough then," Micah said with relief. "I will come back tomorrow afternoon to check in and as my duties allow the other days. If anything changes, I will let you know right away."

"Thank you, Micah," Ahanna said.

Micah pulled a hand through his hair. "It's nothing."

Ellomar guffawed and leaned in close, "Nothing? You're too modest, Lad. Why, you could be hanged for this. Imagine what could happen if they discover you're hiding the Crowned Princess from King Tisus."

Micah looked skyward for patience as Ahanna became more and more distressed and looked at Ellomar. "Hanged!" she whispered harshly.

Ellomar nodded his head with exaggeration, "Oh, yes. They might even charge him with treason."

"Micah!" she exclaimed as she turned her focus back to him with wide eyes.

"I don't think that is a likely outcome," Micah reasoned.

"Are you kidding?" Ellomar replied. "Treason is a grave matter."

Micah glared at the old Ranger and said, "I do not believe King Tisus will see it as such."

"Tisus! No, Lad, treason is handled by The Enclave. It's them you must worry about, and they're a canny bunch. Your sacrifice is—"

A young woman in her mid-twenties approached their cart. "Excuse me?"

Ellomar never finished his thought as he went around them and smiled at the woman. "Yes, madam."

"I'm looking for an elixir for my husband. He has a bit of a sick stomach, I'm afraid."

"Ah, yes, I have just the thing," Ellomar assured and guided her to the other side of the wagon.

Ahanna took Micah by the arm and pulled him to the street. She scanned the crowd, clearly frustrated.

Micah shook his head, silently cursing the old Ranger for worrying her. "Ah... Anna, I'll be fine. Don't worry too much. He exaggerates."

"I didn't think—None of us did," she confessed.

"It's not—"

"Please." She put a hand on his chest as she looked up at him. "Please, Micah. I'm sorry for it. I will not see you hanging for me."

Not for the first time, his mind muddled as she looked at him. Micah gently gripped her fingers. "Ahanna, I will not hang. I promise you."

"Swear you'll be careful. Do not risk your life for my sisters or me."

Micah looked back to the old Ranger near the wagon, and his mentor offered him nothing but a wink. He looked back to her and met her exotic green eyes, and for a second time, his mind turned to mush.

"Promise me."

"I promise," he said.

Realizing how close they were for the first time, Ahanna pulled free of his grip, and they both took a step back. She looked away from him when she said, "Alright then, you'll be careful?"

"Sure."

"Good."

They stood there awkwardly for a few more moments. Then, finally, Ahanna glanced back at Ellomar, who was being crowded by a few more people shopping there. Following her line of sight and seeing the same thing, Micah cleared his throat, "You best go help him."

"Yes. You're right." She took up her skirt in one hand and started back.

A small part of him wanted to stop her, but after a second of deliberation, he turned back himself. As he started walking away, someone gripped his arm and pulled him to a stop. "Micah," Ahanna said.

Elated that she came back, he smiled, "Miss me already?"

She lifted a brow and grinned, "I forgot to tell you, we stabled Soros at the inn around the corner. I am sure he would appreciate a visit."

"Oh. I'll take him an apple later."

She was already turning away, "I'll see you tomorrow then?"

"Yes. Tomorrow," Micah agreed, and she left him there.

THIRTY-SIX

Feylynn allowed Revienah to pull her along the corridor to Resora. As she entered her sister's bed-chamber, she took note of the cloying scents first. The unique stench of sweat, fever, and a rebellious belly, all tucked behind stuffy stone walls, clung stubbornly to the air. Then Feylynn saw the new tapestry, the fluffy replacement bedding, and caught the faint shadow of a smoky aroma.

She almost asked what happened, but Revienah let go of Feylynn's hand. Ignoring the fact that Lord Denaris sat on the opposite side holding Resora's hand, Revienah hurried to the bed. Startled upon their sudden arrival, Denaris popped up to his feet.

The Lord slipped a hand behind his back and one in front, as he bowed formally to the girls, "Ladies. I expected you'd come this way. I wanted to check on Princess Resora to make sure she was up to visitors."

Bothered by his behavior, Feylynn came closer, "Are the

healers not attending her?"

"They do," Enreal answered, "but Lord Denaris makes sure to stop in every day to verify they are doing all they can. He's been very kind."

"Thank you, Princess, for saying so. I am pleased to report that the Princess' fever has ebbed once more. Though I am sorry to say it is likely temporary."

Enreal stepped past him to check Resora's brow, "We'll take whatever time we can get. I appreciate your diligence, My Lord." She took up the damp cloth they used to cool Resora and dabbed her sister's brow gently.

Watching, Denaris said, "It's nothing. I am happy to offer you a reprieve. As the King's friend and advisor, I want to ensure the rest of you do not neglect yourselves. Your father could not withstand the loss of yet another daughter."

Feeling the weight of her choice to leave her sisters while staring at Resora's frail, sleeping form, Feylynn snapped, "He hasn't lost one yet, nor will we lose this one."

Lord Denaris scowled, "Has he not lost Ahanna to the wild? We've had no word from her as of yet."

"That does not mean she is lost. On the contrary, perhaps she is finding herself. *Princess* Ahanna will come back sooner or later," Feylynn corrected.

He stared at her with his knowing eyes, "I see. I would have hoped that you of all people understood any contact with Ahanna must be reported forthwith."

Enreal's lips thinned into a tight line of worry, and she fidgeted with the cloth in her hands as she glanced at Revienah. Their eyes met, and Revienah shook her head to keep a nervous Enreal from interfering. But intent on Feylynn, Denaris did not notice their exchange.

Irritated, their older sister stood taller, prouder, and pinned him with an icy glare, "Lord Denaris, are you accusing me of betraying the Code of Honor?"

"Have you? Did Ahanna contact you?"

"*Princess* Ahanna," Feylynn corrected again.

"She abandoned that title when she ran away and abandoned her obligations to Ranoak," he countered.

Feylynn checked her temper as was expected, but she took a deliberate step closer to Resora's bedside. Revienah shuffled up toward her sleeping twin in the large bed, so she was out of the way and would not be between them.

Nervous now, Enreal set down the wet cloth in the water basin. "Lord—"

Feylynn lifted a hand to stop her sister. "My Lord, as you well know, my father still names Ahanna as his successor," she said with a firm and even tone to avoid disturbing Resora.

"Which defies the treaty," Denaris was quick to point out.

"Not until she turns twenty-three years of age. I have read the treaty and understand the guidelines within it."

Denaris smirked at her admission, but Feylynn offered him no chance to speak, "Until that time or until such time that my father and your King says differently, no matter where my sister is, Ahanna is still the Crowned Princess of Ranoak, and as a Golden Dragon Knight of Ranoak, I will insist that *Princess* Ahanna is afforded the respect that comes with that title. Whether she is present or not."

Denaris tilted his head respectfully. "My apologies, Princess Feylynn. I will endeavor to remember your corrections. Still, I noticed you did not answer my question."

As if the tension in the room disturbed her, Resora stirred slightly and moaned in her sleep, but Feylynn would not let the matter drop. His accusation opened too many dangerous doors. Releasing her tight grip on the sword, Feylynn clenched her fist instead and brought it to her heart. "I have not had any contact from Princess Ahanna since the evening before her departure. If you feel I have lied or deceived you, I accept that your station, *Lord* Denaris, entitles you to request the Masters of The Enclave conduct an inquiry. As a Golden Dragon recruit, I will accept their judgment, whatever it may be."

Enreal put a gentle hand on the lord's arm to plead with him. "I'm sure that won't be necessary. Please, My Lord, we are all grieving here. And as her sisters, we all continue to hope for Princess Ahanna's safe return. We cannot count her as lost to us, for it is too painful to think of."

His jaw tight, Lord Denaris glanced at her, and after a moment, relented, "Of course you are right, Princess Enreal. Emotions are high these days." He offered her a brief smile and patted her hand.

Resora stirred again.

Revienah leaned in close to her twin, "Resora, wake up. I have a surprise for you.

"Revienah, let her sleep," Feylynn admonished. "I have all day and have nowhere else to be. I can wait."

Lord Denaris tilted his head, "Do you not intend to make an appearance at the dinner tonight?"

Still irritated, Feylynn had to invest significant effort to calm her sharp tone. "No, my father has already given us permission to stay with Resora."

By looking at the Lord's face, she realized she was not as successful as she hoped. "Very well, then. I shall leave the young Princess in your care. Do let me know if you should need anything."

Feylynn glanced back at the door one more time. Denaris had never been overly fond of her. In fact he had never been overly fond of anyone, but the encounter left her edgy. She couldn't figure out why he would take such an interest in Resora.

"Right, Feylynn?" Revienah said.

"What?"

"Were you even listening?" Revienah accused.

Enreal smiled patiently, "No. She clearly wasn't."

Feylynn sighed, "I am forced to admit Enreal is correct. My mind was elsewhere. Could you please repeat what you said?"

Revienah's brow scrunched in distaste. "What's wrong with you? Why are you talking like that?"

"I don't know what you mean."

Enreal sat on the bed next to a sleeping Resora, "She is referring to the proper tone you're using as if you're still lecturing Lord Denaris."

"I wasn't—" Feylynn began.

"You were," both sisters said at the same time.

Feylynn sighed, but before she could apologize, Resora groaned again, her brow wrinkled as her head rolled to the side. "Revienah?" Opening her eyes, Resora blinked several times to adjust to the daylight streaming through the window.

"You're awake!" Revienah exclaimed and moved so Resora could see Feylynn. "Look who came to see you!"

Barely awake, Resora lifted her head and followed Revienah's finger. When she saw Feylynn standing there in her room, she started to cry. "Feylynn," she croaked.

Feylynn was there the next second, crowding Revienah as she leaned over and kissed her sister's fevered brow. Taking her hand, she fell to one knee next to the bed. "Can you forgive me, Resora?"

Enreal and Revienah glanced at each other to share in their surprise at Feylynn's action.

"I don't understand," Resora replied softly.

"I did not come when you needed me," Feylynn confessed. The sharp, formal tone from before was gone, replaced with the emotions of an protective older sister. "When I heard you were ill, day in and day out, I could only think about how I abandoned you. Yet, I did nothing to fix it. I left you all here for selfish reasons, and I am not sure I can do it a second time."

Resora took Feylynn's hand, "There is nothing more you can do, and there is nothing to forgive," she croaked.

Feylynn stood to fill Resora's water cup from the pitcher next to it. "Here," she said, handing her sister the drink as Enreal helped her sit up. "This will help your dry throat."

Resora took the cup and sipped. She choked and coughed but drank the whole cup before she regained her voice. "Not even the greatest healers in Ranoak can help me."

Feylynn eased the cup from Resora's hand, setting it aside. "I am here now," she said, taking her hand once more. "And I won't stop looking until we have answers."

Shaking her head in denial, Resora met Feylynn's eyes. "You mustn't throw away your dream to sit here and watch me weaken every day until there is nothing left. I think—I think I am dying, Feylynn."

"Stop speaking in such a foolish manner," Enreal admonished.

"You are not dying," Feylynn insisted. "We won't let you."

Enreal glanced at Feylynn before she said, "They'll figure this out. We'll figure this out."

Despite her strong tone, Feylynn saw the fear in her sister's eyes, and she knew Resora saw it too when watery tears spilled down her cheeks, "I don't think anyone can help. I'm scared."

Revienah slammed her fists on the mattress then jumped off the bed in frustration. "If anyone can help, it's Father! Why won't he do anything? We should tell him that we know."

Enreal was shaking her head before Revienah even finished. "We can't. For whatever reason, and Father must have one, he doesn't wish to speak of it. Micah said he is trying. He went to the elves."

Revienah sighed, "When Ahanna—"

"Stop right there," Feylynn said with her hands out. "Did you not sit on this bed minutes ago and hear Lord Denaris' accusation? You cannot speak of Ahanna when I am present."

"This is so stupid," Revienah said, plopping back on the edge of the bed and yanking a loose thread from the quilt.

Resora let go of Feylynn's hand and laid it on Revienah's, "Let's not talk about this. These times when I feel well enough to enjoy you all are so brief. Feylynn, will you tell us about the Enclave? There must be so many amazing things there."

After a weary glance at Revienah, Feylynn offered Resora a patient smile and sat next to Revienah on the end of the bed, "There's not so much to tell, I'm afraid. My days are spent training and doing chores. I've had very little time to explore."

"I'll bet you've seen more than you think," Enreal offered. "Are the paintings we have here a resemblance?"

"If I am being honest, the artwork, while beautiful, does not do The Enclave justice. Its beauty would be hard to capture in such a way. The main structure was built with perfect continuity within the mountain. The walls are massive pieces of white stone harvested from the mountain itself ages ago. Getting to the gate is no small feat as it is all uphill, and you must cross a stone bridge to reach the main courtyard. From a distance, it does not look so big, as the mountain dwarfs its size, but as you cross the bridge, you realize the enormity of The Enclave is staggering."

"Bigger than Castle Ranoak?" Resora asked.

Feylynn nodded, "I still often get turned around, and I have been there for months. Outside there are vast gardens. And either side, water spills from the mountain above into the river far below. There are two more bridges to separate sections that were added later. The student quarters are on the east side of those bridges, so

I walk them often. Sometimes I am distracted by the might of the mountain waterfalls."

"Where do you train?" Revienah questioned.

"There are training grounds for combat and cavalry education. Inside, there are rooms upon rooms for study as well. Even the library is easily three times the size of ours here, and the histories kept there…" As a lover of knowledge, Feylynn smiled wistfully. "I think that is my favorite place at the Enclave."

"It sounds amazing," Resora observed softly.

Smiling at her wistful tone, Feylynn decided to indulge them further. "When we first neared The Enclave, we came upon an orchard that was filled with crisp, green apples and plump, juicy peaches that were both sweet and tart all at once. Up at The Enclave, they serve them during the early fall. My mouth waters just thinking about them. Of course, those trees are filled with new blooms now.

"In winter, the heavy snow blankets the mountain so thickly that at night, you can stand upon the parapets, and it feels as if the whole realm has been silenced. I spent many bright moonlit nights looking at the mountain's winter splendor."

"What about the other knights in training?" Revienah asked. "I bet some of them are worth looking at too."

"Revienah!" Feylynn admonished, but Enreal giggled, and Resora's lips tilted up contentedly as she laid back against the pillows.

Feylynn couldn't help it, and with twinkling eyes, she grinned as well.

"I knew it!" Revienah said joyfully. "Tell us all about them."

Embarrassed, the heat in her cheeks flared to life, and she rolled her eyes to brush it off. "Honestly, Revienah, most of the men want nothing to do with me. There are only a few recruits that will even talk to me."

Curious, Resora prodded, "Who?"

Feylynn stood. She didn't want to let Resora down, but talking about this had butterflies flitting about in her belly, "Well, there's Irel, and—"

"Wait," Enreal interrupted. "Lord Irel Danoral?"

"Yes."

Enreal's eyes widened. "You should be careful with that one. He's earned a reputation among the ladies even here in Ranoak."

"How would you know?" Feylynn asked.

Enreal blushed, "I heard about him from my lady maids. They told me to steer clear of him."

"But he's so handsome," Resora said. "I watched him last year. All the girls like him."

Revienah stood up on the bed. Then, jumping off again, she said, "I heard he only likes the best girls, so of course he likes our Feylynn."

"It doesn't matter what his reputation is or what he likes. We're only friends," Feylynn insisted.

"Hmm," Enreal said with skepticism, "What's he like then?"

Feylynn shifted and fidgeted with the flowers on the table, "He's a happy sort, and he makes me laugh. He's a devil with swords. He uses two blades at once, and I've never seen the like of it. Irel tried to teach me how to wield two swords, but I much prefer my shield. I've never bested him yet, but then again, there are a few I still cannot best," Feylynn admitted when her last match with Rhushawn popped into her head. She smiled when she remembered Irel's aide at the end of that match. "He's often chivalrous but a bit mischievous."

"He's trying to court you," Resora said sleepily.

"I'd say it's working," Revienah added as she hopped back on the bed next to Resora.

"Stop it." Feylynn protested. "He is doing no such thing."

The twins laughed together, and exasperated Feylynn waved it aside with her hand.

THIRTY-SEVEN

own the hallway, Tisus sat in his receiving room in front of a fire next to his oldest friend. In their youth, Carek and Tisus had trained together from the beginning of their inscription. The rest of their friends came later after Tisus was made captain. Sitting here with Carek had his sentimental mind reflecting on the past. He thought of all his old friends tonight. The ones that were still close to him and the ones he regrettably lost.

Even as a twenty-one-year-old novice captain, Tisus had been smart enough to know paladins were not the only assets in the war. Over time, he cultivated his unit with multiple men of various forms of talent.

Ellomar helped him and the men navigate the wilds, and his aim was unrivaled by even the elves' standards. Kirren, may his soul be at peace, was a faithful follower of Ealoram, but that faith never kept him out of a fight. He was a fierce brawler, and

Kirren's tenacity alone helped his party avoid death more than once. Of course, it helped that he was, in fact, one of the most powerful healers of his time, and whenever Tisus' men skirted death, Kirren kept them on their feet.

Then there was Denaris. Denaris was clever and could often outthink his opponents. As a small man, he had a knack for sneaking into places few would ever dare to go, and he could gather the most useful information as a result. The former thief could pick a man's pocket while staring him in the eye and making him laugh simultaneously. The victim wouldn't even know until it was too late, and he would not even be able to place who had done it. It was not a skill Tisus had always appreciated, but during the war, that skill had led them to find a path to end all the bloodshed, and it also led Tisus to Shelanna.

For that alone, Tisus would be indebted to Denaris for as long as he lived. Shelanna, his sweet Shelanna. She had been the greatest sword master that likely ever lived. And a devoted mother besides. If she were here, Shelanna would have already found a way to help Resora. His heart twinged as an image of her smile flashed into his mind. Out of habit, his fingers rubbed the miniature likeness he kept in his pocket.

Carek set down his glass on the table and sat forward in his chair, "Are you going to tell me?"

Pulled from his musings of the past, Tisus shook his head. "I'm not sure I should."

"How bad is it, old friend?"

The weight of the last months pressed down on Tisus. "I am not sure it could be any worse."

"You did not send word. I would have come."

"I couldn't," Tisus muttered.

"What is it? What has made her so ill?"

Tisus shook his head and stood up. He needed some air. He

needed a miracle. "She's dying. Or at least she might be. Though I am not sure living in her condition would be better. I pray for it every day, but Ealoram has not heard."

"The healers told you this?"

"No."

"Then surely they can do something," Carek insisted. "And if they can't, call on Ellomar."

"No, there is no cure for what she suffers. The healers don't even understand."

"Do you?" Carek asked. His features pinched as he peered into the fire and tried to figure out what Tisus was not saying. "We are too old for these games of half-truths and unsaid words."

Tisus threw up his hands, "It's all I have. I cannot speak of it, and maybe that's best. She's my daughter, and I would die even by your blade to protect her."

Shocked, Carek stood, "Surely you don't think I would ever come against you?"

"I pray for that too."

Tisus' words were so sincere and so tired, Carek found himself surprised. His friend's eyes had genuine fear in them. "Why would I ever—" Even as he started to ask, the possibility of an old truth hit him. "No, surely not," he said in a breath filled with disbelief.

Offering Carek nothing, Tisus turned away once more. He wasn't sure what he'd just done, but some outside force had driven him to this guessing game. If The Enclave found out about Resora, they would haul her away in chains and keep her contained. Still, there was this knot twisting in his gut, and he needed to know where Carek would stand. Because no matter the cost, Tisus would stand in front of his daughter with his sword pointing at any man wishing her harm.

Sooner or later, the truth would come out, and Tisus' first

attempt for help had failed miserably. His second desperate idea had not received any response, and his praying was getting him no closer to a solution. Right then, when it was just the two of them, Tisus had to know if Carek's oath of fealty or even one of friendship could outweigh his oath to the order of The Golden Dragons.

Carek paced the room, "This isn't possible, the line to that... the connection... It's gone. It hasn't existed for a long time."

"What if it wasn't? What if it did?" Tisus asked, standing a little taller. There was no going back now. His chest tightened, knowing he had to choose his words carefully.

"What are you telling me, Tisus?"

"I have told you nothing. What's more, I cannot tell you anything. I merely allow you to make unprovable assumptions. But what if you could prove it? What if your assumption proved true, and it required you to choose a side? Where would Carek Breowyn stand then?"

Scowling, Carek stomped over to stand before his King, "What kind of question is that?"

"A desperate one," Tisus admitted, and this time it was fear that clutched his heart.

Carek didn't even hesitate as he put a hand on Tisus' shoulder, "I have failed you if you feel you even have to ask, but I will always stand by my King. And I will forever stand with my friend."

The tightness of Tisus' stomach eased for the first time in weeks. "I had to be sure."

"Then be sure that my blade is yours. Your family is mine, and my fealty will always be with you, first and foremost."

"Then sit down, my old friend, I have a tale to tell, and I need you to pay attention. I am still bound by my oath and cannot tell you all this night, but I will give you what I can."

As Resora requested, the sisters spent the rest of the day's hours avoiding disscussions about curses, dragons, or Ahanna. Feylynn could not deny Resora such a simple wish when it made her smile. She figured there would be plenty of time for that in the days ahead. In the hours after the sun fell, they heard the noise from the festival filter in, but none of them cared much. Being together after so long was better than any celebration. Eventually, Resora dozed off, and Feylynn sent Revienah and Enreal to get some supper.

Alone now with a crackling fire in the dim room, Feylynn sat on the chair next to Resora's bed, holding her sister's limp hand. With her eyes closed, she whispered a prayer to Ealoram for guidance and hope. The flame on the few candles in the room swayed as the night breeze cooled the room, but that cool air did little to help her sister. Resora slept fitfully as her temperature climbed again. According to Enreal, this was a common cycle.

Lord Denaris entered, interrupting her. "Princess Feylynn. I do apologize. I heard you went to eat."

Feylynn didn't look at him right away. Instead, she silently finished her prayer. When she was done, Feylynn kept her attention on Resora as she replied, "I sent my younger sisters along. They will bring something back. I'll be staying here with Resora as often as my duties allow this week."

"Surely you want to attend some of the festivities?" Denaris suggested.

"Why in the realm would I do that when Resora lies here in such an uncertain condition?" Lifting her head, Feylynn finally met his eyes, "I am not here for games and celebrations. I am here as the daughter to the King, sister to Resora, and a Golden

Dragon Knight."

"Knight in training," he corrected. "Let's not forget you haven't finished the trials or taken the oath yet."

"Oath or no oath, my loyalties, and responsibilities are to my family and my King. It's lucky for me that those both fall in the same category."

Gritting his teeth, Denaris bowed, "Yes, Princess. I will be sure to check on Princess Resora tomorrow for you when your duties to The Enclave pull you away."

Turning her back to him, Feylynn took up the rag to dab Resora's brow, "No need, Master Carek came by minutes before you to inform me that I will be cleared to attend to my family for now. At least until the ball at the end of the week. At any rate, I am sure you have many other responsibilities to see too. So I will sit with her in my sister's absence for the next few days."

"I see," Denaris replied.

"I am certain that between my sisters and Resora's ladies in waiting, we will be fine. While we appreciate your attention and assistance, you may rest easy this week. Lord Denaris, Resora is in good hands."

He hesitated. Feylynn wasn't sure why, but that bothered her the most. His dark grey eyes darted back to Resora's form lying far too still beneath her blanket. "The King—"

"Knows already," she cut him off. "While he is concerned, he understands and trusts me enough to make my own decisions."

"As you wish, Princess. Do call upon me should you need anything or if she worsens," he replied as if she'd punished him.

Denaris abruptly turned for the door, and her conscience got the better of her. She'd been curt and cold to him. After all, by her sisters' accounts, he'd been very kind these last few months. Feeling guilty, Feylynn sighed, "I do appreciate everything you have done for my sisters, Lord Denaris."

He turned his head to glance back at her. "I do all I can for the good of Ranoak, Princess. Be sure that you are doing the same."

Without allowing her a response, he left her alone with Resora. "I'm trying," Feylynn whispered.

THIRTY-EIGHT

The grand room was stuffy, almost unbearably so. Feylynn stood with her fellow trainees as the procession of graduating knights was brought forth. It was the first time she had attended the event in full ceremonial armor. In the past, Feylynn had come in a fancy dress made especially for the ball. Back then, she believed the layers of clothing in the custom dresses were cumbersome, but right now, Feylynn wished for one of Liddia's dresses. Tonight her outfit was far worse, a tunic, breeches, greeves, gauntlets, boots, and padding, along with her breastplate. It was suffocating in a room filled with sweaty bodies.

All of the windows and doors were open to try and create circulation. Feylynn stood in the center of the room with those lining the path to the throne. Much to her dismay, the open windows did little to cool her. Most of the others in armor appeared rather comfortable, and she couldn't fathom how that was possible.

It was a trainee's obligation to line the aisle to the throne and stand in fidelity with the men taking the oath in their full armor. Carek had arranged her place in the line to be near the front. Still, it was the first time she hadn't watched the event with her sisters. She glanced up to the balcony reserved for the Lords and Ladies in attendance and found Enreal and Revienah staring back.

Likely, they were thinking the same thing. In years past, the girls had spent the first long hours of the ceremony whispering and giggling about trivial matters, like dating habits of the staff and the boys their ages. Her life had changed so much since then. She smiled wistfully but realized gossip and fun guessing games seemed so far away in her memories.

Revienah stuck her tongue out playfully, and Feylynn almost laughed. Her sisters meant everything to her, and coming home was so right. But, of course, her sisters were not the only important people to her. Feylynn looked toward Micah in line to make his oath, and she was able to gain some self-control. He stood there so serious and proud.

Feylynn was a little jealous that Micah got to take the oath before she could. He was older, so it made sense technically, but still, she wanted to do it too. Since she couldn't stand next to him, she would stand proudly here in her place as an upcoming knight to bear witness to his special moment. He did not share their blood, but for all the Nacarian sisters, he was one of them. Her mind drifted back to Resora's illness and her own pending departure tomorrow, and the weight in her chest settled fully.

When she glanced up again, Enreal was alone with no sign of Revienah. Her sister gave her a half-hearted smile, and Feylynn knew Revienah had probably concocted some scheme to bide the time tonight. Her frustration rose. One of these days, Revienah was going to get herself into real trouble with her games of cat and mouse.

Irel bumped her with his elbow and whispered, "Your sister,

in the green dress? Isn't that Enreal?"

Feylynn made sure no one was looking. They weren't supposed to be talking. She nodded to confirm his assumption as Master Carek called forth the next paladin to come along and take the oath.

Irel waited until the new knight started talking, then leaned over again, "She's come into herself, hasn't she? Do you think she'd dance with me?"

A pang in her heart made her twinge, but she brushed it aside, refusing to feel jealous of her sister. "She barely turned sixteen this past month."

"So, I am barely twenty."

Across from them, on the opposite side of the aisle, Rhushawn glared at them. Feylynn didn't know why he was so annoyed. He didn't even have the hot, cumbersome armor on, and he refused to stand at attention.

After a minute passed, Feylynn whispered honestly, "She doesn't like to dance much. She doesn't even like people much."

Irel snorted.

Watching Micah's progress, she scowled at him, "What?"

Keeping his voice low and his eyes forward, Irel said, "She better get over that."

"Why?"

"Look around the room, Fey. There isn't an unattached man here that hasn't calculated his chances to court her."

For the first time, Feylynn did look and was surprised to see Irel was correct. Men were glancing at her sister more than they should be. In fact, if it wasn't for Lord Denaris and the house guards standing next to her, Feylynn suspected several would have already tried to engage Enreal in conversation. Six men stood close to her sister, and each eyed not only her, but their possible competition as they were trying to edge their way in.

"Mark my words, your father will have suitors lining up for her now," Irel said from the side of his mouth. "Women like that have started wars."

Feylynn could not disagree, so she said nothing. She was staring straight ahead. Her eyes focused on the balcony column and a small piece of missing stone on the corner. It was no wonder why Enreal hated the fancy dresses and events of court these last two years. The men all gawking at her in such a way must be uncomfortable. Feylynn had always known her sister was beautiful, but she hadn't noticed the effect that beauty had on those around them.

What would all these men think, she wondered, *if they knew Enreal's exotic visage was in large part a result of her half-elven bloodline?* Feylynn knew their reaction would not always be favorable.

She set aside the disturbing thoughts as Micah stepped forward to stand before her father. He took a knee and saluted not only his King, but the man who raised him. As the King's Ranger, Micah was not obligated to recite the paladin's oath, but men like him, the lords, and those of the watch, could make their own oath. Feylynn held her breath as she listened to what he would say.

Micah took a deep breath and began to speak, "On this day, I kneel before my King and swear my fealty to defend him, his daughters, and the people in the realm of Ishreedin. I promise to remain righteous in all of my actions and will protect the weak. Bound by this oath I will not disgrace my King, or my Creator."

Feylynn smiled. Every word was perfect.

Revienah loved the festival. She loved the whole of it, but the last day, in her opinion, was filled with so much fanfare and extravagance it was impossible not to want to immerse yourself within it.

Crowds filled the streets with laughter and music. Blue and gold banners were strung up between the buildings and swayed gently in the spring breeze. Revienah loved the various vendors, competitions, games, and all the performers. The exciting atmosphere of the last night fed her soul.

The variety of food was even better. The traditional foods at the ball were nothing compared to the street vendors' sticky, sweet, and juicy offerings. Knowing her love of food, Revienah's lady attendants had often brought her some of them in the past.

There was marinated venison that was so juicy it dripped through the flatbread wraps onto your fingers and fruity tarts that were glazed with sticky, sweet honey. Then the crispy loaves of bread with herbs that had crackled when she broke them. Revienah's mouth watered at the thoughts of the chocolate-covered sweets, and she quickened her climb down the sidewall.

She dreamed of the endless scents and colors that would drown out the worries and pain. According to the castle staff, the last night, everyone pulled out all the stops and brought out their very best baubles and treats. Revienah intended to make the most of it.

As the youngest daughter to Tisus, walking the market square freely was no easy feat. Especially at night. For her to attend the festival last year, Revienah had to beg and bargain with her father, and she was required to bring Ahanna and an entire contingent of protection with her. She hated the confinement and security part of being a princess. To her mind, it was stupid.

Despite the annoyance of constant supervision, Revienah would never really complain about her station. Being a princess wasn't so bad. She never went hungry, she had a slew of people willing to help her, and Liddia always made her dresses. They were the very best and finest materials. Even better, thanks to the motherly dressmaker, Revienah had access to things like aranath spider silk outfits, like the one she wore now to stay concealed as she crawled along the outside of the narrow ledge leading to the gatehouse. Very few in the realm could afford such an extravagant gift.

Revienah appreciated the diversity of her clothes. Clothes could make you a different person. With her silk suit, she could be a burglar and sneak about the castle. If she attended the festival as Princess Revienah again in full dress, people would all fall over themselves at the sight of her wandering about.

That's what happened last year, people acted so proper around her, and it wasn't the same as being unknown and part of the crowd. Plus, she was surrounded by the castle guards when people made a fuss about her that day, and she missed all the good fun that night.

Tonight, Revienah wanted to be a part of the crowd, not the focus of it. Recently, she learned the art of disguise. She loved being around people when they weren't bowing or trying to impress her father.

Since tonight was the final night of festivities, it offered her the perfect chance to sneak away and find a few of those savory treats. She reasoned that maybe she would check out some of the celebrations too to test her latest disguise. Dressing down was the biggest key to not being recognized tonight. With a servant's help, she'd bought some ordinary clothes on her last visit to the city and hidden them away.

By now, The Enclave leaders would have presented their first potential knights, and from there, the stupid tradition could take hours.

If all went according to plan, Ahanna would be with Resora, which was perfect for Revienah. Resora would not be alone, and hopefully, seeing Ahanna would help her get better. Her fever hadn't ebbed in days, and her sister's dreams were getting worse.

Revienah's dreams were not any better, and for that reason alone, she needed a few hours away from the stuffy castle and the nasty red wyrm that haunted her. The last few months taxed the young Princess emotionally, and it made her desperate for a reprieve.

She feared leaving, but staying with her twin night and day was weighing on her free-spirited soul. Revienah wanted this one experience. She needed a single night to breathe fresh air and set aside her fears for Resora.

I will feel it immediately if something happens, as I do every day these last few weeks when the dreams come. If I feel Resora's in danger, I will go home right away, she reasoned. *In the meantime, Enreal has Feylynn to keep her company at the ball and keep the unwanted suitors away.*

Revienah was only twelve, almost thirteen, but she was observant beyond her years. Unlike Feylynn, Revienah knew that shy, sweet, Enreal attracted every man's attention whether she wanted to or not. It relieved her guilt, knowing stoic and fierce Feylynn would help keep those looking in check.

Then Resora would have Ahanna, she thought again to reassure herself. *And Father has his knights.*

She had about three hours give or take to wander about and get home before she had to be back to meet Ahanna. So for the first time in her life, Revienah would soak up tonight's fun as a regular citizen.

After climbing most of the way down the outside of the eastern wall, she jumped the final distance. She ran to the bushes and took up the sack she'd hidden yesterday, and Revienah covered her black spider silk suit with a brown skirt and plain green top. She'd insisted her lady maids braid her hair earlier rather than curling it, so she could use the cream-colored scarf to cover her ears and most of her hair. To finish it off, Revienah smeared a bit of dirt on her cheek for the perfect effect and hurried along a side street, following the tantalizing scents wafting about in the air.

THIRTY-NINE

evienah entered the market square and heard the lively music. The people crowded at the center of the square where all the best food was. The group started clapping their hands with the steady beat of a small drum, and Revienah was drawn to the commotion.

She worked her way through the press of eager onlookers and smiled when she reached the center and the performers within the human circle. Flowing skirts of purple and orange whirled about as the dancers formation resembled a flower as they turned in perfect time with one another.

Each girl was adorned with tiny gold bells on their wrists and ankles. The dancers were so skilled in movement that they could make the bells ring or keep them silent on a whim. Their feet jumped and turned with precise speed and kept with the rhythm of the song.

Revienah watched with admiration as the dancers performed.

Many in the crowd oohed and awed over flips and tricks as the show reached its climax. Revienah analyzed the movements instead. She was puzzling over the momentum required so she could try such a move herself one day. The crowd cheered wildly as the music, and the dancers stopped with a sudden crescendo.

The dancers curtsied and moved away as a man stepped forward to take his place in the center of the circle. The new performer's skin was a dark umber color. He had a beard that was well-groomed and thin in shape, that came to a strange point at his chin.

Wearing the most ridiculous, plumed hat with orange and purple feathers over a black bandanna. Revienah laughed at his silly, matching stage outfit, but he was handsome and exotic.

"Lords and ladies," he called.

The young ladies giggled and smiled, and as a practiced performer, he bowed, winked, and grinned in response.

Revienah didn't care about any of that though, what drew her attention was his many belts. These were not there as a fashion statement like his hat. The belt around his waist, another one strapped to each of his thighs, and the two belts fashioned in an 'X' across his chest. Every belt was loaded with small throwing knives and daggers.

A hushed sound fell over the onlookers, and people all about the crowd murmured and whispered their speculations.

He cleared his throat, "Death is never far away when playing with sharpened steel." He plucked up one of the six daggers at his waist and threw it in the air, and caught it easily behind his back.

The crowd oohed and ahhed. He flipped the dagger over the back of his hand, then balanced it with the tip down in his palm.

The crowd clapped and cheered.

The musicians picked up a beat to add some levity to his show.

Smiling, the man took up another dagger and threw this one behind his back too. Revienah watched with awe. Before she could blink, he had three. Pretty soon, he was juggling six.

"Just one wrong move, and he's done for," one of the crowd members said.

Revienah was enthralled. Never had she seen such a thing. Every one of his movements was precisely timed. He did trick after trick with his blades, and Revienah loved every single one.

She was so excited by the act that when the knife-wielding man asked for a volunteer, she blurted out, "Me! Me!" and raised her hand before she could think better of it. Most people stepped back, and Revienah was left outside the human line with her hand stretched as high as she could get it.

The knife-thrower smiled widely. "I believe this is a first for me."

Revienah glanced around and realized she was the only one willing to volunteer. She shrugged and returned the man's smile. "Me too."

The crowd laughed at her charming response.

The man gestured her forward, "Come then, let's see if you're brave after we are done, little girl." As Revienah approached him, he asked, "Do you have a name?"

"Rev—" Realizing her mistake, Revienah stopped herself before it was too late.

"Rev?" the man asked with a speculative look.

"Raven. Call me Raven."

"Very well, *Raven*. Do you know how to throw a knife?"

Revienah shook her head, "But I'll bet you could teach me."

The man laughed. "That I could, but I don't suppose I could do it in one night, so how about I do the throwing tonight?" he said with a wink.

Revienah shrugged.

The trickster waved to the side, and another man, a big burly fellow with thick arms and a thicker belly, came forward pushing a large piece of wood.

"Now then, Raven. Let's test how brave you are."

She cocked her head to the side at his challenge, "You're going to be surprised."

He leaned in close and spoke low, "I'm liking you more and more. If you survive this, I may give you a job."

Revienah grinned, "I'm looking for one just now."

He laughed again. "Alright, little bird," he said loud enough for the crowd this time. "If you'll stand right here," he said as he positioned her close to the wood wall. "You'll need to hold very still for this to work."

Feeling sure of herself, Revienah nodded.

The man handed her a purple handkerchief. "Could you hold this for me?" Revienah took the piece of cloth, and he lifted her hand against the wood. "Now, just keep still, alright?"

Suddenly, Revienah realized what he was planning. He wanted her to hold the handkerchief out so he could throw a knife at it. At that moment, as he backed away from her, she wasn't so sure of herself anymore, but she was too afraid to move.

With eyes wide, she watched as the knife thrower pulled one of the long daggers from his waist and took aim. The crowd went still, and Revienah heard a roaring as the blood pumped through her body. As he threw the blade, a sudden fear took over, and she squealed and jumped away from the wall, using her hands to protect her head. The wall vibrated, and a loud *thunk* echoed a millisecond later.

The crowd cheered and hollered.

Revienah glanced around and noticed a few of the people pointing. She looked back to the wood and saw the dagger's blade was buried deep in the wall, and a purple handkerchief hung beneath it. His aim had been so precise the knife had caught the fabric at least three inches below where she had held it.

He walked past her to pluck his dagger free, and Revienah couldn't help herself, "I jumped. I dropped the cloth."

"Not as brave as you thought, eh?" he teased as he pulled the blade free.

"How did you know? I dropped it after you let it fly."

He leaned in close, "Birds are a skittish sort, Little Raven. They always flinch." He winked at her one more time, then turned to take his bows. One of the dancers from before came and led Revienah away from the center stage. Another performer, this time a bard with a lute, took up his place.

The dancer patted her shoulder, leaving Revienah alone as she went back to her companions. Revienah was determined to talk to the knife thrower, but something else caught her attention.

There was a male elf standing at the edge of the crowd, and he was staring straight at her as if he recognized who she was.

She was surprised by the sight of a male elf in Ranoak. Elves were not common on the city streets, or at least she thought they weren't. *It's not like I roam the streets often enough to know,* she thought.

When he saw Revienah staring back at him, the elf turned on his heel so fast that his dark cloak billowed out behind him. Revienah could not fathom what possessed her to follow the lone elf but resolved it was a night of strange impulsive actions on her part, and she was loving it.

It took some work to get free of the crowd watching the street show, and when she finally escaped, she couldn't see the elf anywhere. She took several minutes to search the area and had almost given up when she saw the edges of a dark green cloak dart behind the alley near a blacksmith shop.

Revienah ran after him. If her sisters were here, they would have stopped her, and if she got caught, Revienah was certain she would get the worst scolding of her life. But they weren't here, and Revienah couldn't quell her curiosity as easily as her sisters. There was a strange thrill coursing through her as she pursued him, and for her, the mystery was almost as much fun as climbing steep walls or jumping off high points at the castle.

She hesitated at the entrance to the alleyway. Looking down the dark path, a slight sense of foreboding settled in her belly. She had no torch, and she knew all the city was enjoying the revelry, so the blacksmith would not be here. She wondered what had driven the elf this way. She glanced back to the streets behind her. She still hadn't even gotten one of the fruit tarts, and she didn't have that much time left. Her mouth watered at the thought of those tarts, and she reluctantly turned away from the alley, but then a flicker of strange light caught her eye.

Revienah turned back to the alley, then glanced down the street. People walked back and forth to their desired events laughing and talking. One couple passed with the spiced wraps in hand and ate while they walked. Revienah's belly rumbled. Everyone was having so much fun no one was paying attention to the blue-colored light that filtered out from behind the blacksmith shop.

She wondered how no one even noticed or cared. Yet, as hungry as she was, this was too strange to ignore. In the end, her curiosity won out, and Revienah slowly entered the back alley. She took every step with caution and clung to the shadows as her instinct demanded.

Using her best efforts to remain stealthy, Revienah crouched behind a water barrel to listen for any strange sounds coming from the blacksmith's shop. She waited several minutes there, but when her legs couldn't stand the discomfort of her position any longer, she decided it was safe enough to move. Following the barn's wall, she made her way to the entrance, and she peered around the corner for danger. That's when she saw the source of the light.

In the center of the dirt floor, a strange rock emanated a soft blue glow. The sight before her was familiar, and Revienah licked her lips as excited energy ran through her. The stone's light mimicked the same blue glow her mother's necklace offered if she pulled it out of the hidden pouch she had sewn into her inner waist. She could hardly believe her luck. *That elf must have dropped it by accident,* Revienah thought to herself.

Her eyes began darting about looking for the elf, but she couldn't see him anywhere. She calculated the distance to the stone and wondered if she could retrieve it before the elf returned. If she had two stones, she could give one to Resora. Such a gift could cheer her sister up.

Determined, Revienah sought out the elf one last time. She took her time and tried to look past dark corners for any movement. It seemed too easy, but relatively confident she was alone, Revienah took a deep breath and focused on the stone. *You can do it,* she assured herself. *You're stalling, Revienah. Just go!*

With a burst of speed, Revienah ran as fast as she could towards the stone. She didn't even stop to grab it up. With a racing heart and shaking hands, the Princess slid in feet first. Her fingers grabbed the stone mid slide, and she used her momentum to jump back up then ran for the side door she'd noticed in her previous scans. She'd nearly made it to the door when it opened, and there stood the elf in question. Without even slowing, Revienah took a quick turn for the same entrance she'd came from.

"*Alagos cali,*" the elf called from behind her.

Storm light? Revienah thought for a split second before her world shifted. The stone in her hand sent a shock up her arm. She yelped and dropped it on the ground as the soft light erupted into a bright blinding flash. For a moment, there was nothing but the white light burning away the darkness as well as her eyesight. Stunned, Revienah tripped over her own feet and fell to the floor, blinking rapidly to clear her vision.

Before she could muster up any defense, the young princess was lifted off her feet and held fast from behind. She couldn't see who held her, but he was strong and paralyzing fear took over. She started to scream for help when his hand slapped down over her mouth. Panic took over, and closing her eyes, Revienah put all her strength into fighting back. She started kicking and squirming, but her captor behaved as if he'd played this game a thousand times before.

F❋RTY

Asleep in her bed, Resora was dreaming again. In her mind, she pictured the sparkling stone and reached out to touch it. She could practically feel it between her fingers. She wasn't sure why, but she needed the cooling stone beneath her skin more than anything.

The heat was pumping through her, and it had been days since the fever ebbed. Her head jerked back and forth against the feather pillows as she fought against the overwhelming sensations—the fever and dreams mixed with the intense energy building in her stomach.

Resora didn't know what to do with the monster inside or how to grab hold and control what was happening. It was like a living entity itself had grown beyond her control. Yet, in a strange contradiction, as the energy built in her body, her strength weakened. It was as if her body was feeding her life force to the entity inside her.

In her dream, Feldorathanosh was there as he fought for his life amid the darkened sky. The red dragon slashed his front foreleg with its tail, but the dream changed. This time a jolt traveled up her arm, and pain followed. Then suddenly, instead of a gold dragon gliding above her, Resora saw her sister Revienah falling from the sky, with a terrified scream that was lost in the wind of her fall.

Resora screamed and thrashed about against the bindings of her sheets. Her back arched, and blue fire swirled around her fingers as her bedding began to smolder. Her lady maids cried out in fear and rushed to get the guards.

"She's possessed!" the woman cried as she threw open the door.

The two guards assigned to watch Resora's room scrambled to help. The sight before them had their eyes popping wide, and both of them knew this was beyond their training. "Go get Lord Denaris!" shouted the man on the left.

"And leave you here?"

"Hurry! Fetch King Tisus himself!"

Resora rose from sleep and stood next to her bed. Her eyes were vacant, but she looked around for something only she could see. Without another thought, the guard on the right ran for help. The man left behind stepped back in fear as the dancing blue flame now spread up to her elbows.

Never in all his life had he seen such a thing, but the inexperienced castle guard only allowed himself a moment of fear. He was one of the King's trusted men, and he'd renewed his fealty to Tisus the night before. He meant every word of the oath then, and with the words, by life or death in his heart, he resolved that he would not fail his King now.

He stepped forward with as much bravery as he could muster. "Princess, wake up!" When she didn't respond, he touched her shoulders to shake her. "Princess! You must wake up."

Her eyes turned to focus on him, and the fire died instantly. "Thank The Creator," he said in a relieved breath.

She stared through him with eerie vacant eyes and whispered, "Revienah." Tears fell down her fevered cheeks.

The guard was surprised to see her walking. For weeks Resora had barely been able to make it to the privy without help. This week had been her worst one yet, but the guard found hope in her standing by herself. He blocked her path as she started for the door, and putting his hands on her shoulders, he gently steered her toward the bed. "Princess, wait here. Harron has gone to fetch your father."

Resora's dream was too fresh, and her fear too real. The sensation of his hands on her shoulders assaulted her confused senses. Her hazel eyes flickered with anger, and golden light sparked within them. The golden hue flashed so fast the guard wasn't sure what he saw.

Without a second thought, Resora lifted her hand to push him away. A spark of light arced between them, and the young guard's body seized for a second before he crumpled to the ground unconscious.

For Resora, the only thing that mattered was Revienah. Her twin's desperate fear pulsed through her, and somewhere in her frayed mind, she associated that pain and anxiety to Feldorathanosh's death. Desperate, Resora glanced around the room and saw the drapes flutter as the breeze from outside pressed against them. Her eyes flashed to gold again, and she let go, following the will of the magic in her body.

The ball was in full swing, Lords and Ladies delighted in

the music, food, the art of courtship, and especially the gossip. Feylynn stood with Enreal near the large windows. Irel's revelation set Feylynn on edge, and she was decidedly more cautious than ever before. Enreal had already danced with three would-be suitors, and Feylynn saw how much the attention bothered her sister. Especially the last twit, who was at least twenty years older than her. After seeing yet another man approaching from across the room, Feylynn's eyes darted about for a solution. And she found one that made her cringe.

"Come on," Feylyn said, pulling her sister away.

A little stunned, Enreal asked, "Where are we going?"

"Just follow me, and don't make eye contact with anyone."

She pulled Enreal through the crowd at a hurried pace. She didn't want anyone trying to stop them along the way. Out of the corner of her eye, she saw one of her fellow trainees watching their progress. "Don't look up until I tell you. Just keep your head down."

"What are you up to?" Enreal asked from behind her.

"I'm saving your sanity and your feet," Feylynn said as she pulled Enreal closer and pushed her ahead. "Just remember this next time I need a favor," she said in her sister's ear.

Enreal came up short. When looking up, she realized she stood before the most giant, most frightening man she'd ever seen. She couldn't keep herself from muttering, "Oh dear," as she was pulled next to him.

"Rhushawn," Feylynn said with a nod.

He grunted, and folding his arms, he widened his stance.

"Perfect," Feylynn said with a sardonic grin and guided Enreal to stand next to him. "So glad you understand."

Scowling, Rhushawn took a step to leave.

"Oh no, you don't!" Feylynn snarled. "You owe me, and it's way past time you paid up. I don't care if you understand the words I am saying or not. You will stand here and keep those worthless dandies away from my sister!"

Rhushawn tilted his head to the side curiously.

"Stand here, got it," she ordered, emphasizing every syllable. "Or I swear I will kick higher this time, and the whole assembly will see how your advice works out for you!"

Feylynn could have sworn there was a smile in his eyes. But his lips didn't so much as twitch. To her surprise, Rhushawn assumed his previous rigid stance and obeyed.

"Fine then. That's good." She gestured at the barbarian with her hand, "Enreal, this is Rhushawn."

Rhushawn glared down at Enreal with his dark eyes, and she shrank away from him.

"He's a man of few words, but that's to our advantage."

"Feylynn—"

"Trust me on this. There's not a man in this room brave enough to bother us if we stay next to him. I spent the last several months at The Enclave, and very few men have said more than five words to him."

"I think I can understand why," Enreal said nervously.

After a while, Feylynn glanced around the room and found herself pleased. Her plan was working. Several of the men were looking, but no one was willing to act. When Enreal realized what was happening, her fear of the barbarian abated slightly.

Feylynn noted that not even the confident Irel bothered to come their way. Enreal turned to Feylynn, "What debt does he owe you?"

"Humm?" Feylynn said absently as she scanned the room.

"Rhushawn. What did you do for him?"

Hearing his name Rhushawn looked at Feylynn, and understanding the question this time, she glanced at him as well, "It's a long story," Feylynn said vaguely.

Enreal took her sister's arm, "We have plenty of time. I've nowhere else to be for at least another hour. If you don't tell me, maybe Rhushawn will."

"It's nothing," Feylynn insisted.

Next to them, Rhushawn shifted uncomfortably, but neither answered.

"See, he's a man of few words. I'm not even sure he understands much of what I say."

Enreal glanced up at the tall warrior, "Do you? Understand her, I mean?"

Rhushawn hesitated, and Enreal noted he clenched and unclenched his fists under his folded arms. His hesitation drew Feylynn's attention now. Turning, she frowned at him. After a few more seconds, Rhushawn tilted his head as he grunted.

"Well," Enreal said, "now you know."

"So I do," Feylynn acknowledged and turned away from him. She focused her attention on the crowd once more. When she saw the man heading their direction, she muttered, "I was wrong. There are a select few brave enough to come over this way."

Enreal followed Feylynn's line of sight and grinned. "I am pretty sure he's not a worthless dandy, nor do I believe that one is intent on courting me."

"Princess Feylynn, Princess Enreal, Rhushawn," Carek greeted with a proper bow.

"Master Carek," Feylynn returned with her own paladin bow.

Rhushawn huffed with indifference.

Carek glanced at the big man, "I am grateful to see you are keeping Rhushawn involved tonight. I worried he would intimidate everyone into leaving him alone."

Enreal pressed her lips together to keep from laughing.

"Turns out that's exactly the sort of company we needed tonight," Feylynn replied.

"How does Princess Resora fair this night?"

Enreal's smile fell, and she looked away.

Feylynn's shoulders slumped. "Not well, Sir. Since my arrival, her condition has worsened more each day. Her once frequent afternoon reprieves have shifted, and her fever is now constant."

Carek offered them a look of sympathy. "Your father has informed me that you wish to stay behind when we leave tomorrow."

Taken aback, Rhushawn's eyes left the crowd and centered on her as his arms dropped to his sides.

Enreal pulled Feylynn to face her, "You can't!"

"It's what's best. Resora needs me here."

"If you quit, they will not take you back," Carek explained, "but you know that already."

"I do."

"Feylynn. Why didn't you tell us? We could have helped you with this," Enreal accused, with the pain of betrayal lacing every word.

"It's not as if it matters. Very few at The Enclave would be remiss if I left."

"Only the few that matter, Princess," Master Carek injected.

Rhushawn stalked off without a word.

"It seems to matter to him," Enreal pointed out.

"Trust me. It doesn't. Very little matters to him," Feylynn observed as she watched the barbarian go.

Carek lifted a brow, but young Harron ran into the room with a flushed face and fear in his eyes before he could say another word. Upon seeing them, the guard rushed to Master Carek. "Hurry! You must come quickly! The Princess..." He glanced around the room, and realizing several people were watching, he said quietly, "The Princess is possessed. Fire crawls over—"

Enreal's eyes grew wide, and Feylynn took his arm to demand answers, but a level-headed Carek took the man by the shoulders and turned Harron to face him. "Hold your tongue. You'll set this place ablaze with panic. Take me to her."

"The King—" Harron began.

Carek pulled the man along, "I will inform the King when we know more. Princess Feylynn, you two should come along as well."

They moved to the ballroom entrance purposefully, but Carek would not allow them to run. As they entered the corridor, the Master Paladin spotted Micah at the end of the hallway heading for the door leading to the garden. "Micah," he called.

Micah spun about and waited for them to catch up. He eyed the frightened Harron carefully as they approached and took note of Enreal's and Feylynn's worried expressions. "Yes, Master Carek?"

Carek spoke calmly and chose his words with care. There were still several people in the hallway. "I wonder if you could come with us. There's been a change in Princess Resora's condition. I believe we will need your assistance."

Confused, Micah agreed, "Of course, Master Carek." The Ranger knew that Ahanna was likely chomping at the bit to get the all-clear. He'd already been detained longer than expected by the King himself. Tisus had insisted on introducing Micah to all the Lords of outlying fiefdoms. Regardless of the wait, he figured he should see what was going on first. When they all reached Resora's room to find her missing and an unconscious man on the floor, each of their hearts stopped.

FORTY-ONE

A hanna waited in the stables for Micah to come retrieve her as promised. Sitting on the floor in Freesia's stall and doing her best to stay out of sight, her legs kept bouncing with nervous anticipation. She was jittery, as if spiders were racing through her blood. From Micah's last report just yesterday, Resora had taken a turn for the worse.

This knowledge, mixed with the inability to see her little sister was a knife to the heart, and every minute that passed, the imaginary blade twisted further. Sitting with Freesia and fretting about what would happen to Resora allowed regret to swirl about in her mind.

I am a selfish fool, Ahanna reasoned. *So what if I had to marry a knight? So what if they took me to that stupid prison they called home? At least I could sit with Resora right now as Feylynn had.*

Feylynn was yet another painful wound. And while Ahanna was grateful for the upcoming visit with Revienah and Enreal,

Feylynn's refusal to come cut deep. Understanding the difficult predicament Feylynn faced, it was still a painful reminder of the consequences she had outlined before Ahanna ran away.

Ahanna didn't fully understand those consequences before. At the time, she thought she could handle anything but training at The Enclave, but now, she would take it all back for a single minute with her sisters. She couldn't selfishly ask Feylynn to risk any more than she already had for a secret meeting.

Even now, waiting for Micah to give her the all-clear, she considered turning herself into the masters to gain five measly minutes with Resora and Feylynn. *If Micah doesn't get here soon, I will.* Running footsteps pulled her attention away from her self-pity, and Ahanna held her breath. *Please let it be Micah.*

"Ahanna? It's me," he whispered at the stall door before entering.

She let out a sigh of relief and rose to greet him. "It's about time." The rest of her words fell away when she noticed the pallor of his face.

"Ahanna, something's happened," he said.

She gripped his cloak with tight fists, "What's happened? Resora!"

"Resora has escaped the castle. No one knows how, or where she's gone. The guard she attacked said she was calling for Revienah before she took him down."

"What are you talking about? Resora is a sickly twelve-year-old girl with barely an ounce of strength to spare. How could she take down a castle guard?"

"He says she shocked him, and he fell unconscious."

"Shocked him?" she said a little too loudly.

He checked outside the stall to make sure no one was listening. "Magic, Ahanna. He says flames crawled up her arms and did not burn her, and she jolted him with some sort of power from her hands when he tried to keep her from leaving."

Shaking her head, Ahanna stepped back. "No. It's not possible. That's insane. He probably fell asleep and dreamed about it."

Micah took her hands in his, "Ahanna, her bedding was burned."

Her eyes filled with fear, "Micah, what's happening?"

He shook his head, "I don't know, but we have to find her before the city watch. Princess or not, the people won't handle it well if she uses this magic on the street."

"If she hurts anyone—" A horrible thought struck Ahanna, "Where's Revienah?"

"No one knows. Master Carek has the castle guards searching for both girls in the castle and around the grounds."

"Does my father know?"

"Not yet, but he will soon enough. Master Carek hoped to find the girls before they disrupted the ball. He insists your father need not stress until we know more. He would not allow me to fetch your father. I am supposed to be helping in the search in the gardens."

"Micah, Revienah knows how to get out of the castle grounds. She loves the festival."

"So she's not in the castle?"

"You don't understand. Resora and Revienah have a strange connection. They sense each other's pain. If Resora was crying for Revienah, then she might be in trouble. They might both be in the city, and they might be in danger. Revienah may know how to get out, but she is foolish and naive when it comes to people."

"If they're in the city, then we're all in trouble. If Resora is really using magic and she is still hallucinating, then—"

Ahanna ran from the stall in a mad rush with little care as to who may see her. "We have to find them!"

"Go! I'll get Feylynn and Enreal," Micah said, running

toward the castle. He only made it a few yards before Master Carek rounded the stables and called out to him. Surprised the Paladin Knight was so far from the castle, Micah reluctantly shifted direction to meet him.

"Master Carek," Micah greeted.

"Was that who I think it was?"

"I don't know what you're talking about," Micah said evasively.

"I could have sworn I saw a young woman who looked a great deal like the missing Princess."

Micah shook his head, "Resora's not around here. I was checking the stables."

"I think we both know I'm not talking about Princess Resora."

Micah chose to ignore the Knight's comments. "Master Carek, I fear Resora and Revienah may have left the castle grounds."

"Yes, I fear the same."

"I need to tell Feylynn and Enreal," Micah insisted. "More importantly, we need to inform King Tisus.

"No."

"No? That's his daughter!"

"And there's nothing he can do that we're not already doing. For now, let the Princesses keep to the castle in their search. The last thing we need is another princess to go missing. The King cannot stop tonight's events for more runaway children."

His spine straightened at the Paladin's dig. "King Tisus' daughters are his most important priority."

"Agreed. That's one more reason why it's important we let him keep up appearances. The search for his daughters could take hours, days even. This tradition is important to the stability of the entire kingdom. Calling it off will not be good for anyone. What's more, we do not need the whole contingent of knights searching for the cursed child. Somebody is likely to get hurt, and that somebody could be Princess Resora. Tisus is my friend, and he trusts me to help him. Can you not do the same?"

Micah struggled with the request, but the Paladin's words sank in. "You know."

"I do, but you and I are two of three who do."

Micah hated keeping this from the King, but in a strange way, it was sound reasoning. If Revienah was in danger, then the last thing King Tisus needed was more of his girls in the thick of that danger. On the other hand, if they weren't in danger and Tisus stopped the traditional events for them, it would look bad on his part and would hurt the new paladins that earned the right to attend tonight. Conceding, Micah gave the Paladin Master a nod of assent.

"Very well," said Carek. "According to Princess Enreal, Princess Revienah intended to visit the square. Take the eastern side. I will search the western areas. The girls are not that far ahead of us. We will find them and return them to the King before the night is out. If we have seen no sign of them by the peak of the moon, I will alert the Golden Dragons in attendance, and we shall comb every inch of the city until they all return home."

It did not escape Micah's attention that Master Carek sent him on the same path as Ahanna, and he was grateful to the older man for his discretion. He also heard the clear warning from the Paladin. Ahanna had a little over an hour, and then the whole of the Enclave would come down upon her. Micah would not let that happen.

Held captive by an unseen man, the elf she followed circled her, with his eyes looking her over. "Imagine my surprise when I was trying to get into the castle to retrieve you, and my curious query came to me instead. Does your father know you're wandering about the city unattended?"

Revienah stopped struggling against her unseen captor at the sound of his voice and did her best to turn her restrained head to track the elf and see his face. She wanted to see him up close before she escaped so she could tell her father. He came around to stand before her with the glowing orb in his hand. Breathing through her nose, Revienah glared venom at him as the male elf stood there staring at her with curiosity in his eyes.

She did all she could to memorize his features. His long hair was nearly white instead of blonde, and he wore it styled with several intricate weaving braids. Revienah couldn't remember her mother, so staring at this man with his full-blooded features was odd to her. His ears came to a severe point, but their sharpness matched the high angles of his cheeks and the sharp line of his jaw.

She was used to her own slightly angled ears, and Ahanna's with their sharp, obvious points, but her oldest sister's more prominent elven features did not compare to this male. He was handsome, a mythical kind of handsome, and his appearance held a power of its own. His eyes were the purest green she'd ever seen, and Revienah wasn't sure that color green existed anywhere else in Ishreedin. She'd heard servants in the castle speak about a beautiful, compelling nature in an elf's appearance and how an elf could manipulate humans to do their bidding. Looking at this handsome male now, Revienah could see why there were such rumors.

Coming closer, he smiled, but it didn't feel friendly, and Revienah didn't feel compelled in the least.

"You're a wiley one and in much better health than I expected," he said as he got closer. He took up a lock of her dark hair between his fingers, "You have his hair, but your eyes...

371

Shelanna is in your eyes."

Revienah stilled momentarily. She couldn't fathom what he wanted with her, but she hated that he knew her mother. Tears began to form.

"Look at me, Resora."

Revienah's eyes went wide, but upon hearing his command, she would not look at him. She could not let him see the shock there as frantic thoughts crashed through her mind. This elf thought she was Resora. *Creator, help me,* she prayed. The elf wanted her sister.

Terrified for her twin, Revienah tried to yell again. The sound was muffled, and she knew no one would hear. Her heart slammed against her chest as she renewed her efforts to get free. Kicking and wriggling, Revienah tried hard to bite her captor's hand, but the unseen man behind her held Revienah so tight nothing was working. She had to get away. She had to warn her father. *Resora!* she thought. *What did he want with Resora?*

When Revienah refused to look at him, the elf's brow furrowed in thought. Reaching out, he gripped her chin beneath her captor's beefy hand, trying to force Revienah to look at him, but she shut her eyes tight. She could sense him looking at her as if willing her to open her eyes. For a second, she almost obeyed, but to save her twin, she had to deny anything he wanted. He laid a hand on her chest over her heart, and a strange sensation passed through Revienah. Those haunting yellow eyes from her dreams flashed in her mind. Panicked now, she kicked and squirmed, fighting as hard as she could to get free.

She heard the elf suck in a breath, "Of course," he mumbled.

Revienah stopped struggling as he stepped back away from her. Daring to open her eyes, she saw a passing flicker of emotion in the elf's features, one that she might have mistaken for sympathy if she hadn't known he wanted to kidnap her sister.

"You're not Princess Resora," he accused.

Revienah nodded as best she could to assure him she was her sister.

He smiled knowingly. "No, you are not," he said, pointing at her chest. "Resora has something frightening within her. But you and I know for a fact that what stirs in you is entirely different."

He turned away, pacing the space near her as if thinking about this discovery. Then he spun back to her with sadness in his eyes. "I pity you, child. It has awakened, and there is no stopping it. Have you seen her, I wonder?"

Revienah couldn't make sense of what he was saying.

The elf shook his head, "You have no idea what is coming, and few will ever understand as I do."

Filled with confusion, Revienah was shaking her head. She tried to insist she was Resora through her captor's hand, but it came out as a moan rather than actual words. She was desperate to protect her twin and wanted him to believe she was Resora.

"Twins," he muttered, "It had to be twins." Revienah's tears spilled down her face. The elf stared at her with a hint of indecision in his eyes.

Her breathing became panting as she struggled to get the oxygen as emotion overwhelmed her, and she forgot to breathe through her running nose.

As he turned away from her, the elf brought his hand up to his chin and puzzled over his dilemma. "She never told me." He glanced past Revienah to the man who held her tight. "She must have known."

Revienah's captor shrugged, and the tiny movement afforded her a small chance of hope. His hand over her mouth shifted just a tiny fraction, but it was enough for the wiley Princess. Her teeth sank into the flesh on his middle finger as she bit down as hard as she could. The big man howled, and the grip on her body lessened.

Ignoring the taste of blood, Revienah kicked and wriggled enough that her captor bent forward, and her feet touched the ground.

"Don't let her go!" the elf ordered.

With her mouth free now, Revienah screamed louder than she thought possible, and threw her head back as hard as she could. The strike was true. The back of her head slammed into the man holding her, and the solid crack of his nose against her skull was a clear indication it was broken.

He cursed and let her go. His hands came up to stem the bleeding.

Some of the blood ended up in her lengthy hair, and her ears rang from the blow, but she ignored everything except her desire to escape. Revienah stumbled away from him in her desperate attempt for freedom, but she hadn't expected to be so dizzy. Hitting someone with your head hurts. She tripped and fell to her knees. Before she could compose herself again, someone started pulling on her arm.

She looked up to see the elf yanking her to her feet. He was grinning from ear to ear, "You are a clever girl, to be sure."

There was a slight prick in her arm, and faster than she ever thought possible, her body grew leaden. Her assailant wore a ring with a small needle protruding from its center. The poison coating the needle stole all of her strength. "My father... will kill you," she slurred.

"We'll see," he replied as she slumped in his arms.

The elf's injured companion finally made his way over to them. "That girl has a mean streak."

"Too bad we're not taking her with us," the elf said and glanced around the dark building in search of a solution. "Here, take her," he said as he passed the limp body back to his friend. "Lock her up in that shed."

"What now?" the bigger man questioned as he complied.

"I think Resora will still come to us."

"How do you know?"

"I don't for sure, but I have a hunch."

FORTY-TWO

Resora wasn't coherent or aware of her surroundings. There was a fierce burning for revenge coursing through her, and that need drove her from the castle to the festival. When she looked around, she couldn't fully remember how she got there. The only thing that mattered was helping Revienah.

She wandered the streets like a wraith, hoping to find both her sister and the person who hurt her. Some strange instinct had her walking the side streets and back alleys rather than heading to the market square via the main roads.

She wore her nightgown and a blue cloak. She vaguely remembered taking the cloak from her room, but the thought was lost before it fully formed. She'd even scraped her bare feet twice, but for Resora, there was nothing except the bright growing magic within. She passed through one of the more popular side streets and found herself face to face with a middle-aged man with rotting teeth and breath that smelled of heady fermented drink.

"Hey there, pretty girl. Where ya goin'?"

Resora tilted her head and considered the man with a vacant expression and eyes flecked with bits of bright gold. "Have you seen my sister?"

"No," he said with a wink, "but I'll help you find her."

Even in her dazed state, an inner alarm told her not to trust him. Without another word, she stepped past him.

The man reached out and took her arm, but a blue flame sprung to life where he gripped her. He howled in pain and dropped to his knees holding the burned hand.

Resora ignored him, but several people heard the man's cries and saw the strange girl walking away from him as he pointed at her, calling her a sorceress. It was his drunken state that saved Resora. The man was rambling so much, very few people took notice of him. Those that did shook their heads at his shameful condition.

Micah tried hard to catch up to Ahanna. He wanted to warn her that Carek was in the city. The problem, though, was the crowds were at their peak. Venders, performers, and villagers milled about. To find any of the girls in these streets thick with revelers would be near impossible, but he persistently maneuvered through it all anyway. Micah stepped aside to find a better spot to scan the area and spotted a warehouse with a platform for wagon deliveries. He needed a higher vantage point. He wished for Soros, but horses were banned from the area during the festival to keep the streets clear for the multitude of visitors and events.

Micah took the stairs to the platform two at a time. Once he was there. It wasn't enough. He stepped upon a barrel and launched himself up to the roof, and ran to the corner. He peered out into the crowd below for any sign of Ahanna. The night was in full swing now, and as bright as it was, the moon offered little help. Micah settled in, allowing his eyes to adjust and searching for the long blonde hair he found so striking.

It was not Ahanna he spotted in the crowd first, but rather it was Cirus. His loyal friend soared above the people as if seeking someone. *Ellomar, you're a saint*, Micah thought and glanced around for the older Ranger. When he couldn't spot him, he whistled loudly. The falcon obeyed the call, and raising his arm, Micah offered Cirus a perch as he approached. Well trained, the falcon landed lightly atop Micah's leather gauntlet and tucked his wings to settle in upon his arm.

Micah offered the bird one of the bits of dried meat that he kept in a belt pouch. "Show me, Cirus, show me where they are."

The falcon lifted from his arm and glided above the sea of people. From the rooftop, Micah watched carefully to see where the bird set down and a rush of warm relief spread through him when Cirus set down close to the center of the market square.

With no time to waste, Micah hopped down from the roof and followed the path his companion had shown him. He knew that when Cirus returned to Ellomar, the old Ranger would wait. It was a system they set up during his years of training. Long-distance communication was one of the reasons Ellomar had helped him train the falcon to begin with.

When he spotted Ellomar, Micah was relieved to find Ahanna was with him.

Ellomar gripped his shoulder, "You made good time."

"I didn't have a chance to alert Enreal or Feylynn. Carek is in the city. He's not only seeking the twins, but he knows Ahanna is here as well."

"I don't care. I just want to find my sisters," she insisted.

Ellomar agreed, "I'll deal with Carek. You and Ahanna head

toward the blacksmith. One of the dancers said she saw a young girl about Revienah's age, with the same hair color, dressed in a brown skirt, headed off in that direction. She remembers because the girl volunteered to assist the man with the knives, and she says no one ever does that, and the girl said her name was Raven."

Ahanna's eyes went wide. "That's Revienah!" she said with new hope. "I called her Raven before I left."

"Then we have a place to start," said Micah.

"Go," Ellomar said gently, pushing Ahanna along. "I'll keep looking for Resora. If I see Carek, I'll do my best to keep him away from you."

Already moving, Ahanna took Micah's sleeve to pull him along with her. "Thank you."

Turning to the crowd to seek out Resora, Ellomar mumbled, "Don't thank me yet. The night's not over." Something in his gut wasn't sitting right, and years of experience taught him his gut was rarely wrong.

Revienah pushed through the weight of her drugged stupor as best she could, but it was useless. Whatever he'd injected had caused debilitating effects. A single thought kept her semi-conscious, *Resora*. As badly as she wanted to give in and sink into oblivion, fear for her twin sister would not allow it.

Lying against a pile of wood in the dark, cramped shed, the warm tears slid down her cheeks. She couldn't make the tears stop even with her eyes closed. It was so dark in the tool shed that even if she opened her eyes, she had no hope of seeing the door. Nor would she have the strength to stand and feel for it. It was probably only an arm's reach away, but her body was too heavy to even shift onto her side. It was as if the elf had filled her bones with lead.

"Re-sora," she moaned softly. She needed to warn her father. She needed to warn Resora and those thoughts burned through her mind. Then she realized her stomach was warming. Uncomfortable, she wanted to curl up. She willed herself to move, to pull her legs in, anything to help. Miraculously, she managed to pull one leg up, but her foot caught on the shovel leaning against the wall. It slid across the wall before toppling over and landing on her other leg.

Frustrated, Revienah concentrated on that blasted shovel, forced her leg to move again, and pushed it off. The shovel hit the wall again with a loud clanging sound. "Re. . ." She started to call out, but the word died. The energy to move ate up her reserves. She wanted to sleep so badly.

A strange sound pulled her back. There was a rattle, a scrape, and then there was light. Revienah couldn't open her eyes, but beneath her lids, she saw the warm glow of a torch.

"Revi!" Micah exclaimed. His rough hands picked her up.

Revienah tried to tell them. She needed to warn them, but her tongue was thick, her mouth dry, and she was so tired.

"What have they done to her?" Ahanna said. "There's blood in her hair on her dress."

Micah set Revienah down upon a table as Ahanna shoved tools aside.

"Micah, heal her," Ahanna begged with a shaky voice.

"Help me find the wound," he said as he searched her body for any signs of fresh blood. "It's got to be a head wound. Most of the blood is in her hair, but it's too dark in here. We have to take her back."

"What about Resora?"

Resora! Revienah thought.

"Ahanna, head wounds are dangerous."

"Re-so..." Revienah slurred.

"Revienah!" Ahanna took up her hand and laid her other hand upon her youngest sister's brow, "You're going to be alright. We'll take you home."

Revienah tried to shake her head. "Resora . . . trouble." The effort those words took was immense, but she forced them out. The burning in her belly was constant now, but she ignored it.

"Come on, Revi. Wake up for us," Micah said as he searched her head for the cut. Then, he turned to Ahanna, "I can't find any wound."

"Elf," Revienah grunted. "Pois..."

"Poison? Revi, you were poisoned?"

Revienah gave a weak nod.

"I have to take her back. We can't know what was used."

Ahanna knew he was right, but as he went to pick her sister up again, Revienah tried to squeeze Ahanna's hand with her weak fingers.

"Resora," Revienah insisted barely above a whisper, but Ahanna's sensitive ears heard her clearly.

"Wait!" Ahanna bade as she nudged Micah away with a hand to his shoulder. Micah took a step back, and Ahanna leaned over her sister. "Where's Resora?"

"A-hanna," she said with a weak breath."Elf..." she relaxed again.

"Princess," Micah pressed.

"No! She wants to tell me something." Ahanna gripped Revienah's shoulders, shaking her awake. "What elf, Little Raven? You can do it. Tell me where she is."

The endearment pushed past the sleepy fog, and Revienah found the strength to open her eyes slightly. "The elf... Resora. He wants—wants Resora."

Worried for both girls, Micah asked, "What elf, Revi?"

Revienah closed her eyes again. Her words were thick. "Help her, Hanna."

When she fell limp, Ahanna could not hold back her cry of alarm. She feared she'd pressed her younger sister too hard. "Micah!"

The Ranger checked for breathing. "She's alive, but she needs help."

"Let's take her to my father," Ahanna said, but another fear ruled her thoughts, *How can I help them both now? How can I choose?*

As if reading her mind, Micah gave her an answer before she could even ask. "I'll take her to your father. You're going to find Resora."

"I-I don't know where to look."

"Trust your instincts, Princess. Trust Ellomar's training. You must find her before this elf does. Only The Creator knows what he wants with her."

Ahanna nodded. "Don't let Revienah die, Micah. Please, you have to save her."

He scooped Revienah into his strong arms. "She'll be fine, but you have to go, or else we may lose Resora."

Ahanna kissed Revienah's brow and whispered, "You'll be okay, Little Raven." When she looked up at Micah, their eyes met. There was so much fear between them and far too much unsaid. She squeezed his arm, then, on impulse, kissed his cheek. "Thank you, Micah."

"Be careful, Ahanna."

With a quick nod and new tears forming in her eyes, Ahanna turned and ran for the market square, praying she would find Resora in time.

FORTY-THREE

There was no way to know where to start, but Ahanna kept walking with alert eyes that sought out any sign of her sister. Ranoak was no small village, it was the central city to the kingdom, and right now, nearly everyone living in the outlying lands attended the festival. The Lords of fiefdoms, the farmers on the outskirts, merchants, performers, and even adventurers that made their coin as caravan guards for hire all attend the yearly event. The current population tripled during this week in the spring.

The city watch was out in full force to keep the peace, and Ahanna had to navigate the throng carefully to avoid them. She wasn't sure anyone would recognize her with her stablehand outfit, but she couldn't afford to take any chances.

Everyone in front of her walked with a lazy shuffle as they milled about to enjoy the offered street fairs. Her urgent need to find her sister only amplified as she was forced to the same pace as the people surrounding her. She bumped into another tall, middle-aged man when he suddenly stopped. Filled with annoyance, Ahanna groaned.

Offering a quick apology, the farmer shuffled aside to allow her to pass. Ahanna wanted to feel guilty for being so rude, but she'd been alone with Ellomar for so long, Ahanna forgot how claustrophobic the city was.

Desperate to breathe, she stepped out of the thickest part of the crowd and stood by a vendor selling wood carvings and glass baubles. An older woman wearing a tattered dress and a black shawl that had seen better days approached her. "Are you looking for a gift?"

"Ah no, not really."

Ignoring the reply, the merchant shuffled about her cart of trinkets and started showing off the wares in hopes of making a sale. "We have some nice pieces. I have a lovely horse here. My husband made this one with his own two hands." She laughed a little, "Well, since it's blown glass, I suppose that's not really true. Look at the detail. It's one of my favorites."

Distracted, Ahanna kept her eyes on the crowd for any sign of Resora, the mystery elf, or Ellomar. She didn't even look at the glass pony. "No, thank you."

The older woman wasn't deterred easily and babbled on about a pretty set of goblets, vases, and even a small luck charm that would, in her words, charm gentlemen callers and be a perfect neck ribbon. Ahanna barely heard any of it as she reasoned out a better vantage point.

Discouraged by Ahanna's disinterest, the old woman nearly gave up and even went about resetting the items she'd tried to show Ahanna. However, as she reset the small charm upon the shelf and saw the wooden box she'd set aside earlier, she hesitated a moment. She'd planned to keep that particular item for herself but also knew it would bring in a hefty sum of coin.

Glancing over her shoulder, she eyed the intense young woman and her attire, then wondered about the item in the box. This girl was obviously not looking for pretty neck ribbons, girlish figurines, or even dinner goblets, but that was really the type of merchandise her husband, and she made. Tonight was the last night for good sales, and this festival had been light on them. Despite her travel-worn clothing, something about this girl's mannerisms spoke of money.

Shrugging, the merchant woman picked up the wooden box with her aging hands. "How about something more unique? I have the perfect item here for someone with your particular taste. Mind you, I only have one of these," she said as she produced the small wooden box. "It's one of a kind. Carved from a sacred tree in the Shilesta Wood."

The mention of the Shilesta Wood had Ahanna turning her attention from the crowd to the older woman as she held out the trinket for her.

"The Shilesta Wood?"

"Aye, they say there's still magic in those old trees. And this particular carving was crafted by none other than an elf from those very same woods," the old woman said with the tone of a canny merchant that had bent her customer's ear. "The elves rarely share their gifts with the likes of us. So this here is about as rare a gift as any in the realm," she hinted. As she opened the wooden box slowly to add to the hidden item's mystic, inside was the likeness of a great dragon.

Ahanna reached out, "May I?"

"Oh yes, but be careful."

Removing the carving from the box, Ahanna turned it in her hand to admire the fine details and the beautiful patterns in the polished wood. It was about the size of a man's fist and was made with a smooth dark wood that had darker grain lines swirling in the design. There was something familiar to her about the dragon. Something in her memory as a child, but she couldn't grasp it. "Where did you get this?"

The woman hesitated, but smiled sweetly, "Oh, well, I pick things up here and there in my travels. You know, trading this for that. I'll give you a fair price. Just look at the details. As I said, you'll never find it anywhere in the realm."

"I've seen this before, or at least something like it," Ahanna mumbled absently.

The older woman huffed, "Not likely, child. Only an elf with nimble hands could have made such a rare piece."

The women's defensive reaction pulled Ahanna's attention from the wooden statue. She wasn't sure why it mattered so much to the woman, but Micah told her to trust her instincts, and it was those instincts that drove her next actions. She tried handing the dragon back, "I'm sorry, but I'm certain I've seen this before, and I am more of a collector of rare items."

The old woman put her hands on her hips in frustration, then decided she would have to tell the girl more. "I'm telling you, I sat here yesterday and watched while the artist made it right here at my wagon."

Ahanna's eyes went wide. Sometimes elves came to the festival, but that was in the past. Denaris told her once that the elves didn't know how to have fun, so they hated the chaotic celebration in the city. "I thought you said you picked it up on your travels."

"Well, I did, didn't I? I picked it up while traveling here just yesterday. If you want to verify, the elf is staying nearby at The Slithering Eel. He arrived about the same time as me and paid up until tomorrow."

Ahanna gripped the woman's shoulder. "His name," she demanded.

"I can't tell you that."

"Please, it is vital that I find him."

"I can't tell you because I don't rightly know, as I never bothered to ask," the old woman said with an indignant huff.

Ellomar came upon the scene as Ahanna pulled the frightened woman closer and pressed her for answers. "You must know something. What does he look like?"

"My dear, what are you doing?"

"The elf, this woman knows him," Ahanna explained.

"I do not! Just met him two days past."

Confused, Ellomar moved to extract Ahanna, and he saw the item she held. Following his line of sight, Ahanna forgot she still held the statue. Ellomar offered her no reaction other than a slight pause before he lifted the dragon from her hand to return it to the older woman. "M'lady, I believe this is yours." He took Ahanna by the arm and steered her from the wagon full of wares, "Come, we must go."

"El…"

Ellomar shook his head.

Ahanna almost said his name. Horrified by the mistake, she bit her lip. She stole a quick glance back over her shoulder as Ellomar pulled her through the crowd. Then she turned to Ellomar. "We found Revienah."

"I know. I saw Micah." He did not mention the means by which he'd seen Micah carrying Revienah toward the castle, nor did he mention how he'd tracked Ahanna down so fast. The Princess was not yet ready for some revelations. "Micah had no time to tell me what happened, as Revienah looked quite ill, but I am starting to piece it together now."

"Resora is in trouble. There is a strange elf looking for her. He wants to take her."

Ellomar nodded distractedly.

"That woman says she got that dragon from an elf yesterday, and he is staying at The Slithering Eel. It has to be the same elf."

Ellomar stopped so suddenly Ahanna stumbled, but he tightened his hold to keep her from falling. A small prodding on his thoughts forced him to focus. Closing his eyes, Ellomar ignored Ahanna's proclamation and opened the magical link he'd forged with Cirus. A link few knew was even possible.

An image formed behind his closed lids, and for a few seconds, Ellomar saw the reason for the bird's alarm. The falcon's sight was far more vivid and clear than any human. The falcon located Resora. The young Princess was walking through the back streets in her nightclothes. "This way," he said, pulling Ahanna along.

"Where are we going?" she demanded with frustration.

Ellomar stopped again, but this time what he saw had him turning on his heel and pulling Ahanna the opposite direction. He was walking so fast that she had to jog to keep up with his long stride. Confused, she tried to look back to see what spooked him, but at that exact moment, he shifted direction and gently pushed her between the dark, narrow space between the candle shop and the brewery.

Already frustrated and worried, Ahanna turned on him, "What are you ab—"

Putting a finger to his lips, Ellomar cut off the rest of her words. He stood with his back straight against the wall and used his protective arm to urge her against the same wall to his right. Realization dawned on her. He was hiding from something, or rather someone. Catching on, Ahanna mimicked him and flattened herself against the wall of the candle shop.

The evening's events had turned Ahanna into a mess of nerves, but those nerves made her hyper-vigilant and aware of her surroundings. Forcing herself to focus on slow, steady breathing, as Ellomar taught her to use when shooting, she slid her fingers around the hilt of her blue steel sword to remind herself that she was not helpless.

The shadow of a man stopped near the entrance between the buildings, and Ellomar sighed with relief. He kept absolutely still a few heartbeats more before he turned his attention to Ahanna and whispered, "Carek saw you, saw *us*. I'm sure of it."

"I have to find Resora."

"That you do," he agreed. "But you can bet he's looking for her as well, and if he catches up to you first, he is honor-bound to act on it. I have no way of knowing what actions he will take, but I am unwilling to risk it."

"I don't care anymore. Only Resora matters. Someone is after her. I have to help her."

Keeping his voice low, Ellomar said, "Ahanna, Resora, she's not the same as she was. You must understand this. She is as much a danger to herself as anyone else could be. Tell me you understand?"

"I don't care," she repeated.

"I know where she is, and I was taking you there, but things just got more complicated," he said as he glanced back to make sure Carek wasn't returning. Feeling they had a few more minutes, he gripped her shoulders. "You must listen carefully, Ahanna."

Seeing the worry in his eyes, she nodded.

"I will redirect Carek. Go to your sister and see what state she is in, but I warn you to take caution. Powerful magic flows in her blood, and she cannot control what is happening. Do you understand?"

"Magic? What are you talking about?"

"Ahanna, there is no time. You must trust me. No matter what you wish to do, you cannot touch her. Tell me you understand."

"I understand," but she didn't.

Cirus screeched overhead, letting Ellomar know he had

arrived.

Ahanna glanced up and watched as the avian hunter perched on the roof of the building they used for cover.

"Cirus will take you to Resora. Follow him but keep to the shadows. Stay out of sight at all costs."

"What if I lose sight of him?" Ahanna whispered.

"You won't. He will keep your pace. Trust him, Ahanna. Trust me."

Ahanna nodded again.

"Go then. Find Resora and see if she will return to the safety of the castle."

Cirus screeched again and took to the air.

Ahanna met Ellomar's eyes, and he gestured for her to leave. *Trust him,* she thought and needed no further prodding. Ellomar hadn't steered her wrong yet. Obeying the old ranger, she stayed between the buildings as she ran after Cirus.

FORTY-FOUR

Thinking her helpless and alone, two burglars followed Resora through the dark alleys, and although the young girl feared the threat, the sorceress building within lacked the desire even to acknowledge their presence. One thing drove her forward this night, and that was Revienah.

As the pain of possibly losing her twin resurfaced, Resora's hazel green eyes changed to an unsettling golden hue. Her skin tingled, the hairs on her arms stood up as if electrified by the storm in her body. Whatever was inside her begged for release. It begged for destruction.

Ba-bump. Is that my heart? she wondered. *Ba-bump*, her heartbeat slowed. The steady rhythm was calm compared to the quick panting breaths that escaped her lips. *Ba-bump. Or is time slowing,* she wondered. It was as if every second was a minute, and every minute was an hour. Then, in the space between those heartbeats, she saw something on the ground behind a tavern.

Her heart picked up speed as she approached the small item that glinted oddly in the dark night. *Ba-bump, Ba-bump, Ba-bump.* Tears blurred her vision as she realized Revienah must have been here, and now she was gone. Resora bent down to retrieve the gold ring that had drawn her attention, and she fisted the trinket so tightly that its gem dug into her soft hand. It was Revienah's ring, and Resora wore an identical one on her finger. Her father had gifted them the rings when they turned twelve last year.

Resora closed her eyes against the pain. Tears ran freely down her pale cheeks. *Revienah.*

She heard the scuffle of footsteps and knew the two men who stalked her watched from nearby, but even Resora, trapped beneath the might of power running through her blood, could not bring herself to care about the threat those men posed. Everything outside of the loss of Revienah was inconsequential.

Her twin's anguished cries for help circled in her mind and heart. With the next beat of the heart, Resora threw her head back and screamed from the pain. Something raw and untapped ripped through her. Her beating heart pounded now, and her senses amplified to a painful level. For Resora, a flood gate opened, and she could not stop the roaring waves tearing her apart, nor did she want to. Blue flames came to life around the tips of her fingers. She opened her hand and watched as the fire crawled over her skin and around the small gold ring she held in her palm.

The two men following her realized the depth of their error and ran away swiftly from the girl wielding blue fire.

The smoldering heat that started in her belly weeks before was nothing more than a lump of hot coal compared to the raging wildfire burning through her now. Somewhere in the back of her mind, the young girl cried as she came to the realization that this curse would consume everything around her. Resora tried hard to put it out, but Revienah was missing and hurt.

The power inside was alive, and a sorceress surfaced, knowing she could stop them. *They all had to pay!* Her mind was fuzzy, her thoughts and dreams mixed together. The child was afraid, but then images of the mighty dragon bleeding, dying at her feet, quelled that fear, and anger took over.

"Resora!"

The long-lost voice of her sister broke through her confusion. *Ahanna? Why is Ahanna crying?* she wondered.

Resora tried to cling to the sound of her oldest sister, but she lacked the willpower to control what was happening. Lost images, memories, and nightmares replaced the reality of the scene in front of her. A red dragon's lifeless eyes staring at her with hate even through her last breath. An ancient gold, her friend, struggled to live.

Feldorathanosh! "Don't die," she cried. There was so much blood. Where once a beautiful green meadow existed, a blood-soaked scar took its place. "Please don't die," Resora begged.

Despite Ellomar's warnings and the magical fire writhing like a serpent along Resora's skin, Ahanna could not keep away. She approached her sister with caution, and warmth started around her fox pendant. Ahanna's hand went to the charm.

She couldn't think about it though, Resora needed her. Her sister's eyes were glazed over like she was sleepwalking. Ahanna wasn't sure what to do, but she tried reassuring Resora, "She's alright, Resora. Revienah will be fine. We found her. No one is dying." Considering Revienah's condition when she last saw her, Ahanna didn't even know if that was true, but she was desperate to reach Resora.

Ahanna's voice cut through the mad haze momentarily. Resora found comfort in seeing a familiar face, a face she hadn't seen in too long. "Ahanna? You came back."

"That's right. It's me. I came to see you."

Resora's voice cracked, and for a moment, the pleading child broke through. "Help me, Ahanna."

"I will. I'm home now."

"It hurts."

"I know. You need to rest, just a little rest, that's all. Can you close your eyes? Think of home. Did you see Feylynn today?"

Resora nodded blankly.

Ahanna tried to smile, "What of Father? Tell me about him."

Tears shone in Resora's eyes, but she gave her sister no reply.

"Alright, it's alright then. Do you remember the warm honey cakes? I miss honey cakes."

"Ahanna, please, I can't..."

Ahanana didn't know what to do. She didn't know how she could help, but she refused to give up. "Think of Revienah. She's back home waiting for you."

The anger in Resora rose again, "Revienah! She's hurt!" There was nothing else but Revienah's pain and fear.

Ahanna realized her error too late, "No. No, we found her!"

Fisting handfuls of her long, brown hair, Resora bent at the waist, begging, "Make it stop!"

Ellomar came upon them as Resora pleaded for help, and seeing the young Princess for the first time, his breath caught in his throat. The old Ranger's heart broke for his friend and King. He'd never seen a touched elf before, but he knew the tales well enough to know the truth.

The child's skin was white as a spector's, and her eyes, filled with madness, had shifted to a golden hue. She was far worse than the Ranger expected, and Ahanna seemed oblivious to the danger she was in. "Ahanna! Step back," he cried out in warning.

Resora's eyes darted from Ahanna to this stranger running toward them. Like shattering glass, the full might of the growing magic broke free of the last remnants of her fragile control. She wouldn't allow another sister to find harm tonight. Resora stepped in front of her older sister, and her voice shifted from panicked childlike pleas to one of eerie control and dangerous threats as she spoke two words, "Run, Ahanna,"

Ahanna wasn't entirely sure if Resora was warning her about Ellomar or if she was warning her of the danger she, herself, posed. An odd current stirred about the sisters, and a slight tingle tickled her head. Loose tendrils of hair rose on end, pointing toward the source, as sparks of light formed in Resora's hand in place of the blue flames. Horror poured through Ahanna as she watched her little sister lift her fingers and point them at Ellomar.

"No!" she screamed. Reaching out, Ahanna yanked Resora's hand out wide. At the same time, Ellomar dove to the ground.

A flash of light filled the clear night sky seconds before a thunderous crack stunned anyone within five miles. The bolt of lightning missed Ellomar's heart by a hair's breadth as it slashed across his bicep before he hit the ground. The remnants of Resora's chaotic energy rattled his bones, but luckily he was alive thanks to Ahanna's quick reaction.

Unfortunately, Ahanna was not that lucky. By jumping at her sister and gripping her hand to disrupt Resora's aim, the destructive electricity poured into her. Flying backward, Ahanna's head hit the stone wall.

Shouts echoed in the street as Ellomar struggled to regain his senses, and he saw Ahanna's crumpled body lying motionless on the ground with a trickle of blood dripping down from a large cut on her head.

Resora screamed and threw herself over Ahanna, sobbing. At the sight of her injured sister, Resora's fractured mind once more revisited the horrible place she hated.

She ran a shaking hand over the wound, but she didn't see her sister anymore. Instead, her hand touched the glittering scales of a dragon. Even in the dream, the warm sticky blood beneath her fingers was real, and she begged, "Please don't die."

The acrid scent of smoke filtered about them, and the thatched roof where the bolt landed had caught fire. At the front of the building, people scrambled into the road seeking breathable air amid shouts and cries for help. The Slithering Eel Tavern was burning.

Unaware of anything but her sister, Resora sobbed all the harder, "You cannot die. Please wake up!"

"She will not die. I can help her," Ellomar swore as he tried to approach to offer his student his healing. "Let me heal her wound."

Resora's head hurt so bad she couldn't think, and she was so confused. She still straddled the line between past and present. Resora sneered at him. The words felt like a lie, mainly because they came from the red dragon's evil maw. "You lie! You killed him!"

Every sound, every sensation, it was simply too much for the young Princess. She could not control the tears anymore. Her mind switched back to Ahanna and the stranger. She threw her head back and saw the burning sky filled with smoke. She lost all hope. She knew the ending and had seen it play out constantly these last months in waking nightmares. It was happening right now in her mind. The light of the blood moon morphed into an orange sun tainted by war and death. "It hurts!" she cried.

Ellomar took another step, and a bright blue flame erupted around her and Ahanna, forming a protective ring. Resora closed her eyes and gave in to the pain and grief as she pulled her sister's body into her lap.

Ellomar tried to get past the barrier, but the hot fires rose and scorched his skin anytime he neared the ring. Every second he could not reach Ahanna, was a danger to her. Even from this distance, he knew her wounds were of the fatal sort. He needed to get through the insanity plaguing the young woman, "Resora! You must calm yourself. Calm your mind."

"You think that such an easy feat, do you?" a hooded figure said as he entered the alley.

Ellomar whipped around, his hand reaching for his sword to face the newcomer. "I knew you were coming. Though I don't yet understand your intent. Whatever it is you're looking for, look elsewhere," Ellomar demanded.

"I'm here to pay a debt, nothing more."

Unafraid of the old Ranger, the hooded figure pulled down his hood and stepped from the shadows into the firelight. Ellomar drew his sword, but as the elf walked through Resora's deadly fires without so much as a tiny burn, he made no move to strike.

The stranger crouched down before the young princess wallowing in her grief. Resora ignored him as she sobbed over her sister, stroking her hair while whispering, "I'm sorry," over and over again.

The elf reached out, and placing a gentle hand under her chin, he forced Resora to meet his eyes.

Even in the depths of her craziness, Resora could not resist looking deep into his green eyes. Her sobbing slowed to hiccups almost immediately. His eyes captivated her, and soon after, the raging fire waned unexpectedly. The flashing images of dragons and blood ebbed, and at that moment, there were only his green eyes that flashed to gold and back again.

"No one can help her, Venlare. It's too late. Her mind is broken," Ellomar proclaimed as he sheathed his sword.

"It's not broken," Venlare protested with calm assurance. "Not yet," he whispered to Resora. The rogue elf pulled a jeweled dagger from his belt and held it as if he would strike.

Ellomar flinched, "This can't be the way of it."

Resora did not flinch at the sight of the weapon made of rare blue steel. She welcomed death just then, but instead of cutting her throat, Venlare cut the ties on her cloak free, and it fell to her feet. He did not release her from his gaze, and she did not move when he reached down to her clenched fist. "Open your hand, Resora."

She obeyed and he saw the small glint of shining gold that he noticed when he approached moments before. He took up the ring in his hand and looked away when he realized what it was. Seeing it's twin on Resora's finger, he slipped it free and dropped them to the ground.

Desperate to keep her connection with Revienah, she grabbed his tunic with her hands aflame, but the fire died instantly. He took her chin in hand again and locked gazes once more.

"You must stop," Venlare said calmly. "Put the fire out, Resora." The circle of fire flickered and died suddenly. Satisfied, Venlare nodded.

Ellomar rushed to help Ahanna as the male elf took a brooch from his belt pouch and ran his thumb over the gold dragon head as if to check the texture and weight. Without another thought, Venlare dropped the brooch on top of the cloak.

Still tending to Ahanna, Ellomar heard the calls for the city watch, and shook his head with regret. "The city, the King. Ranoak will not survive this."

Following the flames and the cries from the tavern, Master Carek finally came upon them. He still cursed himself for falling for Ellomar's tricks, and upon seeing the mess in the alley, Carek suspected he would curse about it for a long time.

Without knowing who the stranger was, Carek agreed with what his old friend was saying. "The King's guard is on its way. As well as the whole of The Enclave, I suspect. Ellomar is right. When the people know the truth—"

Venlare pulled Resora to her feet. "What truth is that, Paladin?" he said with disdain. "My truth or yours?"

It was only then that Carek realized who the stranger was, "You!" he spat with disdain. "What have you done to her?"

"I'm here to collect the Princess."

Carek's hand went for his sword. "You will not! Princess, don't listen to him."

Resora turned her head toward Carek, but Venlare squeezed her hand and stepped in front of her again. "Don't look at them, *hina*. Be still."

She obeyed, but Venlare held her gaze to be sure. Cries of alarm still rang out, and people were still trying to put out the fires, but back here, behind the known streets, in the dark places only thieves and beggars frequented, Resora could only hear the beat of her own heart, and Venlare's calm voice. Tears spilled down her cheeks, but her sobbing had gone silent.

"This will kill him!" Ellomar snapped.

Venlare shut out Ellomar's harsh words and smiled at Resora, "Close your eyes, *hina idra*."

She obeyed again.

"I can't let you do this," Carek declared as he drew his weapon. "I will not allow you to kidnap the daughter of Tisus."

"I know you can't, and I figured you would try to stop me." Venlare conceded. "And to be honest, because I know you prefer it, I have no intention of ever crossing blades with you again either. At least not if I can help it."

"You'll have to face me if you think you're taking the Princess on this night."

With his back still facing the Paladin, Venlare smirked, "Actually, I won't."

They all heard an audible *thwack*. A small crossbow bolt found its way into the exposed space in Carek's armor. Stunned, the Paladin fell to his knees as a sharp pain traveled through his nerves. He tried to turn to see the shooter, but he slumped to the ground a couple of seconds later.

Turning to see the prone man on the ground, Venlare said, "I hope that hurt."

Having stabilized Ahanna, Ellomar went to his downed friend. "Are you insane?"

"Depends on who you ask," Venlare said nonchalantly.

"What have you done?"

"It seems I have repaid two debts tonight," the elf said, and he scooped up the small, fragile Resora in his arms. As he pulled her close, Venlare whispered in her ear softly, "Keep your eyes closed. No matter what you hear, keep them closed."

Ellomar bent over his former traveling companion, discerning his condition. He pulled the small arrow free, and Venlare rolled his eyes as he passed them.

The elf's burly companion, who had held Revienah captive earlier and fired the shot that took out Carek, appeared from the shadows with a fawn-colored mare following. Time was short. The festival would slow the city watch, but a fire would bring the whole of Ranoak here. The watch, The Enclave, and any other able-bodied man would come to help.

Venlare could hear the rising chaos around the corner and the distant blare of the Golden Dragon's famous horn, but he had to be very careful to keep Resora's mind cleared. Doing so required a gentle touch and immense concentration on his part. Wrapping her up in a black cloak, he pulled the hood up over her head. Then setting her upon the mare, he said softly, "Hold on now," and he guided her hands to the front of the saddle one at a time.

Utterly spent and feeling a strange fog suppressing her senses, Resora obeyed, but she began to open her eyes again. Venlare squeezed her hands, "Not yet, *hina idra*."

His friend pointed to Ellomar. "You gonna leave him like that?"

Venlare glanced back at the Ranger and the two bodies lying on the ground. He winced at the sight of the unconscious young woman but did not go to her. He saw Ellomar sniff the arrow's point to discern the poison, and Venlare took pity on him. "Give it a rest, Ranger. He won't die. At least not tonight. The arrow is merely dipped in a potent sleeping draught." Venlare grinned wickedly, "Though, I expect he'll wake with a pounding head."

Ellomar glared at him, "Why are you doing this?"

He mounted behind the young Princess and patted the animal's neck as she side-stepped nervously. When he settled behind Resora, Venlare met Ellomar's insidious gaze with one of resolution, "Given a choice between her and the kingdom, which would he choose?"

"It's an impossible choice. No one could make such a choice, not even him."

"Then do not force him to make it. I shall make it for him. You know she's dangerous. Even he knows what will come."

Silence passed between them, and Ellomar's attention shifted to the compliant young girl who nearly killed him without a second thought minutes before.

"Centuries of blood-shed is more than enough. You are too young to remember the reality behind the hatred between my people and yours. The beginning of it was lost. It was lost in the lust for revenge and gold, but this child will dredge everything back up again. We will lose all that we gained, and blood will fill these streets. Think, Ellomar!"

Another horn blew. They were close. Both Venlare and Ellomar knew little time remained. Venlare's sensitive ears could even hear the distant sound of hooves clattering on the cobble-stone streets on their way towards him.

The weight of the decision before him tore at Ellomar, but ultimately, Venlare was right. The kingdom would never survive the truth about Resora, and while Ellomar didn't trust Venlare, he distrusted the collective panic of men even more. "Swear you will not harm her."

"*Nyo aurie agevedim,*" the elf said, bidding him farewell but making no such promise as he turned the mare about. He nodded to his burly companion, "You know what to do."

Without another word, the big man left the alley, and Venlare urged the mare forward. Ellomar's fingers itched to pull out his bow. He wanted to stop them and save Resora, but he couldn't. He wished Micah was close enough to follow, but the young man would not be able to make it back in time.

The horse burst from the dark alleyway onto the main road. Cries of shock rent the already chaotic scene, and men fighting the fire dove out of the way while women, watching the tavern burn, cried out in alarm pulling their children out of harm's way.

Afraid he'd just doomed the entire realm, Ellomar bent over his paladin friend once more and whispered, "Forgive me, my friend."

After reassuring himself that Carek would live, Ellomar gathered up Ahanna in his arms and disappeared into the crowd before the Golden Knights could find them.

FORTY-FIVE

Every year on the morning after the ball, the Golden Dragon Knights left the city with as much fanfare as they arrived. The festival was officially over, but today as the sun peeked over the mountain, the Golden Dragon Knights did not make their usual procession out of the city gates. Nobody lined the streets with roses to wave at the soldiers as tradition dictated. Instead, the horrible news from the night before set a melancholy mood throughout the city.

As the merchants in Ranoak packed up their wares and local shop owners took down decorations, they were abuzz. The shocking news spread like wildfire from vendor to vendor and farmer to farmer. One of their beloved King's daughters had been kidnapped.

As the sun's light filtered into the streets, many of the gold knights were still hoping they could find the mysterious man who had taken her before any harm befell Resora. Another full contingent had been sent outside the walls in the dark hours of the morning to hunt down the kidnappers, and the remaining golden dragons stayed vigilant at the castle to protect their king and the rest of his dwindling family.

The city was filled with whispers and watchful eyes as men searched alleys, taverns, and public buildings for any sign of the mysterious man and the missing princess of Ranoak. At the Falling Oak Tavern, a young barmaid washing the tables asked, "What did this man want with her? She's just a bit of a thing, not even a woman."

Her co-worker, wiping down the chairs, replied, "I can't right figure it out. Maybe someone wishes to start a fight with King Tisus."

"You can bet he'll be roaring for one now. Not so smart, if you ask me."

The other woman huffed a laugh, "No, I suppose not. Everyone knows King Tisus would lay out an entire field of men for any of his daughters. You mark me, There's no bigger fool than the one who picks a fight with King Tisus. I expect he'll be charging out of the gates before long."

The other woman put a hand on her hip and looked around to see if anyone else was around. She leaned in closer, "Well, I heard it weren't no normal man. King Tisus might have to take on a sorcerer of the black arts. That's what stole young Resora."

"What? You're daft! Where on earth did you hear such a thing?"

"Neicery, over at the Slithering Eel, said she saw the whole thing with her own eyes. Lightning, and fire, and the like, come from out of nowhere. Then a shrouded man on a white horse charged straight out into the street, nearly trampling everyone gathered to put out the fire."

Her friend swatted her playfully with the rag. "Neicery's a

fanciful fool. Was just a storm last night. Don't look for dragons where there aren't none, I say."

"She's not the only one," the younger woman said with an expectant expression.

"Magic! What a tale," the older woman admonished.

"I'm tellin' you 'twas magic," the young woman insisted.

Her friend rolled her eyes. "Bah! Wash your tables already." The older woman chuckled and mumbled, "Magic? A fishmonger's tale."

On the steps leading up to the rooms that the proprietor rented nightly, Ahanna Nacarion, barely recovered from her ordeal, sat listening to the two women gossip. As she listened, she chewed on her quivering bottom lip while her fingers absently traced the puckered, healing flesh on her opposite hand. Closing her eyes as they chattered about magic, Ahanna recalled the staggering power of the lightning Resora had used. Her sister had nearly killed her.

With so much swirling about in her mind, Ahanna was horribly afraid. But, she wasn't afraid for herself, for Ranoak, or even for Resora. Ellomar had told her a little more about Venlare. While that information was vague at best, Resora's choices were limited for now.

Ahanna's fear rested solely on her worry for her father. Shelanna's disappearance years before nearly crippled him. She could only wonder what the loss of yet another daughter would do to King Tisus.

She'd nearly run home last night to see him, and if she'd been stronger, Ahanna might have managed it. Her weak condition had made it easy for Ellomar to pour in healing magic and coax her back to sleep last night before she could even manage to rise from her sickbed. Early this morning, when she awoke, Ellomar had reminded her that going home would not accomplish anything. If the golden knights found her, Ahanna would be sent away with

Feylynn to The Enclave and would not be able to help Tisus more than she was now. That truth was the only thing that kept her rooted to these very steps.

The door downstairs opened and closed, and the women quieted as a customer entered. When the silence fell around her, all the stress overcame her. Putting her head in her hands, the haunting echoes of Resora's pleas for help rang in her ears once more. Ahanna kept imagining the sorrow in her father's liquid brown eyes and was devastated by her utter failure from the night before.

As the silent tears began to flow freely, another figure entered the stairwell. Ahanna didn't even bother to look up. Somehow, she knew who it was. Easing down next to her in the narrow space, Micah put an arm around Ahanna's shoulder. Without a second thought, she buried her face against him and allowed herself the time to grieve with her oldest friend.

Back at Ranoak Castle, King Tisus defied all gossip and suspicions. He hadn't charged from the castle with a sword in hand to recover his daughter from the nefarious kidnapper. Rather, upon hearing the news, Tisus left the council of lords without a word as they gave commanders orders to retrieve his daughter and secluded himself to his private chambers. With his heart aching, the mighty King and Paladin warrior of legend sat in his chair, staring blankly at a dancing fire. In his hand, he held a familiar dragon pin.

The trinket had been a token given to him in trust the day he married Shelanna. A precious item given to him by a jaded elf as a symbol of respect. He alone understood the meaning the trinket represented. The King's call for help had come. It just hadn't come as Tisus expected.

A soft knock at his door pulled Tisus from his deep thoughts and memories. "Enter," he bade.

Master Carek, now fully recovered, opened the door. Having wiped away any sign of moisture in her eyes moments before, Feylynn followed her teacher into the room. Carek approached the chair but stopped before he rounded it. He recognized Tisus needed privacy at a time like this. "My King, there is no sign of them along the eastern roads to Brithel, nor have our scouts found any evidence leading me to believe he took her toward Govan. It is a blessing that he is not seeking the refuge of a ship."

Staring at the fire, Tisus pocketed the dragon brooch, and his fingers brushed the small likeness of his wife that he kept there too. He now had two items of mourning to carry, and he closed his eyes against the raw pain slicing through his heart.

"Your Majesty? Did you hear me? He must be heading to Pran. I've sent a small contingent that way. Worst case, Venlare intends to make for Ilirith."

Tisus shook his head and clutched both trinkets in his fist so tightly that the edges of the jewelry cut into his skin. "No, not there," he mumbled.

Watching her father's back, Feylynn wanted to go to him and sit at his feet as she had done as a child during fierce storms. She wanted to lay her head on his knee and listen to him tell her that everything would be okay while he stroked her hair and told her grand stories of adventure.

She'd never seen him in such a state. Even when her mother disappeared, he'd ranted about the castle and charged out ahead of his men to search for her. But now, the hollow man before her was frightening. The lack of temper was far more unsettling than the display of anger years before. When he said nothing more, Feylynn dared to step around her mentor to face him. "Father?"

When he heard the soft voice of Feylynn, his free hand came up to rub his brow as if he'd been pulled from a trance, and he mumbled, "Call them back."

Confusion clouded Feylynn's eyes, and shock covered Carek's features as he said, "I'm sorry. What?"

Tisus stood and went to the fireplace. "Call them all back."

"Father. Resora!"

"You cannot be serious," Carek said with incredulity. "The Princess—"

At the reminder of what was at stake, Tisus kicked the metal stand holding the fireplace poker and shouted, "Call them back! Every last one!"

Feylynn recoiled and stepped back. Not from the temper but the order.

Tisus pinned Carek with his angry eyes, and his nostrils flared. "Not one knight will pursue them! Not one!"

Holding Enreal's arm, a mostly recovered Revienah was making her way to her father when the order echoed down the stone corridor. Startled at the sound of their father's shout, they stopped mid-stride. Revienah could hardly believe her ears. She pulled her sister around the corner and hid so they could listen without being sent away.

Inside the room, Carek was unfazed by the outburst. It was a behavior more fitting for Tisus, but in the end, the show of temper was short. Carek saw the utter defeat take over again. Tisus gripped the fireplace mantel with both hands and leaned into the grip while hanging his head.

Carek moved closer to his old friend, and lowering his voice just above a whisper, the Master Paladin left formality behind, "Tisus, what are you doing?"

"I'm trying to save her," Tisus admitted with watery eyes.

Surprised, Feylynn took a measure of her father and observed the men carefully.

Unable to hear any more than mumbled tones, Revienah left Enreal and ran down the hall toward her room. Understanding Revienah's intent, Enreal sank to the floor softly crying, and Lord Denaris, seeing what transpired, eased down next to the young Princess and pulled her close to offer comfort while he strained to listen as well.

On the other side of the stone wall, Carek pressed Tisus, "Talk to me, My King."

Tisus turned back to the fire and rubbed his greying hair, "While I don't understand his game, if we pursue, Venlare will be forced into the Uninhabited Lands, and that cursed land is no place I would have him take Resora."

"But surely we can beat him there. At the very least, I can."

Staring into the dancing flames, Tisus questioned, "To what gain, Carek? She cannot stay here. People will notice. If the magic doesn't kill her, the city will surely rise against her. How many would die coming after her? How many would I kill with my own sword?" Tisus shifted from the fireplace and pinned Carek with his dark eyes. "Even you must know she is safer with the rogue elf."

"I'll make no such admission!" Carek said. "She belongs with us, among the safety of the knights. You know that is how it is supposed to be. You know the old truths."

"Maybe, but it was long ago. You know better than I that The Enclave has trained many great men, but its original purpose is long forgotten. Politics are now the rule of law. The original oath is dead. If it were not for you, and men like you, who believe in justice and righteousness as well as selfless acts for the good of the people, the council would have fallen into ruin long ago."

Feylynn was stunned by the accusation, but Master Carek only clenched his jaw and stared hard at Tisus.

Tisus straightened up, and Feylynn saw the true strength in her father's demeanor as he said, "I'm asking you, Sir Carek Breowyn, as my friend, to find that sense of right and wrong here. I am begging you to trust me and follow the code of that first oath. It is left to you to teach Feylynn, for she will be needed before the end, and only you know the truth. Whether by sword or by death. . ."

Carek nodded and finished the line for his friend, "I swear to give all that I am to the cause and will utilize all the tools at my disposal to protect truth, honor, and life."

King Tisus sighed as relief flooded him, and he glanced past Carek to the bewildered eyes of his second daughter. He put a hand on Carek's shoulder in solidarity. "Can you give me a moment with Feylynn?"

Carek turned to leave but stopped at the door. "Do you remember the rest of the legend, Tisus? Do you remember the second part?"

"I do."

"Then you'd best keep a careful eye on all of them," Carek warned.

"That is why I have you and Ellomar, my friend. For whom could I trust more?"

Carek tilted his head in acknowledgment and left Tisus with his daughter.

Feylynn still couldn't understand. The conversation between the two men had revealed nothing and confused her more. *Wasn't Ellomar the Ranger dead?* "Father?"

Tisus took her hands and held them tight against his chest. "You must trust me. Can you do that?"

"Of course, I can," she said, staring at his strong hands.

He let go with one hand and tilted her chin to meet his eyes. "Feylynn, I know you have heard of the truth of Resora's condition. For now, I'll beg that you do not tell anyone else. Those who need to know already know, and those that wish to guess need not have it confirmed."

"Father—"

"Swear it, my daughter. Swear you will not speak of it to anyone. At least not for a while yet. Around every corner, someone is listening, especially at The Enclave."

"I swear it."

"Good. I know you wanted to stay home, but you must return to The Enclave. There is much you need to learn."

Feylynn nodded.

"You can trust Master Carek. Learn from him, and he will guide you forward, but you must not place your trust foolishly with just anyone. Pick your friends carefully. The world that you know is about to shift beneath your feet, and you will need allies more than ever, but you will find that enemies are never far away."

"Yes, Father," she whispered.

He kissed her brow, "Trust me to know what is best, and I will see you one year hence when I blow the horn to call you home."

She straightened her spine and stood tall. "And I shall swear my fealty to my King," Feylynn promised proudly.

Tisus smiled, but it didn't reach his eyes. The pain of losing another daughter ate at him. He placed his hand on her cheek, "I love you, my daughter. One day you shall win over the hearts in this kingdom, but always know you have mine every day."

Feylynn threw herself into her father's arms and hugged him as tightly as possible. "Find Resora, Father. Bring her home."

As he returned the embrace, words failed him. Tisus could make no such promise because, for the second time in a year, letting go was the best thing for his daughter's survival.

EPIL⊙GUE

D eep in the market square, the talk was the same as it was within the city's taverns. A small group of performers listened half-heartedly as they readied to leave Ranoak for the port city, Govan. The other vendors around them were also bustling about to prepare for their own journeys home as they talked.

None of them would do much more than gossip. There was nothing any of them could do to help anyway. They'd only seen the Princesses on infrequent occasions, and most people in the city didn't even know what they looked like.

"Everyone knows that the Golden Knights are the King's best hope to recover his daughter," one dancer said.

"That was, if she was still alive, anyway," said the old woman who cared for the dancers.

As Jamas loaded a heavy trunk full of costumes on the bed of the wagon, he smirked at some of the outlandish ideas circulating among the crowd.

"I heard people saw Princess Resora climb up on that horse of her own free will. Not even a little resistance," the cart driver observed.

"I think she ran off. Just like her older sister," the old woman added.

The cartman wagged his finger in the air, "King Tisus shoulda' used more of that famous temper on those girls. They're spoiled, is all."

Grunting with relief, Jamas set the large trunk down amid the other boxes. He always found it interesting how quickly gossip could turn a crowd. An hour ago, people throughout the city were filled with pity and fear. Now, as the day wore on with no answers, those same people created their own speculation and judgments.

Jamas stood to wipe his brow and used his hands to push back his midnight-black hair from his face. He surveyed the group and was satisfied they were almost done. As he turned to shift another box, a curious sight caught his attention, and his hands fell to his sides. A familiar young woman strode purposefully toward him. He smiled and hopped down from the back of the cart. "Little Raven. What brings you about this morning? If you came for another show—" He gestured to the loaded boxes, "I'm afraid we're all loaded up."

"I want you to teach me," she said with determined fire in her eyes. "I want to learn how to throw knives like you." Revienah refused ever to be so helpless again, and she intended to find Resora and kill the elf who kidnapped her. Unlike her father, Revienah refused to write off her sister so soon.

Jamas snorted, "Teach you?"

"Why is that funny?"

Turning his back on her, the knife thrower started to tie down the items in the wagon. "Fly home, Little Raven."

413

"I'm going with you. You can teach me along the way."

He laughed as he threw a canvas cover over the boxes and trunks, "Can I now?"

With a hand on her hip, Revienah glared at him, "I am still curious as to why you think this is funny."

He stopped tying down the load and pinned her with a frightful stare. The hairs on the back of Revienh's neck rose. She immediately realized the playful performer was gone and in his place was a dangerous stranger who could throw a knife faster than a girl could blink. But Revienah needed someone like him to help find her sister.

"I find it funny that you think you can order me around." He turned his back on her again and checked the wheels to his cart. "I have no interest in babysitting a spoiled Lord's daughter. You can't even be more than eleven, and I'm not a nanny."

"I'm nearly thirteen. And I'm no Lord's daughter!" she insisted.

"Neither are you a street waif," he said pointedly. "Your back is too straight, your hands too soft, and your speech is too proper."

"So what! That doesn't make me the daughter of one of Ranoak's lords."

"It makes you dangerous," he countered.

"My mannerisms make me dangerous?"

He smiled derisively as if her prim tone proved his accusation true. "Your mannerisms make you missable, and I'm no teacher. Fly home, Little Raven," Jamas warned again as he finished the last tie on the cart. Then, walking away, without so much as a glance to the young girl, Jamas said over his shoulder, "Hurry along before someone in your rich family sends the watch looking for you."

Her cheeks heated up with embarrassment. She scowled at his back then glanced about to make sure no one had listened to them. She needed this man's help. Surely anyone that skilled with a dagger could help keep her safe until she could defend herself.

This morning, when Revienah heard her father's order to call back the knights who hunted for her twin, she was infuriated. She couldn't understand him. First the secrets, and now he was leaving her sister to the whims of that vile elf.

With little thought about the consequence, the impetuous Princess decided she would find Resora, but she wasn't dumb enough to try alone. Not with her encounter against the elven stranger still fresh in her mind and his poison barely gone from her veins. She'd hoped to trick this rogue into helping her, but he was smarter than she anticipated. *Or maybe,* she thought, *I'm not smart enough.*

With that truth circling in her mind, Revienah glanced at the wood cart and the wood crates set upon it. She eyed the heavy canvas that doubled as a tent and a covering for the wagon load to protect it from rain. As always, the King's youngest daughter acted with little thought. After ensuring no one was watching her, she crawled under the cover and settled amid the cargo, hoping no one would find her until they were far away from Ranoak.